Kylie Chan has a BBus in information technology, an MBA in IT, and an MPhil in Creative Writing. She started out as an IT consultant and trainer specialising in business intelligence systems in Australia, and then had her own consulting business for ten years in Hong Kong. When she returned to Australia, Kylie wrote the bestselling nine-book *Dark Heavens* fantasy series, followed by the *Dragon Empire* and *Council of AIs* science fiction series.

She is a full-time writer based on Queensland's Gold Coast, and her website is at www.kylichan.com.

Books by Kylie Chan

Dark Heavens
White Tiger (1)
Red Phoenix (2)
Blue Dragon (3)

Journey to Wudang
Earth to Hell (4)
Hell to Heaven (5)
Heaven to Wudang (6)

Celestial Battle
Dark Serpent (7)
Demon Child (8)
Black Jade (9)

Novellas
Black Scales White Fur
The Gravity Engine
The Bride with Red Hair
Small Shen (with Queenie Chan)

House of the North
The Serpent Princess (1)

Dragon Empire
Scales of Empire (1)
Guardian of Empire (2)
Dawn of Empire (3)

Council of AIs
Minds of Sand and Light (1)
Bodies of Stone and Water (2)

THE SERPENT PRINCESS

KYLIE CHAN

ISBN: 978-0-6458837-7-0 (Hardcover)
ISBN: 978-0-6458837-6-3 (Paperback)
ISBN: 978-0-6458837-5-6 (eBook)

Published by Kylie Chan
Copyright © Kylie Chan 2024

Cover design and illustration by Ashton Smith
Author photo by Bradkay Photographix
Printed and Distributed by LightningSource Pty Ltd (IngramSpark)

1

Simone drove into the small, open-air parking area under Kwun Lung Lau, unlocked the barrier on the parking space, and reversed the Mercedes into it.

Although part of the 1960s-era government housing complex had been replaced with two enormous modern towers of tiny, hundred-square-foot apartments after a lethal landslide, four of the original, interlinked twenty-two storey towers remained. The older part of the complex was almost exclusively occupied by elderly residents who had refused the government's offer to move to something newer in North Point or the New Territories. Their televisions played at full volume in every apartment, and the sound of TVB Jade, the Cantonese-language television station, echoed around the hillside.

The connected snake of towers formed a semicircle around the hillside, with the inevitable concrete covering the side of the hill beneath them. A road passed through a square arch beneath the building on the end, leading to an open, paved area where there was room for ten parked cars under a couple of tired, dusty trees that sheltered stacks of mops, buckets, and traditional Chinese rice straw brooms.

Simone walked out of the complex through the tunnel that pierced the end building and headed to the shining new Hong Kong Jockey Club Student Village next door The village was halfway up the side of Hong Kong Island and consisted of four massive towers that shadowed the shorter Kwun Lung Lau complex. Simone's boyfriend, Graham Zhou, waited for her the small lobby of the second tower, standing next to the door. There were no security guards, and the lobby was painted white above pine panelling that reached halfway up the walls in a nod to decoration, but was otherwise bare, with a plain, beige-tiled floor. Graham opened the door and joined her when he saw her.

Graham was a half-Chinese, half-White Canadian, and was taller than her, but not nearly as muscular, indicating his scholarly life. He wasn't overweight but his strength was obviously in his intellect. He had brown eyes behind his wire-framed glasses, light brown hair, and fair skin a similar shade to hers. Sometimes people asked if they were related. They'd share a grin about 'mixed kids'.

'Love the outfit,' she said.

He looked down at himself; he was wearing dress slacks, a business shirt, and a tie with a chunky cream-coloured cardigan. 'It's not too much?'

'The tie isn't really necessary ...'

He touched it, unsure.

'But they'll appreciate that you dressed up.'

He nodded, more confident. 'I'm freaking out here. You're *driving* us up there?'

'You're scared of my driving?'

'No. No!' he said, waving his hands in front of him. 'It's just ... a place in Hong Kong that isn't served by public transport? So strange.'

'It is if you're willing to take the green minibus up to the Peak and then a massive hike up the hill,' she said.

'Your family is so wealthy,' he said weakly.

'Don't panic, they're not snobby or anything,' she said. 'My dad will probably be dressed like a hobo. Ready?'

He nodded, smiling at the 'hobo' comment.

'The family car is down in the car park,' she said. 'Fair warning, it's a big Mercedes, because of course it is.'

'Yep,' he said. 'That or a Beemer. Inevitable in this town.'

He followed her back down the hill and into the housing estate with its buildings painted in bright, fading colours, streaked with black car exhaust and mould around the wet laundry hanging on bamboo poles. The cool, damp air was thick with the smell of incense, and frying fish and pork. He stopped at the car. 'How did you get a park here? This car park is always full.'

'A friend of my dad's owns the space,' Simone said. 'She visits all the time.' She left out the fact that it had been to practice martial arts on the building's roof, away from prying eyes during the demolition, and that the Red Phoenix had never bothered to sell the space after the residents moved back in.

She negotiated the car up the overgrown drive close to the top of the Peak, and the electric gate opened to reveal the concreted area around the base of the building. The family's seventies-era apartment block was eleven storeys tall, stained with mould from the dampness, and had an old-fashioned open car park at ground level to house the residents' expensive vehicles. She reversed the car into its space—pleased that Graham had seemed completely relaxed about and trusting of her driving— and guided him past the smiling security guards to the elevator.

'Your family has the whole top floor?' Graham asked Simone when they reached the eleventh floor and there was only one door with a small altar to the Door God on the floor next to it.

'Yeah, and my big brother and his husband have the apartment directly underneath.' She smiled at him. 'Traditional Chinese families, you know. Massive.'

His expression froze and she put her hand on his arm to reassure him. 'It's fine. They're great. They won't interrogate you or give you a hard time, and don't worry about remembering everybody's names.' She reminded him anyway. 'It's just my dad, John Chen, my stepmother, Emma Donahoe-Chen, and my little brother, Frankie.'

'Okay, I guess.' He was obviously still nervous, but nodded and straightened, steeling himself. 'I can do this,' he added under his breath.

'You'll be fine,' she said, and bobbed up to kiss him on the cheek as she opened the front door.

The family was in the living room when they entered. The two top-floor apartments had been combined into a single four-bedroom residence, and the living room was double normal size, with cream carpet, leather couches, and Ming-style antique rosewood coffee tables. The floor-to-ceiling picture windows overlooked the southern side of Hong Kong Island, with the high-rises of Ap Lei Chau clearly visible in the winter sunlight reflecting off the South China Sea to the outlying islands of Lamma and Cheung Chau beyond.

Simone squealed when she saw that Michael and Clarissa were visiting.

'We were just leaving—' Clarissa said, but Simone interrupted her.

'Don't go anywhere!' She quickly turned to Graham. 'Shoes off here. I'll be right back.' She kicked off her shoes and scooted past everybody in the living room to run to her bedroom. She stopped at the door, turned back, and jabbed one finger at Clarissa and Michael. 'Don't go anywhere!' She grabbed the gift from her desk before returning to the living room, where a bemused Emma was presenting Graham with a pair of guest slippers, and he was awkwardly putting them on.

Simone stopped in front of Clarissa, Michael's wife. She was of American–Chinese extraction, with her black hair cut shoulder-length to frame her kind face. Her skin was transparent, with the blue veins beneath clearly visible, and her pregnancy was nearly at term, making her fragile appearance seem even more frail. She leaned on two long-term crutches when she stood, her withered forearms nestled in cups that held her arms from elbows to wrists. Her hands were twisted claws that gripped the braces of the crutches.

Michael looked in his mid-thirties, to match Clarissa, but as a Taoist Immortal, his appearance was by choice. He was half-Chinese, half-White American, and his father was the White Tiger God of the West, the god of metal and autumn, and Michael's shining platinum-blond hair was held in a short ponytail. He wore grey suit slacks and a shirt with a bright yellow sweater over it, inherently drawn to his father's white-and-gold livery. His stunningly good-looking face was a combination of his gorgeous American mother and the Celestial nature of his father.

Simone held the gift out towards Clarissa, who turned to Michael and handed one of the crutches to him. He helped her ease her ungainly, heavily pregnant body to the couch, and she gleefully tore at the gift wrapping, drawing a gasp from Simone's little brother, Frankie.

'You're supposed to wait until you're home,' Frankie said breathlessly.

'Not in the West,' Clarissa said, smiling at him. 'And I think Simone wants to see my face when I open it.'

Simone nodded agreement.

Michael helped Clarissa open the gift, attentively sitting next to her on the couch and taking the shredded pieces of wrapping paper as she clumsily worked on it. She freed the felted teddy bear from the wrapping and held it up with a huge smile, then glanced at Simone. 'Did you *make* this?'

Simone sat on the couch next to Clarissa. 'I did! It's from one of those Japanese craft kits, but I made it all myself and poured all my love for you into it.' She put her hand on Clarissa's where she held the toy. 'Because I want everything to be perfect for you and baby, and I can't wait to be the best Aunty Simone ever.'

'I love it, and the baby will as well,' Clarissa said, and put her arms out. Simone clumsily hugged her from beside her on the couch, working her way around Clarissa's swollen belly. They pulled back, and Simone took Clarissa's hand.

'I'm always here for you, okay? Anything you need, I'm there. Just get Michael to call me, and I'll be there in an instant.'

Clarissa looked from Simone to Michael to the rest of the family, who were standing around with indulgent smiles— except for Frankie, who was hopping from foot to foot, obviously hungry, and Graham, who looked both anxious and confused. 'Marrying into this family was the best thing I ever did in my life.' Michael's face fell, and she put her hand on his. 'Even after everything. I wouldn't change a thing.'

She passed the little teddy to Michael, and he handed her the crutch and helped her stand again.

'We were just filling Emma in on the final details for the hospital and delivery, and Clarissa's mother is arriving tomorrow to help,' Michael said. He turned and shook Graham's hand. 'Sorry to turn up like this while you're being put on the spot. I know how important these first family meetings are—especially with a family as strange as this one.'

'They don't seem that strange, it's been pretty normal so far,' Graham said.

'Oh no,' Clarissa said under her breath, her expression full of realisation that Graham didn't yet know who they really were.

'We're not strange. Come on,' Emma said cheerfully. 'A little bit of weird here and there is a good thing.'

'Yeah, like you showed me a room full of tigers the first day *I* visited this weirdness,' Clarissa said, and everybody laughed.

Graham was beginning to look thoroughly confused and more than a little concerned. Simone stood and linked her arm in his to reassure him. 'Don't worry, I'll explain everything later. Right now, I want you to meet the family, and see how loving and supportive everybody is.' She didn't add, 'Before I toss you into the tiger-filled weirdness.'

Michael guided Clarissa towards the door, helped her with her shoes, and left with many cheerful waves and promises to bring the baby to visit.

'Now,' Emma said, clasping her hands. 'Dinner time, and let's try to be welcoming to poor Graham.' She gestured towards the dining room. 'This way, and I promise, no tigers.'

Simone followed everyone to the dining room and Emma smiled as Graham and Simone sat at the table next to each other, Graham stiff and awkward. The dining room had her father's graceful ink paintings of sea creatures in frames on the wall, and a side table held an open scroll under glass: the original manuscript of the classic, *Journey to the West*. Emma had salvaged it from a corner of Xuan Wu's messy office and put it on display 'where it belonged'.

I remember doing this to my family, Emma said. *When I told them the whole thing, it freaked them out completely. It's a good idea not to reveal anything too wild at this early stage.*

Simone glared at Emma without speaking—talking telepathically was *so rude*—then sat straighter and gestured over the bowls and chopsticks to the lazy Susan in the middle of the ten-seater, round rosewood table. 'Family style, you're familiar with that, right?'

'No problem,' Graham said. 'It's the way we eat at home half of the time.'

'Okay, introductions,' Simone said. 'This is my dad, John Chen Wu.'

Simone's father nodded, studying Graham with his dark eyes. Xuan Wu, the Dark Lord of the Northern Heavens, had taken a mid-sixties human form, with his usual black hair worn long at the back and tied on top, in traditional style. He was wearing his standard at-home uniform of a scruffy faded black T-shirt and a pair of cotton martial arts pants—his 'hobo' uniform.

'My adopted mother, Emma Donahoe-Chen. Technically she's my stepmother, but I call her Mum.'

'Mrs Donahoe-Chen,' Graham said, carefully respectful.

Emma nodded back, with a smile that lit up her face every time Simone called her 'Mum'. She was in her usual late-fifties form, a White Australian with bright blue eyes, wearing a scruffy sweater and jeans. Her greying, mid-brown hair was in a messy bun that wanted to escape and go everywhere.

Simone gestured towards Frankie, who sat between Simone and her father. 'This is my little brother, Frankie. He's twelve.'

'Hi Graham,' Frankie said in a sing-song voice. He changed to a childish whine. 'Can we eat *now*? I'm starving!'

'Food's on its way,' Emma said.

'So how did you and Simone meet?' Xuan Wu asked Graham.

'We were in the same honours year cohort,' Graham said. 'I'm a microbiologist, so I'm in the third-floor labs, Simone is marine so she's on the seventh—'

'We kept running into each other at the coffee shop next to the biology building and complaining about university politics,' Simone said.

'Is that why you stopped coming home and moaning to us about it?' Emma asked.

Graham shot a grin at Simone. 'Glad I could help.'

Frankie piped up. 'What martial arts do you do?' he asked Graham. 'Which style?'

'What? None. No martial arts, I know Simone does it, because she showed me and she's really good, but me, no. Why?' Graham asked, obviously confused.

'Good,' Emma said firmly. 'John will show absolutely no interest in you and will keep himself to himself.'

Simone's father opened his mouth and closed it again, then smiled. 'Promise.'

Simone nodded thanks to her father. She'd asked him to tone down his dark aura of raw power so he wouldn't scare Graham away, and her father was obviously making an effort. She appreciated it.

Graham was completely bewildered, and Simone was ready to paper over the whole martial arts business when Er Hao brought in the first vegetarian dishes, and everybody was distracted putting bowls on the lazy Susan and serving rice.

'This is Er Hao,' Simone said. Er Hao appeared to be a Chinese woman in her mid-forties, wearing the traditional servant's black-and-white uniform from a time before the import of Filipina and Indonesian domestic helpers became more common. 'She and her sister Yi Hao look after the family, and they're really part of it.'

Er Hao smiled, making dimples appear in her cheeks. 'Thank you, Miss Simone.'

'Number One and Number Two?' Graham asked. 'They're people, not numbers.'

'Madam Emma rescued us from an abusive situation,' Er

Hao said with pride. 'We are honoured to serve as her Numbers One and Two.' She hesitated, then spoke carefully as she recited from memory. 'It's a traditional Chinese thing, and we're happy to work here.' She leaned in to speak to Graham in a stage whisper. 'You can offer to help me escape later if you like. One of Simone's friends from university did that and was shocked when I said I am happy here.'

'It's true,' Simone said. 'It really is an old-fashioned Chinese thing, and they won't have it any other way.'

'Truly part of the family,' Emma said, nodding to Er Hao, who smiled around the table and returned to the kitchen. 'So, pass me your bowls and I'll give you some soup.' She lifted the lid of the tureen to reveal a hollowed-out winter melon holding the fragrant broth. 'It's winter melon and straw mushroom. Are you allergic to anything or do you have any sensitivities, Graham?'

'I'm lactose intolerant, but Simone said that wouldn't be an issue. All of you are vegetarian, which is great, because I am as well.'

'You will fit right in,' Emma said with satisfaction. 'Now tell us all about the microbiology. It sounds fascinating. What's your specialty?'

'Local yeasts!' Graham said, lighting up, and Simone smiled as he relaxed into his favourite topic.

After dinner, Simone took Graham past Emma's tidy office and the training room—without opening the training room door—and showed him to her room. He stopped just inside and whistled. 'No wonder you don't want to live in the dorms. A bedroom and your own little living room? This is like a hotel suite—except nicer.' He glanced at the reverse-cycle air conditioner. 'We have to put money on a card to pay for the electricity to run our air con. This is luxury!'

'If you need help with the cost—' she began, but he interrupted her.

'I have a scholarship and I am doing this myself. I will *not* take money from you. Ever.' He saw the window. 'Damn. Look at that view!'

'Come and see,' she said, going further into the bedroom with its double bed and showing him the view over the northern side of Hong Kong Island. The busy harbour traffic shimmered over the water beneath the neon lights shining from the packed high-rise apartment buildings. Christmas decorations had already been strung up on the hotels across the harbour, highlighting brilliantly coloured images of Santa and reindeer that would be converted to the God of Fortune when Chinese New Year came around.

'I can see the student quarters,' he said. 'Next time I'm in my dorm, I'll look up this way and try to recognise this building. I wonder if I can see it.'

'You should be able to,' Simone said. 'Uh … I worked out which room is yours. It's in the second tower on the eighteenth floor.' She pointed, then lowered her voice. 'Sometimes I imagine you're in there, and it's like I'm with you.'

He smiled down at her. 'That's brilliant. I'll be able to look up here and imagine I'm with you.'

She wasn't aware of how it happened, but a moment later, they were in each other's arms and kissing, and it felt wonderful. She lost herself in the feeling of being so cherished by someone who adored her and fell in love with him all over again. She felt him harden against her, and her body responded with urgent need for him. She so wanted to put her hand inside his pants and feel—

Someone coughed outside her room, and they quickly split apart.

'Uh …' He looked uncomfortable. 'Bathroom?'

She pointed at the door halfway down the side of her suite. 'Just in there.'

He slid the door open and stopped again. 'You have your own *ensuite*?'

'Everybody does,' Simone said.

'This place is amazing,' he said, slid the door closed and locked it.

Simone tried not to listen—the door was thin—and

unpacked her bag. She moved the red box with the Jade Emperor's stupid Edict to one side and put her laptop on her desk. Fortunately, she didn't need to hide the elaborately carved Edict box as ordinary mortals couldn't see it. She smiled at the thought of sharing an ordinary life with an ordinary mortal, and only having to deal with ordinary issues that were never life-and-death or full of horror and pain.

Since absorbing the essence of the previous Demon King to end the war and save the Heavens, she was sure she was no longer an Immortal. The prospect of growing old with someone she loved—instead of watching them age and die—was reassuring. What Michael and Clarissa had was so precious and joyful that she couldn't help but wish for something like that for herself. Maybe she could have a life like that with Graham. Her smile widened at the idea of a low-stress, love-filled, refreshingly ordinary future with him.

She opened her email and sighed at the number of messages—most of them were university administrative spam, but some were from her Celestial friends. She flipped through them and deleted all the ones that had the subject line of 'The Jade Emperor Hereby Orders the Princess Simone to Use Her Unique Status to Destroy a Demon' from a variety of senior Celestials. As soon as she had time, she'd add a spam filter for this Jade Emperor nonsense—and maybe ask Emma or her father to speak to him about cutting it out. It bordered on harassment.

Graham came out of the bathroom, and she nearly closed the laptop so he couldn't see the emails from the Celestials, then realised what that would look like, changed her mind, and left it open. 'So, what do you think of my family?'

He sat on the couch across from her little television. 'Your father was quiet, but he didn't seem to hate me, which is good. Your mother—'

'Stepmother,' Simone said. 'My mother died when I was little, remember?'

'Oh yeah, sorry,' he said, then moaned quietly. 'I should have remembered, that's really important to you, and—'

She waved her hands in front of her. 'No, it's okay, I don't mind. I do call her "Mum" sometimes, and she loves it. What about her?'

'She's so down-to-earth! Just so normal. And her Aussie accent is charming.'

'Good. Don't worry about Frankie, he's a little weirdo.'

'Is he on the spectrum?'

She stopped at the question, because it was a good excuse for Frankie's strangeness. She went with the family's established story. 'He's developmentally delayed. Sometimes he sounds twelve, other times he's like a five-year-old.' She wiped her hand over her forehead. 'He was kidnapped and abused by some gangsters when he was small. Emma and Dad paid the ransom and got him back, but he'll have issues for the rest of his life.'

'Abused? Really? What …?' Graham shook his head. 'No, don't tell me. That's awful.'

'I think it says something about the therapy he's been receiving that he's coming along so well,' Simone said. 'We sincerely hope that when he reaches adulthood, he'll be able to fully function as an independent adult.'

'The support of his family—and you—probably makes a difference as well,' Graham said, with a goofy smile full of affection. He rose. 'I have to be out early tomorrow, but what do you think the verdict is? Do they approve?'

'One hundred per cent,' she said. 'I'm sure they adore you. Frankie cannot wait to make your life a living hell. I think he has a notebook full of plans to "annoy Simone's boring boyfriend".'

He took her hand and pulled her up for a quick kiss. 'They seem lovely. So supportive of each other, you know?' His goofy smile deepened. 'Steamboat tomorrow night? Just you and me?'

She embraced him and kissed him on the cheek. 'It's a date.' She pulled back to smile at him, and her heart melted at his besotted expression. 'Come and we'll call a taxi for you, and I'll show you out.'

'Do I need to say good night to your parents? Show them

respect before I leave? I think I should, your dad seems quite traditional Chinese.'

Simone giggled. 'They'll be in their respective offices, doing some late-night crisis-wrangling. Wait until you see *this*.'

2

2

The next evening, Simone charged into the restaurant, breathless, and quickly pulled a chair out to sit next to Graham. He didn't appear fussed by her lateness; he just put his chin on his hand and smiled at her.

'Sorry, the tutorial went over time, and a student wanted me to explain something—' she began, but he interrupted her.

'Not a big deal, I've done it to you,' he said. 'I took the initiative and ordered you everything you like, and vegetable stock. Is that okay?'

'You're wonderful,' Simone said, putting her laptop bag on the seat next to her.

She looked around, admiring the Christmas decorations—everything was wrapped in tinsel and accordion-folded paper ornaments of trees and Santas hung from the ceiling. The restaurant had the standard Hong Kong over-styled décor, with expansive crystal chandeliers on the mirror-tiled ceiling and wallpapered walls above battered wainscoting. The thick, patterned carpet was brown with use in the high-traffic areas, and everything had a low-level dinginess caused by the large amount of people passing through—even though it had been renovated only a couple of years earlier.

The waiter brought a tureen full of stock and placed it over the portable stove set in a hole at the centre of the table, then turned on the gas burner to boil it.

'I really need to learn more Cantonese,' Graham said ruefully. 'But I suppose I'm lucky—they see I'm not full-Chinese and cut me some slack.'

'Same with me,' Simone said. 'We half-Chinese kids are notorious at failing in both languages.'

'Oh, come on,' he said. 'I've heard you speak at least four different dialects.'

She shrugged. 'It's part of what I am.'

'Which is awesome,' he said, and touched her hand, making her smile. He lowered his voice. 'Want to come back to my place after this? We started something last night in your room and I would really like to finish it.'

She moved her head closer to his. 'I need to go home afterwards because I have to be out early tomorrow—but I would love to.'

His grin widened. 'Excellent.' He studied the steamboat. 'I want to rush this now.'

'Eat up, you'll need your energy,' she said.

He laughed and shook his head.

The waiter brought the first set of plates for the steamboat, piled high with fresh leafy greens, four different types of tofu and deep-fried gluten balls that would become tender and full of flavour in the stock.

'Can I ask you something?' Graham asked, scooping some fried bean curd into the stock.

'You just did,' Simone said, and bumped him with her shoulder.

'You finally introduced me to your family, and I understand what a big step that was.' He put the basket down and sobered. 'We've been going out for nearly eighteen months now ...'

Simone's heart fell. Here it came. She opened her mouth to ask him if he really wanted to do this, then changed her mind. Graham was exceptional: smart, funny and great company. Their partnership was one of mutual respect and caring, and she didn't want to lose him. Her heart drifted down to settle somewhere near the floor.

'And I know we're still young and we haven't been together long, but dammit, Simone, you might be leaving Hong Kong soon to go research in Australia.'

'That's a long way off, my PhD topic still has to be approved and you know what a nightmare that is,' she said.

'Either way, your future isn't here and both of us know it.'

She shot him a sharp glance. His smile was innocent. She had taken him to dinner with the family—something that had scared other men away—to be absolutely sure he was human and not another demon plant.

Her father had assured her that he was clear.

He put his hand on hers. 'I think I love you, Simone.' He corrected himself. 'Falling in love with you.' He struggled when he saw the expression on her face. 'You're so wonderful, you know? This feels like more than just a casual thing. And I want to be sure … is it the same for you too?'

Simone's heart fell through the floor and landed in the basement.

He studied her expectantly and an icy breeze wafted through the heart-shaped void in her chest. She sighed and gave up, leaving whatever happened next to the cold hands of fate.

'I love you too, Graham, and I'll miss you terribly if I go to Australia.'

He hugged her, resting his cheek on hers, and she closed her eyes to relish the moment. He pulled back and his face was full of joy. 'I don't think we're ready for marriage or anything just yet—'

A hole opened under Simone's heart, plummeting it straight down to the tenth level of Hell.

'But I bought this …' He pulled out a jewellery box—fortunately not ring-sized—and opened it to show her a little eighteen-karat necklace with a turtle as the pendant. He took it out and held it up. 'Will you be my partner? My only one?'

She turned around and lifted her hair. 'We've been serious for a while, Graham. Yes, of course. And it's beautiful.'

She turned back to him and smiled. He jumped and turned down the gas—the soup was about to boil over.

After dinner, they went back to Graham's place and sat on the bed in his little dorm room. The furniture was cheap, with pine-veneer fittings that were already bubbling from the humidity. There was a single bed with a thin mattress, a built-in cupboard and desk, and not much else. He didn't have many possessions, although he did have a stone turtle on his desk that she'd given him as good luck charm. He had always talked about returning to Canada when his master's degree was complete, and they hadn't discussed their plans after that, apart from places he could show her there. Simone had been happy to live in the moment with him, postponing the day when she told him the truth about herself, but it was time.

Now she would see if the relationship survived it.

Simone summoned the book and pulled it out of her laptop bag. 'There's something I need to show you, Graham.' He put his arms around her, but she moved away from him. 'No, seriously. This is important.'

He nodded and released her. 'If it's what you want, sure. Tell me.'

She flipped the book open to the demon-slaying Shen.

'That book looks really old,' he said, fascinated. 'What's it about?'

'Chinese mythos,' she said. 'I've had it since I was four years old, my father bought for my stepmother, to explain who we are.'

'Your stepmother, Emma, the Australian,' he said. 'That makes sense, she probably knew nothing about our culture.' He shook his head. 'Growing up in Toronto, I didn't learn much about it either.'

'The Chinese pantheon is large and contains many powerful Shen—'

He interrupted her. 'Shen?'

'Spirits.' She connected it with the anime that they both loved. 'Kami in Japanese.'

'Oh. Like Dragon Ball.'

'Exactly like Dragon Ball. The Monkey King is the main

character of Dragon Ball. Now.' She turned the page to the Four Winds. 'These are the four gods of the directions, they're used in fung shui all the time.' She pointed. 'Blue Dragon of the East.'

'Cool,' Graham said.

'Red Phoenix of the South. White Tiger of the West, and this one.' She pointed to the statue of a god with long wild hair, a sword in one hand and a snake and turtle beneath each of his bare feet. 'This is the spirit—the Shen—of the North, the Xuan Wu. He is a powerful demon killer, and a snake *and* a turtle at the same time.'

'How can he be *two* animals?' Graham asked, fascinated. 'Is that canon? That's incredibly weird.'

'Totally canon, and I should know.'

He pointed at the picture. 'But he's a guy here, and the other three are statues of animals. He's not a turtle or a snake. They're under his feet.'

'He conquered his demonic turtle-snake essence and now spends most of his time human.'

'So weird.'

She snapped the book shut and took a deep breath. 'Okay, this is the part where it will be difficult for you.'

'As long as I'm with you everything is easy,' he said with confidence.

'He's my father.'

That stopped him dead and he froze as he tried to work out what she was telling him.

'That God, Xuan Wu, is my father. The gods are real, and my father is one of them.'

'I saw your dad last night in his disaster of an office, and he definitely didn't have reptile feet.'

'He does sometimes. He can change. He's a god, Graham.'

His mind stopped. He knew she wasn't delusional or mentally ill. This was just so far out of his cognitive experience that the gears ground to a halt. Then he came to the obvious conclusion and grinned broadly.

'No,' she said patiently. 'I'm not joking. I mean it.'

His features filled with confusion.

'Now for the hard part,' she said, and called her father.

Xuan Wu tapped on the door, and Simone let him in.

Graham shot to his feet and put his hand out for Xuan Wu to shake. 'Sir. Mr Chen. Good to see you again.'

Xuan Wu took Graham's hand and spoke to Simone without looking away from Graham. 'Are you sure you want this?'

'It's time,' she said with defeat.

Graham was full of forced smiles as he shook Xuan Wu's hand. 'I'm so happy that your daughter has allowed me into her life—'

'Come with me and help him,' Xuan Wu said, and teleported out, taking Graham with him.

Simone followed them to the basketball courts in front of the Pak Tai Temple on Cheung Chau Island.

'Do you know where we are?' Xuan Wu asked.

Graham staggered, and Simone rushed to hold him up. 'What just happened?' he asked.

'Graham,' Simone said urgently into his face. 'Do you trust me?'

He stared at her with his mouth open, then nodded. 'Uh. Yes. I do.' He looked around. 'What happened? I just lost like … is it the same day? I just lost a massive amount of time. I don't remember coming here at all. Did I hit …' He ran his hands over his scalp. 'What happened?'

'It's a special Chenco VR art installation,' Simone said. 'It's harmless. Dad wants to show it to you.'

'No, Simone—' Xuan Wu began, but Simone waved him down.

'Trust me, Dad. And you, Graham, do him a favour, and just go with it? Behave like we're really here at Cheung Chau.'

'That's where this is?' Graham asked, turning on the spot. 'It looks so real! This is amazing. Can they build games in this? I cannot wait!' He touched his forehead. 'Did you put a headset on me? I can't feel it.'

'This is the wrong way to go about it. I may have to

directly manipulate his mind to make him believe us,' Xuan Wu said, and headed up the stairs to the temple. It was the size of a large suburban house in the West, with a main building flanked by two smaller ones. The tennis and basketball courts spread two hundred metres from the temple in the centre of the island to the sea to ensure that there was no blockage of the fung shui energy. People were playing basketball under the lights, their shouts echoing across the space. Clouds of insects flew around the lights, and small bats flitted in and out of the halos to catch them.

Simone helped Graham follow Xuan Wu into the temple. They approached the head priest at the visitor's desk next to the front door, working on a spreadsheet on a slim modern laptop behind stacks of incense and lucky tokens. He was in his mid-sixties, wore slacks and a business shirt and jumped to his feet when he saw Xuan Wu.

'My Lord!' He saluted them both. 'Princess Simone. And who is this?'

'Simone's new boyfriend,' Xuan Wu said. 'Since the West Courtyard is complete, I thought I'd make use of it. Anyone else here, Ming?'

'No, my Lord, we're closed, I was just doing the books.'

'My Lord?' Graham asked, then to Simone, 'Princess?'

'This is Pak Tai himself, the Dark Emperor of the Northern Heavens, Xuan Tian Shang Di,' Ming said with pride. 'And his *mighty* daughter Princess Xuan Si Min Simone, the Saviour of the Heavens.' He saluted them again. 'You are a lucky young man! You're *blessed* to be chosen by the Destroyer of the Two Loathsome Kings and Router of the Two Dreadful Hordes.' His expression faltered. 'What about your oath, my lady? Is this young man capable of defeating you and the Dark Empress in battle, and then touching the Primal Yin?'

'Ugh,' Simone said, and swiped her hand over her forehead. 'I only killed one king. Frankie took the other one out, okay? I don't need to worry about that stupid oath until I'm thinking about marriage, and that's a long way away. And just Simone Chen. Please?'

'This is the best game *ever*,' Graham said with enthusiasm.

'See? Big mistake,' Xuan Wu said. 'This was so much easier when itinerates wandered China pretending to be Immortals and stories of their illusions spread through the community.' He gestured. 'This way.'

Simone held Graham's hand and they followed her father past the effigies of the patron gods of the temple in the main hall. A statue of Simone's father—portrayed as a large dark-faced fearsome god with wild hair, holding his sword with the seven stars on it, with a snake and turtle under each of his bare feet—stood in the middle. They passed through an open door on the side of the hall to a small, paved courtyard, surrounded by high concrete walls, topped with red terracotta tiles. One wall was inlaid with a bas-relief of the White Tiger in True Form, and there were a few dusty potted plants around the edge next to the wall.

Simone's father turned, raised his hands, and summoned a sparkling illusion that filled the courtyard. It showed the heavens, full of stars, and the twelve animals as glittering motifs around the edges, from rat to pig.

Graham made a soft sound of astonishment.

'The sky is divided into twelve sets of roots and branches,' Xuan Wu said, making the illusion spin gently around them. 'You know of them?'

'Well yeah, everybody knows the Chinese zodiac,' Graham said. 'I'm a rat.'

Xuan Wu snapped his wrist and the illusion shifted. The zodiac animals disappeared and were replaced by the Four Winds, each at their corner of the heavens.

'The Red Phoenix of the South. The White Tiger of the West. The Blue Dragon of the East,' he said. 'You know them?'

'Vaguely, Simone just showed me in her book,' Graham said. He grew excited. 'Do we fight them in this? I just remembered—we used to fight them in an old Final Fantasy game! That was great fun.'

The illusion focussed on the Xuan Wu, the combined snake and turtle, and the other three Winds disappeared as it grew to fill the whole image. 'The Shen of the North, the Xuan Wu, is a combination of a snake and a turtle.' The Serpent writhed around the Turtle's shell and the two heads stared ahead, one above the other.

'It was only a turtle in the Final Fantasy game,' Graham said, and became even more excited. 'Culturally authentic! Fantastic.'

Simone filled with dismay. 'I think I've made a mistake, Daddy.'

'I sincerely hope I don't have to do this the hard way,' Xuan Wu said sadly. 'There's always a small chance of damage when I modify their minds directly.'

The depiction of the Xuan Wu, in its combined snake and turtle form, changed to his human Celestial General form, wearing traditional Tang-style armour with his sword Seven Stars strapped to his back. The armour fitted over his robes, was black with silver trimmings and had the character for 'North' embossed on his shoulders. He was massively muscled and had a small beard on his square, ugly face.

'The Xuan Wu has many forms, one of them is the First Heavenly General, the Destroyer of Demons. He is the Right Hand of the Jade Emperor, and leads the armies of the Celestial ...'

The image changed to show Simone's father in the Celestial Palace, standing before the Jade Emperor, with the Legions of the Thirty-Six—her father's army with its thirty-six generals—in ranks behind him.

'Excellent,' Graham said with enthusiasm.

The image shifted to Xuan Wu's normal human form, still wearing traditional armour with his hair long and wild. 'He also has a human form and lives on the Earthly.'

'Wait, what?' Graham asked, looking from the illusion to Xuan Wu.

'In nineteen ninety-three, the Xuan Wu was on the Earthly at a performance of Western Opera.' The image changed to a stage where Simone's French-Canadian mother was performing *Tosca*. She wore a white Napoleonic-style dress and a huge wig as she silently sang an aria, her pale skin glowing in the spotlight. 'He fell in love with her at first sight, and she came to love him. Two years later, they were married and had a child.'

The image changed to Xuan Wu and Michelle, both holding the baby Simone, their expressions full of love and bliss. Simone's mother had shoulder-length hair, in a honey-brown the same colour as Simone's. Simone looked away, because the clarity of the images meant they were still vivid in her father's memory.

'The wife was killed by demons. The father raised the child with the assistance of a brilliant Australian woman who loved Simone as her own.' The illusion shifted to show Emma, her father, Leo and Simone herself at the top of the Eiffel Tower when she was four years old. 'When his daughter was five years old, Xuan Wu was killed by demons, returned to his animal form, and wandered the Earth, without memory, for ten years.'

'Oh, God,' Simone said quietly, wanting to forget those lost years.

'While he was absent, the Asian Demon King allied with the Demon King of Europe, and they built their joint strength for an attempt at our Asian Celestial Heavens. The Xuan Wu returned just as a great army of demons—from both East and West—attacked the Heavens.' Xuan Wu showed the awful attack on the Gates of Heaven, with the Jade Emperor standing on top of the gate as the demons threw themselves at it. 'The demons defeated the Celestial armies, took over both Heaven and Earth, and installed Simone's little brother Frankie as a puppet Jade Emperor.'

'This is an *amazing* backstory,' Graham said.

The illusion changed to the Demon Kings' throne room in their mock-Versailles palace. Simone's father was on his knees in front of Frankie on the throne, flanked by both of the Kings. 'Princess Simone ran the Resistance by herself from hiding, sheltering refugees and protecting the innocent. And when the demons tried to destroy her father, she killed them.' In the image, Simone raced up to the Asian Demon King and plunged her swords into him. The dark essence of the demon swirled around Simone and was absorbed into her, then her father grabbed her, and they both disappeared. 'She is tainted by the dark essence of the King she killed and can no longer visit the Celestial Heavens. She saved the world—and has suffered for it ever since.' The illusion disappeared and the contents of the courtyard returned to normal. 'And here we are. I am Xuan Wu, the Dark Emperor of the North, and Simone is my daughter. As the attendant noted, she is a Celestial Princess, Destroyer of the Demon King and Saviour of the Heavens.'

'And who can I be?' Graham asked. He turned to Simone. 'You said this was experimental? This will be an absolute winner, thanks so much for showing it to me! Can I be involved in the alpha testing?'

'It's real,' Simone said. 'My father really is Xuan Wu.'

'It is *so* real!' Graham said, spinning back to speak to her father. 'I felt like I can touch it!'

Simone's dismay deepened. 'Take us back, Daddy, I think we need to do it the hard way.'

'I'm sorry, Simone,' Xuan Wu said, and took them all back to Graham's dorm.

Graham felt his scalp again. 'How the hell did you do that? I didn't feel a headset, where is it?' He dropped his hands. 'That was *awe—*.'

Graham stopped dead and flopped to sit on the bed with his eyes wide when Xuan Wu hit his brain. The room's temperature dropped, and Simone sat next to Graham, ready to catch him when her father released him.

'Nearly done,' Xuan Wu said, then, 'All right. I told him everything and I've commanded him to know it's the truth.' He shook his head. 'He will have a mighty headache when I release him.'

'Did you tell him about my vow?' Simone asked.

'No, because I doubt you'll get that far with him.'

'Thanks a *lot*, Daddy.'

'He's human, he can't help it.' Xuan Wu said and released his hold.

Graham drifted for a few heartbeats, his eyes fluttering,

then looked from Simone to Xuan Wu, yelled and plastered himself as close to the wall as possible.

'Sorted,' Xuan Wu said. 'Leave him to it.'

Graham curled up against the wall with his head in his hands.

'You broke him!' Simone said.

'The headache will pass,' Xuan Wu said. 'All of this would be much less trouble if you'd just date Celestials.'

'I can't go to Heaven, so they don't want anything to do with me—the ones that aren't scared to death of me, anyway. Would you prefer I dated demons?'

Xuan Wu made a soft sound of amusement. 'At least they'd know who you are.'

'Very funny,' she said.

'He's okay,' Xuan Wu said. 'But we probably need to leave him for a while to sort it out.'

'Please don't hurt me,' Graham whimpered, still covering his face. 'Don't kill me, I have a family.'

'We won't hurt you,' Simone said without attempting to touch him. 'I'll be back later, and we can talk about it. If you feel up to talking, just ping me on my phone.'

Graham didn't move.

'Thanks, Daddy,' Simone said, and Xuan Wu disappeared. She removed the necklace, put it on the bed next to Graham, then took her bag and went out the dorm's door, closing it softly behind her.

3

Two days later she sat at her little desk in the postgrad cubicles and attempted to work on the final version of the prospectus literature review. The existing body of research on turtles was extensive, but there wasn't much that was Asia-based; it was mostly from Australia and the Pacific, with some in the Indian Ocean. Thankfully, the spam filter for JE nonsense was working well, and she wasn't being constantly distracted by emails from Celestials ordering her to kill a stupid demon.

Her phone pinged and she grabbed it, full of dread. The dread turned to brittle hope when she saw it was Graham.

Hey you

Hi Graham, you okay?

Can we talk?

Oh shit. She tapped a reply.

Sure. I'm in the cubicles on the seventh floor

Omw

She put the papers to one side and wiped her eyes. At least now she would know whether their relationship was over or not. She plastered a false smile on her face as he came through

26

the door and stopped to study her. She pulled an empty chair closer for him.

'Sit, Graham,' she said.

He sat on the chair across from her—just out of reach—clasped his hands and looked down.

'Did your father hypnotise me? What did he do to me?'

'He just told you the truth about us.'

'Like a hallucination. But real.'

'Sorry about that, but it's a lot to cover, and he can do it with complete certainty so that you know it's true.'

'Do you know how mind-blowing that was? Do you have any idea?' He shook his head. 'I know it's true, but it's still unbelievable. It's breaking my head. I didn't know anything about the Chinese gods. My mom said it's "old people's superstition". Why doesn't anybody know about this? I mean—gods are real, but nobody talks about them?'

'I think there's been a concerted effort by high-level demons to destroy any references to the gods, so that people won't call on them when they need help.'

'So the supernatural world ... magic ... all of that exists?'

She nodded.

'Demons? He said that demons exist? Like ... the demons that fung shui consultants protect us from—they're *real*?'

She nodded again. 'But my father drove them into Hell a few thousand years ago ...' She saw his shocked expression at these revelations and plunged on. 'And they aren't allowed on the surface to hurt people. You'll always be completely safe with me.'

'We're *scientists*, Simone,' he said with exasperation. 'The obvious scientific explanation is that your dad hypnotised me. How am I supposed to believe all of this? Can you prove it?'

'I don't think you're ready for me to prove it in person.' She tried to stay calm and logical, respecting his legitimate scepticism. 'I've chosen to live an ordinary life away from all of that, but you had the right to know because it's part of who my family are.'

'He said that you made a huge sacrifice—thinking that

you'd die doing it—and saved everybody,' he said. 'Now that I know you well, that's the most believable part of it.'

She lowered her head. 'Thanks.'

'You really did that? Killed the King of the Demons? You *murdered* someone?'

'It's complicated, but it's what the Demon King wanted, and he ordered my father to do it because it would destroy Dad as well. I just made sure I was the one who did it, instead of my father. I wanted to spare Dad from the consequences. I thought it would kill me.'

'So doubly a sacrifice.'

'I don't see it that way,' she said.

His eyes bored into hers. 'If you were some sort of superhero like he said—'

'Absolutely not a superhero,' she said. 'And I said, I'd prefer not to—'

He cut her off. 'What sort of things can you do? He wasn't specific, he just said that he's one of the gods ...' He hesitated. 'I can't believe I just said that. And you're his daughter. He said you can do things.' He pulled his chair closer to hers. 'Like what?'

She didn't lead with "Destroy the planet and all life on it", and gave up trying to avoid the topic. 'He's one of the most powerful Shen in the heavens, and I'm his daughter. There isn't much that I can't do.'

'Fly?'

She nodded.

He looked hopeful. 'Wings? Like an angel?'

'No wings. Like Superman.'

'Really?'

She nodded again.

'Super strength? How much can you lift?'

'When you reach my level, it's hard to measure with weights, because I can deadlift an A380.'

His mouth flopped open.

'Uh ... with one hand.'

'Damn.' He moved his chair slightly away. 'What if you ...

If you're that strong ... When we're being ...' He shook his head again. 'You could easily kill me if you lost control. You could crush me like a bug!'

'It doesn't work like that,' she said. 'My normal strength is normal. Even when I'm excited. If I want to use the extra strength, I have to make a really big effort.' She reached out to touch his hand and was thrilled when he didn't move away again. 'You'll always be safe with me.'

'It could all be a lie. I mean, everything you say defies science—and we're *scientists*. Is there a way you can physically prove to me that it's not just your father hypnotising me?'

'Sure. At this point what I usually do is take you to a completely inaccessible place—somewhere really high, like the top of Burj Khalifa or something, and take selfies with you. But the last guy said it could be a greenscreen, so I—'

'What last guy?' he asked sharply.

'Graham, I'm twenty-five. You aren't the first man I've dated.'

'What happened to Burj Khalifa guy?'

'He said that I was insane, my father was insane, it was definitely a hoax and we drugged him then put greenscreen photos of us on his phone. He put a restraining order on me and every member of my family.'

'It can't be a greenscreen if I choose where we go and we go right now,' he said. 'How about the top of the Sydney Opera House? If we made a video there, we'd get a million YouTube views.'

'Most of those insane videos of heights and parkour on roofs are actually Shen showing off,' she said. 'I wish they wouldn't do it. Humans emulate them and get killed.'

'*Humans*?'

She looked away.

'You're not human?'

She sighed. 'Define human.'

'Me.'

'I'm not you!'

'Okay. My sister.'

'If your sister is the baseline for human, then in many ways I am, and in many ways I'm not.'

'I think you're avoiding the issue here, Simone.'

'In every way that counts, I'm a human being. How about that?' She sliced one hand through the air. 'I want to be ordinary! I don't want to do anything like that, I want to have a normal, happy life—'

'And be able to lift a superjumbo and fly to the top of the Sydney Opera House.'

'Effectively, yes. Practically, no, because I'm not allowed in Australia.'

'But you were planning to do research on the Great Barrier Reef?'

'The Grandmother negotiated ...' She saw his face. 'That big rock in the middle of Australia. Uluru?'

He nodded, then his face filled with wonder. 'It's alive?'

'Many stones are alive. Anyway, the Shen ... Kami ... of Australia are pissed with me because my mother climbed Uluru a long time ago. Uluru's a sweetheart, and she's given me a special dispensation to research the turtles on the reef from the station on Heron Island, but I am not to step on the mainland of Australia.'

'Okay then ...' He thought about it. 'Top of the Empire State Building. Higher than the viewing deck. Take some selfies, and it's all proven to me. Do you have a magic carpet we can ride there?'

'No, but I can do a Dragon Ball-style cloud for you,' she said, and felt a bolt of hope as he grinned at the idea. 'You'd do that? For me? Let me prove everything to you?'

'I know it sounds weird, but I'd like it to be true.'

She stared at him. 'There is something seriously wrong with you.'

'Well yeah, I'm dating you, god-lady.' His smile widened. 'This is a whole new field of study, you know? Even though I have to keep it a secret, I can learn more about ... everything. And riding Goku's cloud? I'm in!'

'I can make a Goku costume for you when my prospectus

is done and I have time for cosplay again,' she said slyly.

'Doubly in! How long will it take to go to New York? That's the other side of the world, and we have work to do. Next week? After your presentation?'

She checked her watch. 'It's five pm right now. I can have you there by midnight and back here tomorrow morning.'

'Midnight photos on top of the Empire State Building—' he began.

'It will be the middle of the day there. Yesterday.'

'Damn!' He hesitated, looking at her, then grinned again. 'Let's do it.'

She held her hand out. 'Take it.'

He took her hand, still grinning like an idiot.

'I'm going to teleport us.'

He snatched his hand away. 'What, really?'

She nodded. 'You'll feel dizzy when we arrive, but you'll be perfectly safe, and I can catch you if you fall. You'll be *safe*. Understood?'

He nodded, then held his hand out again and she took it. His smile had returned.

She teleported them to the top of the biology building, in the centre of the roof so he couldn't fall off if he passed out. It was high above Hong Kong Harbour on the Western side of Hong Kong Island, close to the top of the Island's highest point. She held his hand as he staggered, then righted himself and shook his head. He looked around, still clutching her hand.

'Shit, we're a long way up,' he said. 'There's no railing!'

She stepped up into the air and floated just above the rooftop, still holding his hand. 'We don't need a railing, Graham. I won't let you fall.'

He stared at her, then lowered his head to see her feet. He pushed his free hand under her feet, then stood again. 'It's true.'

She dropped back to the surface of the roof and summoned a cloud. 'Ready to go?'

'We'll be higher,' he said, staring at the cloud as if it was a deadly animal. 'With no railing. On a cloud. For a long way.'

'We can skip it if you don't want to,' she said quickly.

'How do I get onto it?'

She moved the cloud so that it was directly next to them, and he put one hand out—still holding hers with the other—to touch it. He pressed his hand through the surface of the cloud until it met the hardness beneath. 'That's remarkable.' He grinned at her. 'Just like all the martial arts television series. Riding on a cloud. Wild.'

'Just step up,' she said, and helped him onto it. She stepped up behind him and turned him so that his back was against her chest.

She had a sudden flashback of doing this when her father had been lost to her. She and Emma had led a Celestial strike team to the mountainous region of Guilin. Michael had gone along with them, summoning a cloud for Emma to ride on. He'd sung the Magic Carpet Song from the Aladdin movie, and his voice had been so sweet—

'Is there anything I need to do?' Graham asked.

She put her arms around his waist and leaned her head on his arm so she could see around him—he was a few centimetres taller than her. 'Just stand still—you can sit if you want—and I'll take us. You can't fall off, I have you. Okay?'

He nodded and she slowly lifted the cloud higher.

He clutched her arms where she held him around his waist, gripping her so tight it hurt.

When they were fifty metres above the rooftop, he started to yell. It was a single long sound of terror, then he managed to form it into words.

'No, no, no, too high, too high, fuck! Take me down, this is too high! Simone, enough!'

She gently carried them back down the rooftop.

'Down to the ground! Please!' he said.

She teleported him back to her cubicle without letting go of him. He staggered away from her and fell to sit in one of the chairs.

'You won't be sick, will you?' she asked with concern.

He shook his head, gasping, and bent over his knees. He breathed faster and more heavily: he was having a panic attack.

She put her hand on his arm and calmed him just enough to ease his hyperventilation. He settled back in the chair and stared at her.

'You did something to my mind,' he said, his eyes wide with shock.

'I am so sorry,' she said, still with her hand on his arm. 'It's okay. Really. We don't need to do anything to prove it.' His eyes were glazed. 'I'd prefer a normal, ordinary life, hopefully with you. We can forget that this conversation happened and go back to just being us. I won't do anything like that to you ever again. Okay?'

'I need a drink,' he said, then stood and lurched down the corridor to the exit.

She didn't follow him.

'And you haven't seen him for two days?' Emma asked from behind her desk in the Peak apartment.

Simone shook her head.

'Not even a text?'

'No.'

Simone's father poked his head into Emma's office, his long hair falling over his shoulder. 'I'm taking Frankie for his bath and putting him to bed.' He saw Simone's face. 'Are you okay? Is there anything I can do?'

'We're talking about human relationships,' Emma said.

'Really not my area of expertise. I'll leave you to it.'

'Let me know when to say goodnight to him,' Emma said.

Xuan Wu nodded, pulled back and softly closed the door behind him.

'Have you seen Graham around the campus?' Emma asked Simone.

'I think he's avoiding me.' She leaned her forehead on her hand in the visitor's chair. 'He's terrified of me.' She wiped her eyes. 'This is the third one, Emma.'

'He's not scared of you, silly Simone,' Emma said. 'He's embarrassed. He probably thinks that you see him as a terrible coward for being afraid of something that he should have enjoyed. Scared of heights? Not Goku after all? He had a panic attack right in front of you! He's mortified.'

'Oh,' Simone said.

'Write him a letter,' Emma said. 'No, send him an email. Tell him it's fine, it's okay, and that he's normal.'

'And I'm not,' Simone said. 'I want to be normal, and I'm not!'

'No, you're completely exceptional,' Emma said. 'Wait until your father has a chance to tell Graham that *you saved the world.*'

'He already did, but I don't think it went in amongst all the weirdness.' Simone tilted her head back and stared at the ceiling. 'I'd rather save this relationship. He's a total sweetie.'

'Go to your room, pull out your computer, throw all the words at it and send them to him,' Emma said. 'If he comes around, he's worth it.'

'And if he doesn't?'

'Then he's not.'

Simone rose to leave, and Emma stopped her.

'When's your prospectus presentation? I'd like to go along and cheer for you.'

'Four more days, Thursday morning.' Simone leaned on the desk, hesitated, then decided to be frank. 'Could you not come? No family? I'd like to do this one hundred per cent myself.'

Emma wasn't fazed. 'No problem. Do it, succeed, then come home and we'll have dinner to celebrate. Do you want to invite your uncles and aunts?'

'No, but dinner with the close family would be great.'

'Done.' Emma waved her away. 'Go. I have a hundred Dark Disciples to induct into the Mountain schedules and your father keeps stealing them, taking them to remote mountaintops, and teaching them esoteric martial arts that they aren't ready for.'

Simone smiled. 'He's the God of Martial Arts, Emma, I think he knows what he's doing.'

Emma raised both hands. 'One of the new disciples has been on the Mountain for a week already and still hasn't provided me with a contact for next of kin!'

'None of my business,' Simone said with satisfaction, went out the door and closed it behind her. She re-opened it and poked her head back in. 'Thanks, Emma.'

'I love you!' Emma shouted at the screen.

Simone went into the apartment's training room to think. It was the size of her suite and had modern gymnastic mats covering the polished-wood floor. One of the long walls was mirrored, and a short wall had a collection of her father's favourite legendary weapons—of all types—hanging on hooks. A stand next to the picture windows held Emma's weapon, a gorgeous Japanese-style katana called 'Scales of Wisdom'. The sword had been a wedding gift to Emma from Xuan Wu and was decorated with his Serpent skin wrapped around the handle and pieces of his Turtle shell inlaid into the *tsuba*, the guard. Emma had presented Xuan Wu with a silver filigree crown that also had skin from her Serpent form inlaid into it. Each had been delighted with their respective wedding gifts, claiming that the essences in the sword and crown would enhance them through the love they shared. Simone thought it was strange and a little creepy for them to carry around pieces of each other's dead bodies, but respected their relationship enough to keep quiet about it.

Simone was aware that her father and stepmother had a … creative private life. He was a snake and turtle at the same time, and could take two human forms, male and female. Emma was a Celtic serpent, and capable of taking a big black snake form. They made it very clear, way too often in Simone's opinion, that they found each other's reptilian forms intensely attractive, and she didn't want to know the details. But she did sometimes wonder what it would be like to be with Michael in his Tiger form, and to bury her hands into that soft golden fur …

She called her swords and they appeared in her hands. They were khopesh-derivative, shaped roughly like sickles, with curved blades that were lethally sharp on both sides and perfect for tearing demons to pieces. The forge on the Celestial

Mountain had made them specifically for her in a deep blue that mirrored her own livery, with seven holes through each blade to hold her energy chakras. She had named them Bo and Bei after the only two women who were Heavenly Generals in her father's Thirty-Six. She smiled as she remembered the generals' horrified reactions to having Simone's weapons named after them and how she'd told them to shut up and take the compliment.

She moved into a wide defensive stance and began a top-level Shaolin double-sword set. The movements helped her shift into a meditative trance and allowed the words to flow freely in her imagination as she composed an email, in her head, to Graham. She really wanted to salvage this relationship and hoped that he could learn to deal with her weirdness. She wished she could fill the indentations on her curved short swords with her chakras, but since she'd killed the Demon King, her essence was tainted and she couldn't use Celestial abilities or enter the Heavens.

Need a sparring partner? her father asked her telepathically.

Always, she said, and he appeared on the other side of the room. His own double-handed Chinese great sword, Seven Stars, appeared in his hands and he lit the indentations in it, filling the room with glowing colours. He changed the sword to a spear and spun it, still glowing, in his hands, then stood on one leg with the other toe on his knee and the spear pointed at the ground in front of him in a classic 'Monkey King Prepares for Battle' stance.

'You keeping your skills sharp?' he asked.

She crossed her swords above her head in a salute and moved into a defensive stance as well. 'An hour every day, because high-level demons still occasionally try me out.'

'Good to hear.'

He moved too fast for the human eye to see and went straight for her face. It wasn't a feint, so she slid to the side and attempted to take his feet out from under him as he passed. He jumped and span in the air to stab at her abdomen, but she blocked the spear with both blades, then used all her strength to force him down and back. He hit the floor and slid backwards a metre.

'Nice,' he said, then swung the spear in his hands in a big swinging blow at her head.

She saw the feint, jumped over the spear as he lowered it to target her feet, used her left blade to guide the spear in the direction it was already going, and stabbed him in the side with her right, slicing right through him so that point of the blade came out in the middle of his back.

The look of astonishment on his face was matched by her own horror at what she'd done. She dropped both blades, but Bei was still lodged in his abdomen. His face was pale with shock, and he dropped the spear, then fell like a dead tree onto his back.

'Daddy!' She ran to him and knelt next to him. She took his hand in hers. 'I am so sorry. What were you thinking? You let me stab you!'

He raised his hand as he gasped. 'Minute. Take the sword out.'

She studied him desperately. Removing the sword would hurt like anything. 'Do you need me to block the pain for you? Do you need Emma to help?'

He smiled through the agony. 'Don't tell Emma, she'll never let me hear the end of it! Just take the sword out. I have it, the pain's under control.'

She winced, took the handle of Bei and wrenched it out of him. The wound was huge and horrendous, and blood fountained from it.

'Ugh. What a mess. Minute,' he said, and changed.

He transformed into his True Form, the Turtle and Serpent. He was so large that his shell pushed her back; his smallest form was a good three metres long and he filled the room. The Serpent writhed around the Turtle's shell, with its head above the Turtle's.

'Much better,' they said with male and female voices in unison, before changing back to her father's normal human form. He fell to sit on the mat and put his head on his knees. 'Wah, lost some blood. Give me a minute.'

She knelt next to him, carefully avoiding the puddle of blood they'd made on the mats. 'Why did you let me do that? That must have hurt like anything! What were you trying to teach me—'

He raised his hand to stop her speaking and took a deep breath. 'Simone. It wasn't intentional.'

She stopped. 'What?'

He grabbed her in a fierce embrace, then kissed her on the cheek. 'You bested me! Finally. Someone who can take me down.' He pulled back, his eyes glistening with tears, and hugged her fiercely again. 'I am so damn proud of you. I must tell Emma. This is ...' He shook his head. 'Magnificent.'

'I'm better than you?' she asked weakly. 'That's not possible, Dad, you're the freaking *God of Martial Arts*.'

'You aren't better than me,' he said. 'But you are close to my equal, and I underestimated you. I was careless and paid the price.' He lowered his voice. '*Finally*. Someone who can take me down if I turn.' He took both her hands and shook them. 'Thank you.'

'What?' she asked, aghast. 'What do you mean, take you down if you turn?'

'There is always a small chance that I will return to what I was,' he said. 'The Bodhisattva Kwan Yin has helped me, but that demon is still there, inside me, and it is immensely powerful. Now I know: the Heavens are safe. You and Emma, working together, are more than capable of destroying me if I turn.' He leaned his head back and closed his eyes. 'The Heavens are *safe*.'

'I could never do that.'

'I will do my very best to ensure that you never have to.' He rose and put his hand out to help her up. 'I owe you a cup of my best tea. The Tiger gave us these mats and will make my life hell about getting blood on them again. And Emma will want to take my head off for putting you through that.'

4

Still shaken, Simone finished throwing 'all the words', as Emma had suggested, into an email for Graham, closed her eyes, made a wish, and sent it. She raised her head as she heard shouting from her father's office: Michael's father, the White Tiger God of the West, sounded furious. Simone's father replied, his usual calm self, and then Emma loudly and defiantly said something unintelligible. Simone didn't attempt to listen to what they were saying. They were probably both giving Simone's father grief about allowing her to stab him and the damage to the mats, which Simone wanted nothing to do with it. She left them to it and pulled up her prospectus to work on it for an hour or so before she went to bed.

After twenty minutes of the Tiger yelling in Xuan Wu's office, the Tiger and Emma both spoke into Simone's head at the same time.

Don't listen to him, Emma said.

Children will die and you're the only one who can save them! the Tiger said.

What? Simone asked the Tiger. *Children?*

Come into Ah Wu's office and I'll show you.

Simone made a loud sound of annoyance and pushed her chair back, then stormed into her father's office. It was the usual disaster area, with papers strewn everywhere, and a large

Ninja Turtle figure next to his computer monitor. Emma and Xuan Wu were in their usual black Mountain martial arts uniforms, and the Tiger was wearing a tailored, three-piece, gold-coloured suit with a white shirt and gold tie. He was the same height as Simone's father and heavy muscled, with a shock of white hair and the square, gold face of the people of Western China. His long white sideburns covered his cheeks, and his tawny eyes were full of desperation.

'You don't need to do this,' Emma said.

'Don't listen to the Tiger, we'll find another way,' Xuan Wu said.

'There is no other fucking way!' the Tiger shouted. He gestured angrily towards Xuan Wu's computer screen. 'Watch this and tell me there's any alternative, Simone. It can only be you or Michael, and Clarissa's due any day so it can't be Michael. It has to be you, otherwise these poor kids will die.'

Emma waved one furious hand at Simone as she spoke to the Tiger. 'After killing the King, she absorbed most of his essence. You know she can't travel to the Celestial.' She spoke with more force. 'She may have lost her Immortality!'

'Oh,' the Tiger said, dropping his arms and deflating. 'Really?' He glanced from Emma, to Simone, to Xuan Wu. 'Are you—'

'Don't you *dare* ask me to confirm the truth my wife just shared with you,' Xuan Wu said, glowering.

'Never mind, then,' the Tiger said. 'I will find another way.'

Simone ignored them all, went to the monitor, and pressed 'play' on the video. The Tiger's Number One, Katie, was giving a voice-over as someone wearing a headcam walked between snow-covered trees.

'Do you sense anything?' Katie asked, her voice clear.

A woman replied through the patchy audio of the headcam, her voice a whisper through the throat mike—she was the one walking through the trees and carrying the camera. 'I don't sense anything. No demons around here at all.' She slowed. 'Humans ahead.' The view from the headcam lowered as she crouched and crept through the snow-covered undergrowth. 'There they are.'

Two women in bulky fur coats stood together under a snow-covered tree.

'Clear,' the woman holding the headcam said.

'Who is that carrying the headcam?' Simone asked without looking away from the screen.

'It's one of the Mad Fucking Witches, Katie's little strike team,' the Tiger said. 'Don't know her name, daughter number thirty-something. One of the good ones.' He turned and spoke to Simone's father. 'You should do that too, have an elite woman-only strike team. They're fucking awesome.'

'We don't need to,' Xuan Wu said. 'Our Disciples are completely mixed, all races and genders. The borderline Disciples are screened in the first week, and if they fail a basic test on treating a vulnerable person with respect then they're expelled.'

'I couldn't do that, I'd be throwing out all the White Horsemen except for the Seraglio guards,' the Tiger said, then added under his breath, 'even some of them too.'

'Which is why the Mountain doesn't need an all-female strike team,' Simone said.

'Hopefully, the younger generation are a bit more aware,' Emma said. 'Even the Horsemen.'

'Clear to approach, Katie?' the woman behind the camera asked.

'Go, Sid,' Katie said.

Sid stood and the women spun, alert, then noticeably relaxed when they saw her. She walked up to them and shook their hands.

'I'm Sid. Katie sent me,' Sid said.

'Ilyana,' the younger, dark-haired white woman in her mid-thirties, said. Her appearance had been altered by extensive plastic surgery to make her look younger and much more attractive than was natural.

'Galina,' the older woman said. She'd had similar major surgery done, making her look in her forties when she was probably much older.

'Katie said that your husbands had been in contact with Ineke Prochazka and that their behaviour had changed dramatically afterwards.'

'Yes!' Galina said. 'Before, my husband was all about our national purity. Our way of life, our language, our independence from the Soviets. We fought so hard for our freedom when the Soviet Union fell, and now?'

'Now both of them—father and son—are obsessed with pleasing the Russian masters,' Ilyana said. 'They've steered the entire country in a completely different direction.'

'This is one of those small Eastern European states that turned into a dictatorship after the Soviet Union fell?' Simone asked without looking away from the screen.

'Precisely,' the Tiger said. 'Wife of the current President, who's been in control since the mid-nineties, and wife of the President's son.'

'And then this happened,' Ilyana said, and Galina pulled her in and held her as Ilyana leaned on her. 'My little girl—she was only twelve—he gave her everything. He loved her! And then he met with Prochazka, and changed, and he ... he ... did awful things to her ...' She gasped for breath and clutched Galina's hands. 'And then he killed her! I found him standing over her body and he turned to me, and he smiled ...' She looked directly into Sid's headcam. 'I never want to see a smile like that ever again. His mouth was ... full of blood.' She screwed her eyes shut, as if to reject the mental image. 'He said, "Oops. My mistake. She shouldn't have resisted, I don't know my own strength. Humans are so fragile." And then he laughed and looked down at my little girl, lying on the floor dead and cold, and said, "What a waste of good blood." Vampires? Vampires aren't real.' She turned to the older woman, still clutching her hand. 'Galina, tell me vampires aren't real.'

'Vampires aren't real,' Sid said with conviction. 'But you are in danger, and I think your husbands, both your husbands, have been replaced, and we need to move you and your children somewhere safe.'

'Replaced with what?' Galina asked.

'We'll explain everything after we have you safe,' Sid said. 'Where are your husbands right now?'

'They're in their offices in the capital square,' Ilyana said. She made an obviously massive effort to control her grief and anguish and nodded. 'Can you help us escape?' She turned to Galina. 'What about the other wives?'

'For now, just you, me, and the children,' Galina said to Ilyana. 'I don't trust any of the other wives—they might tell our husbands. We will contact them once we're free and safe with Sid and Katie, to arrange something for them.'

'All right,' Ilyana said with determination. 'Can we pack some things?'

'Where are the children?' Sid asked.

'At school,' Ilyana said. 'It will be a few more hours before their bodyguards and nannies bring them home. They were hysterical about losing their sister, and my husband ...' She took a deep breath. 'He *beat* them. He never laid a hand on them before, but this time? He *enjoyed* it. And then he sent them, wailing, with the bodyguards and nannies—he hit one of the nannies as well, when she tried to stop him—'

'You need to go right now,' Sid said. 'I'll call in a couple of other Witches—that's my unit—and we'll transport you to the school. You pull the kids out of school, and we'll take them to a safe house.'

'But their clothes and things!'

'Leave them,' Sid said. 'They can track you with anything you own. Let's go.'

Ilyana and Galina shared a look, squeezed their hands where they held them, and nodded to each other. They turned back to Sid. 'Thank you.'

'Katie, send two more Witches, we have a group of people to transport,' Sid said. Her hands appeared in the cam's view. 'Take my hands, hold your breaths, and close your eyes.'

'You can't teleport humans!' Simone said, turning back to see the Tiger and Xuan Wu.

'If they're in danger from demons, damn straight she can,' the Tiger said, crossing his arms over his chest. 'What we *can't* do, though, is take down those demon replacements on their home turf before they kill the rest of the family's children "by mistake". The demons are too big for even the Witches to handle, and they haven't attacked us, so we have no authorisation to go in.'

'Collect the rest of the family and put them somewhere safe,' Emma said.

The Tiger shook his head. 'The other wives are brainwashed into believing that all they need to do is love their husbands harder and they'll stop hurting them. The dynasty has a total of fourteen children in the second generation, and Sid only managed to get three to safety.'

'We will not ask you to risk your mortal life, and we will find another way, Simone,' Emma said, crossing her arms in front of her chest to mirror the Tiger's posture. 'Go to bed. You have a prospectus in four days.'

Simone pushed away from the desk. 'Are these the demons the Jade Emperor has been harassing me to deal with? It's becoming ridiculous—the red box never moves from my desk, and he's started sending me emails about it. He's ordering officials—and even my friends—to send me emails about it as well.'

The Celestials shared a look and a shrug—they didn't know, the JE wasn't telling them anything.

'If the Jade Emperor is encouraging me to go, it won't kill me.' Simone sighed with defeat. 'If it shuts the JE up and protects little kids, I guess I'll do it and get it over with before my prospectus presentation. Can Katie show me where to go?'

'You really don't have to do it, girl,' the Tiger said. 'We can find another—'

Simone cut him off. 'Call me "girl" again and I will force you to use full Imperial protocol every time you address me.'

Xuan Wu made a soft sound of amusement.

The Tiger fell to one knee. 'I beseech you, Imperial Highness, to help these children by destroying the demons that have taken the place of their fathers and grandfather,' he said. 'You are the only one who is not constrained by Celestial protocol that prohibits any sworn Celestial from acting when our dominions have not been attacked.'

'And Michael can't do it because Clarissa's about to pop,' Simone said, understanding.

'Michael would probably be as unable as any of us because he is still sworn to serve the Jade Emperor,' Emma said. 'No sworn resident of the Celestial can attack a demon unless the demon attacks them first.'

'It must be you, Princess,' the Tiger said, rising gracefully to his feet despite his muscular bulk. 'Your unique demon-filled nature means that you are neither a Celestial nor a demon and can act as an independent agent.'

'All right then, show me where to go,' Simone said.

'I'm going too,' Xuan Wu said. 'To watch Simone's back. As Emma said, we're not sure that Simone is still Immortal, and I won't see her life at risk.'

'You can't go,' the Tiger said. 'You can't act in that arena unless your heritage is part-European. Believe me, I already tried. Only my half-European kids can do anything there. We're limited by our regional affiliation.'

'Daddy's so powerful it doesn't matter,' Simone said. 'He's been to Europe—he's lived in Europe—for years and had no trouble destroying their demons.'

The Tiger studied Simone's father, and then nodded. 'You're our biggest tactical asset, so I guess you're the best choice to watch her back.'

'He's more of a doomsday device.' Emma uncrossed her arms and gestured towards the living room. 'Suit up and let Ah Bai show you the way. I'll stay here and mind the family.'

They went into the living room. The ceiling was too low to change, so Simone and her father jumped through the glass of the living room windows to float outside them before changing into their Celestial forms.

The living room windows were tinted. The interior was visible, but Simone saw her reflection clearly in the glass and turned away. Her father was his usual majestic self; nearly four metres tall, in black and silver robes with his black enamel armour over the top and his massive broadsword, Seven Stars, strapped to his back. His long black hair writhed with a life of its own and he had a thin black beard on his square, ugly face.

Since destroying the previous Demon King and absorbing his essence, Simone's Celestial form had become a more demonic version of herself. She was nearly the same height as her father, and her robes looked like holes in reality; dark blue with glowing, tiny golden stars within them. Her skin was no longer a more radiant version of her ordinary human form. She was covered in black, glittering scales and her black hair was in thick twining strands that looked almost like tentacles. Her face was reptilian, with two slits for a nose and an almost non-existent chin. She'd tried to control the form, even the bare minimum of making her hair look a little more normal ... but she couldn't. This was who she was now—more demon than Celestial. She saw her own huge completely black eyes widen when Er Hao escorted Lord Venus, the Jade Emperor's personal emissary, into the living room.

Venus glowed gently as he floated above the floor. He was in the form of a slim, elegant man in his mid-thirties, wearing traditional Tang-style robes of many layers of shimmering violet silk, with the front of his long hair held in a small gold crown on top of his head. He saluted Emma and Xuan Wu with a small bow, and they nodded back.

Simone's heart fell when Graham rushed into the living room behind Venus. 'The door was open, and I got your email and—'

Venus interrupted him. 'I have an Edict from the Celestial Himself for the Dark Emperor of the Northern Heavens and his daughter, the Princess Simone.'

Graham fell to one knee and bowed his head, then said, 'Ten thousand times ten thousand years.' He glanced around, his eyes wide and his mouth open. He tried to speak, but nothing came out.

Emma, the Tiger and Simone's father knelt, her father still floating outside the window. In unison they said, 'Ten thousand years,' then rose again.

As someone who wasn't sworn to obey the Celestial, Simone didn't have the same forced response. 'Venus that's my *boyfriend* and he's *human*—'

Venus turned and smiled down at Graham. 'Completely human? How is he coping?'

Graham looked about to have another panic attack. He was gasping.

'Not well at all!' Simone said, ducking back through the window and retaking human form to wrap one arm around Graham's shoulder. 'Graham, it's okay. Nobody will hurt you.'

'Simone?' Graham pulled himself clumsily to his feet, still gasping. He stared at Simone's father floating on the other side of the window, then back to Simone. 'That was you, wasn't it?'

'That's my working form,' she said.

'It had *scales*,' he said with distress. 'And *swords*. You were—'

Venus cut him off. 'I bear an Edict from the Jade Emperor himself, may he reign for ten thousand times ten thousand years.' He glared at Graham. 'And it is highly unusual for the Emperor's subjects to so *flagrantly* ignore his Edicts.'

Graham fell to one knee like a puppet and bowed his head. 'Ten thousand years.'

'Better,' Venus said. He opened the scroll. 'I bear an Edict from the Celestial Himself. He directs that in the mission to destroy the demons that have taken control of the country in Europe, the Xuan Wu is not to proceed in support of Princess Simone. The Empress of the North, the Dark Lady Emma Donahoe, is to travel in support of Princess Simone and the Dark Emperor Xuan Wu is to remain in the East.' He rolled up the scroll. 'Ten thousand years.'

'Ten thousand years,' everybody said.

Graham was still on his knees, gasping, and clumsily attempted to rise. Simone put one hand under his arm and helped him stand. He looked around at everyone, his eyes wide, then focussed on Simone. 'You said you didn't do the superhero thing any more—that you wanted to lead an ordinary life. Did you *lie* to me? You ...' He pointed one quivering finger at the windows. 'You were out there, with *scales* and *flying!*'

'This was just a one-off,' she said, guiding him the couches. 'After this, no more.'

'I've heard that before,' Graham said, sitting on the couch and putting his head in his hands. 'From my dad, about the drinking. "After this, no more".'

'I mean it,' she said, and turned to the rest of the group. 'This is the last time, everyone, okay?'

'We support you,' Simone's father said, shrinking to human form and floating back through the windows to land softly on the carpet. 'Did he say why Emma and not me?' he asked Venus.

'The Dark Lady has a pure European heritage. The Jade Emperor believes that her abilities will be more effective on demons outside our Centre.'

'Valid, I guess,' Emma said. 'My energy capabilities are certainly more powerful against European demons.' She held her hand out to the side, and her sword, Scales of Wisdom, appeared in it. The black lacquer scabbard glittered in a scales pattern that shifted under the living room lights. 'I'll watch your back, Simone, and this is definitely the last time, Graham. Xuan Wu will explain why this is so important.' She nodded to Simone. 'Did your uncle tell you where to go?'

'Uncle Bai?' Simone asked.

'Here,' the Tiger said, and pushed the location straight into Simone's head.

'I am no longer needed here, I'll leave you to it,' Venus said. 'Lunch soon, Emma. We haven't had cheesecake in *ages*.'

'My people will contact your people,' Emma said to Venus. They shared a quick hug, Venus nodded around to everyone, and disappeared.

'This is too weird,' Graham said.

'You get used to it,' Emma said. 'I was an ordinary human when I joined the household twenty years ago.'

'Never,' Xuan Wu said.

Frankie ran in from the bedrooms. 'Did I miss anything?'

'You missed Venus,' Emma said.

Frankie scowled. 'I like Venus.'

'Is he like … the actual planet Venus?' Graham asked.

There was a roar as loud as a jet engine, and Katie flew up to hover outside the living room windows on a cloud. She was half-Chinese, half-British, with short-cropped blonde hair, and was nearly as tall as Xuan Wu's human form. She was wearing the white-and-gold enamel armour of the Tiger's army, the White Horsemen. She had the striking good looks and bone structure of her British actress mother, and the heavy muscular build of her father, the White Tiger.

'I gave up waiting for you. Come on—we need to save these kids!' she shouted from her cloud.

'I have to go,' Simone said. She gave Graham a quick kiss where he sat, still gasping and wide-eyed. 'I'll text you when I get back, we have a lot to talk about. Thanks for coming over, I hope we can sort it all out. This is definitely the last time, I promise.'

'Wait, are you going to be in danger doing this?' Graham asked, staring at Emma's sword.

'I'll protect her,' Emma said.

Simone and Emma jumped through the glass of the window and took Celestial Form. Simone's scales glittered in the reflected living room lights. Emma's Celestial form looked like a large version of her human form; taller and more muscular with long black hair and wearing black and silver armour that was similar to Xuan Wu's.

Graham yelled, jumped up from the couch, and backed up to hit Xuan Wu, then jerked away from him.

Xuan Wu put his hand on Graham's shoulder. 'Nobody will hurt you. Come and have tea with me and we'll talk about everything.' He nodded to the Tiger, who nodded back and disappeared.

Graham made a high-pitched noise at the back of his throat.

'Come *on*, the President is planning something. We need to stop these demons!' Katie shouted.

'Go back to bed, Frankie,' Emma said through the window.

'I'll come and tell you all about it when I'm home.'

'Okay, Mum,' Frankie said, but didn't move.

Katie turned, and she and Emma roared away. Simone glanced back at Graham, cowering in the living room, then regretfully turned and followed Emma and Katie towards the West. She had a sudden bolt of premonition.

She would be returning alone and full of rage and grief, having lost someone vitally important to her.

She caught up with Katie and Emma and studied them. She had no idea about the timeline for this loss, only that it would be someone close to her. She opened her mouth to ask Emma if she felt something similar, but changed her mind. Sharing a vision of the future could make it a self-fulfilling prophecy. If she told Emma, it could ensure the loss of her stepmother.

She would just have to be careful. And Emma was an Immortal, so if she did lose her, it would not be permanent, and Simone would tear Heaven and Earth apart to get her back.

Emma moved her cloud closer to Simone's, and from her smile, she obviously didn't have the same foreboding. 'Don't worry, Simone, your dad will talk to him.'

Simone swiped her hand over her scaled forehead. 'That's not very reassuring, Emma. Daddy's one of the most terrifying things on the planet.'

'Your father will explain about the kids, and why you're doing this, and why it's important. Graham will understand.'

Simone looked away and didn't reply.

'I'm still a baby Immortal, Empress or not,' Emma said. 'This will take a while. Would you like to practice your doctoral prospectus presentation on us while we travel?'

'It's pretty boring ...' Simone said, well aware that it was an attempt to distract her from Graham's distress.

'I want to hear, Princess,' Katie said. 'Go for your life.'

'Okay, just let me know if I'm too boring and we'll talk about something more interesting, like different types of slope stabilisation to halt erosion.'

'Fascinating,' Emma said.

'So, there are two populations of turtles in this part of the world …' Simone began, and Katie and Emma moved their clouds closer to listen.

They arrived four hours later, early in the evening local time. The Presidential palace stood in front of a massive, empty square nearly as big as Tiananmen, dusted with a recent fall of snow that hadn't been cleared. The stars shone brilliantly in the frozen sky; many of the streetlights appeared to be non-functioning, and the houses were similarly dark. Plain-clothes police dotted the square and the front of the palace, standing together and failing to look casual.

The snow-covered palace was a mock-Renaissance construction with many cupolas and decorated stonework. It had a central courtyard and Emma made Simone invisible to teleport into the palace's entrance hall.

'Follow me,' Katie said, and led them through doors that opened into a long hall that smelled musty and stale and had a faded linoleum floor. The walls were institution-olive in colour, and the paint on the ceiling was peeling from damp.

Simone followed Katie through an oversized pair of hardwood doors at the end of the corridor and the interior changed. The floor was now golden hardwood laid in an intricate herringbone parquetry pattern, the walls were decorated with plaster reliefs picked out in gold, and massive crystal chandeliers hung from the ceiling. The furniture was ornate-gilt-rococo style with blue velvet covers, and the walls were covered in large landscape oil paintings.

Simone stopped to study an alabaster copy of an ancient Greek statue and shook her head. The luxury seemed immensely fake.

Katie gestured ahead and they followed her past a couple of alert guards in ornate Western-style uniforms and into what appeared to be the President's apartment. It had a comfortable sitting room with an overstuffed leather sofa, a kitchenette and a dining table big enough for six.

The President lives in this little hole? Simone asked Katie.

No. He has a massive palace just outside town with its own golf course. This is for when he doesn't feel like making the trip, Katie said. *They're in here—both him and his son.*

She teleported into the bedroom, and they followed her. The two demons—father and son lookalikes—were obviously in the middle of having sex. The corpse of a little boy lay dead, drained of blood, on the floor at the foot of the bed. The demons leapt out of bed, one of them grabbed a gun from under a pillow, spun and sent a flurry of shots in their direction. The noise and flash were blinding and deafening.

There was a blur in front of Simone as Emma jumped in front of her to block the bullets with her body. Simone was blinded by a spray of blood, which she wiped from her face as Emma toppled to fall in front of her.

One of the bullets had gone through Emma and hit Simone in the shoulder. She put her hand over the wound, pulled the bullet from her shoulder, healed it, then stormed up to the demon who was still attempting to fire with the empty weapon. She grabbed him by the throat, lifted him, crushed his windpipe and dropped him again. She turned in time to see Katie take the other demon's head off.

Emma was lying deathly still on the ground next to the child's corpse. The bullet had torn out the side of her throat and she lay in a pool of blood. Simone ran to Emma and took her hand, then put her other hand over Emma's throat to heal it.

She felt rather than saw Katie kneel next to her. 'She's losing a lot of blood, Simone ...'

Simone grunted with concentration. 'Not on my watch. I am *not* losing her.'

Emma tried to speak, but no words came out. She desperately mouthed the words, her eyes wide and intense, but could only make gasping wheezes.

'Shut up, I am healing you and we are going home,' Simone said.

I love you, Emma said telepathically. She let out a huge breath and her shen energy, her spirit force, left her.

'She's an Immortal, Simone, this isn't the end, you know that,' Katie said.

'We're in a different region,' Simone said, wiping the blood from her hands and face and rising. She focussed on Katie. 'I had a premonition. On the way here. That I would lose someone ...' She bent and gasped, then pulled herself together. 'Important.'

'You can't lose her, she's an Immortal—' Katie began, but was interrupted by the door flying open to reveal a massive demon in the form of Ineke Prochazka, the previous European Demon King's crime-lord persona.

His smile disappeared and his face filled with shock. 'No. Emma!'

He raced towards them, and Simone stopped him with one hand on his chest. 'Don't come any closer.'

'Simone.' The demon pulled her hand off its body with alarming ease but didn't attack. 'I'm obviously too late. Thanks for taking them out, you saved me the trouble. I gave them this country on the *strict* understanding that they'd behave like humans and do as they're told.' He gestured towards Emma. 'She's not dead, is she? Tell me she's not dead.'

'She's dead,' Katie said.

'No. After all this time, I finally have a chance to meet her, and she's dead?' The demon bent and clenched his fists with frustration, then straightened. 'Things work differently here in Europe. Hell is controlled by ... a god. Shen? Whatever. A Celestial! The last one remaining. He has a cohort of demons that serve him, and I have no authority over them. If Emma's in Hell, I can't get her out.'

'I knew it!' Simone shouted with horror. 'How do I get her out? Which god?' She strode to the demon and grabbed his designer suit lapels to lift him up to her height. Her tentacle hair writhed at the edges of her vision. 'Tell me!'

'Hell's controlled by a Celestial?' Katie asked. 'There's still one around? Hades?'

The demon pointed at Katie, seemingly unfazed by Simone's grasp. 'That's the one. He has no idea who you are. He has no idea who Emma is. You need to get down there and stop him from giving her the waters of the River Lethe and sending her back up here as a mortal with her memory erased and no way to identify her.'

'I can't go ...' Katie began.

'I can, my dad's been there and showed me the way,' Simone said.

'You changed since he did that!' Katie said. 'You're mostly demon now, and you could be stuck there!'

'Why are you so concerned about Emma?' Simone asked the demon.

'Because she's my fucking *mother*, stupid!' the demon shouted, and disappeared.

Simone knew better than to believe anything a demon said. 'Go home,' she said to Katie, and concentrated on the location of European Hell.

5

She landed in a dimly lit and deserted underground cavern. The floor of this Hell was like the surface of the Moon—absolutely dry and covered with fine grey powder. No plants were present, and the walls were too distant to be seen. The invisible ceiling was like the night sky with no moon or stars, and without her enhanced senses it would have been too dark to see. Simone checked around and found no other source of chi energy—people, animals, plants, insects … nothing. Emma could be anywhere, and if this Hell was as big as the Asian one, she could be searching for days.

She lifted off the ground and sent her senses out, trying to find her stepmother and failing. She sensed some demons a great distance away, so she flew towards them.

After flying towards the demon presence for ten minutes—without sensing Emma anywhere—Simone noticed a shape near the wall of the underground cavern and stopped. A massive stone throne—big enough to hold her father's largest Celestial form—stood at the base of the wall. She landed in front of the throne to check it.

The ground was covered in footprints, but the throne itself looked untouched and was grey with dust. She lifted off the ground to study the wall behind the throne more closely and discovered that it was carved into a bas-relief all the way up, as

55

far as she could see. The carving was eroded by time, and she summoned a light and moved closer, noticing that it had been filled with rich colours—red, blue and gold—a long time ago, but that they had worn away to nearly nothing.

She distinguished the curve of a jaw, traced it with her finger, and her touch filled the sculpture with light. Brilliant gold filled the short curly blond hair and tightly bound beard, and the radiant colours flooded the carving to form the image of a naked man standing side-on and wielding a thunderbolt in his hand. The entire figure was nearly as tall as her father's eleven-storey apartment building.

'Zeus,' she said softly.

The colours shimmered across the wall, ignited by Simone's energy, and showed Poseidon with his trident. He was dark-haired, bearded and also naked. As she worked out what she was seeing, she recognised more and more of the ancient European pantheon until she had revealed the brilliant images of nearly twenty gods, goddesses and titans. She drifted down to the throne again and studied its sides for more carved artwork—to find nothing. It was completely plain and featureless.

'I wish you could have met my dad,' she said to the throne. 'He's not into ornamentation either.'

When she touched down, the ground beneath her feet sprang to life. The dust around the throne receded to reveal mirror-shiny black-marble tiles, inlaid with decorative gold edging. The restoration worked its way up the throne, regenerating black marble, again inlaid with simple gold accents. She felt the tug of energy being pulled from her as a pile of purple and blood-red cushions appeared on the throne.

The floor tiles spread, until they reached a line of life-sized, brightly-painted marble statues along the sides of the tiled area—

Simone realised with horror that this Hell was draining her energy to reconstitute itself, and if she didn't stop the drain, it would kill her. She might be mortal enough to die in this Hell and be stuck here.

She controlled her breathing as the life was sucked from her, lowered her head, and concentrated on her energy centres. The main drain was from her shen energy, her soul. This Hell was eating her soul ... She controlled her panic and concentrated again on stopping the drain. The location fought her, greedily grasping at her spirit, but she slowed the drain to a trickle, then nearly halted it. She made a massive effort to block the last leaking of energy and couldn't. The place was killing her, but she had at least twenty-four hours before it would succeed. She could easily teleport out before the drain became critical.

Emma, on the other hand, didn't have that level of control and could easily be ... eaten within a couple of hours.

She looked up at the mural, then shook her head. All of them gone. What a stupid thing to do, to decide you've caused enough damage to humanity and destroy yourselves. They hadn't even ensured the safety of cross-regional visitors like herself—probably confident that no other regions' residents would be able to travel this far.

She turned, ready to take off again, to find two European demons kneeling in front of her. They were really big ones; even kneeling they were as tall as her working form. They were human-shaped and black-skinned, with bat-like heads and wings and long claws on their hands. Their knees bent backwards, and their feet had similarly long, sharp claws.

The tiles emerged beneath their feet, and a row of planter boxes grew behind them, gradually expanding, black and shiny, and filling with purple-blossomed shrubbery.

'Highness, we greet you,' one of them said.

'Do you wish to wait here for your Lord, or will you pass on immediately?' the other asked.

'My Lord?' Simone asked. 'Oh yeah, my father has been here before. But I'm looking for my stepmother.'

Both of the demons' heads shot up. 'You're his child?' one of them asked.

The other grinned. 'A child!' He grabbed the first demon's shoulder. 'They're coming back. After all this time. Finally.'

'I'm looking for my stepmother. White skin, brown hair, wearing armour? Have you seen her?' Simone asked.

'The Queen doesn't usually wear armour,' one of the demons said, confused.

The other demon studied Simone suspiciously. 'You're mixed race, with a lot of demon there, and you're not from here. That's not right.'

Simone wanted to shake them with frustration. 'If there was another Celestial here, would you know? Where can I find her? How do I know if she's here?'

'Celestial?' the first one asked, confused.

'Someone like me!'

The second demon tilted its head. 'We don't call you "Celestials", I've never heard that term before. You're a strange demon mix. What are you?'

'I think we need to tell the boss,' the first one said. It rose to its feet and bowed to Simone with an extra flourish. 'Ma'am. If you'd like to come with us?'

'Yeah, I don't think so,' Simone said, and pulled her phone out of a pocket in her robes. It was difficult to unlock it with her long claws, but she didn't change back to human. The phone had no signal: even the combination of the Blue Dragon's advanced technology and the Golden Boy's high-level magic couldn't pick one up this far from anything.

She grunted with frustration and put the phone away again. The only way to be really sure that Emma was here, was to check the East and confirm that she wasn't there. And if Simone left Europe, there was no guarantee that she would be able to break into European Hell again. Every time they'd made it into Heaven or Hell in the past, the door had been locked behind them when they left.

The demons were both standing now, and their attitudes had changed from obsequious to menacing. A number of other, smaller demons that looked similar—black, spikes, wings, horns and carrying spears—flew in to land behind the two big ones.

'You're going to attack me?' Simone asked them,

incredulous. 'Look at me. I can take you all without even touching you. Are you really that stupid?' She had a moment of disorientation when she realised that she sounded *exactly* like her father when he talked to idiot demons, then waved one hand at them. 'Find your boss. Find the biggest demon here—hell, find the Celestial boss-God himself so I can talk to him. I want Emma Donahoe. If she isn't here, I'll leave without causing trouble.'

One of the big demons spun its spear in its hands and gestured for the others to attack.

'Your technique is *terrible*!' Simone shouted as she summoned her swords, and they didn't come. She ducked beneath the demons as they ran for her, then did a couple of backwards somersaults with her robes flying around her and stopped to yell at them again. 'I don't want to destroy you. Cut it out!'

The smaller demons obviously had no choice but to follow the bigger ones' orders. Simone summoned a few simple, low-grade chi balls and blew them up. The backlash was stronger than the chi return from Asian demons, and she gasped at the intensity of the energy rush. The area around her sparkled into life, triggered by the growth of the energy within her. The tiles glowed with dark purple luminescence, and more planters emerged from the ground.

She'd left the two biggest demons alive, and they stood holding their spears and staring at her.

She stormed up to them, stomping in time to her words. 'Find. Me. Emma. Donahoe.'

One of the demons jabbed at her with its spear so she knocked the spear out its hand, grabbed the demon by the throat with her left hand, and lifted it. She held it with its feet dangling above the ground as it clutched at her hand, attempting to free itself.

The other demon ran at her with its spear lowered. Using her free hand, she grabbed the spear before it hit her, and flipped it so that the demon holding it was forced to do a near-perfect pole-vault over her head, flying off the spear and landing some distance away. Still holding the first demon with her left hand, she tossed the spear to turn it around, then threw it to impale the other demon before it could climb to its feet.

'Now,' she said glaring into the first demon's eyes as they rolled with terror. 'I'm going to lower you, and I won't kill you if you take me to your boss.'

'Yes, ma'am. Understood, ma'am,' the demon said, its voice strangled.

She put it back on its feet and it fell to its knees. 'I'll take you to see the boss.'

'How long will it take?' she asked.

'If you can fly, about ten minutes?'

'I can.' She waved one hand at it. 'Up. Show me.'

It rose and cocked its spiked head at her. 'If you don't mind, ma'am? I need wing space.'

Simone lifted off the ground and hovered above it. It spread its massive bat-like wings and with a couple of powerful thrusts, lifted into the air, then gestured for her to follow it as it flew in the direction she had been travelling.

She followed it for another ten minutes, unable to move close enough to it to ask questions because of the spread of its flapping wings. They arrived at a crumbling, ruined building with its rear wall set hard against the stone walls of Hell. Its front portico was held up with columns—Simone's perception shifted, and she realised she was seeing a traditional Greek or Roman temple, as large as the Parthenon in Athens, but it was obviously falling apart. She followed the demon to land in front of the temple. The area around the temple appeared to be paved with white stone for some distance, but it was covered in the dust. Similarly, the planter boxes and gardens arranged around the temple in a geometric design were filled with nothing but dust.

Simone's touch brought the surroundings to life, and the white tiles emerged from the dust. The tiles had veins through them like marble, and each tile was etched with gold patterns in geometric designs. The repair flowed up the stairs towards the temple, each tread healing to a similar white marble. The columns reassembled themselves, and long black and purple banners with complicated motifs on them fell from the temple's gable to flank its entrance.

A European man in his mid-forties, short and plump, trotted down the stairs with a huge smile on his face. He wore a standard modern business suit and stopped at the bottom of the stairs to stand clasping his hands in front of his chest.

'Princess Simone, is it? The King of the Demons warned me you might come. Welcome, welcome!' he said. He gestured at the temple. 'Please, come inside, I hope you can help us.'

'Where's the River Lethe?' Simone asked him as he went back up the stairs. 'I'm here to make sure you don't remove my stepmother's memory. Has she come through? White woman, brown hair, Immortal, wearing armour?'

He turned at the stop of the stairs and smiled down at her. 'I don't think she's here, ma'am, but once the formalities are taken care of, it won't make a difference.' He turned back to the temple and entered it.

'No wait!' she called after him, but he had gone inside. She followed him up the stairs.

The temple continued to reassemble itself as she went inside. The ceiling had collapsed, leaving a pile of rubble in one corner on the vague outline of the tiled floor beneath the grey dust. The dust rose from the floor and the columns flew into the air to became fluted white pillars with delicate carvings at the top, their features picked out in bright hues and gold leaf. The ceiling solidified and became embossed with brilliant colours in more geometric designs high above her.

The demon spread his hands and beamed up at the roof. 'So long since it has been this beautiful.' He lowered his hands and bowed Western-style to Simone. 'I thank you, Highness.'

Gilt benches with red cushions appeared against the walls, and a large desk emerged from the far end of the room, in front of an imposing blood-red chair big enough to hold her father's Celestial Form.

A big conference-style table, made of white marble, appeared in the centre of the room, and a three-dimensional image coalesced above it, like a hologram from a movie. It showed three tiers of landscape: the lower one fiery, then one that was obviously the grey emptiness she was in, topped by an idyllic forested level with grass and trees.

Stone tables coalesced from the dust in the air, and plates of fruit—grapes, pomegranates and figs—and steaming tureens full of pungent roast meat that smelled like goat or mutton appeared on their tops. The demon pulled a knife from the back of its suit, saw Simone's face and raised it along with its other hand.

'I haven't had food in eons,' it said. 'I eat the old-fashioned way—if you don't mind? Come, and I'll show you your new dominion while we eat.'

She waved one hand at the demon as she passed it to approach the desk at the end of the room. The surface of the desk vibrated, and an enormous scroll—at least thirty centimetres high on each rolled side—erupted from it, sending a shower of dust into the air.

The demon was busy carving pieces of meat, skewering them with the knife and eating the pieces from the blade. It spoke with its mouth full. 'Would you like some, ma'am?'

'No thanks,' Simone said, standing behind the desk to study the scroll. It was so high that in her normal form she wouldn't have been able to see over it, but in this form she was as big as her father's largest Celestial Form. The writing on the scroll was all in capitals and there were no spaces between the words, but she knew exactly what it was—the list of judgements of people who had died in this region, and where they were sent. She placed her hand over the flat paper between the massive end rolls and ordered it to search for 'Emma Donahoe'. The scroll rolled until a list came up of hundreds of names and their associated notations. Many were marked as 'Given the waters of the River Lethe and returned'—the European version of reincarnation, but some very early ones from thousands of years ago had been 'Granted a place in the Elysium Fields' or 'Sentenced to a hundred years in Tartarus'—an interesting European analogue to the Ten Levels of Hell that she was familiar with from Asia. She wondered where all the souls in this Hell had gone and had the unpleasant realisation that since the gods had left, everybody had their memory erased and were reincarnated by default, never having the opportunity to achieve a higher plane of existence.

She narrowed the search to only the current day, and nearly collapsed with relief when the scroll rolled to a blank page. Emma was in Asian Hell, and her premonition had been wrong—that sometimes happened when the timeline changed and the future was redirected.

'Find what you're looking for, ma'am?' the demon asked, waving the meat-skewered knife at the hologram. 'Would you like to see your palace? I can show you more of your administrative areas and the other two zones of this region's Hell, if you like. We have a great deal of work to do.'

'No thank you,' Simone said. 'I found what I needed, and I have a doctoral prospectus to present later this week.'

She changed back to human form in jeans in a sweater and teleported out of Hell and back to the Earthly plane, landing inside the ruins of the Parthenon in Athens. A couple of tourists studied her with the confused expression that humans used in the presence of Shen abilities. They knew something had happened, but they weren't sure what.

Simone jumped onto the top of the temple and pulled out her phone. It took a maddening few seconds to connect to the network and establish its Celestial roaming service—and then forty-three missed calls and dozens of messages popped up. She scrolled through the messages and fell to sit on the top of the structure with her legs dangling to study them.

There were nearly twenty from her father, frantically concerned about her safety. Some were from other members of the Celestial family, and there was even one from that ancient ugly bastard, Er Lang, the Second Heavenly General, stiffly notifying her that he was worried about her as well. She raised her head to the early morning sunshine and concentrated.

Daddy, I'm fine.

What happened? Are you all right? Where are you? Katie

said that you went to European Hell—

Is Emma okay? Is she in our Hell?

Yes ... Judge Pao is making her sit in the cells awaiting trial, and I was just about to go down and give him a piece of my mind ...

Simone wiped the tears of relief from her eyes. *I'm in Athens now, but Katie's right and I travelled into European Hell. I'm on my way back, and wow! Do I have a great deal of information about it. Hold tight and I'll see you when I get there.*

I love you, he said.

Uh ... Daddy, please let the rest of the Celestial know that I'm okay, because I have a bunch of missed messages and I'll be going too fast for my phone to keep up.

Will do.

Simone rose, stepped off the beam, and screamed towards Asia, carefully waiting until she was over the ocean before she sped up enough to break the sound barrier. The sonic boom made clouds of condensation appear around her. The premonition struck her so hard that she dropped in the air and nearly hit the water. She would be returning this way again but crippled with grief and loss and so full of fury that the air would burn around her. The knowledge was like a punch in the chest.

In Europe, in the near future, she would lose someone immensely important to her. *Again.*

The family were waiting for her when she arrived back at the Peak two hours later. She charged through the window without damaging the glass, and threw herself into Emma's arms.

'I'm so glad Pao let you go,' she said into Emma's shoulder as her father patted her back and Frankie wrapped himself around her waist. 'I'm sorry I was too slow to save you.'

Emma pulled back to smile at her. 'It all worked out in the end. You were in European Hell? I want to hear all about it.' She glanced down at Frankie. 'Back to bed, young man. You have school tomorrow.'

'I want to hear about their Hell,' Frankie whined.

'I'll tell you tomorrow. It's the middle of the night, and I need to quickly bring Mum and Dad up to speed ...' Simone saw Emma's warm smile at being called 'Mum' and her voice softened. 'And then I need to go to bed too. I'll come in and tuck you in later. Okay?'

'Okay,' Frankie said. He gave them hugs all around and went to his room.

Simone followed Emma into her office and Emma sat behind her tidy desk while Xuan Wu and Simone sat in her visitor chairs.

When Simone had finished telling them about her European escapade, Emma spoke.

'So, the big question is: is she Immortal?' she asked Xuan Wu. 'We're still not sure what affect all the demon essence is having on her soul.'

'She didn't die, so we still don't know,' Xuan Wu said.

'But I teleported out of their Hell,' Simone said.

Xuan Wu spread his hands. 'It's a good sign.' He moved his hands to his knees. 'But keep yourself safe, because it's not absolute proof. Na Zha did it before he was made Immortal.'

Emma ran her hands through her hair. 'Damn Immortals and their non-answers. So frustrating sometimes ...' She smiled wryly. 'Yeah, I know.'

'And the demons were positive that there was one Celestial remaining in Europe?' Xuan Wu asked Simone.

'The European Demon King and the demon in their Hell claimed it, but we all know how much they lie,' Simone said. 'It could be a ploy to have me go there and have all my energy sucked away, because I'm such a threat to them.'

'That's the most interesting part of this—the way it was draining your life force,' he said. 'European Hell didn't do it to me when I went in there. So it's your unique heritage.' He turned to Emma and opened his mouth.

'No,' Emma said without looking at him, 'and don't even think about it. I have too much happening and a small, traumatised child to care for. I will not let myself slowly die so you can rebuild their Hell and bring back the Western Shen.'

'Europe's managed for two millennia without any gods,' Simone said. 'They can wait until Michael's kids are grown, and he can go and investigate. Now if you don't mind,' she stood. 'It's the middle of the night, I'm covered in Hell dust, and I have a meeting with my supervisor first thing tomorrow morning.'

Xuan Wu rose and kissed the top of her head. 'You saved those European children. Be proud, Simone.'

'Is Katie okay?'

Emma nodded. 'She's still on her way back, as she can't move nearly as fast as you. She provided a full report—and as your father said, Simone, well done. Now that those two demons posing as the President and his son are dead, there's a political power vacuum that the Tiger is facilitating towards democracy. We've sent info on the inter-demon conflict through to the Higher Ups in the administration, and they're working out a strategy to exploit it.'

'Which means I'll be pulled into another interminable meeting with them,' Xuan Wu said.

'You're one of them, don't deny it, Your Highness. So come on,' Emma said, took his hand and pulled him out of the office. 'It's nearly three am, Simone, get some sleep. Mission accomplished, and you did great.'

'What she said,' Xuan Wu said.

They went to their bedroom at the end of the hallway, and Simone opened the door to her own, next to Emma's office.

'Wait!' Simone said as Emma opened their bedroom door. 'How did the talk with Graham go after I left?'

'I reassured him that you won't be doing any more of this,' Xuan Wu said. 'He understands, and he trusts you, but asked for some time and space to put his head back together.'

Emma had gone into their bedroom and poked her head back out into the hallway. 'If he returns to you, he's worth it,' she said. 'If he doesn't, he isn't.' Her face went strange. 'Well, that wasn't helpful at all. Damn Immortals.' She smiled at Simone and tugged Xuan Wu inside their bedroom.

Simone went into her own bedroom and saw the red box

on her desk. Maybe if she opened it this time, it would disappear for good—because she'd finally done as that ancient bastard had ordered her to.

She placed her thumb on the clasp and the lid of the box flipped up. She opened the scroll to find that the text had changed.

The Princess Simone is commended for her actions in the European Centre. She is ordered to contact the Celestial administration immediately with regard to the destruction of another demon in that region of the world—'

She growled under her breath, tossed the scroll back into the box, and closed the lid. Unbelievable—she'd done as he asked and now he was asking for more. Whatever. She decided to ignore the box. Time for her to move her concentration down from Heavenly to Earthly matters, take a shower, worry about finishing and presenting her prospectus, and try to save her relationship with her boyfriend.

Are you okay? Frankie asked her.

I'm just fine and not going anywhere, Squirt. I need a shower and then I'll come and check on you.

His voice sounded sleepy and content. *I love you, Simone.*

I love you too, Frankie.

6

Simone entered the tutorial room where she was to present her prospectus. It sat twenty people in four rows, with a whiteboard and projector at the front. The décor was universally grungy white, with some ragged cork pinboards on the wall, and the floor was ancient tan-coloured linoleum. A sad string of tinsel had been strung above the windows in a cursory nod to the upcoming Christmas break.

The room smelled of impatience and desperation—but the desperation could be her own. Half-a-dozen of Simone's postgrad cohort were in the room to give her moral support, sitting behind the three professors who were at a table directly in front of the podium with papers laid out in front of them. She wasn't surprised to see that Graham had failed to show.

Time to give up on him and move on. Again.

Simone smiled around the room and set her laptop up on the podium. She connected it to the projector, took a deep breath, and moved in front of the professors.

'Go ahead, Simone, you're right on time,' Simone's supervisor, Mei Yi Li, said. She was in her early thirties, had a kind smile and was nearly as enthusiastic about turtles as Simone herself.

'Thanks, Doctor Li. I'm Simone Chen, and this is my prospectus to perform a comparative study of the migration habits of marine turtles in the Asia-Pacific Region.'

'*Doctoral* prospectus,' Professor Chow said, his voice dripping with condescension.

Professor Chow was the head of the biology school, and he was notorious for hating both women and white people—boxes that Simone emphatically ticked. He was thin and sallow-looking, and his face was set into a permanent scowl.

Simone shot him a cut-glass smile and pulled up the first slide. 'Yes, of course. Doctor Li advised me not to include the level in the title of the thesis, because everybody would already know. Would you like me to change it?'

'People need to know. I think you should change it,' he said. He waved one hand at her. 'Continue. You've barely started. Let's get on with it.'

Simone pulled up the next slide, the map of the region.

'The data on the migration, feeding and mating habits of marine turtles—specifically green and leatherback turtles—is fragmented across the Asia-Pacific region,' Simone began, and pulled up the next slide. 'Previous studies have concentrated on single populations, following their migration patterns within a small region. MacPherson's recent study is only on turtles in the Great Barrier Reef, and further studies by ...'

Simone mechanically reviewed the previous literature on the subject. It had taken her six months to collect the information and she could summarise it in five minutes.

'My study will collate the existing information, and I will add to the knowledge by attaching transponders to a number of turtles in both the North Queensland and South China Sea regions. I am hoping to discover whether the two populations interact.

'Past studies have shown that the turtles migrate around the region, and I would like to—'

'Will. You will,' Professor Chow interrupted to correct her.

'I will ...' She nodded to him. 'Also pull samples of DNA from both populations to see if they overlap. This will significantly add to the knowledge on the extent of turtle reproductive interfaces between populations within the region, and the degree of travel for the two groups. If there is reproductive interaction, that gives us a viable opportunity to import Australian turtles to bolster our local population.'

She outlined the project for twenty minutes, working around Chow's constant petty interruptions. When she finished, all her student friends applauded politely. Doctor Li was smiling and nodding, but as Simone's supervisor she'd been there every step of the way. Professor Chow looked constipated, but he always did. The other professor was someone from the biology faculty who she didn't know, a man his mid-forties, wearing a cheap polyester suit.

'You ask for questions now,' Chow snapped.

'Of course, Professor.' Simone felt her smile become even more brittle. 'Any quest—?'

'Yes,' Chow said loudly, without letting her finish. 'As your literature review clearly stated, there has been a great deal of research already done into turtle migration conducted by Australian universities. This is just duplicating the work. You're not doing anything new here. How are you adding to the knowledge?'

Simone stared at him. Had he listened to a word she'd said?

'This study is to ascertain whether there is interaction—and possible reproductive interaction—between the two groups on either side of the Equator,' Simone said. 'If the local population is limited to the South China Sea, there is much greater survival pressure. If we have the additional genetic diversity from the southern populations, the local population will be more robust, and we can even bring—'

He interrupted her. 'Is this really important? Do we really need to know this? You're treating them like two separate populations. What if it's just one big population that moves around?'

Simone looked to Doctor Li for support. Her supervisor seemed tranquil and unaffected by Chow's unreasonable haranguing.

Simone took a deep breath and pushed down her desire to chop this asshole's head off. Since she'd destroyed the previous

Demon King and been filled with his essence, her temper had been shorter, her visions crueller and her tolerance for people like Chow much narrower.

'That's the question I'll be answering with this study,' Simone said. 'Are they two separate populations, or one big one?'

'Then why didn't you say that at the start?' he asked.

She took another deep breath. 'I did. *Twice.*'

He scowled, and she immediately regretted baiting him.

'I'm not sure we even need to know this,' he said. 'The University has limited resources and should be focused on more worthwhile research. People are dying from ciguatera poisoning from eating contaminated seafood, and we haven't found a solution for that. This ...' He waved one hand. 'Isn't adding to the knowledge.'

Doctor Li's expression changed to resigned sympathy. Whoa, Simone was in trouble.

'Will this in any way help the turtle population's survival?' the other professor in the polyester suit asked. 'All we'll discover is whether they'll die out sooner or later—this has no practical application.'

'I think every scrap of knowledge we can collect about them will help,' Simone said. 'If it's a single population, we can bring turtles from Australia to boost—'

Chow ignored her and turned to Li. 'Is there another species she can study that has more meaningful outcomes?' He turned back to Simone. 'Were you considering another topic?'

'I've worked for six months on this topic and never considered another,' Simone said, feeling the ground shifting beneath her.

'You should have given her a backup topic, Mei Yi.' Chow looked down at his papers. 'The next round of funding is in March next year. You should rethink your project and come back then.'

'We can work together to see if we can come up with something more acceptable,' Li said, still maddeningly serene.

'All right. Do that.' He glanced up at Simone, his eyes

sharp. 'Talk to your supervisor about doing something more worthwhile. This project isn't it.' He spoke to Li. 'You should have told me at the start, Mei Yi. The School is done with turtles.'

'I understand, Professor,' Doctor Li said, nodding back to him. 'We'll see what we can do.'

He pushed himself away from the table. 'Waste of my time,' he said under his breath. He collected the manila folder full of her prospectus—with the red marks he'd scribbled all over it—and went out.

'Come and see me in my office, Miss Chen,' Doctor Li said. She nodded to the other professor. 'Thanks for your time, Ricky.'

'My pleasure, Mei Yi.' The other professor went out, and Mei Yi Li followed him.

Simone busied herself unhooking her laptop from the projector and was blinded when the projector went to the brilliant blue of a lost connection. Her friends gathered around her, all obviously confused.

'What did you do to him?' Abigail asked.

'I have no idea,' Simone said, holding the emotion down. 'I've never even spoken to him.' She shrugged and tried to keep the tears from her voice. 'I'd better go see Doctor Li.'

Abigail patted her on the shoulder. 'Come see us at the café after you're done with Mei Yi.'

'Yeah, okay.' Simone put her laptop into its bag, shoved her papers in haphazardly next to it, and went to Doctor Li's tiny office.

'Come in. Don't look like that.' Mei Yi rose and came around the desk as Simone arrived. 'I knew we were taking a chance, but you're so eloquent and enthusiastic I thought …' She went past Simone to close the door, then lowered her voice. 'We'd be able to break through his prejudice.'

'You knew he'd reject my prospectus?' Simone asked, frozen with betrayal.

'You told me yourself, Simone, you're from a wealthy

family and you don't need the scholarship money, just the university's endorsement.' Mei Yi returned to her desk and sat behind it, gesturing for Simone to sit in the visitor's chair. 'Most of the work is done, we only need to find you another topic and you can go ahead in March. Redo the literature review between now and then. If you were to research—as he said—ciguatera poisoning, you'd have his complete endorsement. His father died of it after eating contaminated *Serranidae*.'

'I can't believe you used me like this,' Simone said.

'I didn't use you, Simone, I genuinely thought you'd manage it. You're so obviously intelligent and eloquent—'

'He *hates* strong, smart women, you know that! I even made myself appear more nervous than I was, so I would be less threatening to him!'

'I saw that, it was masterful. This is why I let you go ahead. Unfortunately, it didn't work. So ...' She placed her hands on her battered, paper-strewn desk and smiled at Simone. 'Doing post-graduate study is one disappointment after another. One rejection after another. Pick yourself up and move on.'

'But this research is so important. If we can transplant turtles from the Coral Sea in Australia to boost our diminishing population here, we can—'

'I know that, I helped you write it. He didn't listen, and he only skimmed through your prospectus to mark all the grammatical errors.'

'Incorrectly,' Simone said under her breath.

'Spending significant time overseas and using standard international English rather than the local variant is just going to make him hate you even more. You're rubbing his nose in his limited local experience.'

Simone sagged. 'Yeah.'

'I heard your friends say that they were heading to the café. Take a break for the holidays to think about what you want to do, maybe revise the literature, then come back and we'll work on a new topic for you.' She walked around Simone to open the office door again. 'This sort of setback is typical, and there'll be many more before we're finished. It's just academic life.'

'Thanks, Mei Yi,' Simone said, and went out.

The small café on campus was a busy social centre for the students. It was on the pedestrian overpass connecting the fifth levels of the main library and the Kadoorie Biological Sciences Building. The café was a pop-up to one side of the walkway, with five folding tables and chairs along the edge to allow students to easily travel through.

Simone's friend Abigail waved when Simone approached, and Simone staggered to them and flopped into a chair, resting her head in her hands.

'I'll get you a coffee or something, you need it,' she said.

'Green tea, thanks Abby,' she said into her hands.

'What did Mei Yi say?' Winston asked.

'Exactly what Chow said.' Simone dropped her hands onto the table. 'Redo the literature review and find another topic.' Abigail put a pot of green tea and a cup in front of Simone, who gave Abigail some money, then poured the tea. 'Six months of work wasted, and I won't be able to do turtles.'

'Did you have any other ideas at all?' Winnie asked.

Simone shook her head, then raised it when an Immortal passed nearby. It was Hong, the red dragon who ran Celestial High, in human form. He was wearing his usual teaching outfit of chino pants, a red long-sleeved polo shirt under a red puffer vest and socks with Birkenstock sandals. He was tall and slender, like most dragons, and had a shock of red hair that he'd toned down for the Earthly to appear like it was dyed.

'A stone Shen saw the emails and told me what happened, Simone,' he said, sitting at the table. 'Have you explored other options?'

Simone's cohort gaped at him.

'This is Professor Hong, visiting from Todai,' Simone said to clarify for the dazed humans. 'I did my undergrad study with him.'

'Pleased to meet you,' Hong said, shaking everybody's hands and making them even more bewildered. Like most Shen, he had a hypnotic effect on people, and they instinctively knew that he should be respected and was absolutely trustworthy.

'I got sucked into academic politics,' Simone moaned.

'Welcome to the Earthly,' he said expansively, spreading his hands and nearly tipping her teacup over.

'Oh geez,' Simone said with dismay. Her father and her stepmother had just teleported onto the overpass, completely unnoticed by anyone.

Hong saluted them without rising. 'Lord Xuan, Dark Lady.'

Simone's friends' expressions became distracted as Xuan Wu approached.

'Uh, I'll catch up with you later, Simone,' Abigail said, and fled. The rest of the group quickly grabbed their bags and left as well.

'That wasn't a nice thing to do, Daddy,' Simone said. 'They're my friends.'

'He didn't do anything,' Emma said. 'He has that effect on people, particularly young ones.'

Xuan Wu sat at the table. 'The Princess Simone ...' His eyes went wide. 'Is ordered to contact the Celestial immediately to receive orders that will result in the destruction of a demon that threatens the entire realm.' He went grim. 'Unbelievable.'

'He forced you to say that?' Simone asked, incredulous.

'Bastard!' Emma said, then her face went slack as well. 'The Princess Simone is ordered to report immediately to the Celestial. The importance of this order cannot be underestimated. Report to the Celestial at once.' She scowled. 'The hell?'

'I refuse,' Simone said. 'Did he force you to come down here and harass me? I asked you to stay away and let me do it!'

'We heard you were rejected and thought you'd need us,' Emma said. 'That Celestial order business is both new and unacceptable and we'll stop it as soon as we can speak to him about it.'

'Thanks, Emma,' Simone said. She swiped one hand over her eyes. 'It's all I need with my doctoral study in tatters.'

'Did the lecturer really reject your prospectus purely because you're white and female?' Xuan Wu asked, his voice echoing.

'Tone it down, Daddy, and I'm not white but ...yeah. He did. He's also very over turtles.'

'Well, that's just insulting,' Xuan Wu said.

'Damn straight,' Emma said. 'So, plans, Simone? What did your supervisor say?'

'You could always return to the Imperial House of the North and run our Earthly—' Xuan Wu began.

Simone interrupted him. 'My supervisor suggested I try again in March with a more politically correct topic.'

'Not turtles?'

Simone shook her head.

'You should go back to Todai,' her father said.

'I think the Blue Dragon was watching my grades in my honours year, to ensure that I wouldn't fail.' She tapped her teacup on the table. 'I want to do this myself, dammit.'

'What about doing it in a university in Australia?' Hong asked. 'It's a popular postgrad destination for my local students. There are some excellent marine research stations on the Barrier Reef and the water might help to purify you.'

'I can't,' Simone said. 'The Grandmother of All the Rocks has made it very clear that anyone who is even remotely related to someone who—and I quote her directly here—"sullied my surface with their filthy feet"—is not welcome anywhere in Australia. She's given me a dispensation to study the turtles as long as I don't touch the mainland.'

'I should have been more firm when I told your mother—' Xuan Wu began.

'You were never able to tell her anything,' Simone said. 'That much I remember of my mother.'

'Pop over to Tokyo, talk to the Blue Dragon,' Hong said. 'See if his Todai connections extend to Australia, to do the Barrier Reef thing.'

'I need a research station here in the South China Sea as well,' Simone said.

'And HKU has one?'

'Yes.'

'No, you are not going to lean on the head of the university, don't even think about it,' Emma said to Xuan Wu without looking at him, and he closed his mouth before he could speak.

'The Blue Dragon might be able to help with that too,' Hong said. 'He has a lot of input into the university in Japan, he keeps a close eye on all the research. Pop an email through to him, tell him that you only need access to the program and research stations, and that he's to butt out otherwise. He'll be glad to help.'

'Do you want me to send an introductory Imperial Edict?' Xuan Wu asked. 'Making it very clear that you want to do this research the hard way?'

'Not an order—maybe just an … Imperial Memorandum?' Simone asked.

'Even a memo from your father has the force of an order, you know that,' Emma said. 'Are you sure?'

Simone ran her hand over the top of her head and pulled her hair out of her eyes where it had blown into them. 'Yeah. I think I need all the help I can get. Thanks, Daddy.'

Simone returned home with her parents to find Frankie waiting on the couch in the living room next to Yi Hao. A live fir tree was standing in the corner of the room next to the picture windows, still in its protective netting. An unopened plastic storage bin of ornaments sat next to it. The tree was in a water-filled stand and was tall enough to nearly touch the ceiling.

Frankie shot to his feet when he saw the family. 'It arrived! I want to do it now! Can we do it now?'

'I'm sorry, Frankie, but Simone just had some bad news, and she may not feel—' Emma began.

'No,' Simone said. She put her hands on her hips and studied the tree. It had already started to fill the living room with the crisp scent of pine needles. 'Let's set it up and decorate it.' She turned to smile at Emma. 'It's a beauty, Emma.'

Emma approached the tree and summoned a knife to cut

away the sleeve, releasing the branches in a cascade of green. She stepped back to study it, then fluffed the branches to make it more full. She nodded. 'The ones in Australia aren't generally this gorgeous. You're right, it's a beauty.'

'Can I open the decoration box?' Frankie asked, full of excitement.

'Go right ahead. Come on, everyone, let's make this one special.' Emma turned to smile at Xuan Wu. 'You too, this is for family.'

Frankie opened the box of decorations and made small sounds of delighted wonder as he sifted through the tinsel and baubles. He picked up a glossy, gold-printed box from one of the Japanese department stores. 'What's this?'

'Yi Hao, could you find Er Hao and Smally?' Emma asked, taking the box from him. 'John.' She handed the tinsel to Xuan Wu. 'You're the tallest, so wrap this around the tree from the top down.' She opened the box, revealing carefully packed glass baubles with names on them in English and Chinese. She held up the one with Frankie's name on it. 'We'll put these on last.'

Xuan Wu smiled affectionately as he took the tinsel and checked the contents of the box. 'You had them made for the demon servants as well?'

Yi Hao was standing next to the kitchen door with a stricken expression. Emma took a bauble out with Yi Hao's name on it and showed it to the stunned demon.

'You're family too.'

Yi Hao burst into tears, spun and ran into the servant's quarters.

'You hurt her feelings?' Frankie asked, unsure.

'No, she made her the happiest demon on the planet's surface,' Simone said. 'I can't wait to see Er Hao's and Smally's faces when they see they have them as well.' She handed a plain bauble to Frankie. 'Let me show you how to do this.'

Frankie wiped one eye, nodded, and allowed Simone to assist him to attach the bauble to the tree. He was glowing with happiness.

Dinner was still an hour away when the tree was finished, so Simone retreated into her room and ran listlessly through her emails. The usual academic spam from the university that wasn't supporting her, more than twenty requests for her to contact the Celestial administration to kill a demon, still nothing from Graham—and one from the Blue Dragon.

To: Simone Chen
From: Seiryu Ten
Subject: Shift your doctoral research to Tokyo U.
Hongie told me what happened, no need for your father to send me any Celestial formalities. I'm not surprised those buffoons at UHK are giving you trouble, politics was always their first priority and they're a backstabbing collection of trash. Send me what you have so far—a synopsis for me to read would be the best, and I'll pass the full prospectus on to my people in Tokyo U's biology department. No niece of mine is falling victim to bullshit human political nonsense, what you're doing is too important.
Uncle Qing

Simone smiled at his usual brusque over-compensation for being such a huge softie and composed a reply.

To: Seiryu Ten
From: Simone Chen
Subject: Re: Shift your doctoral research to Tokyo U.
Thanks for the assistance, Uncle Qing. I've attached the prospectus and synopsis. I appreciate you giving me the opportunity to work on my own topic rather than one the University forces onto me. One condition, though: no interference! Please let me do this research myself, so I know that I'm good enough!
Attachments: synopsis.docx
Possible_Reproductive_Interaction_Between_Multiple_Populations_of_Asian_Turtles.docx
Many hugs,

Simone

She sent it and heard whispering outside her door.

One voice was obviously Frankie, and the other ... was Freddo? She cocked her head to listen.

'No, you go first,' Frankie hissed.

'You're her brother, I'm just a tame demon,' Freddo said.

'What if she cries?' Frankie asked.

'Then you hug her 'cause I can't,' Freddo said. 'If you think she's going to cry then we can just leave it until next year ...'

Simone went to the door and opened it to see Freddo's massive bulk—he was a good-sized palomino warmblood stallion—nearly filling the hallway and unable to raise his head to its full height without hitting the ceiling. Frankie was somewhere behind Freddo.

'You two want to ask me something?' Simone asked.

Freddo looked back, the whites of his eyes showing with nervousness, then at Simone. 'Both of us do, yeah.'

'Come on. Into the living room where there's more space,' Simone said, and guided them down the hallway.

'Gentle on the carpet!' Emma shouted from inside her office.

'He's got his new shoes on, he won't hurt anything,' Simone called back. Freddo was wearing new high-tech, clip-on acrylic foot covers instead of metal shoes, which tore up the carpet every time he came to visit.

When they reached the living room, boy and horse stopped to admire the tree, which was glittering with baubles and tinsel all the way to the ceiling.

Simone had a quick, desperate bolt of guilt. If Frankie had pointed out the named baubles for family or if Freddo had noticed them ... there wasn't one there for the horse, who was a tamed demon just as much as Yi Hao, Er Hao and Smally were. Simone had neglected Freddo while she was working on her thesis, and she should have visited him sooner.

Freddo and Frankie shared a look, and Frankie leaned against Freddo's shoulder for support.

'Go on, what were you about to ask me?' Simone asked.

'Freddo wants to teach me to ride,' Frankie said.

'Ride natural horses,' Freddo said, explaining. 'Hands, heels, seat, all of that.'

'That's a great idea,' Simone said, relieved that they would be spending time together, and making Freddo feel less neglected.

Frankie's voice was small. 'At Nanna's house.'

'That's the obvious choice, they have plenty of room and even a sand arena there,' Simone said. 'You don't need to ask me, why are you here? Just go and do it, guys. It's a terrific idea.'

'For two weeks, during the Chinese New Year break,' Freddo said. He spoke faster. 'All the cousins will be there, and we can have group lessons, and both of us can stay at the house with the family, and the Tiger gave them some really top-class ponies and—'

'We all want jumping lessons, and Freddo will teach us, and—'

They stopped when they saw Simone's face.

'Sorry, Simmony,' Freddo said.

Simone tried to compose herself. She couldn't go to their grandparents' estate in the Heavens, so she'd be stuck on the Earthly alone while the family went to spend Christmas there. The Peak apartment was too small for all the extended family, so the plan had originally been to spend a small, family Christmas in Hong Kong, then for the others to head to the Heavens. Chinese New Year, three weeks after Christmas, was a busy time for the Emperor and Empress as they had a great many formal ceremonies to perform in their realms—both the Northern Heavens and the Mountain—to assure good luck.

Having Frankie at his grandparents while Xuan Wu and Emma were busy on the Celestial Plane made perfect sense, and she'd reassured them that she was fine staying in the apartment while they were gone. She thought she'd be busy preparing her research plan and spending time with Graham, who was also stuck in the Territory away from his family during the holiday break. Now Simone would spend the holiday alone in the apartment with her failed doctoral thesis, her failed relationship and nothing to do while her friends were busy with their own families, as the entire city shut down.

She plastered a false smile on her face. 'What a great idea! You'll have a terrific time with them.' She rubbed Freddo's forehead enthusiastically. 'You're the only one I trust to teach him properly and keep him safe, and it's about time you visited your grandparents, young man, they miss you. We'll spend the Christmas break learning the basics together out at the country club, and then you two go and spend Chinese New Year with the rest of the family.' She patted Frankie on the shoulder. 'Sound good?'

Both Frankie and Freddo perked up and Frankie grinned broadly, then threw his arms around Simone. 'Thanks, sis.'

She ruffled his hair. 'No problem, Squirt.' She banged the side of her head against Freddo's. 'I'm looking forward to spending more time with you, Freddo-frog, now that the prospectus is out of the way.'

'It's still early, want to head over to the country club and go for a twilight ride with me?' Freddo asked.

'You'll be okay, Frankie?' Simone asked.

'Can I come too?' Frankie asked.

'Not until you have proper riding gear and a helmet,' Freddo said. 'Let me and Simone talk about a lesson plan. You can come riding on me tomorrow, and we'll have our first lesson with a saddle and bridle and everything.'

'Okay,' Frankie said, unfazed, and ran to Emma's office to bellow, 'Hey Mum guess what!'

7

Simone pulled herself onto Freddo's back and he teleported them to the riding trail at the country club.

It was early evening, and the cloudy sky was rose-pink as the sun set. A pair of Asian koels shouted back and forth between the trees, their distinctive calls echoing around the valley that held the country club.

Simone didn't need to guide Freddo as he followed the bridle trail that passed across the golf course and then through a small glade between the fairways.

'I saw your face,' Freddo said as he stepped carefully along the gravel path. 'You were so disappointed. I'm a demon, and I can visit the Northern Heavens, isn't there some way for you to go too? Without you being tamed? I was born there and lived there before I was tamed.'

'Destroying the Demon King made me King-level,' Simone said, running her hand over the smooth gold of his coat above his withers. 'I can visit the Heavens with permission—as if I was a King going to parlay—but they have to take down the seals to let me in. While I'm in the Heavens, they can't put the seals back up again. Daddy tried, and the seals he put up disintegrated. My presence in the Heavens would put everyone at risk.'

Freddo shook his head and didn't reply.

'So we have to do as the Buddhas say, and be patient,' Simone said. 'You and I both should live long enough for me to clear this stuff out of me so I can return to Heaven.'

His ears pricked up. 'You confirmed you're Immortal?'

'No, but I'm so much demon that I'll live as long as one. At least a hundred years, maybe more.'

Freddo lowered his head and blew air out his nostrils. 'At least me being demon is useful for teleporting, and I can help look after Frankie when he's up in the Heavens.' He lifted his head again. 'Incoming. Can you make us invisible?'

'Not any more,' Simone said, and a rider turned a corner onto the path in front of them. It was the chief instructor, a local named Daniel, riding one of the club's eventing horses.

'Hi, Daniel,' Simone said, raising one hand.

'Hey, Simone. Look at you!' Daniel said with enthusiasm. 'No tack at all—wonderful training.' He went serious. 'But no helmet either, young lady. You know better.'

Simone reached behind her, conjured a helmet and put it on. 'Yeah, I know. Sorry.'

'That's better. Even with a horse as well-trained as Freddo, you shouldn't be taking chances with your head.' His expression faltered. 'Can you stop and talk for a minute?'

'Uh, sure,' Simone said, and Freddo stopped so they could talk.

'My wife and I are leaving Hong Kong,' Daniel said, his horse shifting with impatience under him and swishing its tail. He raised one hand. 'We didn't participate in the protests, so don't worry about us being arrested, but the environment has become ...' He searched for the word.

'Hostile,' Simone finished for him.

'That's the word. The club will be bringing in new ...' He searched for the word again.

'Politically correct?'

'That's the words again. Instructors from China.'

'Are you having a farewell get-together?' Simone asked.

'No, we're leaving quietly. We have Canadian passports, but they still may ...' He hesitated again.

'They may try to stop you from leaving. I get it,' Simone said.

He bowed over his horse's neck to her. 'I wish you all the best, Simone, and greet your father for me. And if you can leave ...'

'I'm talking to people in Japan.'

He nodded, satisfied. 'And you,' he said to Freddo. 'Glorious animal. I will miss seeing you around.'

Freddo whickered.

'I swear sometimes that horse understands us.' He took up his reins. 'Please don't tell anyone I'm leaving, it will be quiet, but ...' He went wistful. 'I remember you coming for riding lessons when you were a little tiny thing, galloping around on that fat pony with your father, and then Emma came and made you even happier, and now you have this gorgeous animal ... keep going up and up, Simone. And say hello to them for me.'

'I will.' She touched his arm and his smile turned sad. 'Thank you for everything, Daniel, and if you have any problem leaving, ping me on my phone and I'll bring my dad in to sort it out for you.'

The sound of hooves became audible from further down the path, and riders speaking Putonghua.

Daniel's expression filled with concern. 'Later, Simone,' he said urgently, nodded to her and pushed his horse into a trot to head back to the stables.

'I liked him,' Freddo said when he was gone.

'Shh,' Simone said. 'They'll hear you.'

Freddo snorted and shook his head.

A pair of riders on thoroughbred club horses came around the corner, still speaking Putonghua. It was a couple of men who she didn't recognize, one on a bay and the other on a chestnut, so she nodded to them and Freddo moved to pass them.

'Why are you riding without saddle or bridle?' the man on the chestnut asked Simone.

'My horse is extremely well-trained, I don't need them,' Simone said.

'That's dangerous. He could escape at any time,' the man on the bay said.

Simone glanced down at Freddo's placid expression, then up at them. 'Really?'

Chestnut Man became fierce. 'You are a danger to yourself and others. You are breaking regulations by riding a dangerous stallion without proper equipment.'

Bay Man chimed in. 'Return to the office immediately and hand in your ID. You should be expelled for endangering valuable Jockey Club equipment.'

'What equipment?' Simone asked. 'I'm not using any.'

'The horse!' Chestnut Man said.

'He's mine.'

'All horses in Hong Kong are property of the Jockey Club,' Bay Man said smugly. 'You are mistreating this animal and will be expelled for it.'

'Not in this case,' Simone said, fighting to keep her voice mild. 'Freddo is my personal property. I imported him myself.'

'Return to the clubhouse immediately to be disciplined,' Chestnut Man said. 'You are endangering yourself, your horse and every other rider in the club with your flagrant disregard for safety procedures.'

Simone hesitated, watching them. Both of them were on the boil with this petty power-play.

'Are you the new instructors?' she asked as sweetly as she could.

'*Senior* instructors,' Bay Man said.

She bowed over Freddo's neck. 'It's lovely to meet you. I'll see you back at the clubhouse.' She pushed Freddo into a crisp canter to pass them, and their thoroughbreds reacted just as she'd hoped. Both of the highly-strung horses had been fidgeting at standing for so long, and they erupted into rabbit jumps, scurrying in circles, and the instructors had to fight to get them back under control. They yelled for her to come back, which made the horses' behaviour even worse, but unfortunately neither of them fell off.

'I need to wear tack to teach Frankie anyway,' Freddo said

with resignation when they were out of earshot.

'I know you hate it. We'll find somewhere else,' Simone said.

There was an email from the Blue Dragon when she checked her computer after dinner.

> To: *Simone Chen*
> From: *Seiryu Ten*
> Subject: *Re: Re: Shift your doctoral research to Tokyo U.*
> *Can you call me when you get in? I have a place for you at Todai.*
> *xxx Uncle Q*

She checked the time—it was two hours later in Tokyo than Hong Kong, but 10:30 pm was still not too late by local standards. She called him on his mobile.

He answered as a video call, showing him sitting at his desk, and she switched to video as well. Qing Long, Blue Dragon of the East, Emperor of Spring and Wood, was in his tall, slender human form with short, blue-tinged hair and bright blue eyes. He appeared to be working late as he was still in his spacious office on top of his office building in Shibuya and wore a grey silk business suit. The city skyscrapers spread behind him, lit up with moving billboards for electronics companies.

'Simone,' he said with concern. 'You okay, little one?' His expression shifted to disbelief. 'No. I do not ... I cannot ...' He straightened and changed to ultra-formal Japanese. 'The Emperor of the East reminds the Princess Simone that she is to present herself to the Jade Emperor and receive direction to hunt and dispatch a number of demons causing suffering and chaos in the mortal world.' He grunted. 'Sorry about that. Ignore—I can't tell you to ignore it!'

'I am ignoring it anyway. I refuse. You can ignore it as well,' Simone said. 'Dad and Emma will talk to him and tell him to leave me alone. So, about the university ...'

His expression softened, and he switched back to informal Japanese. 'I heard what happened, that was ridiculous. Your research could do so much good.'

Simone's throat filled at the support. 'Thanks, Uncle Qing. University politics, ne?'

'Stupid,' he said with scorn. 'The university year here starts in April, but as you're a postgrad we can get you in before the winter break. You can do the orientation, have the vacation, then start work on the research. How does that sound?'

Simone wiped her eyes with one hand. 'That sounds great.' She remembered. 'What about marine research stations?'

He waved it away. 'Let me handle that. If you need resources, you tell me, and I'll arrange it. Anything you need.'

'I want to do the work,' she said with force. 'I don't want to coast through it.'

'Of course you don't,' he said. 'But what you don't want, is to have to deal with stupid human obstacles, so let me handle that side of it. Let's see if we can't save the turtles in this region.' His smile turned smug. 'You can call me "Saviour of the Turtles".'

Realisation filled Simone. 'Holy shit, Uncle Qing, are you trying to upstage my dad?'

'Hell, yeah,' he said with satisfaction. 'Let's tweak his scaly tails, shall we? He should have given you more help from the start.'

'I did ask him to butt out so I could do it myself,' she said. 'And now, I hit my first obstacle, and I'm asking for help ...'

'This first obstacle is big enough to shut the whole thing down, and you—and the turtles—deserve much better.' His grin turned sly. 'I have the resources to help, and I'm just assisting my Sovereign.' He moved his mouse around, checking the screen below the camera. 'Can you meet me in Ueno Park tomorrow morning, about ten? I'll introduce you to the biology professor and we can get this underway.'

Simone gasped with relief. 'Thank you!' She filled with enthusiasm. 'I can do it after all. Thank you so much!'

'Not a problem at all, see you tomorrow.'

The ornamental cherry trees in Ueno Park in the centre of Tokyo were leafless, and the clouds threatened snow. The swan-shaped paddle boats were all locked up to one side, and the café near the water was shuttered. Trees around the lake blocked the view of the high rises of central Tokyo, and the surrounding buildings were all five storeys or less. Some taller residential towers stood behind Simone, blocking her view of the university campus.

The demons had less of a hold on the Earthly administration in Japan, resulting in the fresher air and more vibrant plant life in the park. The smell of diesel and the brown, choking sky were so pervasive in Hong Kong that they were a background to her life. Her father had mentioned that after she had freed the Celestial, there were still demons in control of government positions on the Earthly, and the Celestial administration was quietly removing them as they were identified. This was probably what the Jade Emperor was harassing her about—a demon that was too powerful for the Imperial Guard to handle. She squared her shoulders. She'd done enough for the Celestial, and it was time for her to do what *she* wanted and take a break from the constant violence of demon destruction. The Jade Emperor could find someone else to do his dirty work.

The Blue Dragon surged out of the water in True Form—the length of a bus, shining blue and silver, and completely unnoticed by everybody around. He changed to his human form—tall and elegant with long turquoise hair and wearing a western-style silk suit in shimmering silver.

He bowed to her Japanese-style, and she bowed back.

'The Emperor of the East reminds the Princess Simone that she is to present herself to the Jade Emperor and receive direction to hunt and dispatch a number of demons causing suffering and chaos in the mortal world.' He shook his head. 'Again! This is—'

'Ridiculous,' she said. 'I refuse.'

'I am calling your father the minute I'm back in my office,' he said. 'Insane.' He held his arms out. 'And it's good to see you looking so well, niece.'

Simone gave him a hug and he patted her back.

'Don't worry, I'll sort this study business out for you. Your research is far too important to be stopped by ridiculous human politics.'

'Thanks, Uncle Qing,' she said into his chest, immersed in the floral fragrance that surrounded him.

He pulled back and smiled at her, his blue eyes intense. 'Let's go talk to the head of the biology school, he's a half-human son of one of my dragon daughters. Don't give him any grief about not being able to transform into a dragon, please, he has a huge inferiority complex about it already.' He waved airily at a luxury high-rise residential building overlooking the lake. 'I have a couple of empty apartments in this one. If you want to use one just let me know.'

Simone glanced up. 'Home is only thirty minutes away ...' she started, then remembered that home would be empty for at least three weeks over Chinese New Year. 'I'll think about it.'

They went through the gardens of the campus, following the wide, paved paths between a mishmash of buildings from different eras. The campus was nearly deserted; the Christmas break had begun, and classes wouldn't recommence until January. Only postgraduate researchers like herself could choose to work through the break.

The biology building was ten storeys high, square and unremarkable. They entered the single-storey lobby, which was filled with exhibits of the school's research, bulletin boards, and some small meeting couches and tables. The entire building echoed with emptiness in the absence of the undergrad students. She followed the Dragon to the lifts, up to the top floor and through a secure door to the offices beyond. A brown-carpeted corridor lined with dark wood laminate on the walls stretched the width of the building, flanked by offices for the senior staff. They went to the end and the Dragon knocked on the door of the department head.

'I can't speak to you right now, I have someone important

coming,' the professor said through the closed office door.

'It's me,' the Dragon said. The professor's hurried footsteps approached, and he opened the door.

'My Lord. I apologise! Please.' He raced back to the middle of his untidy office and fell to one knee in front of the Dragon, bowing his head. 'Imperial Highness, Imperial Princess. Welcome. I have all the paperwork here.' He rose and bobbed his head. 'A thousand apologies, Celestial Worthies, I just received the message that you would be coming in person. I wasn't expecting such a distinguished visitor.'

'Relax,' the Dragon said, and flopped into one of the visitor's chairs. 'Just complete the paperwork, it's fine.'

'Of course!' the professor panted, then raced around his desk and flipped open a manila folder. 'Imperial Highness Princess Chen Si Min Simone, welcome back. I have your prospectus here and I've already approved it. Take these ...' He passed her a set of documents with many chop marks on them from official stamps. 'To the administration office on the seventh floor, and they will allocate you a study space. Wait.' He turned the paper around, found a red pen, and scribbled on it in Japanese with many exclamation marks. 'This is to ensure that you receive the best study space on the floor, and if it isn't suitable—'

'You really don't need to go to all this trouble,' Simone said.

'No trouble,' the professor said. He pushed the papers to her, and she took the folder. 'Come back to me when you're ready to graduate and we'll do the formalities. Welcome back.'

'I want to do this the hard way—supervisor, examiners, possibly even publication, everything,' Simone said.

The professor stopped and stared at her. 'Why? Provided the research is a valuable addition to the knowledge—in your case to saving the turtles of the South China Sea—the rest is a formality.'

'The House of the North is famed for doing things by the rules,' the Dragon said. 'Be as tough on her as you would on an ordinary postgrad student.'

The professor blinked at his grandfather and his mouth quivered. 'Yes. Of course, my Lord.'

The Dragon stood. 'Look after her.'

The professor shot to his feet. 'Of course, of course.' Simone stood as well, and the professor came around his desk and put his arm behind her back to escort her out. It trembled against her, then he quickly pulled it away, so he wasn't touching her at all. 'If there's anything you need, my Lady, just let me know. Anything at all.'

She allowed the terrified professor to escort her out of the office, and the Dragon shut the door behind them. 'He's so worthless.'

'What did you do to him?' Simone asked as they headed to the lift.

'Nothing, they're beneath my attention if they can't transform,' the Dragon said. 'It was his mother. Horrified that he was a live birth not an egg, horrified that he's human and not dragon, and particularly horrified that he's ...' He snorted a quiet laugh. '... ordinary human levels of average appearance. He was raised by his human father, but she'd occasionally drop in, abuse the hell out of him for being ugly, then leave. He's scared to death of us.'

'Charming,' Simone said.

They entered the lift, and the Dragon straightened his immaculate silk suit sleeves. 'Do you need me for the rest?' He waved one hand at the document folder. 'It looks sorted to me.'

'I can handle the rest—'

The Dragon disappeared before she could finish.

'Thanks, Uncle Qing.'

She arrived at the seventh floor. There was a window with 'Student Administration' in English and Japanese, and she went up to it. She pushed the document through to the woman on the other side, who eyed her suspiciously.

'Professor Yoshida gave me this and said you'd arrange a study space for me?' Simone asked.

The administrator relaxed and smiled when Simone spoke fluent Japanese. She flipped through the documents, then quickly picked up the phone and had a short conversation with Professor Yoshida. She put the phone down, pulled out a binder and placed the documents into it.

'He said to give you room eight but Mohinder's in there,' the administrator said. She closed the binder with a snap and walked around to the office door, exiting to join Simone. 'He should move anyway.'

She guided Simone down the hall to room eight. It was a small office with carpeted floor and walls covered in the same dark wood laminate, and a narrow window that overlooked the street outside. It contained a simple, battered wooden desk, a filing cabinet and a small, empty bookshelf. A young South Asian man, wearing a khaki turban and with a kind face, was sitting at a desk, flipping through references on his laptop.

The administrator tapped on the open door.

'You have to move out,' she said without preamble.

'No, it's fine, if there's another room—' Simone began, but Mohinder jumped up and desperately began to pack the office.

'No, no, I can move. I can go anywhere,' he said in broken Japanese, furiously putting books into a cardboard box. He wrenched the power cord from his laptop, snapped it closed and shoved it into a backpack. 'I can go anywhere.'

'You're set up here,' Simone said. 'I can go—'

'This will be your office, Miss Chin,' the administrator said, using the Japanese version of Simone's family name.

'No problem at all,' Mohinder said, breathless, as he grabbed the box and the backpack and rushed out the door. 'I'll be right back to get the rest.'

'But you don't even know where you're—' Simone began, and the administrator interrupted her.

'Cubicle fifteen,' she said.

'Got it,' Mohinder said, and raced away. He returned, bowed to Simone with a smile, and then ran off again.

'He should not be in here anyway,' the administrator said stiffly, then became more friendly. 'This will be your space. Nice to see a good Japanese girl here, the international students are so difficult—I don't know who is worse, the Indians or the

Chinese.' She smiled at Simone. 'I hope you do well.'

Simone opened her mouth and closed it again. The administrator was seeing—and hearing—what she wanted to, and Simone would gently correct her about being Chinese later.

The administrator passed the binder to Simone. 'Here's all your paperwork, and Professor Yoshida will be in touch soon to arrange your student ID. He says he'll supervise your thesis personally.'

The administrator went out, and Simone put the binder on the desk. She looked out the small window and saw the street below with a couple of courier trucks and many bicycles parked on it. She brushed her hair out of her eyes, sighed with feeling, and went to the desk and flipped through the binder, then put her head in her hands. She tried to hold the emotion in for a while, then gave up, pulled out her phone and texted Emma.

I could use a heart-to-heart if you're free, evil stepmother.

She went through the documentation and did ten minutes of the health-and-safety nonsense on her laptop before Emma appeared on the other side of the office and sat across the desk from Simone. 'You are again reminded to contact the Celestial administration about a most important task.' Her expression filled with fury. 'This is completely unacceptable.'

'Yeah, Uncle Qing did it too,' Simone said. 'Looks like he's ramped it up.'

Emma studied her. 'What happened? Was your research rejected again?'

Simone ran her hand over her face and felt the damp of tears. 'I don't need to do the work. The head of the school will sign off anything. They evicted a South Asian student from this office ...' She pulled a tissue out of her bag and wiped her nose. 'I'm receiving special treatment and I don't want it!' She blew her nose. 'If I stay in Hong Kong, I can't do the research at all. If I do it here, I'll never know if I'm good enough.'

'Oh, Simone,' Emma said, went to her and pulled her into a hug. 'Do the stupid work anyway. It's worth it.'

A flash of premonition—something big and bad was

coming—hit Simone and knocked the breath out of her. 'What the hell?'

'I saw that,' Emma said. 'I felt nothing. What was it?' Emma's phone pinged and she checked it. 'Clarissa's gone into labour. I'd better head back.'

'Wait,' Simone said, and held Emma's arm. 'Something big. Something bad. And something very close. To us. Our people. Bad!'

'Family close?'

Simone nodded, choking with fear.

Emma checked her phone again. 'Oh no. Oh shit. Your Dad's on the Celestial, in the middle of strategic war games with the Heavenly defences. The Jade Emperor won't release him for a single human woman, even if she is Michael's wife.' She glanced up into Simone's eyes. 'I really wish you had your Celestial alignment back, you would be a great help if she's in trouble.'

'You and Michael can handle it. Go!' Simone said, and Emma disappeared.

Simone turned back to the health-and-safety with dread, then gave up, picked up a few documents she'd found in a drawer, and went to the open space in the centre of the floor. There were eight cubicles of desks with dividers between them, none of them occupied. Mohinder had already spread his books on one of the desks and was browsing references on his computer.

'You forgot this,' Simone said, placing the documents on the desk. 'I'm sorry I forced you out like that.'

Mohinder jumped to his feet and bowed low to her, Japanese style. 'It's not a problem. I knew it would happen—' His voice trailed off. 'You speak Punjabi like ...' He studied her. 'You even know my dialect?'

'No, I'm just a bit of linguist,' she said. 'So, what did you do to piss off administration? She really hates you—more than just everyday racism.'

He lowered his voice and looked around, but nobody else was present. 'I dated a local girl. The love hotel was her idea.'

'A really bad one,' Simone said, just as softly.

'I know. I trusted her. She said it would be fine.' He wiped one hand over his face. 'It wasn't. The hotel owner took our IDs and contacted the university. The university contacted her family—we were in love, you know? We were making plans for after we graduated. I have family in the Netherlands—we could go there together.' He sniffled and looked around for a tissue. 'They banished her into the countryside, to live with elderly relatives. I have no idea where she is. I was very lucky not to be expelled, but I'm fully paid up with all my fees until the end of the program, so I've just been shuffled way down to the bottom of the list of priorities.'

Simone checked her phone, then realised what she was doing and turned back to Mohinder. 'Sorry. A very close friend is in labour. She's like a sister to me.' She sighed. 'I won't have anything done until I'm sure that both she and the baby are okay.' She brightened. 'Could you show me around the campus? Where are the good kombini and vending machines?'

He studied her for a long moment, then said, 'I want to find my fiancée again ...'

She raised one hand. 'Just as friends. I haven't made any friends yet, and you've been here longer than I have—'

He interrupted her. 'That's another bad idea. If you're seen around campus with me, you won't make any friends at all. It's for the best if you avoid me.'

'I don't care about that,' she said.

'I do,' he said. 'So if you'll excuse me, I have work to do.'

He sat again and pointedly ignored her. She sighed and returned to her bare, empty office. She sat at the desk and checked her laptop—5 pm. She decided to shuffle through her research and make sure it fitted the Todai research standards before heading home to Hong Kong for dinner with the family.

8

The apartment was quiet when Simone returned home from Todai at the end of the day. Neither Emma nor her father were there, but she sensed Er Hao and Frankie were sitting together in the television room. She kicked off her shoes and went into the room to find them on the couch in front of an Australian children's show, with Frankie nestled into Er Hao's side. He jumped up and ran to Simone to give her a hug.

Er Hao muted the television then stood and shifted uncomfortably. 'I need to prepare dinner, my Lady.'

Frankie spun to stare at her with his mouth open, then visibly cringed.

'No you don't, young man,' Simone said, clasping his shoulder. 'Nobody's mad at you, and you didn't do anything wrong.' She nodded to Er Hao. 'Go, but nothing too fancy, okay?'

Er Hao nodded and went out.

Simone pulled Frankie back down to the couch and sat him in her lap—he was nearly too big, but she didn't care. 'I know Mum's still with Clarissa at the hospital, but where's Dad?'

'John's at work, he says he'll be home soon.' Frankie never referred to their father as 'Dad' or 'Ba Ba', because that brought back too many memories of abuse from when the demons had kidnapped him to act as a puppet Jade Emperor. He always called their father by his English name 'John' instead, and Xuan Wu was infinitely patient with him about it. Frankie hesitated, then leaned into Simone. 'Everybody's really worried about Aunty Clarissa. Really worried. Is she going to die? You can't die just by having a baby, can you?'

'It can happen,' Simone said, wishing that Emma and her father were present—with their Immortal wisdom—to handle this instead of her. 'It used to happen a lot more, and modern medicine has made it safer, but it still happens.'

'If she dies ... will she go to Hell?' He stiffened with shock in her lap. 'She wouldn't be with the demons in those ... places, would she? She's a nice person!'

'Did you see any of that?' Simone asked, trying to be as gentle as possible. 'You never mentioned it before—I know you were down there for a long time, but—'

'Mummy—fake Mummy—took me a couple of times,' he said, referring to the previous Demon King that Simone had destroyed. 'She wanted me to like what happens in Hell.' He shivered. 'I didn't.'

'Oh Frankie,' Simone said, and hugged him. 'I wish I could take all those memories away from you.'

'No,' Frankie said. 'When I talked to Doctor Au about it, she said that it's better for me to remember everything, because if I blank it out and there are gaps, they'll come out later and hurt me even more.'

'She's right, I guess,' Simone said. 'You're here now, and we love you, and that's all that's important, right?'

'But what about Aunty Clarissa?'

'She'll be fine,' Simone said, hearing the lie in her voice. Clarissa was so incredibly fragile, and Simone could see the future. It was grim. Frankie probably had a good idea about the future as well, given how powerful he was, and that was probably why he was asking.

'But if she dies? What happens to her? What happens to them? I *saw* things down in Hell, Simone, and Mum and John won't talk about it.'

'I'm probably the only one who can tell you about it,'

Simone said with a sad smile. 'Because I'm the only one the Jade Emperor can't order around. He tells everyone else not to say anything.'

'Yeah, Mum and John said that. They have to do what he says, and we have to trust him, but sometimes he's *really annoying*.'

'Okay.' Simone shifted him to beside her on the couch. 'What happens is …' She hesitated, to see if she could tell her brother, and relaxed when she could. She was too demon to have any Celestial alignment and owed no allegiance to the Jade Emperor. Up yours, JE, he had no control over her. 'Good people, like Clarissa, have their memories wiped and they're reborn to a new life, to have another chance at gaining Immortality.'

'That's nasty! Why wipe their memories?'

'Let's say Clarissa's baby is born with all the memories of their past life. What if they had a husband or wife in that life? And children? A *baby* remembering having children? Everything would be a mess. And if they had bad things happen to them in their previous lives, then they'd remember all of it. And when bad things happen to you, they leave…'

'Marks. Scars. Doctor Au says she's a doctor for hurts in your head.' He lowered his voice. 'She just talks to me, and I talk to her, and every time we finish talking, she makes me feel …' He sighed slightly and relaxed. '*Cleaner*. In my head.'

'What if someone lived hundreds of lives of suffering? Even if they could talk to someone like Doctor Au, it would still break them.'

Frankie nodded. 'Okay. I guess it makes sense. What about Immortals? They remember.'

'If someone gains Immortality, they don't have the memories from the lives before they were Raised, but they do from after. And if someone gains Enlightenment, they remember all of it. All their lives. The memories are never really lost—they're just on hold until your brain is big enough to deal with them.'

'John says Ms Kwan gained Enlightenment?'

'Kwan Yin.' Simone nodded and squeezed him. 'That's why she's so special. She's one of the Buddhas and helps us.'

Frankie sat and thought for a while. The children's show was still running, muted, on the screen in the background and Simone fervently wished that her brother lived the simple life of an ordinary child.

Frankie nodded. 'I get it. But what about the people down in Hell who ... are with the demons?'

'Those are people who did *really* bad things when they were alive. They're being punished.'

'But if they won't remember—what's the point?'

'You are so wise sometimes,' Simone said. 'Dad negotiated this system with them a long time ago, to keep the demons happy so that they would stay in Hell and not come up and cause trouble here. He's regretted it ever since—and I want to change it. It shouldn't happen.'

'I'll help you when I'm Immortal too,' Frankie said with confidence. 'I hope Aunty Clarissa will be okay. I really like her.'

'I do too,' Simone said. 'Now, dinner's ready, let's go eat. I'm starving. I'll tell you about Japan.'

'Okay.' He hopped off the couch and went out, with her following and shaking her head, certain that she'd just told him way too much, messed everything up and set the child's recovery back by years.

After dinner, Simone played with Frankie for a while, then let the demon bathe him and tuck him into bed. A couple of hours later, her father arrived, teleporting directly into Frankie's room—she felt him—then he went into his office. She followed him to find him reading an Imperial Edict from a pile inside one of the red boxes. She sat across from him and swiped her hand over her forehead.

He dropped the Edict. 'Thank you for talking to him about it. Neither I nor Emma had permission.'

'I thought that may be the case. The future looks grim, Dad.'

'I know.' A new Edict appeared on the desk in front of him,

already open. 'Oh for ffss …' He didn't finish it and she smiled. 'Again? Every time we sit down together.'

'It's fine, Dad. Just do it and get it out of the way,' she said.

'Humph.' He straightened and spoke formally, looking her in the eye. 'The First Heavenly General reminds the Princess Simone that she is to present herself to the Jade Emperor and receive direction to hunt and dispatch a number of demons causing suffering and chaos in the mortal world.' He sagged. 'Sorry. I have no choice.'

'I refuse.' She hesitated, then said, 'But there's something important I need to tell you.'

'I thought it went well in Tokyo? You said it was a good plan. You look concerned?'

'Nothing to do with that. A couple of things happened— one of them related to the demons—while I was in Europe, and I need your advice as the resident expert.'

He leaned on the desk, clasped his hands and concentrated on her. 'There's usually a great deal of jostling for the top spot after a King dies, but this new one that's taken the old European King's place appears to have a sufficient level of cunning and viciousness to keep the job.'

'That's not what this is about. The new European Demon King said something after Emma was dead, and I wasn't sure that she should know about it, so I waited until she was out to tell you.' She looked up into his dark eyes. 'The European King said that Emma was his *mother*. Is it possible? And should I tell her if he is?'

'Entirely possible,' he said, completely calm. 'The previous Kings were engaging in a massive breeding and cloning program, both here and in Europe, and stole one of Emma's ovaries to use in seeding it. The Tiger's people have sighted big, powerful demons that are outwardly identical to Emma—'

Simone interrupted him. '*Emma copies*?' She realised she'd nearly yelled it and lowered her voice. 'What? Really? Why didn't you tell me?'

'I'm sorry, I should have. I thought you would never encounter one, as they've only been seen in Europe. I would not be surprised to learn that the new European King is one of Emma's progeny.'

'How many do you think they made?'

His eyes turned inwards as he thought about it. 'I found three nest cavities in the facility in Wales. There was the underground one where you found Leo—eight more nest cavities there. Six eggs to a nest? It depends on how many more nests there were, and how many of the progeny were eaten by the mother before they were pulled clear.'

'That is a *lot* of demons.'

'Powerful demons if they have inherited anything from their Emma-clone Snake Mother. The Welsh serpent people were powerful enough to hold back an entire Roman invasion force.'

'Does Emma know about the copies?'

'Yes. She had nightmares where she was inside the heads of some of the clones—the Snake Mother ones—and it took us a while to work out that she was somehow mentally linked to them.'

'I remember those nightmares,' Simone said. 'They really freaked her out.'

'Since gaining Immortality, she says that the dreams have stopped. Her essence is now too pure to be affected by the clones.'

Simone cocked her head. 'What does she want us to do with them? If we run into one?'

'Emma's an Immortal. She doesn't deal in absolutes. If you encounter one, decide for yourself.' He looked down at the desk. 'There's something else you should know about these copies.'

'There are some of me,' she said.

He nodded. 'Take care if you see Emma, or Michael, or yourself, or another member of the family in an unexpected place. The previous King worked very hard to make the copies undetectable, and some of them aren't aware of their true nature. I can identify them, but more junior Celestials see them as human. Double-check with our code words.'

'Have you encountered any that were undetectable and thought they were the real Emma? Or the real me?'

His dark eyes were full of pain. 'I did meet one. I was with the Tiger in the Western part of his dominion, reconnoitring a big Nest. We entered the tunnels, I heard my name called and Emma ran towards me.' He clasped his hands on the desk. 'It was so delighted. Screaming with joy, screaming my English name …' He looked away. 'The Tiger and I were both stunned at its resemblance to Emma. It threw itself into my arms and exploded, killing us instantly.' He turned back to concentrate on her. 'Take care with them. Some of them are programmed to self-destruct in a spray of demon essence.'

Simone studied her own hands, then dropped the camouflage on them to reveal that the tips of her fingers were black with demon essence—it looked like she'd dipped them in ink. 'At least I don't absorb the demon essence and become more demon every time I kill one.'

'You are still yourself, uncontaminated by the essence within you. Still pure and kind, and I am very proud of you.'

'Thanks, Dad.' She glanced up at him. 'Should we tell Emma that the European King claims to be her child? This is horrifying.'

'Regardless of whether you choose to tell her or not—I will. I have vowed never to keep a secret from her.'

'I didn't know that!'

'So be careful what you tell me if you don't want her to know. Even about gifts—I won't withhold information from her. Take care.'

'You didn't do the whole standing-up, hand-on-the-desk, freaky-voiced-promise, complete-silence-then-cold-wind thing, did you?'

He just smiled.

'Did you at any point tell her, "Be careful what you wish for?"'

His smile didn't shift. 'I may have said something to that effect. Now she will never receive a surprise from me, good or bad.'

Simone leaned back and studied him. 'I'm sure she prefers it that way.'

'She absolutely does.' His face filled with delighted wonder. 'You can help me! For her next birthday, I can point you at her wish list, you can buy her something, I won't know what the gift is, and I'll be unable to tell her.'

Simone chuckled. 'What did you buy me for my birthday, John? I didn't buy you anything, Emma.' She sobered. 'I had a premonition while I was on my way back from Europe—'

He stiffened. 'Clarissa needs me. Mind your brother?'

'Oh no,' Simone said weakly, and her father disappeared.

Simone was woken at 2 am by her phone pinging. She picked it up and checked it. It was a message from Emma.

Group text FYI. Nobody needs to do anything and please do not contact Michael. Clarissa Huang-MacLaren passed away in childbirth at 1 am, Hong Kong time. Her daughter was successfully delivered and is a healthy girl. Clarissa haemorrhaged and died of blood loss and organ failure. Clarissa's mother Christine Huang and other members of the Huang family are assisting in the care of the child. Again: Michael asks for privacy during this time of loss. You will be notified of funeral arrangements when they're made.

Simone stared at the screen, too shocked to feel anything. Her premonition had been right—her father had failed to heal Clarissa. This was unheard of because the Xuan Wu was the mightiest healer on any plane. Perhaps something to do with modern technology and Clarissa's donated kidney? Simone would have to ask him about it. Then the realisation hit her that she would never see the delightful woman again, and her eyes filled with tears. Michael would be so traumatised. She threw the covers off. She needed to go to Michael, to help him. He would be—

Her phone pinged again.

Simone, this message is just for you: don't contact Michael, please. He's really taking this very badly and you can't help. Throw yourself into your work or something because he's going to need a lot of therapy to handle this after losing his mother, so tragically. Don't worry about the baby, she's fine and we're all pulling together to look after her. We're at the hospital arranging things and won't be home for a while, so please mind Frankie for us.

Simone rolled out of bed, still in her fluffy winter pyjamas, and went into her father's office. Frankie was asleep, and the demon servant, Er Hao, was dormant. The bottom desk drawer was the only one not hanging open, and she unlocked it with energy and took out the fancy bottle of expensive French cognac that her father had hidden there to share with his Celestial friends.

She pulled the cork out and took a big swig, feeling the burn all the way down, then teleported to the top of the apartment building. The roof was covered in slimy tiles, thick with mould, and the lift machinery sat to one side, silent so late at night. The rooftop wasn't used as an outdoor area by the family—there was a much nicer playground behind the building at ground level—so she walked to the edge, cleaned it off with energy, then climbed over and sat with her legs dangling. The cloud cover was complete, thick and grey, and so low that she felt as if she could reach up and touch it. The sky shimmered with the reflected colours of the city's lights far beneath her, and the Peak around the building was covered with thick scrub and wild azaleas in the areas that were too steep to build on. She took another big gulp—probably at least five hundred dollars' worth—and closed her eyes as it went down.

She quickly pulled herself to her feet when she felt a massive demon presence nearby. It hovered just out of range of the building's powerful seals, and it was at least Prince level.

The words sounded like they were spoken right next to her by a child. 'Truce, Princess. I wish to parley.'

'Talk to my father, I don't do any of that anymore,' Simone said out loud.

'I believe you were just in European Hell.'

Simone stiffened. How did the demon know that?

'How's Frankie? Tell him I miss him,' it said.

'Who are you?'

'I'm the Demon King's Number One Son.'

Simone let her breath out in a long hiss, then took another swig of the cognac. 'Edu.'

'Congratulations on getting rid of the competition, Princess. My spies told me what Michael said to you when he was imprisoned in Hell—that the two of you are destined to be together. It must be a huge relief to have the little human wife out of the way.'

Simone nearly roared with rage, then swallowed it. Becoming angry with a demon was pointless, it would never understand why.

Edu's voice was sly next to her. 'I know you Celestials are all about doing the right thing, but if you need a favour, I have human nurses in the hospital who owe me favours. I'd be happy to provide an accident for the baby—'

Simone doubled over with horror. 'You do not touch that precious child. If any harm comes to her, I will come after you myself. You hear me?'

'Fine, fine, whatever. I didn't realise you wanted the child for yourself.' Edu sounded bored. 'I guess that's more strategically sensible, even though it'll be in the way of your relationship with Michael. I'm just trying to help.'

'I do not need any help from you. Piss off, go torment some smaller demons or plot against the new King or something.'

'The new King's weak.' Her voice was full of derision. 'I have an offer for you, if you're interested. Build some connections, make some money, kill some demons? It'll keep you occupied until you're ready to make a move on your man.'

'Go. Fuck. Yourself.'

'I don't need to; my harem is absolute top-quality. Would you like to see? I'm sure there's a young man here who is just your type. Tall, muscular, blonde, half-European ...'

'You *scum*. Go to Hell. Go back to Hell.' Simone took another swig and wiped her eyes. 'Leave me alone.'

Edu's voice changed to that of a sweet and caring child.

'Sorry, that was uncalled-for. I'll never forget how well you looked after us when my late father kept us incarcerated in that awful little house in Hell. You taught me about kindness and empathy—'

'Cut the bullshit,' Simone said, and took another drink. She was starting to feel nicely light-headed. 'You are all spite, poison and malice from top to bottom. Go. Away.'

Edu's voice changed back to businesslike. 'Come visit me on my yacht in Aberdeen Harbour. You can't miss it, it's the biggest one there. I have information that could bring back the European gods—the old Kings were preparing to put a tame god into the European heavens to start things up again. Apparently one of them is still around.'

'Sure. I'll come visit you on your yacht full of teeth and venom.'

'Teeth and venom won't hurt you, dear, you're as much demon as I am. Come to the yacht whenever you feel like it. If I'm not present, my wives will call me, and I'll come and give you the time of your life. They are unforgettable. Extremely talented.' Edu's voice filled with humour that sounded way older than her ten-year-old-girl persona. 'All of them are in the form of bright, handsome young men, and they're willing to do anything to please you.'

Simone remembered her comment about dating a demon instead of humans, who were unable to handle her nature, and wanted to kick herself.

'The only thing I am interested in is removing the demon essence filling me and becoming full Celestial again,' she said. 'If you have a way of doing that, I'll talk. Otherwise, leave me alone.'

Edu sounded delighted. 'Seriously? Let me look into it, I have some great people. Start thinking of something you can do in return for me. Getting rid of that worthless pile of shit in charge and giving me the throne of Hell would be a good start.' Her voice filled with enthusiasm. 'My father helped Emma clear the demon essence from her, and now I can help you. Fitting. I'll be in touch.'

The demon's presence disappeared.

Simone took another swig of the cognac, feeling she'd made a massive mistake by letting Edu know what she wanted, and given the demon leverage over her. She put the bottle down, sat back down on the edge of the roof, and let the tears flow. Clarissa had been like a sister to her: so warm, and normal, and caring. Simone's heart ached at the thought of never seeing her again, and Clarissa's lovely daughter would grow up motherless.

Sometime later, her sobs petered out to gasps. Her father appeared next to her and held his hand out. She handed him the bottle and he took swig, then raised his head and closed his eyes as it went down.

'Too many hospital staff,' he said. 'The placenta ruptured, and she bled out. They moved her to the ICU, and she was surrounded by doctors and nurses trying to save her. They threw all of us out into a waiting room and Michael was yelling at me to do something …' He took another drink. 'I couldn't change into my Serpent to heal her and hide my appearance from that many humans at the same time. I tried to explain to Michael that he needed to handle their minds, that Emma doesn't have the strength to control them without causing damage, but he was too distraught to understand me. Then Clarissa flatlined, and he realised that if he'd kept his head and wiped their memories, I could have fixed everything.' He drank again. 'The baby's fine, but Michael's close to catatonic and in the mental health ward. The White Tiger wants to take him to the Western Heavens to recover, and it's probably a good idea. Emma and Clarissa's mother, Christine, are arranging for Christine to take the baby back to Canada with her and care for her there until Michael is capable.' He pushed the bottle at her and she took it. 'What a mess.'

She took another drink to top up the buzz. 'Emma told me to stay away from them.'

'That would be for the best, yes. Everybody knows that you and Michael are fated to be together. It would not be a good idea to rub that in his face right now. He feels guilty enough as it is. He's ...' he sighed. 'He started loudly blaming himself for not being completely devoted to Clarissa, convinced that he hesitated because he *wanted* her to die. Clarissa's mother took this as meaning that Michael had been unfaithful and had a mistress—like Clarissa's father did. Clarissa's mother laid into Michael in the waiting room, and it ramped up his guilt. Emma tried to moderate but ... it became ugly. The worst part was that Michael was agreeing with her, saying that he could have saved his wife if he had his head on straight.'

'This is because of me?' Simone asked.

'And now you're blaming yourself as well,' he said. 'Nobody is to blame. Sometimes life doesn't work out the way we want, and we do our best with what we have. Laying blame doesn't change the situation. Everybody needs time to work through their feelings and rebuild themselves. Until Michael works out that this isn't his fault, and isn't your fault, it might be best to do as Emma says—go to Japan and throw yourself into your work.'

Simone took another swig, enjoying the burn. 'I was just contacted by the Demon King's Number One Son. That piece of shit, Edu.'

Xuan Wu held his hand out and wiggled his fingers. She handed him the bottle.

'Oh yes, what does she want?'

'The usual bullshit. She wants me to take out the King and give her the job.'

'Interesting. That means she doesn't have the strength to do it herself. She really is too young and naïve to be Number One, I'm surprised she has lasted so long.'

'The biggest yacht in Aberdeen harbour is her Nest, if you want some carnage to make you feel better.'

'What would make me feel better,' he said, stretching, 'is a hug from my wife and my youngest son and daughter, and the knowledge that in the end, everything will be okay.'

She put her arms out sideways and they shared a seated embrace.

He summoned the cork stopper and sealed the bottle. 'Go

back to bed,' he said. 'Tomorrow, you can decide what you want to do. Do you need help to go back to sleep?'

She hesitated, then, 'Yes please, Daddy.'

'Okay. Let's go.' He disappeared.

She arrived in her bedroom and crawled into bed. He pulled the covers over her and kissed her on the forehead, making her eyes spring with fresh tears at the feeling of his love after so many years of being apart.

He put his hand on her forehead. 'Oh, and the *really* good alcohol is in the storeroom in a plastic bin next to the demon jar. Go for that next time.'

9

The next morning, Simone woke, thought about her prospectus ... and couldn't find the energy to go to Todai. The rest of the family weren't home, but her father had left a note on the dining table saying he was back to work training his martial arts students on Celestial Wudang Mountain, and she could call him or Emma any time. Emma had taken Frankie to her parent's house in the Northern Heavens to stay there for a few days—probably a good move since she seemed to be full-time arranging things for Michael's new daughter.

She sat at the kitchen table for breakfast and checked her phone, hoping for a message from Graham. She choked with horror. Celestials ... so many people that she knew, or didn't know ... had messaged her, on all her social media platforms as well as by email. She ran through the messages and saw their subjects with dismay.

Jade Girl: *Ignore them, all your real friends know the truth.*

Jade Flower: *Is it true you'll get together with Michael now?*

Wide Eagle: *Did you set it up? We all know you feel about Michael and wouldn't blame you. You're a much better fit for him than that weak human wife. You can tell me*

Plum Blossom: *You need to call me right now because people are saying the most insane things!*

Precious: *Me and Sylvie have a place in Shanghai if you want to hide. Plenty of room.*

Virtuous Scholar: *So the way's clear for you to hook up with Michael now, right? I'm jealous, girl, that man is fire!*

She ignored them, and opened the messenger app. It was full of similar distastefully gossipy requests. She denied them all, then composed a message to Graham.

Hi Graham, I hope my father and I didn't scare you too much ...

She deleted it and started again.

Graham, I know it's a lot to take in, but ...

She deleted that one too.

Graham, I meant what I said, before I probably exploded your world ...

Simone leaned back, ran both her hands down her face, deleted the message and tried again.

Hi Graham, I know what you saw was pretty awful, but please know that inside, I'm—

Simone's phone pinged and she checked it, then sagged. It was the long-awaited message from Graham.

I thought about what your father said. You're a hero, Simone, and I'm privileged to be with you.

Simone choked a short, sad laugh. She didn't feel like a hero, but privileged? Maybe there was hope. Another message from him came through.

Would you like to meet up and try again? Battersea, at noon?

Simone's heart lifted and the tears of pain turned to joy. He wanted to try again. He was so courageous and understanding, and she was lucky to have him. Her research was back on track, and she could spend the Christmas and New Year breaks with him. The future suddenly looked a great deal brighter.

She tapped on her phone to respond to Graham, agreeing to meet at the café in Western district at noon.

Simone didn't bother driving the car, because Graham knew who she was. She simply teleported to the street where Battersea Café stood. It was one street back from the Harbour in Western District, below the Jockey Club Student Village and a popular meeting destination for HKU's international students.

Western district had been one of the first areas occupied by the settlers escaping the Cultural Revolution and had always held tight to its working-class roots. The area was known for low-budget cramped apartment buildings and government-sponsored housing estates, like Kwun Lung Lau, strung with ad-hoc electrical wires; ancient, rusting window air conditioners; and bamboo poles holding wet laundry. Since the government had built a new MTR station in the middle of the district, it had become more modern, and the vintage apartment buildings were disappearing, replaced with tall towers of multiple smaller and more modern flats. Its 'rejuvenation' had attracted the Territory's last remaining expatriates looking to find cheaper housing west of the luxury of Mid-levels, and a number of Western-style food places had sprung up to accommodate them.

The wealthier expatriates had mostly left the Territory, moving to new business hubs in Shanghai and Singapore, now that Hong Kong had lost its free-wheeling nature and become 'just another Chinese city where you have to be careful what you say'. Political oppression was present in Singapore, but the police weren't as brutal as Hong Kong's roaming, menacing presence, who stopped and searched anyone they didn't like the look of, taking them away and locking them up if they showed any resistance. Bookstores were closing, journalists and academics were in jail or overseas exile, and business was slow everywhere as the atmosphere was full of uncertainty about the Territory's future.

Simone passed a group of police checking ID cards as she approached the café in Western. Her mixed-race appearance usually led her to be stopped and she already had her wallet out of her bag when they gestured towards her.

'ID card,' the hard-faced cop said, waving one hand at her. One of the other policemen leered.

She took her ID card out of her wallet—she used to keep it

in a windowed pocket where it was safe, but lately she'd been pulling it out of her wallet so often she'd started keeping it with her credit cards. The policeman took her card and studied it, then turned away and went to a small station they'd set up on a folding table under a portable gazebo, taking notes as he spoke on his mobile phone. He called her ID number in, and she felt the same bolt of anxiety she did every time they did this—would she be pulled into a station for interrogation this time? She seemed to be targeted more and more. The cop spoke on the phone for longer than she was comfortable with, then returned, still stony-faced.

'Phone,' he said.

Silently thanking the Blue Dragon's technology expertise for the Celestial special phones, Simone made a performance of finding her phone at the bottom of her bag and pushed the power button four times as she wrestled it out. Its screen was still flashing with the wipe-and-replace app as she handed it to him. He took it with a satisfied grunt, then returned to the table and connected it to a laptop.

No nudes on it, asshole, she thought at him as he unlocked it with the override that was compulsory on all phones sold in the Territory and scanned the photo album contents. He didn't find what he was looking for and disconnected it, obviously disappointed.

'No more than two people in a gathering,' he said in Cantonese as he gave her the phone and ID back. 'Restrictions on gathering. For your own safety.'

She relaxed, relieved. She'd done this dance before. 'I'm not in a gathering, I'm on my lunch break.'

'Work where?' he asked.

She pointed up the hill. 'University.'

His Mainland accent started to come through his Cantonese as he spoke with distaste. 'Pah. Bad foreign ideas up there. Not patriotic.'

'I'm studying fish and turtles, not ideas,' she said, attempting to placate him so he would let her go.

He cocked one eye at her. 'Why? We catch them, we eat

them. That's all you need to know, isn't it?'

'I want to make sure there are always fish to eat,' she said.

'Of course there are. You just need to go out and catch them,' he said, and waved her away. 'Go back to America and study the dirty fish there. Polluted.'

She opened her mouth to tell him that she wasn't American but closed it again. If she argued, he would hold her up even longer. Emma had been pulled in a couple of times for questioning, and Simone didn't need the added complication of her relationship with the targeted Australian woman coming up. She nodded to the policeman. 'Thank you.'

'Got a boyfriend?' he asked, eyeing her with the avarice of a man coveting an expensive car.

'Yes, sorry,' she said, smiling ruefully and hating every second of this game. She gestured with her head. 'I can go? I'm meeting him for lunch.'

The cop pulled out his notebook and gave her his phone number. 'If you get tired of him, or he cheats on you, call me and I'll punish him. I'll take him to the station and beat him up for you.' He grinned. 'I'm a good guy.'

She took his number, not wanting to touch his hand. 'Thank you.' She turned and walked quickly away, wiping her eyes with relief. It was only a matter of time before she would be pulled in for 'a cup of tea' with them. She checked her watch. The police had kept her for more than ten minutes and she was running late to meet Graham. She hoped he would wait for her.

Simone and Graham often shared meals at the Battersea Café. It was decorated in a modern style with dark timber tables and comfortable, teal-coloured chairs lined up along the floor-to-ceiling windows that faced the street. It had a timber bar with a selection of specialty alcohol behind it and was lit with rustic industrial-style light globes. The head chef regularly travelled to London to discover the latest trendy dishes, and the menu was small, fresh and always being updated, with multiple vegetarian options for them.

The café next to Battersea also served Western food but was in the old-Hong Kong style—dingy Formica-topped tables, folding chairs, greasy walls and an enormous A3-sized laminated menu offering at least fifty different dishes, from pizza to spaghetti to thick-cut French toast with lashings of maple syrup and a card advertising the Borscht-derivative set lunch that had never been anywhere near Europe. There were no vegetarian options at all—if traditional Hong Kongers wanted vegetarian food, they went to a specialty restaurant that provided mock-meat dishes with thick, sweet sauces. Simone enjoyed both styles of Western food, but Graham was accustomed to the modern dishes, so they went to Battersea more often.

Simone stood, frozen, when she saw who was sitting across the table from Graham, and immediately knew why she'd been held up by the cops. It was the Demon King's Number One Son, Edu, in her ten-year-old girl form. She had twin braided pigtails and was wearing a black gothic-style frilly dress, looking like something out of a horror movie. Graham sat across from her, eyes wide and mouth hanging open, riveted with horror as she spoke. He saw Simone through the window and jumped, and Edu turned to see Simone as well. She smiled and gave Simone a cheery wave, then disappeared.

Simone rushed in and sat across from him. 'Everything she said is a lie!'

'She warned me that you'd say that,' he said, obviously distressed. 'What the hell? She was so damn creepy ...'

'That was a senior demon,' Simone said. 'The "little girl" thing is just a façade. She's a really nasty piece of work.'

'That was a demon? She looked human!' He cast around with alarm. 'There are *demons* everywhere? How many are there? Will they hurt us?' He looked on the verge of another panic attack.

'Relax.' She put her hand on his and clutched it. 'They have a treaty with us. They won't hurt any humans. They can only come out of ...' She didn't continue with the concept of Hell, that would freak him out even more. She could explain it all later. 'You're safe. As long as you're with me, you're safe.'

'And when I'm not with you?' Graham took a sip of water

with a shaking hand. 'She said some things. Some really nasty things.'

'It was all a lie.'

'She said ask you some questions and make you promise to tell the truth. Will you promise to tell me the truth?'

Simone's heart plummeted again, and she squeezed his hand. 'Ask me anything. I will never lie to you. I promise.'

'Your mother was human?'

She nodded a reply.

'She's dead. What happened to her?'

Simone hesitated, then said, 'Demons kidnapped her and …' She sighed. 'Murdered her.'

'So much for the treaty. They killed her because she was married to your father?'

Simone nodded and looked away. 'I was two years old. They were planning to hold her to control my father, but they killed her …' She knew how bad this would sound but told him the truth anyway. 'By mistake when they tortured her too hard.'

Graham didn't lose his intensity. 'Was your human housekeeper—a helpless British woman, who wasn't involved in anything—did she have her head chopped off by the same demon for no reason whatsoever?'

'Yes, but that demon is dead. I destroyed it.'

'I'm sure I'll be terribly grateful if that happens to me and you kill the demon after I'm dead,' he said, his voice heavy with sarcasm. She tried to speak, and he waved her down, his voice fierce. 'How many innocent people have died, just because they were close to your family?'

She stopped and tried to work it out. Did the war count? So many innocent refugees …

'The fact that you have to stop and think about this is worse than you knowing the number off the top of your head,' he said.

'We were at war—'

'The man we met the night I went to your house. Michael MacLaren. His wife's hands were broken and twisted, and she looked so frail. The little girl said that demons did that to her—

they *tortured* her for no reason other than they enjoyed it. It was a random act of violence, that happened because she married into the family. Yes?'

Simone hesitated, looking him in the eye, then her heart broke as she said, 'Yes.'

'She said that you and Michael grew up together? He's a demigod who was a trainee bodyguard for you? He lived in the same house as you for years?'

'Yes. I turned out stronger than him, and I didn't need a bodyguard.'

'But he's not a blood relation, is he?'

'Uh ... no? More like a really good friend.'

He took a deep breath and studied her carefully. 'Are you destined to be with him?'

Her throat thickened, then she answered bluntly and truthfully. 'Eventually, yes. We both know that. We try to work around it.'

'Why aren't you together, then? Why is he married to someone else, and you're dating me? Why don't you just give in to this and stop hurting other people?'

She choked at the thought of poor, tortured Clarissa, who had known about it and loved Michael anyway. 'We didn't know until it was too late. He's ten years older than me, and I was only fifteen when he proposed to Clarissa. I was too young to be in a relationship, and he had too much integrity to pursue anything with me. He went to America, made a life for himself there and met Clarissa.' She shook her head gently. 'He adores her. Like I adore you.'

'But do you love him?'

She was taken aback at the question and quivered with the effort to lie to him. She wanted to reassure him, to bring everything back to what they had before she exploded the relationship. 'I ...' She lowered her head and whispered the answer. 'Yes.'

'I think you should stop dragging us helpless mortals into your dangerous world, Simone.'

'I don't want to live in that world anymore!'

'But you can't avoid it, can you? It follows you around. And if I stay with you, I'm going to end up either tortured like that poor woman or killed. I can't live like that—watching my back all the time.'

'I will protect you.'

'Like your father protected your mother? Your housekeeper? Michael's wife? All those people who died?'

She choked on the truth of his words. 'What we have is so good, don't throw it away.'

'I'm not throwing anything away, I'm running.' He took a big gulp of water. 'Because I'm scared. I'm a coward. I'll never be a fraction of what you are or what you need. I'll never be your equal, and I can't live like that.' He rose and placed the turtle necklace on the table in front of her. 'Keep the necklace, eh? And friends. Best friends. But please, Simone ...' He touched her hand. 'Stop dragging us poor humans into loving you, because your life is way to terrifying for someone as ordinary as me.' He bent and kissed the top of her head where she sat hunched over the table with misery. 'I'll give the restaurant some money for sitting here without ordering, so leave when you feel like it, and I do love you, but you scare me to death.'

'I love you,' she said to table, but he'd already gone to the cash register to give them some money. He negotiated with them to pay for a small cover charge, nodded to Simone and left.

After ten minutes of paralysing misery, she teleported straight to her room at the Peak, fell onto the bed, buried her head in her pillow and cried.

Her father came into the room without knocking. He sat on the bed, pulled her into his lap and held her as she wept.

'He broke up with you?' he asked, his voice rumbling through his chest.

She nodded into him.

'Do you want to talk to Emma?'

She shook her head and clutched him, wordless.

'Okay,' he said, and held her.

When her sobs had petered out into gasps she spoke without looking up from his soaked black T-shirt. 'How did you do it?'

'Do what?'

'Keep Emma around. Without freaking her out. Graham broke up with me because he's scared to death. He thinks the demons will get him ...' She shook her head on him. 'He's terrified of the life we lead. How did you get Emma to stay? When I was a child, it was a hundred times scarier than it is now. There were demons after us all the time, and she seemed to ignore the danger.'

'It's her heritage. Emma, your mother and Michael's mother, Rhonda—they all had that Celtic extraction. They were Celtic serpent people.'

'Oh.' She rested her head on his chest again. 'The gods of Europe were so damn stupid. They created people who were a human-demon-serpent mix as an enhanced army—then killed themselves, leaving these poor people with this streak of savagery and no way to control it. So of course, Emma was never an ordinary human, and you didn't freak her out. I see.' She smiled up at him, with her chin on his chest. 'Maybe I should head over to Europe and check out these Celtic serpent people that can handle the violent life we lead.'

'That's actually a very good idea, because Graham is correct about us forming relationships with ordinary humans.' He squeezed his arms around her. 'Better now?'

She nodded into his chest again. 'Thanks, Daddy.'

'We're right on top of the Christmas break, and we Chinese don't do much for it, so there's no "family commitments" involved like the Westerners have. If you want to go to a resort somewhere with some of your friends, like Jackie or Eva, let me know and I'll arrange it for you. The Blue Dragon's place in Kota Kinabalu, or the Phoenix's place in Phuket, or a ski resort in Japan—just say the word.'

'Thanks, Daddy, but I'd prefer that nobody knew about me breaking up with my boyfriend the day after Michael's wife died.'

'Oh.' He hesitated, then said, 'Point taken. I won't tell anyone.'

She smiled through the misery. 'Except Emma.'

'Always.'

'I think I'll go back to Todai and check out one of the apartments that the Blue Dragon offered me in Ueno. It's as good a time as any to make a fresh start—and maybe try living out there on my own.'

'That's my girl.' He pulled back and brushed a stray lock of hair out of her eyes. 'I am immensely proud of you. Every day. And all you have to do is call, and I'll be here.'

She kissed him on the cheek, making him smile. 'How many people are yelling at you to go do things for them?'

'Right now?' He cocked his head to listen. 'Six, but Er Lang doesn't count, he never stops yelling at me.'

She hopped off his lap. 'Go and do your stuff, First Heavenly General.'

'At least the Jade Emperor didn't make me ask you to go kill demons,' he grumbled quietly as he went to the door. 'I am so tired of that bullshit, and we have a standing appointment with him to tell him to cut it out.' He straightened. 'Dammit!' He looked her in the eye. 'The First Heavenly General reminds the Princess Simone that she is summoned to the Jade Emperor's presence to receive orders. The demon threat at the top levels of the human administration must be removed.' He sagged. 'I am so sorry, and we will talk to him about this. It's harassment.'

She waved one hand at the red lacquer box on her desk. 'Two at the same time. New record. Don't worry, Dad, it's at the stage now that it would feel weird if you didn't do it.'

He pulled her back in for a hug, kissed the top of her head, and went out.

She came out of her little ensuite later that evening to find Michael sitting on her bed, looking shattered. His blond hair had come out of its tie and fell around his face in a wispy tangle, his face was as swollen as hers was, and his eyes were red. He was wearing his signature white jeans and gold-and-white-striped sweater, but his clothes were crumpled and looked like he'd slept in them.

He saw her, bounced to his feet and ran to her, enfolding her in a huge embrace. She fell into his arms and held him, relishing the feeling of his strength and integrity and the pain they both felt. His Shen energy glowed in her inner vision, and it thrummed against hers in perfect harmony with her own—even though hers was tainted with demon essence. His essence was nearly as powerful as hers, and she didn't need to diminish her brilliance in his presence—he would never be afraid of what she was, because he was a match for her.

They held the embrace for a long time, then he pulled back and gazed into her eyes, his tawny ones full of pain.

She wanted to lose herself in those eyes so much that it hurt. She realised with a jolt of dismay that Graham had looked a lot like Michael—the resemblance was so obvious that she wondered how she'd missed it. She resisted the urge to kiss those lush lips. Instead, she pushed him gently away and guided him back to sit on her bed. She sat next to him and put her arm around him, trying not to savour his unique, musky scent. He leaned his head on her shoulder and they sat without speaking as she waited for him to tell her without pushing him.

'This is wrong,' he eventually said, his voice hoarse.

'We're not doing anything,' she said. 'Friends. Sharing our grief.' She pulled back to see his pain-filled eyes. 'Don't feel guilty, Mikey, I'm here for you. Whatever you need.'

'I can't help but feel guilty when my ...' He choked out the word. 'Wife isn't even cold yet, and here I am. This future we have together, you and me? It sits like a doom over us. Everything I do to try and live my own life, yet there's a voice in the back of my head saying, "You will end up with Simone. Stop trying to love anyone else".'

'How's your daughter?' she asked, hoping to change the subject to something less hopeless. 'Is she okay?'

'Emma and Christine are looking after her.'

'Christine?' Simone asked, then, 'Oh. Clarissa's mother.'

'Christine's locked me out because ...' He barked a short laugh. 'I've gone crazy and I'm not safe with the baby.' He released himself from Simone's arm and bent to put his head in his hands. 'I had a big, loud mental breakdown in the hospital, and I'm supposed to be in the mental health ward under heavy sedation, but of course that doesn't work with us, does it? I wish ...' His voice thickened and he curled up further. 'I wish it did.'

'Why are you here and not in your father's palace in the Western Heavens?' she asked gently. 'He has people there who can help you.'

He dropped his hands and studied her. 'I came here looking for ... I don't know why I came to you. Solace? I don't know.'

She put her arm around his shoulders again and tried to ignore the feeling of the sculpted muscles of his back and shoulder moving beneath her hands. *Inappropriate for the grieving widower, Simone.*

'I thought if I came to see you, it would make the pain go away. "Here's the woman who loves you, who's destined to be with you ..."' He looked away. 'I thought it would help to see you. Instead, here I am, running to you the *minute* Clarissa's gone. I reassured her so many times that she had nothing to fear from ...' He waved one hand towards Simone. 'Us. And she trusted me. I never gave her a reason to be jealous. And ...' His voice broke. 'She's been gone for less than a day? And here I am. I'm *scum*.'

Simone sat silently, letting him get it out. They never talked about their joint fate and how it affected their lives, they just tried to live around it and avoided each other while Michael was married to someone else. To hear him talk about it so openly—and so full of bitterness about its effect on him— broke her heart.

'I understand you're hurting,' she said. 'But I think you need to go find help that I can't give you.'

'Yeah, I shouldn't be here, if your boyfriend finds out— Graham, was it? He'll break up with you and it's bad enough that one of us has to be alone.' He rose. 'I'm sorry, Simone, I shouldn't have come. You're right, I'll go to the Western Heavens and leave you to your life, the way you want to live it, without this ... fate ... hanging over us.'

She had to warn him. 'That's a good idea, because the gossip mill in the Celestial is already spinning our stories out of control, and if anyone discovers that you were here so soon after ... losing Clarissa ...'

'Oh god,' he said, and dropped to sit on the bed with his head in his hands again. He sat silently and it took her a while to realise that he was weeping into his hands. The sobs came harder, and his shoulders shook. 'What am I doing here?' he asked through the gasps. 'The last place I should be. Am I completely stupid? This is so wrong—'

He disappeared.

10

Simone stood at the base of the Blue Dragon's headquarters the next morning and looked up. The building was in the main financial district in central Tokyo, surrounded by similar towers, and across the road from the moat that surrounded the Imperial Palace and its extensive gardens. The original building had been an elegant five-storey structure with graceful Corinthian columns along its façade, and the Dragon had kept the older building and built a magnificent glass-and-steel skyscraper above it, with the historic structure contained under an enclosed glass atrium.

She held her phone up to take a photo of the interesting architecture to send to Graham, then lowered it again. He'd been a comforting presence at the back of her mind, someone to share little fun parts of the day with—and now there was a huge gap where his support had been. She wiped the annoying tears away—it was time to stop crying and get on with her life—and pushed down the feeling of desperate loneliness.

She entered the towering glass lobby of the newer building and approached the front desk. The uniformed security guard asked her name and then waved her straight through to the lifts. There was a smiling tame demon in the form of a woman in a pink uniform and matching pillbox cap at the lifts. She bowed to Simone and pressed the lift button with her white-gloved hand. The lift doors were matte black and embossed in silver with images of the Dragon himself in True Form. The demon held the door for Simone when it opened, then went into the lift, pressed the button for the top floor, smiled and bowed to Simone again, and exited without saying a word to her.

Simone brushed the tears away again and thought about the ramifications of moving to Tokyo as the lift went up. This would be her first time living away from home, and she didn't know much about things like housework and cooking—she'd always had demon servants to manage that for her. Her gap year had been fun, but it had mostly been spent eating fast food and staying in cheap backpacker hostels. She squared her shoulders as the lift doors opened. Time to grow up and manage these things by herself. Her family would still be there for support when she needed it. Even if they were on the Celestial most of the time and she couldn't see them.

The double-height atrium she stepped into took up half the top floor of the building, with big windows overlooking the tops of the other skyscrapers in the district. A generous area spread before Simone, with a reception desk, another smiling, uniformed greeting-demon and glass stairs up to a mezzanine level that probably held Qing Long's office. Potted palms and comfortable tables and chairs were spread around the area, making it look like an upmarket hotel lobby. She approached the desk and the greeter stood and bowed formally to Simone with her hands clasped in front of her, then guided Simone up the stairs. Simone followed her to the mezzanine, which had an entire wall of smoky glass, etched with brilliantly coloured duplicates of the famous paintings from one of the waiting rooms in the Shogun's palace in Kyoto—elegant pine trees, highlighted with gold. The doors slid open, admitting Simone to his office, which took up the other half of the top floor of the building. The room had massive windows on three sides, with sliding glass doors to a wrap-around balcony and a view that overlooked the Imperial Palace across the road.

The Blue Dragon was sitting behind his desk in human form, flipping through documents and spreadsheets on five of his technologically advanced—and exclusive—floating screens. He swiped one hand down to collapse them into the desk, rose and came around to her. He embraced Simone, kissed the top of her head, and said, 'You look terrible. This whole thing is awful, and I'm here for you.'

She wiped one hand over her gritty eyes. 'Thanks, Uncle Qing.'

He dodged back to his desk and collected a set of keys from it. 'Come with me, it's all set up.' He straightened and froze. 'No.' He sagged, and switched to ultra-formal Japanese, sounding defeated. 'The Emperor of the East reminds the Princess of the Northern Heavens that she has an appointment with the Celestial two days hence and is required to attend to receive direction on the destruction of a number of demons that have infiltrated the highest levels of the human administration.' He straightened again. 'Sorry.'

'No problem, I'm really used to it,' she said. 'Forget that it happened.'

'I am speaking to the Celestial as soon as I can obtain an appointment with him, this has to stop,' he said. 'Come on, I'll show you your new apartment. I hope you like it.'

He changed to his biggest dragon form—nearly filling the huge office with his bulk—walked out through the windows onto the perimeter balcony and took off. His blue-and-silver scales glowed in the pale winter light, and his massive head was the size of a small car. Simone didn't change, simply walked through the glass behind him and followed.

'I can't make myself invis—' She began, and he interrupted her.

'I have you. I can see what that demon essence is doing to you. The Celestial needs to pull his finger out of his ancient pompous ass and help you fix this.' He writhed with indignation, making his scales clatter. 'He's having all of us harass you instead—your father and stepmother have been ranting about it, and I agree with them. Not good enough.'

They arrived at the Ueno Lake where she'd met him earlier that week. He landed on the garden across the road from the residential tower, changed back to his tall, elegant human form, and escorted her across the street. He used a key fob to open the doors, then passed the keys to her as they entered the lobby, which occupied a generous corridor along one side of the ground level. A Zen fountain of sand and stones lined the area, with tables and chairs on a raised platform. He led her past the wall of mailboxes to the lifts.

'A lot of the residents are away for the break, but a few kids should be on the viewing terrace,' he said, pressing the down button. 'Let me show you where the facilities are before we go up. Your apartment will be on the twenty-seventh floor.'

The lift arrived and he showed her how to use the fob to access the interior floors. They went down to the basement, and the Dragon led her along a plain, white-painted concrete corridor to the parking area. Car parks lined the wall, each capable of holding two cars—one above the other—with a motorised lift. Every space had an identical turquoise electric runabout in the upper lift, and some of them had an expensive sports car on the lower level.

'The little blue car comes with the unit.' He gestured. 'Twenty-seven A, that's yours. Do you already own a car?'

'No need,' she said.

'That's fine, if you want to go for a drive in the countryside, take the blue one, that's what it's here for. It has an app with all my charging stations in it on the console, and if you run out of battery and have to leave it somewhere, *please* contact the service centre and have it towed before it rusts away. It might even get *stolen*, that's been happening more often lately.'

'Thanks, Uncle Qing, that sounds like fun,' Simone said. Graham would have loved the idea, he had his own car back in Canada and they had made plans to go on a road trip there, camping together. She wiped her eyes again.

He guided her through another door. 'Bike storage. Just look for the stand with your unit number on it. You don't need to lock your bike in, everybody in the building is a Celestial.'

This area was nearly empty as well, with only a small number of light-weight carbon fibre racing bikes stored on the racks.

'All right,' he said. 'That's the boring stuff. Let's go see your new flat.'

They went up to the twenty-seventh floor and the Dragon used the key to open unit A. The unit was about a hundred square metres—smaller than most condos in the West, but large by Asian standards. It had a kitchen and living/dining area leading to the balcony, and two small bedrooms to one side. The floors were all timber laminate, the walls were painted a mid-beige, and the kitchen had dark brown stone benchtops and similarly coloured timber laminate cupboards.

'Two LDK,' the Dragon said.

'What does that mean?' Simone asked, checking the gas stove in the kitchen for a wok burner and nodding with satisfaction when she found one.

'Two bedrooms, living dining kitchen,' he said, opening one of the kitchen cupboards and running his finger along the interior to ensure it was clean. 'Standard Japanese measure of apartment type.'

'Oh, okay, thanks,' she said. 'I've never had my own place before, this is all new.'

He smiled gently at her. 'Ask anyone in the building for help, they're all in much the same situation as you—first time away from home, studying across the road, and confused as hell.'

She didn't mention that so far, the building had seemed empty, and the lonely feeling intensified. She smiled back. 'Thanks.'

'This apartment's never been redecorated, unfortunately it's still in original condition—' the Dragon began, embarrassed.

'No, no, Uncle Qing, this is fine,' Simone said. She went past the kitchen to the small modular bathroom, the walls, floor and fittings were all made of cream-coloured fibreglass in a single installed unit. The toilet was in its own powder room, then there was a central bathroom basin, and a sliding door to an area for washing with a shower head and the ubiquitous

Japanese deep bath with a complex electronic control system and a bamboo cover to keep the water hot. She eyed the bath—it threatened snow outside—and thought about buying some bath salts and oils. The only bathroom that had a bath back at the Peak was her father and Emma's ensuite, and she'd felt strange using their bathroom.

'Okay?' the Dragon asked. 'I can give you a few names for furniture suppliers that are owned by my conglomerate.' He wagged his finger at her and spoke sternly. 'No Ikea or Donki.'

Simone scoffed. 'Don Quijote is awesome. I bought some fantastic luggage there, and terrific flashing LED bunny ears.'

He sighed and rolled his eyes, then guided her out again. 'Let me show you the rest of the facilities. Parkview room on the twenty-third—there's a meeting room there as well, with a kitchenette—and the Skyview lounge on the top floor where most of the residents meet.' He took her back to the lift. 'The building is mostly occupied by young dragons studying across the road or working in the city, but we have a few other reptiles in the building as well, like yourself.'

'No swimming pool?' she asked.

He waved one hand. 'We're *dragons*. There's the big pond across the road, and the ocean is about five minutes flight away. We don't need one. I can put one in for you ...'

'No, of course not, I can swim in the ocean as well,' she said. 'Is there a place where I can practise the Arts? I try to spend at least an hour a day practising sword sets, occasionally a big demon will lose a bet or something and come after me, and I need to keep my skills sharp.'

'There's a gym on the first floor, or you can work out here, I'm sure the other students would love to watch,' he said, and the lift dinged. 'Here we are, Parkview lounge.'

She wasn't so sure about having an audience, but the lounge was deserted. It had some chairs facing the window overlooking the park and lake, and enough space in the middle to do a high-level set, so it would do. Simone's loneliness intensified at the emptiness, and she reminded herself that she could go back to the Peak to see her family any time—when they weren't in the Heavens. She wiped her hand over her eyes again.

'They'll all be on the top floor. Come with me,' the Dragon said, and led her out again.

The Skyview lounge was a comfortably furnished meeting-and-study area that took up most of the top floor and had a large outdoor terrace overlooking the park. The room was full of the buzz of quiet conversation as more than twenty Shen of various reptilian types—mostly dragons, but some turtles and snakes as well—were reading, drinking tea or coffee and chatting in small groups or playing board games. Most of them were younger than Simone—undergrads—but a few were her age, mid-twenties, and some were older, up to their thirties. Simone heard the soft words 'Saviour' and 'Michael' a few times and winced.

A girl squealed at the far end of the room and ran to Simone to give her a huge hug. It was Simone's friend Jackie, whose dragon mother, the Jade Girl, had worked for Simone's father as the House of the North's public relations manager for years. She was five years younger than Simone, and her hair was in a blue-green pixie cut that was a mix of colours from her dragon parents, the Jade Girl and the Blue Dragon. The Dragon smiled with pride at her.

'You didn't tell me you were coming!' she said to Simone.

'I didn't know you lived here, I thought you were still with your mother,' Simone said.

'I hang out with Dad when Mama's with her major husband,' Jackie said.

'Excuse me,' the Dragon said, interrupting with false indignance, 'but *I* am your mother's major husband, as I am the more senior Celestial.'

Jackie ignored him and winked at Simone. '... And Papa Ma's house in the Northern Celestial Palace is too far for me to come down and study, so I stay here.'

'We take turns looking after our daughter,' the Dragon said with pride. He put his hand on Simone's back, in a silent show of support that she appreciated. 'Simone will be doing her PhD across the road, and she's taking one of the flats here. Look after her, okay?'

'Sure,' Jackie said. 'Come and meet everybody. We were planning a pub crawl later, would you like to join us?'

'Uh, yeah, that sounds great,' Simone said.

'You can bring your boyfriend if you like?'

Simone had the lie ready for her. 'He's gone home to Canada for the Christmas break.'

'Good, we have you all to ourselves,' Jackie said with feeling. She waved to half-a-dozen dragons lounging in a corner playing a board game, and a few of them waved back. A female dragon, Hickory, jumped to her feet and rushed to embrace Simone.

'I haven't seen you since Celestial High!' She pulled back and smiled. 'Welcome to the insanity. Where's your boyfriend? Isn't he in Hong Kong?'

'He's in Canada,' Jackie said.

'Not ready for you to meet his family?' Hickory asked.

Jackie waved it away. 'We can talk about all of that later. She's moving into the building while she studies here!'

'I want you all to look after Simone,' the Dragon said firmly. 'Help her set up her apartment.'

'We will,' Jackie said.

Simone hadn't expected to have so many potential friends here and felt relieved. 'Uh, thanks. I have to buy furniture ...'

'Can we help?' Hickory asked, full of enthusiasm. 'I'm studying interior design. Let me help!'

'I'll cover the cost, and expect a good job,' the Dragon said.

'Done, Daddy,' Jackie said, and gave her father a quick hug before turning back to Simone. 'Come and meet everyone, and we'll go have a look at your place and make plans for it. We can help you move your stuff in, and if you don't have a bed yet, someone can arrange a futon for you until it's set up.' She gave the Dragon a gentle shove. 'You can go back to your high-powered executive nonsense, Daddy, we got this.' She grabbed Simone by the hand and pulled her towards the group.

'Thanks, Uncle Qing!' Simone called back as Jackie

dragged her away.

His face lit up into a genuine smile, and he disappeared.

'What are you studying?' Simone asked Jackie as they approached the group, and others who were on the floor gathered to join them.

'I'm second year, economics and finance.' Jackie's voice went wistful. 'I'm really enjoying it.' She stopped in front of the group.

'You all know Simone, right?' Hickory asked.

There were some stunned expressions and a general feeling of discomfort from the group, so Simone rushed to reassure them. 'I moved to Todai to do some postgrad study, and this is my first time living out of home. I'm *so* confused.'

The emotional aura eased—they could definitely relate, and their expressions changed from suspicion to sympathy.

'Which apartment is it?' Hickory asked Simone.

'Uh ...' Simone checked the key fob. 'Twenty-seven A?'

'That's a two LDK.' Hickory rubbed her hands together. 'Shops are still open, let's go have a look at furniture and fittings, and then get some ramen and hit 5-Chome.'

'What's in 5-Chome?' Simone asked as everyone in the group grinned and put the game away.

'Bar Neko!' Jackie said

'Bar Cat?' Simone asked.

'The cats are adorable,' Jackie said, wrapped her arm around Simone's waist and guided her back to the lift lobby.

'Dark is modern,' Hickory said as the six of them entered the little noodle shop in Ueno. They'd had a delightful couple of hours arguing about the sort of furniture Simone should select for her little apartment. 'In here.'

They took a booth to the side. It was still a little early for dinner, but they needed to eat something before hitting the bars. Hickory and Jackie had brought along a male dragon, Ash, who insisted with an obvious lie that he wasn't Hickory's boyfriend, and the other two guests, Rowan and Hazel, were a lovely couple of young male dragons who kept smiling sheepishly at each other.

They ordered at the counter and sat in the booth.

'I want lighter colours, though,' Simone said. 'I mean, yeah, the dark is trendy, but I want my place to be bright and welcoming, not dark and …'

'Cosy,' Hickory said. She raised both hands. 'Your choice. So.' She ticked the items off on her fingers. 'Dining table and chairs, a nice *light-coloured* bed, desk and shelves for studying in the second bedroom, I'll do that up as a cosy office—'

'You *sure* you don't want a gaming chair?' Ash asked. 'I love mine.'

'A normal office chair is fine,' Simone said.

Ash shrugged. 'Come down to my apartment and I'll give you a sit in mine anyway, so you know what you're missing.'

Hickory smiled. 'Ash's apartment has a futon, a couch, a massive television with six gaming consoles, a big gaming computer with three screens—and that's all.'

'It's clean and it's the way I want to live,' Ash said with a huff.

'No argument here,' Simone said. 'I like the sofa bed we chose for the office. I can have my little brother to stay with me.'

'Little brother?' Hickory asked, obviously confused.

'Prince Franklin,' Jackie said.

The noodles arrived in twenty-centimetre-wide bowls with chopsticks and small ladles for drinking the miso-flavoured broth. The ramen were nested at the bottom of the broth, with a few pieces of pork, pickles, vegetable and egg decoratively arrayed over the top, and a sheet of seaweed to one side. Simone tasted some of the broth and smiled. 'This is really good.'

'One of the best,' Jackie said. She winked at Simone. 'I feel like crepes at Akiba after this.'

Rowan waved at Jackie's noodles. 'Eat them first and see if you have room. Our booking at the cat bar is at six thirty, remember.'

'Okay, after,' Jackie said, and slurped the noodles again.

The world surrounding them went still and they all glanced around. Simone sagged with dismay; Emma had just materialised on the other side of the restaurant. Simone's stepmother was wearing a pair of faded denim jeans and a white shirt under a V-neck jumper and was in her middle-aged human form. The chefs behind the open bar eyed her suspiciously—they had obviously had some bad experiences with scruffy, foreign middle-aged tourists.

She approached the table where Simone was sitting with her friends and her face went from smiling to stiff. 'The Empress of the Northern Heavens hereby orders the Princess Simone to present herself to the Jade Emperor for direction in the removal of an extremely dangerous demon that is menacing the entire world. The consequences of her disobedience could lead to disaster.' She sagged and wiped her eyes. 'I am so damn sorry.'

Simone rose, edged out of the booth and gave her a quick hug. The dragons sat frozen with confusion, looking from Emma to Simone.

One night out with friends, and the Jade Emperor had to ruin it. And by proxy, as well; Emma obviously had no say in the matter. 'It's okay, Emma, I know it's not you doing this to me,' Simone said. A quiver in her voice betrayed that this constant harassment by the Jade Emperor, on top of everything else, was starting to get to her. 'That one sounded really major, can we at least find out what's going on and why he needs me so urgently?'

Emma's face went from sympathetic to rigid again. 'Any information provided could exponentially increase the catastrophic consequences of your wilful disobedience.'

'Okay then, no, I refuse,' Simone said, then turned and sat next to Jackie again.

'I'm one hundred per cent with you,' Emma said. 'I'm on my way to yell at the Jade Emperor, and I stopped here to give you a quick heads-up.' She changed to telepathy so that the other people wouldn't hear. *Michael is in the Tiger's mental health facility in the Western Heavens, and Clarissa's mother has taken the baby—her name is Larissa—to Canada. I thought you should know, so that if you see Michael, you can send him straight back up there. This whole thing has broken him.* She waved at the stunned dragons. 'Hi. I just dropped by to ask Simone if she needs anything.'

Simone studied her noodle bowl. 'Can you tell the Jade Emperor that it doesn't matter how often he orders me, the answer will always be "No"?'

'I've had a standing request to speak to him for two weeks, that he's obviously been ignoring, and I finally have an appointment to see him in half an hour. This is an obvious attempt at one last order before I tell him to cut it out.'

Simone sagged over the noodles, then picked up the small wooden ladle that passed for a spoon. 'Thanks, Emma.'

The dragons across from Simone suddenly and obviously realised who Emma was. They charged out of the booth, looking horrified. Ash was sitting on the inside from Simone and Jackie and couldn't rush out, and he looked like his ass was covered in ants, wanting to rush out as well. Hickory fell to one knee, grabbed the boy next to her by the elbow, and pulled him down as well.

'Ten thousand years,' they said in not-quite-unison.

'Rise, kids, no need, at ease,' Emma said, and nodded to them, making them relax. 'I'll leave you to it and appreciate you sharing your time with my stepdaughter.' She touched Simone's arm. 'Hopefully, that was the last time, and I am so glad to see you smiling.'

Simone waved Emma away. 'Shoo. Go and talk to him. I really appreciate it.'

'I dunno, those ramen look really good, and *I'm hungry,*' Emma said. 'I'm heading to the Celestial now to suit up and give him a piece of my mind. It will stop.' She looked around at Simone's friends. 'Simone is well within her rights to say no to the Jade Emperor. He's asking more of her than he has a right to. She's not giving consent, and you all know how that works.'

'Saying no to the Jade Emperor,' Rowan said weakly.

'The JE—' Emma began, and Hickory cut her off.

'The who? Oh!' she said and bobbed her head. 'Sorry!'

'Is being a stiff-arsed old fart about this and won't leave her—or us—alone and I will tell him to cut it out, and find another way,' Emma said. 'What he's doing is wrong and I will fix this.' She smiled. 'I'm glad Simone has friends here, and I hope you all look after each other.' She nodded to Simone. 'I'll leave you to it, have fun.' She disappeared.

Simone's friends stared at her. They edged back into the booth.

'Did that just happen?' Hickory asked weakly.

Ash held his head in his hands and moaned. 'That was the Dark Empress of the Northern Heavens. That was the Dark Lady. If my parents find out that I sat here like an idiot for *five minutes* and didn't kneel before her, they will *kill* me.'

'To be fair, she always looks like a scruffy Aussie tourist, so it's understandable,' Simone said, and they all gasped.

'That was the *Dark Empress of the Northern Heavens*!' Hazel said, protesting. 'She's …' His voice trailed off. 'There's a statue in Dragonhome of her, and the Dragon King put it there himself!'

'There's one of me there too,' Simone said. 'Doesn't mean anything.'

Jackie's eyes went wide. 'The Dark Empress just relayed an order from the *freaking Jade Emperor* and you're telling him …' Her voice became weak. 'No?'

'No,' Simone said with relish. 'I'm telling him to go all the way to Hell, just like my dad did.'

This somehow broke the ice—the story of her father telling the Jade Emperor to go to Hell when he was refused permission to marry Simone's mother was legendary—and everyone laughed.

'Sometimes I forget who you are,' Hickory said, raising her chopsticks and spoon.

'Good,' Simone said, and returned to her noodles.

11

Jackie and Hickory laid the futon—a thick pad of cotton wadding—out onto the living room floor of Simone's unit, then placed a thinner memory foam mattress on top. Hickory passed Simone a traditional silk quilt with a Japanese quilt cover—it only covered the edges on the top side—as they put the sheets onto the mattress. They staggered slightly—everybody had had too much to drink at the bars in Akihabara—and giggled as the sheets got away from them. Jackie put the case over the pillow as Simone passed the end of the quilt to Jackie and they laid it on the futon together.

Hickory put her hands on her hips and nodded. 'Do you need help with the groceries?'

Simone wobbled to the kitchen and started pulling the vegetables out of the bag. 'No, I'm good.' She checked her watch. 'It's past midnight! Oh no!'

'The trains have stopped, and we're *stranded*!' Jackie said with mock horror.

Hickory giggled again.

'Go home, I'm taking a shower and passing out,' Simone said. She brightened. 'I'm going to use my new bath!' She pulled some cherry blossom-scented bath salts out of the bag. 'And the onsen in Odaiba tomorrow, yes?'

Hickory leaned her arm on Jackie's shoulder and gave Simone a thumbs-up. 'Absolutely!'

Simone escorted the other girls out, closed the door on them and sighed with bliss. The little bed looked super comfortable, she had furniture arriving in a few days, and a luxurious bath in a haze of cherry blossom sounded wonderful. She went into the kitchen to finish putting the vegetables away, admiring the pristinely perfect Japanese mandarins she'd found at the supermarket. She looked up and saw out through the balcony's sliding glass doors to the glowing city beyond, blurred by the glittering flurry of snowflakes. It was as delightful as Hong Kong's skyline, and with much less pollution.

She would be okay.

Simone, I need you, Frankie said, and her head shot up. *Mum's in jail! Help!*

What? Simone asked. *I can't come to the Heavens if you're there ...*

I'm at the Peak. Please? It's awful!

Simone landed at the Peak living room half an hour later, to find her father sitting on the couch with a pyjama-clad Frankie in his lap. Frankie was gasping with sobs and clutching the front of her father's Wudang uniform. Frankie jumped up, ran to her and grabbed her to pull her down into a tight embrace. Simone's father rose and stood uncomfortably behind him.

'The Jade Emperor put Mum in Hell!' Frankie said. 'We need to go down and get her *right now!*'

'Why on Earth did the Jade Emperor send her to Hell?' Simone asked her father.

'She insulted him to his face—among other things,' Xuan Wu said, quietly amused.

'She does things like that,' Simone said, and pulled away from Frankie to see him. 'She'll be back soon, Frankie—'

'For *thirty days*!' Frankie wailed. 'She'll miss *Christmas*! We have to go down there and get her out *right now*!'

'We promised the Demon King we wouldn't go down there, and we keep our promises, remember?' Simone said. 'He behaves himself as long as we stay away from him, and that means he doesn't hurt people.' She pulled him in to an embrace again and glared up her father. 'Why did you let her insult the Jade Emperor right before our first Christmas all together?'

'Do not, for one second, think that I ever "let" my wife do anything,' Xuan Wu said.

'You really like saying that don't you?' Simone asked.

He stopped. 'Saying what?'

'Your wife.'

His normally stern-and-serious First Heavenly General expression melted into something soft and sweet. 'Yes, I do. She makes me so damn proud sometimes. She lost her temper with the Jade Emperor because he was being stupid, then she insulted him to his face, and here we are.'

'What was he being stupid about? That's not like her to lose her temper, it must have been something really major,' Simone said, then realised. 'Oh. Me.'

'Among other things.'

She pulled back to see Frankie's face. 'Why did you ask Mum to bring you down here, though? You're much safer up on the Mountain or in the Northern Heavens with Nan.'

'I needed you,' Frankie said, and sniffled. 'I didn't want to stay with ... with John. I needed *you.*' He glanced at their father, whose expression was carefully controlled, then back at Simone. 'Can you stay with me while Mum's in jail?' He threw himself into her arms. 'She's gone!'

Emma should have left him in the Heavens where he's safe, Simone said to her father.

I took him to the Mountain, and tried to look after him there, Xuan Wu said. *I bathed him and put him to bed, and he fell asleep—and then woke up screaming an hour ago. He was inconsolable. I asked if he wanted to return to Emma's parents, but he only wanted you. He shrugged. I had to bring him down.*

Simone stared up at her father. 'You brought him down? Only a child's mother can carry them in and out of the Heavens ...'

Frankie gripped her tighter. 'We thought I was stuck up there for thirty days, but John made his Turtle and Serpent parts separate, and the Serpent's a lady, and she said she'd try, and we did it.'

Xuan Wu sagged and looked away. 'Uh. Yes. I guess I'm Frankie's mother as well as his father. My turtle is Frankie's father, and Emma and my Serpent are both Frankie's mothers.'

'Does Emma know?'

'I didn't know myself, but I will tell her as soon as she's back.'

'And she's stuck in Hell, and we need to get her out,' Frankie said.

'I know it's stupid, but we have to follow the rules,' Simone said. 'How about we have Christmas when Emma's back?'

Frankie wiped the back of his hand over his nose and sniffled. 'Can we do that?'

'Come on.' Simone took his hand. 'Let's write an email for Nan and see if we can't postpone it.'

'Does "postpone" mean "do it" or "not do it"?' he asked. 'I get "cancel" and "postpone" mixed up.'

'It means do it later.'

'Okay.' He smiled up at Xuan Wu. 'Can you get her out sooner, John?'

'Let me see what I can do,' Xuan Wu said. 'But remember that you aren't allowed to visit her, because you can't go down to Hell. Maybe we can arrange for her to obtain a phone, so she can video call you.'

'I would like that.' Frankie tugged Simone's hand. 'Come on, let's write an email to Nan. Can she leave her Christmas tree up until Mum comes back?'

'I'm sure she can,' Simone said, and guided him into her room. She turned back to her father. 'Get her out, Daddy, that's unnecessarily cruel. Nothing is worth getting sent to Hell for that long, tell Emma to let the Jade Emperor be stupid. I can put up with the orders, I just ignore them anyway.'

'In this case, I don't think she will.'

Simone stayed in her room at the Peak, because Frankie became completely hysterical if she even mentioned going back to

Tokyo. At five am she was woken by the sound of his muffled sobs coming from his room. She raised her head, wondering why Emma hadn't gone to him, then remembered that Emma was in Hell. Her father was in the Celestial Palace, so she checked the demon servants. Er Hao was in the Peak apartment servant's quarters in the demon equivalent of sleep. She silently cursed the Jade Emperor. If she could go to Heaven she would give the JE a piece of her mind, and he probably knew it.

It was possible that their father was up early doing something that nobody else could do, and after the destruction of the wars with the previous Demon King there were a great number of things that he had to catch up on, but sometimes he was too dedicated to the security of the Heavens. He would get a piece of her mind later as well, and Emma would help when she returned.

She slipped next door to Frankie's room. Frankie was curled up in a little ball in the middle of the bed, a heartbreaking reflection of the small, lonely child he'd been when held in Hell at the mercy of the Demon Kings.

She went to him, sat on the bed, and put her hand on his back. 'Hey.'

He curled up tighter. 'Sorry I woke you up.'

'You lonely without Mum and Dad?'

He nodded under the blankets. 'The house is really empty.'

She pulled him into her lap. 'I'm here.'

'You're going away to live in Tokyo.'

'I know. I will yell at some people tomorrow. The JE is being a turdface. He sent Mum away and Dad's stuck somewhere doing stuff for him.'

He giggled and wiped his eyes with a shaking hand. 'JE turdface.'

'Want to come for a fly? We can go sit on top of a mountain.'

He pulled back and wiped his eyes with the corner of the sheet. 'It's the middle of the night?'

'We are the darkness,' she said theatrically. 'I'm awake now, we might as well.' He jumped out of her lap and opened his closet. 'No need to get dressed. Stay in your Batman pyjamas, nobody will see us. Just put your robe around you, it'll be cold up there.'

He slipped his robe on, turned, and put his hand out. 'Can we have a lesson tomorrow? I want to do things like flying by myself.'

'Dad's the one who should be teaching you,' she said, and railed at the JE again in her head. Their father had spent hours every day teaching Simone to defend herself when she was a child—and now was absent from his son's life for at least ten hours a day, reorganising the defence of the Heavens. Their parents weren't neglecting Frankie—Emma saw to that—but the gap from her being stuck in Hell would be a huge one. Again, time to talk to the Jade Emperor. The next time he summoned her to an audience, she just might go.

She teleported them to the sky above the Peak building. The lights of Hong Kong blazed below them, and the sky was yet to lighten with the coming dawn.

'You ever thought about putting another banner up on Lion Rock or something?' Frankie asked her as she guided him—he was flying himself, a little wonkily but still managing to hold himself in the air—towards Kowloon. 'That was awesome. "We Want Universal Suffrage" in big characters.' He looked confused. 'What is universal suffrage anyway?'

'The right to vote. Everybody should have the right to choose our leaders, not just a few select elite.'

'But that's how it works in the Heavens? John has a Council, but nobody votes for them, he chooses them.'

'We're going to change that too,' she said with determination.

He studied the Lion Rock mountain's side as they flew level with its top and passed it towards Tai Mo Shan. 'You should put another banner up on it.'

'People not responsible might be arrested if I do it again,' she said. 'I can't risk innocents being hurt. The government has arrested and jailed other people for stuff I've done. I can't do that any more.'

'Just get them out of jail!' he said.

'I can't even get Mum out of jail,' she said bitterly.

He went silent.

They landed on top of the Tai Mo Shan tourist lookout and the little restaurant below them was closed. They sat facing north, with the Hong Kong new town high rises visible around the dark country parks, spreading to the border and the lights of the dense high rises of Shenzhen beyond.

'I like your dress,' Frankie said as he settled to sit beside her. 'I want John to teach me more, so I get some cool clothes too!'

Simone looked down at herself. She'd changed to Celestial Form to make the travel easier, and the robe was deep navy blue, highlighted with golden stars. Frankie didn't seem fazed by her black, shining scales or twining, snake-like hair, and she wanted to hug him.

'You just tried on fantastic new robes that Mum had made for you,' she said. 'Next time we go flying at night you can wear them—but the batman pyjamas are cute anyway.'

'Batman,' he growled, and raised his arms. 'We are the night. Fighting bad guys and kicking ass.'

'You are too little for that,' she said, pulled him in and gave him a squeeze. 'And it's a lot more complicated in real life. Hold off on the superhero stuff until you're old enough to not get other people in ...' She took a deep breath. 'Trouble.'

'Really in jail because of stuff you did?' he asked, his voice small.

She nodded and wiped her eyes. 'The judge steamrolled everything and sentenced them for looking at public government records—when I was the one that did it. And then the government tried to jail the lawyer for defending them—so she had to hide in New Zealand for a while.'

'Isn't Mum trying to send some of the people over to Canada or something? I heard her having meetings about it.'

'Yeah. Dad told me what happened.' Simone lowered her head. 'The Jade Emperor won't let her send them somewhere safe. So she got mad at him, and yelled at him, and used some very choice words, and ...' She pointed down.

'*That's* why she's in Hell?'

Simone nodded.

He straightened. 'You should have told me that. If she's down there because she wanted to help people to escape from all of this ...' He waved one hand to indicate the Territory around them. 'Then I'm proud of her.'

'I'm proud of you,' she said.

'We can go home now. I'll go back to sleep okay.'

Their father appeared next to them in his human form, wearing his armour and carrying his sword on his back. 'Why are you two still up? It's way past your bedtime, young man.'

'You sound like Mum,' Frankie said.

'Good.' Xuan Wu pulled Frankie into his lap. 'Couldn't sleep?'

'Nobody was around except Simone, and it was really quiet, so we came for a fly.'

'Good idea. Sorry I was out, little ones. I was trying to arrange remote video visits with Emma for you. The Jade Emperor was being ...' He searched for the word.

'A turdface!' Frankie said and giggled.

'You teaching your brother bad words?' Xuan Wu asked Simone.

'He'll need them. The life we lead—we need to have an outlet, to blow off steam. The words help.'

'Yes, they do.' Xuan Wu rose, still carrying Frankie in his arms. 'How about I take you home, flying really fast?'

'Yes please!' Frankie crowed.

'Try to keep up, Simone,' Xuan Wu said, then he rose into the air and shot away so quickly that she was nearly knocked off the roof, leaving a cloud of vapour behind him.

Simone came out late the next morning and went to the kitchen to see what Er Hao had in the way of breakfast. She thought of the thick-cut sweet Japanese toasting bread and the mini toaster oven back at her own apartment and smiled. When Emma returned, Simone would have a cosy little nest ready to move into and enjoy with a circle of friends.

She opened the bread bin, pulled out slices of Western-style toasting bread, and popped it into the toaster. Er Hao had boiled the urn, so she sat with some green tea, summoned her tablet and brought up the news sites.

Her eyes widened with horror as the reports filled her screen. She selected a video and watched with dismay as tanks rolled across a snowy landscape in a location similar to where she'd been when they rescued the families of the demon replacements in Eastern Europe. An armoured personnel carrier followed the tanks, and a unit of soldiers exited it, then proceeded to shoot at families who were running towards the camera. Children fell, obviously dead, and she winced and turned the video off. She returned to the news sites and flipped through the articles to discover that the invasion was limited to a couple of Eastern European countries, and the general reaction from the press was bewilderment—the governments who'd invaded had been holding 'training exercises' on the border, and then suddenly crossed into their neighbours and attacked everything.

A red box appeared in front of her on the table and she understood. The action taking place in Europe was a shadow of what was happening on their Celestial plane—the demons had found a working portal and were moving back into the European Heavens. Another report popped up onto her feed— more bewilderment at the viciousness and ferocity of the invading forces' actions. They were targeting civilian centres rather than military ones and taking a great deal of pleasure in cruelty and destruction.

It had to be a major demon influence. She paused the video, thumbed the clasp of the red box, and pulled out the dun-coloured vellum scroll, tied with a red ribbon. She opened it and saw that it was written in vermilion ink in the Emperor's own hand, and he hadn't put his official seal on it, so it looked more like a personal note.

It's too late now, their leader is in the Heavens and has

opened the way for their army. What could have been solved with a couple of quiet assassinations has now turned into a major cross-platform incident. Before I said the results could be catastrophic; now the worst-case scenario is a hundred times as bad. You are the only one capable of fixing this. I ordered you when I should have asked you nicely and admit that was the wrong way to go about it. I am asking you nicely now. Please. You have no idea how important this is. Noon at the Hyatt.

Please.

JE

She dropped the scroll into the box, and it resealed itself, but didn't disappear—allowing her to read the missive again if she wanted. The toast popped up and she buttered it as she considered the implications. The JE was right, and this was a catastrophe. He was also probably right about her being the only one who could fix it, as the only one who could kill a demon without provocation. Her resolve to not be used as a workaround assassin wavered. She put the toast onto a plate, sat back at the table and continued to scroll through the news reports with growing horror and dismay.

At noon, Simone teleported to the large lay-by next to the hotel's entrance, where battered red taxis and expensive chauffeur-driven cars lined up to let their passengers out. The doorman opened the glass door for her with a smile, and she didn't really notice the soaring ceiling and marble floors as she passed the tired travellers and harried-looking locals on her way through to the side door to the event spaces. The corridor was decorated in dark tones and an empty urn sat on a big side table with stacks of coffee and teacups next to it.

The hotel's meeting room was one of the smaller ones at the end of the corridor. She went in and stopped. It was set up in a traditional Chinese meeting-style with three sofas in a U-shape with tea tables between them, and the Jade Emperor, as serene as ever, was sitting on the central one facing Imperial South. The emperor wore his full Celestial regalia of gold silk robes embroidered with brightly coloured six-toed dragons and a hat with a veil of beads that stopped anyone from looking him in the eye. Er Lang, the Second Heavenly General, stood at the emperor's right hand behind his sofa, appearing as a thirty-year-old warrior wearing green scaled armour and holding a halberd.

Michael was on one of the other chairs, his eyes blank with grief. He was wearing crumpled white hospital scrubs—inpatient attire from the Tiger's mental health facility—and his hair looked unwashed and tangled.

Simone skipped the obeisance—making Er Lang scowl—and waved one hand at Michael.

'Let him go back to the West and grieve. He just lost his wife, and his child has been taken from him! This is reprehensible.'

'Sit, Princess,' the emperor said, maddeningly calm. 'As I said: please. I have something of vital importance to tell you.'

Simone gathered her robes—she looked down, surprised, at her Celestial form, stars and all. Obviously she had some of her Celestial alignment back while she was willing to listen to the emperor. The scales were gone, and her robes were holes in reality, a portal into the universe of gold glittering stars. She sat with the robes flowing around her, then lifted her butt, tugged her long golden hair out from under it, and pulled it to one side over her shoulder. She leaned forward to speak to Michael. 'Whatever he wants, I'll do it and leave you out of it. I'm on your side, Mikey.'

Michael's eyes were still blank.

'You two are destined to be together, and you both know it,' the Jade Emperor said.

Michael collapsed over his knees and made a wordless sound of despair.

Simone threw herself to her feet and summoned her swords. 'What the fuck is wrong with you?'

'Sit!' the Jade Emperor said, and Simone ignored him. She strode forward to take his head off, and ran into Er Lang, who blocked her with his halberd held diagonally in front of him.

'Out of my way, asshole,' Simone said.

'Just a reminder, Simone, that if you take his head, you have conquered the Heavens and you gain his position and title,' Er Lang said. 'I don't think you want that.'

'I don't know,' the emperor said wistfully. 'A few years in the Peach Garden with my wife sounds awfully peaceful.' He lowered his voice. 'It's been a long time.'

Simone made a loud sound of disgust, dismissed her swords and sat. Her hands were covered in scales again, and she returned to human form.

'If you don't do what I'm asking, Prince Michael will never recover from this loss,' the Jade Emperor said. 'He will never be mentally competent enough to care for his daughter and will only see her once more in her lifetime.'

Michael didn't move, still collapsed over his knees.

'You don't know that,' Simone said.

'Yes, I do,' the emperor said. 'I can see the future, and in any future where I do not send him on this mission, the damage is permanent. He will see her once more in her lifetime, and she will tell him that she hates him and never wants to speak to him again.'

'Oh god,' Michael moaned into his knees.

'This is unnecessary cruelty to all three of us,' Simone said. 'Why are you doing this?'

'It is the only way. Believe me, I have searched for kinder options, and there are none. Your love for him will help him heal to the point where he is capable of rebuilding the relationship with his daughter—'

'Oh, fuck you!' Simone shouted, rose and stormed to the door.

Michael didn't respond at all.

'This really is very important, Simone,' Er Lang said, breaking Celestial protocol. 'You can stop the war in Europe. Listen to him.'

Simone stopped and turned, astonished. Er Lang *never* broke protocol, he had a cast-iron pole up his butt.

'The fate of the whole world—Celestial and Earthly—is at

stake, and only you two can save it,' the emperor said. 'You cannot live as a couple for some time, but right now he needs to do this to pull him from his grief, and you need to go with him.' The emperor raised one hand and a Celestial Palace fairy appeared next to him. She passed him an iPad, and he turned it so they could both see it. 'I believe that performing this task may also return your Celestial alignment, and he will do anything to give that back to you.'

'You overestimate my desire to return to the Celestial,' Simone said. 'I will not torture him to allow you to order me around again.'

'I am already ordering you around,' the emperor said. He raised the tablet. 'This is a European Shen. There appears to be one left—and he is not Semias, the spirit of the city that you met when you were abducted and taken there, Michael. He is— to put it in plain terms—a European god of the highest order.'

Michael's head shot up. 'What? No.'

'Yes. Your father's agents have found one. He is weakened and appears to be stuck on the Earthly in human form, but he seems to be the last one.' The tablet showed a small, overweight middle-aged white man who didn't look anything special. 'He is so weakened that we can't even ascertain his alignment. He could be any of them.'

'Where is that?' Simone asked.

'Paris. You two are the obvious choice to locate and negotiate with him. If you can find the new portal, both of you are capable of entering the European Heavens—'

'Emma would be a better choice to go than either of us,' Simone said. 'She's been in the Western Heavens and she's a Celestial Shen of the first rank with a pure-European heritage.'

'I agree,' Michael said. 'Shoving Simone in my face right after I lost Clarissa will not help me heal.'

The emperor raised the tablet. 'This is a Heavenly Shen of the first order. Excuse the term, but in this case, I must send my biggest guns, and that means the two of you. You are both descended from the Celtic Serpent People of the West from your mothers, but you are also children of the most powerful

Shen in the Eastern Heavens through your fathers—something that Emma is not.' He laid the tablet on the tea table next to the tea pot. 'Er Lang will pass you the full details of the mission.' He poured the tea for himself, picked up the teacup, and studied them in turn over the edge. 'This is the only way. Any other action we take will have catastrophic consequences—and not just for the three of you. Trust me. I am securing your futures.' He put the teacup down, and his voice softened as he looked away. 'You can hate me for it later.'

'I just lost my wife. My mother-in-law took my daughter from me. I'm not emotionally capable—' Michael stopped mid-sentence. His voice dropped to a low growl. 'You complete fucking *bastard*.'

'My apologies, sir,' the emperor said. 'I will return your grief when your mission is complete.'

Simone struggled to speak, but words failed her.

'Do you require assistance to focus as well, madam?' the emperor asked.

She lowered the temperature of the room and her breath fogged as her voice returned with a vengeful echo. 'Touch my mind and I will kill you—then give your throne to my little brother.'

'Good,' the emperor said. 'Er Lang will provide you with the rest of the information and a European base of operations.' He rose. 'If there's nothing else—'

'One question,' Michael said.

'Yes, she is,' the emperor said, and Michael collapsed with relief.

'What ...' Simone understood. 'Am I Immortal. You knew, and you never told us. My family have been frantically worried about me dying before I could regain Immortality, and you knew all along that it wouldn't happen.' She lowered her voice to a growl that mirrored Michael's. 'You complete fucking bastard.' She looked him in the eye. 'I will do this on one condition.'

The emperor leaned on the arm of his chair to sit again, suddenly looking very old. 'If I release Emma from Hell, in two weeks she will discover that you are in a life-threatening position, rush to your side, be killed, and land in European Hell, unable to escape. It will eat her soul before you can save her. The only way I can stop that from happening is to keep her incarcerated for thirty days—safe in a place she cannot escape from.' His voice sharpened and he shot Simone a warning glance. 'Do not tell her why, or it will happen anyway.'

'What about Frankie?' Simone asked. 'With both me and his mother gone, and you running my father off his feet—'

'I am granting the Dark Lord parental leave for thirty days,' the emperor said. 'It will be good for him to spend time with his son, so they can build their relationship. Er Lang and the Thirty-Five will pick up the slack.'

Er Lang's expression filled with horror. 'What? No! I can't—'

'Too late, Number Two.' The emperor rose again, this time with more energy. 'Show them their base in Europe and give them the briefings.' He shot Simone another warning glance. 'Don't permit Emma to follow you there. If she does, she will never return.'

He disappeared, and the room reconfigured itself so that Simone and Michael could sit across from each other with a large meeting table between them. Er Lang waved one hand and a three-dimensional map of Paris appeared on it, looking like a satellite image.

'Your base is the Tiger's hotel in the fashion district,' Er Lang said, and the map zoomed in to the street with its elegant art deco buildings. 'He has put aside a suite for you already. Travel there at your earliest convenience.' He placed two thick binders containing stacks of paper onto the table and pushed one to each of them. 'This is all we have on the European Shen. The Tiger's European agents will meet you at the hotel after you arrive. Any questions?'

'The emperor didn't provide us with a goal for completion,' Michael said. 'We know that the demons have invaded the Heavens, we know that there's a Shen there—but what is he expecting us to achieve?'

'That depends entirely on what you encounter over there,' Er Lang said. 'The main goals are twofold: clear the demons from the European Heavens, and through that, stop the war on the Earthly.'

Simone flipped open the folder and shuffled through the briefing notes. More information on the Shen—they'd been following him around for a while—and a list of the biggest protagonists in the ongoing war in Europe, with speculation on which of them were demons. She closed the folder; she could read it on the trip over there.

She turned to Michael. His face was set into a grim mask. 'I need to go say goodbye to Frankie,' she said. 'He'll probably have a meltdown.'

'His father will handle him,' Er Lang said with confidence.

'No, he won't,' Simone said with similar conviction. She spoke to Michael. 'Pack your bag, meet me at the Peak apartment, and we'll set out from there?'

Michael nodded and disappeared.

Simone picked up her binder and tucked it under her arm.

'Before you go, Princess,' Er Lang said.

She scowled at him. 'What?'

'Thank you.' He nodded to her. 'For making this sacrifice. Again, all the Heavens are in your debt. You truly are one of the Celestial's greatest heroes.'

'I'd rather be a doctoral student getting drunk on Friday nights with a group of stupid friends,' she said, then teleported back to the Peak.

12

The Peak apartment was empty when she arrived. She went into her room and pulled her suitcase out from under the bed as she telepathically contacted her father.

Daddy, where are you? The JE's sent me on a mission to Europe—

'I know, he just told me,' Xuan Wu said from the doorway, with Frankie peeking out from behind his robe-clad legs.

'I don't have a choice. I have to go.' She turned and sat on the bed, then gestured towards Frankie. 'I'm sorry, Squirt, but the JE's being a turdface again.'

'What happened?' Frankie asked as he walked hesitantly into her room. He glanced at the suitcase as if it was a dangerous predator. 'You're leaving? You said you'd stay until Mum came back.'

'I have to go to Europe. There's a war there, and I can stop it,' Simone said.

Michael's gleaming presence appeared outside the apartment's living room windows, and their father went to let him past the seals.

'I'll come with you,' Frankie said.

She pulled him into her lap—he was nearly too big to fit—and held him. 'You can't. It'll be really dangerous, and I might have to go to their Hell, and I could be the only one who can come out of it. If you go with me, you could get stuck there.'

'Are you ready to go?' Michael asked from the door. He had changed his appearance back to his pre-grief self, and the difference was striking. His glossy blond hair was tied back into a neat ponytail, and he wore jeans and a long-sleeved polo under a beige V-neck cashmere sweater, looking like the Harvard graduate that he was. 'The Celestial is on my case about going there in a hurry, because Dad's agents have spotted that Western Shen again.'

Simone stood and returned Frankie to his feet. 'Everybody out, I need to pack.' She pushed Frankie towards their father, but he refused to move. 'Frankie, please. I'll save lives. I'll be back soon, and I'll keep in touch ...' She had an idea and knelt to speak to him. 'How about I send you some cool postcards of the places I go in Europe? And send you selfies?'

'No,' he said. 'Stay. Don't listen to the JE. You said you don't have to listen to him!' He grabbed her again. 'Stay here with me. You promised!'

'Remember when you asked me to put another banner on Lion Rock?' she asked.

He was silent a moment, then spoke, his voice small, 'I didn't mean it.'

She pulled back to see his desperate face. 'This is more than that. People are dying, there's a war, soldiers are shooting and blowing up—' She didn't say "children". '—families, and I can help save them. The Jade Emperor says I'm the only one who can do it, because I'm the only one who can go into their Hell and come out again.'

'Uncle Michael can do it,' Frankie said, glaring at Michael.

'The Jade Emperor needs his most powerful warrior to handle this, and that's Simone,' Michael said. 'She's way more powerful than me. I'm just going along to support her.'

Frankie fidgeted, moving from foot to foot, then turned back to Simone. 'How long?'

'I don't know. Stay with Dad and look after him for me? The JE's given him some time off, so ask him to take you to all the cool places he took me when I was a kid. And he can teach you, like you wanted.'

'I don't want him, I want *you!*' Frankie shouted and ran into his room, thumping both Xuan Wu and Michael with his fist as he passed them. The howls of rage and pain from his room were clearly audible and everybody winced.

'Go,' Xuan Wu said. 'I will handle him.'

Simone wiped her hand over her tear-filled eyes—she would need to see the House of the North's resident therapist, Audrey Au, again when this was done—and waved them away. 'Out.'

Michael nodded. 'I'll wait for you in the living room.'

'You're doing the right thing, Simone,' Xuan Wu said, and they both left her to it.

'I wish everyone would stop saying that,' Simone said and started sorting through her underwear.

Her father was standing with Michael in the living room when she wheeled her bag in, and both of them had the guilty expressions of men who had been discussing her in her absence. Frankie's miserable presence was a dark, sulky aura coming from his bedroom.

Michael leapt through the living room windows onto a cloud.

Simone hesitated in front of her father. 'I have a request.'

'I will watch over him—'

'No,' Simone said. 'Don't attempt ...' She hesitated, unsure of how much the JE would allow her to say. 'To get Emma out of Hell. She has to stay there for the full thirty days.'

His dark eyes searched her face, then he spoke. 'I understand.'

She relaxed with relief, threw herself into his arms and hugged him, then jumped onto a cloud of her own. As they set off, she sat on her cloud and pulled the folder out of her backpack to study while they travelled.

The premonition slammed into her again, and she hesitated with the folder halfway out of her bag. It was even stronger this time. She would return alone, full of rage and pain after losing someone important to her. All her breath left her as she looked up and saw Michael, sitting on his own cloud, engrossed in reading his binder.

Oh no *way*. After all he had lost? Really? His wife had just died, his daughter had been taken halfway across the world, his father, the White Tiger of the West, didn't give a damn about him and his mother had *exploded* in front of him when her Celtic Serpent nature had rejected the Elixir of Immortality. She picked up her cloud's pace to match Michael's. She had a difficult decision to make, and again chose not to say anything to avoid the risk of it happening. She would just have to guard Michael and ensure he returned.

Michael looked up from the binder, noticed her regard, and smiled at her in a way she'd yearned for ever since she realised her feelings for him. For years they'd deliberately avoided each other to prevent hurting Clarissa, who they both adored.

The Jade Emperor really wouldn't be that cruel, would he? But after what he had just done to Michael, anything seemed possible. She wiped her eyes, drawing her hair out of them, and returned to the binder. Her hair blew into her eyes again and she quickly braided it and summoned a hair tie to hold it. When she had originally gained Immortality, her hair had been long and flowing free, and it had been a damn nuisance ever since. Even if she had it cut short, the next morning when she woke up, it was long again.

It became apparent after ten minutes of travel that Simone's cloud was at least twice as fast as Michael's. She slowed her cloud, enlarged it, and stood to gesture towards him. 'I'll carry us.'

He nodded, dismissed his cloud, and flew over to hers.

He smiled. 'Remember me carrying Emma on my cloud to Guilin? And when you didn't know how to summon a cloud in Thailand? We had to use one of mine, and I wasn't strong enough to make the full journey. You've come so far—this one is bigger and faster than any I could produce.' He sang the first few words of the 'Aladdin' magic carpet song, and it pierced her heart.

She raised one hand. 'Let's just go through these briefings. The Shen appears to be so normal it's unbelievable—Katie says he even sees a counsellor for psychological issues. What do you think?'

'Frankly, I have no idea,' he said, then he sat next to her and opened his own folder.

The White Tiger's hotel was on a side-street off Rue Faubourg, the main strip where all the couture fashion houses had their shop fronts—and the location of the Presidential Palace, where the Tiger probably schmoozed local politicians. The narrow one-way street had four- and five-storey, limestone-faced mansions lining its sides, and the hotel opened directly onto the street, across from a big Asian makeup house's European headquarters. The entrance had double doors leading to a lobby the size of a suburban double garage. They went in to find a few of the White Tiger's many wives gathered with a couple of seraglio bodyguards in preparation for a shopping trip.

The wives watched Simone and Michael give their bags to the concierge with open curiosity. One of the bodyguards approached and nodded to Michael.

Michael nodded back. 'Ahmed.'

The bodyguard glanced from Michael to Simone, to their bags being held by the smiling human concierge, and then up at them again. His expression went stony, and he turned back to the wives.

'What's his problem?' Michael asked quietly.

Simone stared at him. He honestly didn't know? His expression was open and innocent, and she understood—after the Jade Emperor had messed with his head, it was very likely that his reactions would be inappropriate until this whole thing was finished. Her shoulders slumped and she followed Michael to the reception desk.

'Hey, Kim, good to see you,' Michael said cheerfully to the woman behind the desk.

Simone recognised the woman and desperately searched her memory for who she was. She was a couple of years younger than Simone, had blonde hair held back in a bun and delightful freckles, was half-European and was obviously a daughter of the Tiger. Kim, Kim—Simone couldn't remember.

'Simone!' Kim said with a slight Australian accent, smiling at her. She nodded to Michael. 'Michael.' She studied his face. 'So sorry for your loss.'

'Uh, thanks,' he said, still cheerful, and shot Simone a knowing grin that she'd longed to see her whole life. 'I keep forgetting. It's awful.'

Kim looked from Simone to Michael, wide-eyed and speechless. Simone tried to tell Kim that the Jade Emperor had messed with Michael's head—and failed. Obviously, this was information that the JE didn't want shared—and now that she'd agreed to this stupid sortie, she had to obey him. Wonderful.

His head is a bit messed up, Simone said silently to Kim. *We're here for something to do with Celestial politics. Help us out?*

Kim nodded understanding. 'It must be really top-level because Er Lang and Dad both told me to give you the suite that Dad usually uses on the top floor. Let me show you around.'

She took a couple of old-fashioned metal keys on security fob rings from the desk, rose and came around it. She stopped and raised her voice so that everyone in the lobby could hear her. 'Dad said you needed two separate bedrooms because you're not here together.'

The wives stood in stunned silence for a couple of seconds, then gathered to have a soft conversation about what they'd just heard.

Simone relaxed. 'Thanks, Kim, but I don't think they'll believe it.'

'Why not?' Michael asked.

Kim and Simone stared at him, then Kim gathered herself and guided them through the lobby to a glass-roofed, conservatory-style restaurant next to the hotel's internal garden, which was surrounded by the high courtyard walls.

'The restaurant has a Michelin star, you can have food

ordered up to your suite or come down here any time,' she said, standing at the entrance and nodding to the maître d', who was another son of the Tiger. 'Katie and Gabriel are on their way to meet with you here, they should be about ten minutes.' She glanced up at the glass roof, streaked from the rain that had fallen recently. 'A bit cold right now for eating outside, but it's lovely in the summer.' She gestured towards the hotel's internal courtyard garden. 'Indoor pool and day spa on the other side, just walk around the corridor to get there.' She guided them to the narrow lift lobby with two small lifts. One of the lifts arrived and a couple of wives exited, talking with enthusiasm, and rushed to join the rest of the group in the lobby with many loud greetings and air kisses.

Kim guided them into the lift and pressed the button for the top floor. It only held five people and wasn't big enough to carry the concierge with their bags as well, so he smiled and nodded as he waited for the next one. When the lift door closed, Kim turned to Simone.

'You saved our lives,' she said. 'Me, Eva, Jackie—you couldn't even tell our parents we were okay, because you were in hiding while you worked to take the demons down. I'll never forget your kindness.' She lowered her voice. 'And your sacrifice. Anything you need ...' She held the keys out to Simone. 'Food, help, housekeeping, *anything*, you give me a call.'

Memory blossomed in Simone's head. When the Demon King had occupied the Heavens during the war, he had imprisoned three girls to serve as wives for Frankie—Jackie, the Blue Dragon's daughter, Evie, the Red Phoenix's daughter, and Kimberley, the daughter of the White Tiger. 'I remember, Kimberley. The three of you were so brave, it was really scary. I had to slip food and water to you for a couple of days because the Demon King forgot about you—you could have starved!'

Kim held Simone's hand in both her own and shook it. 'You saved us and freed the Heavens.' She glanced at Michael, who was standing with a proud smile on his face and scowled. 'What the hell is wrong with you? Are you deliberately trying to spread rumours about Simone? You need to stop this!'

Michael appeared confused as the lift stopped and the doors opened, then his face filled with horror. 'That asshole has messed me up. I am so sorry.' He wiped one hand down his face. 'Shit. We *are* in separate rooms, aren't we?'

'Er Lang arranged it,' Kim said, leading them out of the lift and down the corridor. This floor only had two doors on it. She opened theirs. 'Unfortunately, you're in a suite that shares a living room in the centre.'

They entered the room and Kim closed the door behind them. The living room was the size of a double bedroom with a couple of barrel chairs and a coffee table, a narrow window that overlooked the roofs across the road, and two doors that led to the bedrooms. The entire area was luxuriously furnished in bleached ash and gold-and-white satin, but it was tiny, which was normal for a converted European townhouse like this.

'Michael, I don't know what you've done to yourself, but you are *not* acting like a man who just lost his wife and daughter. You're acting like ...' Kim waved one hand at Simone, her face taut. 'You're making her look awful.'

'I know,' Michael said. 'Can you put me in a separate room? Not in the same suite? Even a different hotel would be better.'

'The Christmas markets are on, it's the middle of the high season and the entire city is full, so no,' Kim said. 'We had to send three wives home to accommodate you here, completely messing up the harem roster system. I suggest you think of something in a *hurry* to clarify to the Celestial gossip mill— since you're right smack in the middle of it, here—that you two are *not* taking advantage of the fact that your wife just passed to spend time together.'

'This is absolute bullshit,' Michael said. He turned to Simone. 'I—'

'Forget it, let's just get this done in a hurry so I can get ...' Simone hit a barrier and couldn't say, "my stepmother out of Hell." 'Your head back together.' There was a knock on the door. 'There's our bags. We'll unpack, meet with your father's agents downstairs in the restaurant—completely professionally, and you had *better* look grieving—and then go out and find this Shen.'

Michael nodded once sharply, his blonde ponytail flipping with the movement, and went to the door to let the concierge in.

Simone's room was barely bigger than the double bed in it, but it was comfortably decorated in white and gold, and immaculately clean. Another attic-style window opened to a small balcony that again overlooked the roofs across the road. The bed had a pile of cushions and a fluffy comforter on it, and she quickly sorted through her clothes and placed her bath stuff in the ensuite, then carried her briefing binder out to the living room to find Michael already there, sitting in one of the barrel chairs and reading his copy.

He stood. 'You take the lead on this. You're more powerful than me and can sense things more clearly than I can. Don't bother explaining anything if we need to move quickly—just run and I'll follow. Draw your weapons, and I'll draw mine.'

'No,' Simone said. 'This is a partnership ...' She stopped and winced at the reflection of Graham's words. 'Of equals, so the same goes the other way. If one of us misses something, the other picks it up. Okay?'

He nodded, went to the door and held it open for her. She walked out to the lift lobby, pressed the button, and when the lift arrived, she held the door for him. He saw what she was doing, shot her a quick smile that pierced her through, and they went down to the lobby together.

The restaurant was doing the lunch service and was nearly full. Simone and Michael stopped at the entrance and Simone looked around for Katie but didn't see her. She didn't know what Gabriel looked like.

The maître d' swept up to them with a smile. 'Michael.' He shook Michael's hand with both of his, grinning ruefully. 'So sorry about everything.'

'Thanks, Louis,' Michael said, freed his hands, and wiped

one over his eyes. 'I didn't want to come on this mission but apparently it's important and we can do something about the war.'

Louis saluted Simone Chinese-style with his hands clasped in front of him. 'Princess. This way.' He guided them through the restaurant—with everyone's eyes following them—to a private room at the end. He opened the door revealing the standard Chinese setup of a ten-seater table, folded mah-jongg table to one side and karaoke screen on the wall.

Katie was waiting for them, sitting at the table with a man Simone didn't know. He was obviously a son of the Tiger, but his mother was Black, giving him dark, glossy skin, a sculpted face with a generous mouth, and short straw-coloured hair that was a startling contrast.

Michael and Simone nodded to them as they saluted, then sat at the table.

'Can I get you anything? Katie? Gabriel?' the maître d' asked.

'How about a luncheon tasting platter in the middle, family-style?' Gabriel asked. 'Vegetarian for the Princess.'

'Sure thing. Drinks?'

'Green tea please,' Simone said.

'Water,' Katie said.

'Same,' Michael and Gabriel said in unison.

Katie had her laptop open and pressed a button, turning on the wall-mounted television and bringing up the photo they'd already seen of the Shen—short, middle-aged, white and not looking anything special.

'He's a boring mid-level manager at a trading company,' Katie said. She flipped to another photo of him sitting at one of Paris's outdoor café tables alone, brooding over a glass of red wine. 'Married, no children, divorced a long time ago. Seeing a psychologist for relationship issues. Gabriel?'

Gabriel nodded and took over, his expression grim. 'My wife's a stone Shen, and she was directed by the Celestial to investigate his psychologist's case files on him.' He scowled. 'She didn't want to do it, but an order's an order, and we have to trust him and do as says.'

'His wife ...' Michael's face filled with horrified realisation. 'Oh lord he's making me miss my *wife's funeral*, and I *don't care*.'

Katie and Gabriel both nodded, unsurprised.

'He told us what he did to you and asked us to "cut you some slack",' Katie said. 'This had better be worth it because he's leaving a trail of trauma behind him.'

'Yeah, my stepmother's in Hell and my little brother may never speak to me again,' Simone said. 'We want this done quickly.'

Gabriel folded his hands on the table and studied them. 'My wife read through his case files and the synopsis is: the Shen is seeing the psychologist for standard single-man issues, loneliness, unable to find the right woman, and apparently the marriage fell apart because he lost interest in his wife and couldn't explain why.'

'That would fit if our suspicions are correct and he's the god Hades,' Simone said, and the others nodded. 'He's looking for Persephone, the love of his life, and she's gone forever.'

'Does everyone here know the story of Hades and Persephone and how he ran off with her and she had to stay in his realm for half the year?' Katie asked.

Michael touched his binder. 'I do now.'

'But the demons in Hell asked me if I would wait for my Lord,' Simone said. 'They thought I was Persephone. Is she still around?'

'The demons may have no sense of time or know that she's gone,' Katie said.

'So we have a choice here,' Michael said. 'Approach Hades and ask him nicely if he can let us into the Heavens so we can clear them or go straight to Hell and background him first.'

'Hades himself can't go into the Heavens,' Simone said. 'It's a big part of the mythos that he was trapped down in Hell because of his asshole brothers.'

'If Persephone's around she can let you in,' Katie said. 'She's allowed there in winter, and we're in the middle of it right now.'

Michael turned to Simone. 'Talk to Hades, or go to Hell?'

'I've already been to Hell and there's nothing there,' Simone said.

The platter arrived and it was large enough for everyone, with a selection of sandwiches both club-style and open on a variety of different breads. Michael immediately grabbed one with chicken and salad on it and attacked it as if he hadn't eaten in days. Simone took one with roasted Mediterranean vegetables on a slice of sourdough. She took a bite and realised she was starving as well. She poured herself some tea to go with the food.

'Eat, stay strong,' Katie said, placing a croissant from the platter onto her own plate and tearing it open. 'The Shen— Hades—is at work right now. At five pm, he will go from his office to the café where we took the photo. He has a glass of wine there by himself, looking miserable as all hell, then collects a take-away dinner from the owners of the café and heads home on the train to a little one-bedroom apartment in the outskirts of the city.'

They arrived at the café just before five. It was too cold to sit outdoors on the icy pavement, so they sat inside, at a booth in the furthest corner from the door, with glasses of an excellent house red wine. The café was on the corner of two busy roads near the train station, which obviously handled freight because large trucks rumbled past carrying rail containers. Simone and Michael pretended to be young lovers, and it was agony for Simone because the pretence was effortless.

Michael smiled at her over the table. 'Once this is over, would you like to come back here with me and just hang out in all the fun places?' Charming dimples that she'd never seen before appeared in his cheeks and his voice turned sly. 'I can take you to the Eiffel Tower and the Science Museum. You loved them when we were little kids.'

Simone swiped one hand over her forehead and pulled the stray hair out of her eyes. 'You keep forgetting that when this is all over, you will remember that fabulous woman who you loved with all your heart, who just gave her life to bring your child into the world. And the child who is in another country and you may not see again.'

His expression fell. 'I do. Thanks for reminding me.' He studied the surroundings—the café's interior was warmed by a fireplace to one side, and vintage Parisian posters decorated the walls, some of them appearing genuine antiques. He turned back to her. 'The pain is there, but it's kind of behind a wall, and I can't feel it. Please don't stop reminding me. While I'm like this—I'm a monster. Heartless.' He lowered his head and shook it. 'This had better be worth it. When he takes the wall down, the guilt over my awful behaviour may destroy me.'

She sighed. 'We have to trust him to know what he's doing.'

'During the war ...' he began and stopped.

'Ask,' she said. 'You can always ask me anything.'

'How accurate was the Jade Emperor's vision of the future? Did he know that you and Frankie would be the ones to save the Heavens? Did he manipulate everybody to ensure it would happen? So many people suffered ... that time I spent in the Hell of the Trees of Swords ...' His eyes went unseeing, and he lifted his glass to take a big gulp of wine, then spoke bitterly. 'Oh, the aftermath of *that* I can definitely feel.' He put his glass down and touched her hand. 'And if it wasn't for you, I'd still be there.'

She pulled her hand away, and his expression filled with hurt, then understanding.

'Emma said that the Jade Emperor seemed just as delighted as everyone else when Nu Wa intervened and it looked like it was all over,' she said. 'I think he has a clearer view of all the future possibilities than anyone else, but he has to be very careful and only nudge things in the right direction, otherwise he'll cause the butterfly effect. I'm sure it's exhausting.'

'Does Frankie talk about what it was like to be the emperor and have his enhanced vision?'

'Frankie doesn't talk much about anything.' She looked away. 'Barely a couple of years old, and having to see all that—'

She turned back to Michael. 'Neither of us had a normal childhood, and it shows.'

'Clarissa had the right idea,' Michael said. 'If you have the choice, stay out of Celestial politics, go to the Earthly and live a quiet life away from all of it.'

'I was trying to,' Simone moaned, and took a gulp of her own wine.

The bell on the café's door rang and the air filled with the lively, uplifting presence of a Shen. It was him. He seemed even smaller in person: plain, bald and overweight, with a lined face full of kindness and an edge of ages-old sadness, but he was smiling. He wore a thick overcoat over a worn, dark blue polyester suit and carried a small, battered briefcase under his arm. He looked around the café and chose a small table in the corner, next to the window overlooking the street, and the café's owner brought him a glass of wine without being asked. They shared a few words and the owner patted him on the shoulder and left him.

Hades appeared energised and positive, very different from the melancholy man in the photo. He tapped his wine glass on the table and stared out the window.

Simone half-rose to go and talk to him when the bell rang again, and the air filled with life. The fresh scent of greenery filled the café.

'Another one,' Michael breathed.

Simone sat back down to watch. This one was a woman, in her sixties, with a lined, weathered face and wispy grey hair under a knitted beanie. She was rotund and plain-faced, and wore work trousers and steel-toed boots with a high-visibility shirt under an ancient, battered puffer vest that was streaked with dirt. She looked around the café and her face lit up when she saw him.

Hades rose and smiled when he saw her. She rushed to him, touched his face, and they embraced, then fell to sit. They twined hands together and gazed into each other's eyes, their expressions full of joy.

'Oh lord, he found her,' Simone said under her breath. 'We

have a way in.'

'There's no mention of a girlfriend or partner in any of the briefings,' Michael said, 'and they've been following him around for months.'

'Text Gabriel, ask him long they've been together,' Simone said. She studied Hades and Persephone, who made the entire café light up with their joy at being together. The humans around them were infected with their delight and the atmosphere lifted.

Michael tapped his phone and it pinged in his hand. 'Last time they tailed him was three days ago, and he was alone and miserable then.' He looked up at the rapt couple. 'This is new.'

Persephone leaned in to say something to Hades, and he laughed gently. She looked away from him, saw Simone and Michael and a look of confusion crossed her face. She gestured with her head towards them as she said something. He turned and saw them as well, and his eyes widened. He took her cheek in his hand, spoke urgently to her—

'Quick, he's saying goodbye,' Michael said, and climbed from the booth with difficulty.

Simone and Michael struggled to get out of the booth to grab him in time, but they weren't fast enough. The Shen stood, cast around and ran out of the café faster than any human could.

'No, no, no ... Simone faster—' Michael panted, but neither of them made it. The Shen ran straight into the path of a truck and was mown down. Simone ran to him and crouched, then turned away at the sight. His head was smashed like a melon. She rose and approached the woman, who had staggered clumsily out of the café and was glaring at her.

'Do you know how many years we'd been searching for each other?' the woman asked. 'We'd just found each other. We only had a few days together. Why. Why?' She leaned on the back of one the café's outside chairs, distraught. 'Who was he? Why was he like that? Even he didn't know.' She slammed her hand onto the back of the chair. 'He glowed like the sun! He didn't know why he was special, or why we knew we were destined the minute we saw each other. Then he saw you, said goodbye, and ran.'

'We need to go to Hell,' Simone said.

The woman jabbed her finger in Simone's face. 'Yes! Go to Hell!'

'Give me your contact details so that we can find you again,' Michael said. 'Quickly! We need to stop him. We can bring him back.'

'He's dead, child. There's no bringing him back.'

'You know that's not true, otherwise you wouldn't still be functioning,' Simone said. 'Like he said. Details! We'll come back. I promise.'

The woman raised her phone and said the number. Simone called her, she answered, and they both hung up.

'Take my hand,' Simone said, holding her hand out. Michael grabbed it and she teleported both of them to European Hell.

13

Simone and Michael arrived in the empty, dust-filled cavern of European Hell. There was a bright light, like a searchlight, some distance away. It was probably Hades.

Simone felt the energy drain start again, and Michael went rigid with his eyes unseeing. She took his hand in hers and helped him to moderate the drain so that it was reduced to a trickle, but again she couldn't stop it completely. She concentrated and did it for herself.

'That's what you were talking about?' he asked.

She nodded. 'That's it. Look.' She leaned closer to speak to him. 'If the drain becomes life-threatening, get yourself out of here. The old-fashioned Immortal-In-Trouble way if you have to.' He opened his mouth to speak, and she raised her hand to stop him. 'No. Don't worry about me, I have better control. But you *do not*—' She spoke with emphasis. '—let yourself die down here, okay? Because it may be soul destruction, and you'll be gone.'

He nodded back. 'I understand.'

'Don't make me worry about you,' she growled. 'We have enough to deal with. Okay?'

He smiled and it struck her like a beacon of warmth. 'Okay. Trust me.'

She turned towards the glow in the distance. 'Let's go.'

They both lifted and flew towards the light, the dust

170

disappearing as they travelled, being replaced by a wide, green lawn with the occasional scraggly tree. The cavern's ceiling brightened until it seemed that they were in warm daylight. The transformation had an obvious source, and they followed its direction for a kilometre to find the Shen sitting on the stone throne Simone had located previously, his elbows on his knees.

The entire area glowed with life, even more than when it had taken Simone's soul—the wall fresco behind the throne glittered with brilliant colours and golden highlights, reflecting the sun-like glow from above. The floor was mirror-polished black tiles. Hades looked exactly as he had when he was alive, in his mid-sixties, short, plain, overweight and balding in a blue polyester suit.

Simone and Michael landed in front of him, but he didn't seem to see them.

'Sometimes I don't meet her,' he said, watching three demons as they approached and fell to their backward knees in front of him. 'Sometimes, I spend a whole lifetime without her. I'll think that I've fallen in love with other women, I marry— but sometimes, I run into her during my life, and ...' He looked up at them, his gaze full of pain. 'Everything else fades away and it's just me and her.'

'She is your Queen, Lord,' one of the demons said.

'Persephone,' Simone breathed.

'We have her contact information,' Michael said. 'You will never be parted again. We can help you.'

The Shen waved one hand in the direction of the temple containing the scroll. 'I drink from the River Lethe and cleanse my memories before I leave. It hurts too much to remember what I've lost, and staying in this prison is torture.'

'What name do you prefer?' Simone asked.

The Shen laughed softly. 'So many. So many that my story has been told and retold until I hardly recognise myself. Ithas, Hades, Pluto, Lucifer, Satan ...' He glanced up at them. 'One of my first names was Prometheus, the strategist. I gave humanity fire. I gave them light. I gave them knowledge, and ...' His hand swept around at the landscape as their surroundings reconstructed themselves. 'Received this gift in return. I was cast out for treating humanity with kindness and respect, and when my brothers and sisters departed, they left me here to suffer alongside the humans I adored.' He shook his head. 'I wouldn't go with those bastards anyway. What they did was wrong. Their ridiculous lies about eternal reward and punishment—of course it didn't make humanity better, it just made them give up. And then those Eastern demons came in and they've used our region—*my* region—as a staging ground for the enslavement of all humanity.'

'Can you enter Heaven?' Simone asked him.

He laughed bitterly. 'No. Cast out a long time ago.' He rose and brushed the dust off his pants. 'It's been lovely talking to you, but there's nothing here for me, and if you don't mind, I'll just drink the water and go searching for her again.'

'We can bring her here. Alive. You can be together—' Michael began.

Persephone appeared next to Simone and ran to Prometheus. She looked slightly younger, in her mid-forties, but it was the same woman—generously proportioned with large breasts and wide hips. The empty planters around them filled with shrubs that immediately bloomed into brilliantly glowing crimson and purple flowers.

'Lightbringer!'

He stepped down from the throne, took her in his arms and smiled sadly down at her. 'Lifegiver. You shouldn't have done that, but ...'

She finished it in unison with him. 'I do it every time.' She turned to see Simone and Michael, still in her lover's arms. 'Who are you, and why are you here? You look different.'

'We're from the East,' Simone said. She bowed to them old-fashioned Chinese-style, with hands clasped in front of her. 'I am Princess Xuan Si Min Simone, only human daughter of the Dark Lord of the Northern Heavens, that he bore with a human woman of Celtic serpent extraction. This is—'

'Michael MacLaren,' Michael said. 'That's it.'

'That's one of the Celtic Serpent names,' Persephone said.

Michael bowed slightly to her.

'But you're a big cat.'

Michael bowed again. 'My father is the Chinese God of the West, the White Tiger.'

'There are Chinese gods?' Prometheus asked, intrigued.

'A whole pantheon of them,' Simone said. 'Maybe even more than you lot.'

'Are they still around?' Persephone asked, equally intrigued.

Simone nodded. 'My father is one of the biggest. We've been attempting to contact the Shen ... gods of other regions so that we can co-ordinate our response to the demon threat. The demons are way ahead of us when it comes to infiltration and conquest across regions.'

'The war,' Prometheus said. He shook his head. 'Humans. Always at war. I thought it was my ugly nephew who caused this constant strife, but it seems to be intrinsic to humans and Ares was a symptom, not the cause.'

'The presence of the demons in the Heavens is making it exponentially worse,' Simone said. 'My father drove all of our demons into our Hell, and we've had centuries of peace since then.'

'I would like to meet him,' Prometheus said.

'Will you help us?' Michael asked. 'The demons are in your Heavens. Again. Their presence is wreaking havoc all through your region. We are powerful enough to stop them, but we can't get in. The demons have closed all the gateways.'

'Not my Heavens,' Prometheus said. He turned and sat back on the throne, waved one hand and made an identical throne next to his own for Persephone, who went to it and sat. Her grubby pants and puffer jacket transformed to an emerald-green flowing silk gown in modern style with a tie at the waist.

Prometheus now looked in his mid-thirties, with short black hair, coppery Southern-European skin and strikingly blue eyes. He had grown in size and muscular bulk, and the suit shifted to one of a better fit in finer black cloth. He put his elbow on the arm of the throne and his chin in his hand as he spoke to Simone. 'You are part-demon. Why do you want to enter our Heavens and clear your own kind from them? Do you want to take over yourself?' He turned to Michael. 'You are pure God. Why are you with this demon?'

'She absorbed the essence of a Demon King when she selflessly destroyed it,' Michael said. 'She thought it would kill her. Instead, she's ended up like this—and she's still a kind, generous, loving person who deserves much better.'

'Your assistance to clear this demon essence from me would be most appreciated,' Simone said.

'The Food of Heaven may fix it,' Persephone said to Prometheus, musing. She also appeared much younger, in her early thirties, and her hair was a red-gold thick braid to her waist. She was still shorter than average and generously proportioned. 'But anyone sitting on the Throne of Heaven can do it easily.'

Simone felt a bolt of hope. 'Can you help us enter Heaven? All the gateways are closed.'

'What do you think, Penny?' he asked.

'Stopping the war and clearing the Heavens would be good. If they can achieve that, we can even do something about the environmental degradation. We should help them.' She turned to Simone and Michael. 'I can't go up to Heaven myself until Spring, but we may have a way to assist you.'

Prometheus spoke to the demons, still on their knees in front of him. 'Tell Baal to get his ugly ass here right—'

The demon that Simone had met at the temple appeared in front of the throne with a pop, still in the form of a middle-aged man in a tailored suit. He clasped his hands and bowed to Prometheus. 'Boss.' He grinned at Persephone. 'Boss Lady. Nice to see you both together again.' He saw Simone and Michael, and lit up. 'The Princess who visited! You could use the scroll!'

Prometheus shot Simone a swift, calculating look. 'You've been here before?'

'My stepmother died in this part of the world, and I came to ensure that she wasn't stuck here and to get her out if she was,' Simone said.

'Honourable,' Persephone said.

'What are your plans once you enter the Heavens?' Prometheus asked.

'Our main goal is to clear out the demons,' Michael said. 'We will find Semias, who is still around somewhere, and then set things up for someone—hopefully neither of us—to take over, re-open the Heavens, and severely limit the demons' activities in this part of the world.'

'Semias is still around?' Persephone asked. 'What of his city? Does it still stand?'

'Typical,' Prometheus said with scorn. 'Kill themselves and leave the spirit of one city alone up there as a caretaker.'

'Semias will slowly go mad without a population to serve,' Persephone said. 'What *cruelty*!'

'Baal,' Prometheus said.

'How can I help?' Baal spread his hands. 'Look at your dominion, springing to life at your touch.'

'Yeah, fuck that,' Persephone said. 'This place *sucks*. I'd rather be a lonely, mindless human than here.' She glanced at Prometheus. 'Sorry, my love.'

'I agree with you, it's why both of us lived as lonely, mindless humans,' he said. He turned to Baal. 'You're the Secretary of Hell, so you have all the contracts we agreed to since the beginning of this whole shitshow. If Penny got these kids into our Heavens, they cleared out the demons and then one of them sat on the Throne of Light ...' He took a quick breath. 'Could they open the way for *me* to take the throne before they went home?'

'Oh shit,' Michael said under his breath. 'Lucifer on the Heavenly Throne.'

Prometheus shot Michael a quick grin. 'Precisely.'

'All the documentation with regard to the Throne of Light is up there, not down here, my Lord,' Baal said, still jolly. 'All I have here is the terms of your responsibilities to this realm and the agreements on procedures for dealing with the souls of the departed.'

'The residents of Heaven can do whatever they want, and

we have to put up with it,' Persephone said.

'That's always been the gist of it, my Lady,' Baal said.

'My mother never got over me running off with you,' Persephone said wistfully. Her voice hardened. 'The fact that I was happy with you made her even worse.' She spoke to Simone and Michael. 'I know of a few gateways, I worked near one during my life just past. I cannot follow you in until Spring Equinox, but by then you should have a good idea of the layout and a plan of attack.' She glanced at Prometheus, who nodded support, and turned back to Simone and Michael. 'I am not a fighter, I am a life giver, and if they catch me, the demons will kill me on sight, and I will be back here again. But I can support you with whatever logistics you need as soon as I am able to join you. If we can get darling Hades up there, he'll run them out in no time. He's the mightiest demon fighter of us all, and they locked him up down here because in a fair fight he'd beat his brothers easily.'

'I never wanted to fight them,' Prometheus moaned. 'Insecure assholes. My therapist would have been set for life dealing with their neuroses.'

'Should we wait until Spring so she can come in with us and show us around?' Michael asked Simone.

'No, we need to do this now,' Simone said. 'Our presence in the Heavens will weaken the demons' effect on the Earthly just by our being there, so we should move.'

'Good point, and we can start looking for a way to clear you—find this Food of Heaven—immediately.' Michael turned to speak to Prometheus. 'A couple of years ago, I was kidnapped by the demons and held in Semias's city in the Heavens. If I can go back there and find him, then hopefully he can be our ground support.'

'He can help you until I have access,' Persephone said. 'It's a solid plan.'

'Please show us the gateways, and we'll see if we can go in,' Simone said.

'Sure,' Persephone said, and changed her appearance back to the sixty-ish year old woman in the battered puffer jacket.

'Follow me.'

'Adorable,' Prometheus said with genuine affection. 'Return soon, my love, we have plans to make.'

She grinned at him. 'Put the pavilion back together, there's a few things we need to do first.'

He smiled back. 'Never change.'

Persephone took them to an open-air area outside the city, on a windy, cold plain. There was a car park bounded by tall shrubs next to a metal shed the size of one of the largest supermarket warehouses Simone had ever seen. At first Simone thought it was a logistics centre for a delivery service, but a cheer went up inside it as a loud radio-announcer voice echoed from a public address system, and Simone realised that it was an indoor arena. The area in front of them was surrounded by a chain-link fence, covered with tattered canvas to hide whatever was inside.

Persephone conjured three big bunches of pink and red silk roses and handed a bunch each to Simone and Michael. She led them to a boom gate staffed by a bored-looking uniformed security guard.

'Already? It only seems like last week you were putting them in the Alice garden,' the guard said in French.

'The tourists take them faster than I can shove them in the bushes,' Persephone replied in the same language. 'My nephew and his girlfriend will help me this time.'

'Go on through, Madam Bernard.' The guard smiled at Simone and Michael. 'Make sure she gets home before midnight this time, eh?'

'We will,' Simone said as she followed Persephone around the boom gate and into the screened yard at the back of the arena.

The yard was stacked with random shipping containers, parts of scaffolding, traffic control signs, and piles of gravel. Another big cheer went up inside the stadium. Simone turned back and recognised the distinctive fairy tale castle on the small hill.

'Euro Disney?' she asked.

'I was their forensic gardener,' Persephone said. 'They wanted to create a French cottage garden on this windswept mudhole. Nothing survived, it's too cold and windy, and the soil is rocky and barren. They saw some topiary I did for a private contract, and called me in, and offered me more than I was making as a designer to bring their gardens to life.' She led them past more piles of construction debris to a small shed with flowerpots piled in front of it and a portable greenhouse. 'Of course, it wasn't the great deal I thought it was—this is a big American conglomerate after all. So much unpaid overtime with no recognition. So many arguments about how to keep the plants alive—I wanted to provide windbreaks and thick mulch, and they said it "wouldn't fit the aesthetic". They wanted roses—roses!—blooming all year round, and when I said that was impossible, they made me shove these ...' She raised the silk flowers. 'Into the azalea bushes. They paid me well, but I was at the bottom of their hierarchy of sleek architectural designers, and because I'm old and fat and ugly they didn't want to be seen with me. They'd just call me in when things needed to be fixed.' She took the roses from them and threw them onto the ground next to the shed's entrance. 'Of course, my touch was the only thing keeping it all going, and now that I'm gone, they'll struggle to keep the plants alive. They'll go back to digging them up and replacing them when they constantly die.' She opened the shed door to show rows of seedlings on shelves against the walls.

'I never knew why I asked to be put here,' Persephone said. 'Now I do. Step back.'

Simone and Michael did as she asked. She stood in the doorway, raised one hand, and opened a glowing portal to Heaven inside the greenhouse with a sound like steel over ice.

'Can you go in, Simone?' Michael asked.

Simone opened her mouth to say 'of course' and then closed it again. She couldn't go into the Asian Heavens because of her demon nature. She carefully stretched one arm towards the portal and felt nothing as her hand entered it. She pushed her whole arm in, then stepped through.

'Too many demons up here,' she said. 'I'll have to keep an eye on myself, though, if the Heavens are cleared, I may be at risk.'

'Take care, there will be no way of contacting me to let you out. You're stuck for thirty-three days in there,' Persephone said.

'I'll make sure you're out before that happens,' Michael said to Simone, and turned to Persephone. 'Thank you. We have it from here. We'll see you at Spring Equinox.'

'Stay alive, kids, if you can give my darling Promy the throne, we can make things around here much better. Go with my hopes.'

'Take my phone anyway, it's special and may be able to contact Simone's,' Michael said, and handed Persephone his mobile phone. He nodded to Simone. 'Want to go back and get our stuff and some support—like Katie—and return?'

'No, we have to go now, because as soon as they sense the gateway's presence they'll close it,' Simone said. 'Semias can provide for us if we find our way into his city.'

Michael nodded and stepped through onto the wide, grassy plain under a star-filled night sky to join her. 'Let's go find Semias.'

'Good luck, children,' Persephone said, and closed the portal behind them.

'I hope we didn't just make a huge mistake,' Michael said. 'Any signal on your phone?'

Simone checked it. 'No, but we're Immortal. We'll be fine.'

Michael turned on the spot. 'Similar to the Heavens back home—zillions of stars, fresh clean air—it's lovely.'

Simone breathed deeply, appreciating the fresh scent of the air. She looked up to see multitudes of stars blazing in the sky, free from light pollution and with the clarity of the higher plane. It had been ages since she'd been on the Heavenly Plane, and her eyes stung with tears—she'd really missed it.

Michael's head shot up. 'Demons coming. Fight or hide?'

She felt it as well—big demons heading their way, moving

incredibly fast.

'Hide,' she said, looking for cover, and finding none. They were in the middle of the broad plain occupied by the outskirts of Paris and the Disney Park on the Earthly plane. 'I can't make us invisible—'

'I can't either.' Michael held his hand out as the thumping roar approached. 'Shit, I can't pull my weapon to me here. What about you?'

She concentrated and her swords didn't come. 'Me neither.' A helicopter appeared in the sky to the south, rushing towards them. Simone grabbed Michael's hand and he whooped with surprise as she shot straight up into the air—to double the altitude that the helicopter was flying at—and hovered above the portal to watch. He released her hand and hovered next to her.

The demons in the helicopter didn't seem to notice Simone and Michael floating above them. The helicopter landed, making the grass ripple, and five demons stepped out. Three were big Western ones like those they'd encountered in Western Hell; black and spiked with bat-like wings and horned heads with many misshapen teeth. Two were smaller and appeared human, looking like White British skinheads, but their demon nature was obvious to Simone.

One of the bat-like demons pushed the two human-types towards where the portal had been, and one of them moaned with terror.

Can you see what's happening? Michael asked telepathically.

Five demons, standing and looking at where the portal was, Simone said. *They don't seem to have noticed us.* She watched the demons as they walked around the location of the portal, discussing it. The bat-like ones had an animated argument, waving their arms, while the two human-types cowered.

That's right, it's not worth closing and locking, Simone said to Michael. *It was a mistake.*

Can you share your vision of them? Michael asked. *I can't see much from this high up.*

Simone hesitated, not wanting that sort of intimate connection with Michael as it would probably reveal more of her feelings for him than she was comfortable with. *Sorry, no.*

Okay. Tell me what's happening?

Sure.

One of the demons obviously made a decision, grabbed one of the human-types, carried it to the location of the portal and smashed its head between his hands, then spread them, covered in red goo. The portal opened and the other demons stared at it, then shared a grin.

They killed one of their own—a human-type—and its essence was red, not black.

Like those weird copies my dad found in the West?

Yes. The sacrifice opened the portal.

Ew.

Simone agreed with him. The other human-type fell to its knees, obviously pleading for its life, but the big ones ignored it. The big ones had an animated discussion, gesturing angrily at each other, and Simone guessed that a few of them wanted to go through and cause some havoc, but probably had orders to stay and guard. One of the big ones strode to the kneeling human one, grabbed it and smashed its head in the way the first one had been destroyed. The portal closed again.

They locked it back down the same way, Simone said. *With a sacrifice of red demon essence. I really don't want to do that to leave here ...*

Semias was able to open a portal to help Emma escape, Michael said. *Or we can wait for Persephone. No need to kill what appears to be human.*

The demons slapped each other on the back, obviously delighted at a job well done, and returned to the helicopter. It took off and Simone waited for it to disappear over the horizon before letting herself and Michael drift back down to the ground. She concentrated on the portal location and shook her head. 'Yeah. It's gone.' She turned to Michael. 'Do you remember where Semias's city was?'

'Absolutely,' he said. 'About five hundred clicks north-west, where the Netherlands is on the Earthly. Can you teleport closer? Something's blocking me.'

She concentrated a moment, then shook her head. 'Same. We have to fly. You good?'

He nodded. 'Let's go.'

They flew together over wide meadows and thick, tall forests, all completely empty. Simone slowed when they approached a village and flew lower to see it.

There were ten generously sized houses with whitewashed walls and high, pitched thatched roofs that had fallen in. The grass was waist-height around the houses and the fences behind them had fallen over. The roads had disappeared beneath the greenery.

'This must have been delightful when they were here,' Simone said, hovering over a shattered fountain in the town square. A fallen sign next to one building suggested that it was an inn. 'I wonder what happened to the humans who lived here when the Shen decided to kill themselves?'

'Probably ended up on the Earthly, confused and disoriented and a hundred years after their own time because of the time differential,' Michael said. He cocked his head. 'Aren't there folk tales about that?'

'The small number of tales suggests that these Shen were selective about having humans in their dominion,' Simone said. 'Only the best and brightest?'

'Or prettiest,' Michael said. 'I think Hades might be an asshole, but he's the least asshole-y of them.'

'Persephone seems all right, though,' Simone said.

'I don't trust either of them, something's off about them, particularly Hades,' Michael said grimly.

'Yeah,' Simone said, and looked around. 'Which way?'

Michael pointed. 'There.' He turned to her. 'You okay? Not feeling the stress of the demon nature against the Heavenly nature?'

'No, I feel right at home,' Simone said, and lifted herself further. 'Let's go.'

After two hours of flying through the clear, bitterly cold night in companiable silence, they arrived at the city. It was completely dark and the soaring stained-glass towers—which Michael had previously visited and described in a report that Simone had read with interest—were just slender shapes against the star-filled sky. Apart from about fifty demons that she sensed were gathered at the centre of the city, it was heart-wrenchingly deserted, gloomy and lifeless.

Simone felt the cold of the loneliness again and tried to push it away. The last time she had broken into these Heavens, she had found them completely deserted and for an hour of terrifying panic, thought she would be stuck on that continent completely alone for the rest of her life. But Michael was here with her now, and she could feel his warm, reassuring presence next to her.

She flew up to enter over the wall but hit an invisible barrier above it. She ran her hand over the barrier—it was an energy shield. She'd never seen anything like it before.

'Down here,' Michael said, and she landed next to him in front of the city's wall. It was twice as tall as them and made of rippling glass joined by shining silvery metal that framed the massive glossy pieces.

'My heart should be broken to be here,' Michael said bitterly. 'The Demon King had copies of my wife and mother—both of them!—alive and claiming to be the real Rhonda and Clarissa, kept here as captives.'

'You never mentioned demon copies in the report,' Simone said, running her hand over the slick glass wall. The starlight had drained it of colour, and it appeared plain grey.

'It hurt too much to mention,' he said. 'I did something really stupid and destroyed them by accident.' He lowered his voice. 'Mind-bogglingly stupid. I didn't think at all. What's worse, is that I should be glad that they weren't the real women, because it would have killed them.' He shook his head. 'So stupid.'

He waited for Simone to ask him, but she didn't, not wanting to open this wound further.

Michael turned back to the wall and raised his voice. 'Semias, I hope you can hear us. I'm Michael, I'm back, and we're here from the East to clear the demons from your Heavens and install Hades as replacement ruler. Can you respond through the city?'

The wall vibrated beneath Simone's hand, and she jerked it back, then realised what it was doing and put her hand on again.

'Isle of the City,' the wall said. 'Help. Michael? He ...' The voice trailed off

'Isle of the City?' Simone asked, then understood. 'Île de la Cité. That's the centre of Paris, close to where we started.' She glanced at Michael. 'Twenty yuan says it's a city chock-full of demons.'

'Stealth, then,' he said. 'Follow me, let's see if we can get into this glass city before we head back there. We may be able to find useful supplies and rest.'

'No,' Simone said. 'There are fifty demons in the middle of this city, and they may ambush us if we sleep in there. I don't need that much rest. Let's go now, and hopefully be at Semias's location before dawn to do a night stealth raid.' She studied him. 'Unless you need to rest?'

'Good point, but at the speed we've been flying, we'll get there just on dawn and have to decide then what to do,' he said, then nodded to her. 'I'm fine. Let's go.'

14

Simone noticed with concern that Michael dipped occasionally in the air as they flew south through the cold, crisp night in silence. The stars blazed overhead in the clear sky, and she was again struck by its beauty. She missed the Heavenly Plane.

Michael lagged fifty metres behind her and kept rising and falling in the air, so she spoke to him telepathically.

Stop for a minute and land, please.

Okay.

They landed on a grassy knoll overlooking a stand of forest that appeared to be half-dying—probably from having so many demons present. Michael looked around. 'Go behind a bush, I can look away.'

'What?' Simone asked, then realised what he was saying. 'Oh, no. I don't need to go—I can handle that with manipulation of water, like my dad. What about you?'

'Yeah. Give me a minute,' he said, and headed down the knoll to stand behind a tree.

She sat on the grass as he returned, looking significantly relieved. He fell to sit next to her with a grunt.

'Please tell me when you can't keep up,' she said. 'You're not much use if you're half-asleep.'

His expression filled with understanding, then went wry. 'Pride before a fall? It must be bad if you're noticing.'

'You should have pushed me harder to rest in Semias's city,' she said, and rose, brushing the grass off her jeans. 'We can't stop here, but keep an eye open as we travel. If we see another inn we can stop and let you have a break.'

'You're really absolutely fine?' he asked with wonder.

She nodded.

He gestured towards the east, where the sky was touched with a tinge of pink. 'The nights are longer because it's winter, but daylight is coming. How far do you think we have to go?'

Simone concentrated, released a ball of her remaining chi, moved her awareness into it and lifted it high into the air.

'I can see the river,' she said. 'Not far, maybe twenty minutes? I think I can see the heavenly analogue for Paris as well, there's something there that looks like a structure, but it's a blob of red dropped onto the river. Red and white. It looks like a giant blood clot over bare bones.'

'Ew,' Michael said, and shook himself out. 'Reconnoitre, find somewhere to rest, and then infiltrate tonight?'

'Sounds like a plan,' she said, pulled the chi down, and lifted herself into the air. 'I can't generate a cloud here, you'll have to carry yourself. You okay?'

'I can make it,' he said.

'I've heard *that* one before,' she said, teasing. 'We all ended up in the Andaman Sea.'

His expression softened. 'You know me too well. Let's find a place for me to rest.'

She nodded and he lifted into the air to join her.

The city did look like a clot of blood surrounding bare bones. The red blood-like substance covered the area around the distinctive boat-shaped island in the centre of the Paris analogue. Hundreds of rib-like white struts of various heights stuck out, up to four storeys high, some archways and others as single curved columns. They filled an area nearly as large as the original Parisian city, and strands of red were strung over the river, with dirty white sheets hanging off them. It looked like the meat hanging off the bones of a giant dismembered corpse.

'Smells vile,' Michael said. 'Like mould.'

'Yeah.' Simone concentrated, sending her senses out. 'No demons here. The city is dead and empty, except for a faint energy … thing … on the island.'

'That's probably Semias. I can't sense anything at all.'

Simone approached one of the red structures and crouched at the edge of it. The dusty smell of dead mould was stronger closer to it. The structure consisted of thick bright crimson threads of goo strung between slender white wooden supports. Sheets of white, parchment-like skin had collapsed around the red goo.

'I don't want to touch it, it looks poisonous,' she said. 'Like red algae that blooms in the ocean and kills everything.' She rose and shivered. 'Gross.'

Michael peered up at it. 'Is the red stuff taking over the rotting city? Like mould growing on it? It smells like mould, but slightly sweeter.'

'That's because it's dead and rotting, but those struts look like wooden structural supports? Oh!' She gasped and stepped back, still studying the red goo. 'I think I know what it is.' She lifted into the air again, then flitted backwards and forwards, clarifying what she was seeing. 'Up here.'

Michael rose to join her.

'Many of the buildings in Paris are Haussmann-style architecture, like the hotel we were in, right?' she asked.

'This does mirror the size and shape of that, if you imagine walls around those rib things,' he said.

'And then art nouveau. Flowing, plant-like decorations on everything.'

'Particularly in Paris, yes,' he said. 'This city used to be plants?'

'No,' Simone said, and swept one arm around at the collapsed red goo. 'This was a *Fairy Mushroom City*. The buildings were made of red fungus.' She dropped again and touched the white parchment-like sheeting that hung, tattered, from the goo. 'The red fungal threads were underneath, connected to the wooden structural supports, and then this white leathery stuff—like skin—was on top.' She flew back. 'The city was made of the fungus. They grew the fungus over the supports.' She turned to Michael. 'I wouldn't be surprised if this dead fungus is toxic, so the demons don't want to occupy the city. They left Semias here to suffer.'

Michael concentrated, his noble features intense, and nodded. 'I can sense him now. You're right, he's on the island in the middle. Let's go.'

A haze of red dust hovered at head-height over the collapsed fungus, so they carefully flew over it towards the river. It was a bright, clear winter morning and the island in the centre of the river—the heart of the city of Paris on the Earthly—held square buildings on one side that mirrored the Earthly hospital, and on the other side was a building located where the Notre Dame cathedral stood. All of it was ruins, with the wooden ribs poking out of the red goo. Michael guided Simone towards the hospital side, and he must have realised at the same time she did.

'The little chapel you used to love visiting when we were kids,' he said as he flew next to her. 'What's it called?'

'Saint Chappelle,' she said, and lowered herself next to the tumbledown set of ribs sticking up in the shape of the chapel. There were a large number of them standing in the shape of the building, closer together and more slender than for the other buildings.

'More pillars to hold the stained glass,' he said. 'Did the fungus make stained glass too? Imagine that.'

'It would have been even more beautiful,' Simone mused. 'I wish I could have seen it.'

'I wonder if Persephone can restore this when we give her back control? It is plants after all.'

'I hope so.'

They landed on the fungus-covered square in front of the ruin. The goo had hard, blackened parts in geometric shapes within the red, suggesting that it really had grown in different transparent colours to make the glass.

Something shifted within the goo. Simone shot up into the air and back with horror, then floated towards it again as she understood.

'Semias are you in there?' Michael asked.

The goo shifted again. There was a human-sized pile of it in the centre of the chapel building.

Michael put one hand out and used his chi to burn a hole in the pile of goo.

'Tell us if it gets too hot,' he said.

'You're talking to him?' Simone asked, opening her Inner Eye onto the pile of fungus. Semias's glowing presence was present in the centre of it.

'No,' Michael said. 'Help me?'

The smoke from the burning goo hit Simone and she said with disbelief, 'It smells delicious? Like barbecued mushroom?'

'Maybe it's edible when cooked,' he said.

Simone added her own careful chi blast to Michael's. The fungus burnt to ash and blew away, leaving behind the rich aroma of roasted mushrooms.

'I'm *starving*,' Michael said as the fungus burned away, then added, 'Stop. There.'

The fungus remained in a lump over Semias's energy signature.

A voice whispered from under it. 'Do the rest. Please.'

'Can you see him underneath?' Michael asked.

'I can see his shape, yes. His energy is something I've never seen before, but I recognise it now,' Simone said.

'Burn the fungus off above a hand, and he can stick it through to us.'

'Okay.' Simone moved closer. She tuned her chi to a smaller ray and carefully worked around the edges of Semias's energy aura. It was hard to tell the difference between the spirit and the fungus surrounding him.

'Stop,' Semias said from within the fungus, and she did.

A bony, grey hand poked through the remaining goo. 'Pull?'

Michael dashed down to the hand, grabbed it, and pulled

up and out.

'Burn around it at the same time,' Michael said, gasping with effort. 'It's like glue!'

Simone carefully worked her way down the wrist and arm, burning the fungus away, and more flesh was revealed. Semias's skin was lined with red—the fungus had worked its way into his body and was growing on him. Michael pulled Semias up and out of the goo as she released him, and eventually they freed the old man with a wet, sucking sound. Trails of goo clung to him, and she worked carefully to remove them, but it was still growing on him, and she didn't have the skill to eliminate it all.

Semias was naked and severely emaciated, with grey skin around the fungal growth. His ribs and pelvic bone were clearly visible, and his eye sockets were filled with the red goo. He grinned at them, and the effect was macabre.

'Michael. Took your time,' he wheezed. 'Is this Simone, the woman you told me about?' He nodded to her. 'Lovely to meet you. I suggest you clear out of here as quickly as you can, this stuff will kill even you.'

Michael shifted Semias to hold him in his arms like a child, and Semias kissed him on the cheek and beamed up at him.

'I knew you'd come eventually,' he said. 'You promised you would.'

Michael's face went grim. 'I should drop you and leave you here. You knew Clarissa was sure I would come for her. And for the real Clarissa, I never did.'

Semias's face fell. 'Sorry.' He glanced at Simone. 'You burn like a dark sun, and control demon essence like ... oh, he was your father.' He placed one hand on Michael's cheek and his voiced lowered to a throaty rasp. 'Take me to my city. I can clear this awful red shit from me and look after you there. I'm having difficulty ...' His head wobbled and his eyes closed. 'Staying conscious.'

'Are you okay to carry him back?' Simone asked. 'I can do it.'

Michael nodded agreement and passed Semias to her.

'We can stop on the way back for you if need,' she said, hoisting the old man in her arms. He weighed nearly nothing, and his grey skin was slimy with the goo.

'I'll let you know if I need to rest,' Michael said. 'I almost said go ahead and leave me, but in these Heavens ...' He looked around. 'Probably not a good idea.'

'Absolutely not a good idea,' Semias wheezed. 'Take me to my city, and we can work together to remove those demon assholes.'

'Let's go,' Simone said.

Simone had to stop twice and land, holding Semias, so that Michael could flop to sit and put his head between his knees for twenty minutes each time. The fungus around the city spirit tried to enter her and she held it back without difficulty, but she was concerned that Michael could have it growing in him, and its toxicity would kill him, Immortal or not.

They arrived back at Semias's city close to midday and the glass spires glittering between the silver metal framework were magnificent. Michael guided Simone to the shattered entrance gates and she carefully flew over the large shards of glass scattered over a wide avenue that appeared to be made of white marble and paved with blue-green glass tiles.

'Semias said that destroying these gates caused him torture-level pain,' Michael said.

As they passed through the gates, the avenue rose on slender supports to second-storey level and continued into the city between the stained-glass buildings. Dead trees lined the avenue, with empty planter boxes on generous footpaths to either side of it.

'Stop,' Semias said, and his form shifted to mirror the nature of his city.

He became immensely heavier in Simone's arms and changed to an automaton made of glass himself. He appeared to be small pieces of deep blue glass held together within a silver framework, exactly like a leadlight window and the buildings of his city. A brass-like clockwork mechanism became visible inside the glass exterior, and she found herself holding a clockwork mannequin with a blue-grey glass casing.

She moved to put Semias down but stopped when he said, 'No, please wait.'

She stood holding him like a child, watching with wonder as the stained-glass automaton changed back to an elegant, middle-aged White man with long, light brown hair and green eyes. His hair braided itself and his naked form was covered in a soft tan-coloured robe within her arms. He opened his eyes, no longer tainted by the fungus, and quickly kissed her on the mouth, making her jerk back and scowl.

'Ask permission,' she growled.

'We talked about this last time I was here!' Michael wheezed from where he sat.

Semias grinned apologetically. 'Sorry. It was my way of thanking you. You are a remarkable young woman, and I can see why Michael is destined to be with you.'

She turned her scowl on Michael—how much had he told this old asshole?—but Michael was sitting on the ground next to her, his head on his knees.

'Can I put you down now?' she asked, and Semias nodded.

She lowered the spirit and he knelt next to Michael. 'You have the fungus in you, and we need to clear it out.'

'I'm sorry, I'm definitely not powerful enough to be doing this,' Michael said into his knees. 'Can you heal me?'

Semias looked up and his expression filled with bliss. 'Finally, no longer sundered, and one with my structure. Unfortunately, there is an outpost of at least fifty big demons in the centre of me, who regularly patrol my districts. You'll have to remove them before I can care for you.'

Michael grunted and clumsily pulled himself to his feet. 'Can we take them?'

'If you were rested, yes, but—' Semias said.

Simone put her hand on Michael's shoulder.

'What are you—' Michael began, then his expression filled with horror.

She shared her Shen energy with him, taking a part of her glowing silvery soul and feeding it into his exhausted body. It lit him up along his acupuncture points like a string of Christmas tree lights, and burned the fungus out of him, leaving his aura clean.

'Simone, no—' he began again, then the energy hit his lowest cauldron, the centre of his sexual Ching energy, and it flared bright red within him.

His knees buckled and he fell to all fours, then quivered with spasms, his face rigid with the pleasurable release. He bent his head and gasped for air.

Simone jerked her hand back and covered her mouth.

'Oh Lord, I am so sorry,' she said. 'I've done that for my father and didn't know that it would do that to you.'

Semias chuckled next to her, and she rounded on him.

'Your father didn't tell you?' Semias asked.

'When I gave Daddy energy, it was an innocent sharing of our love for each other, with no sexual component whatsoever,' she said. 'Just like a big warm hug between father and daughter.'

'Mirroring the purity of your relationship,' the spirit said. He gestured towards Michael. 'That mirrors the nature of *his* love for you. It's a much more common reaction.'

She bent next to Michael, whose eyes were glazed in the aftermath. 'Are you okay? I am so sorry.'

Michael gasped a few times, then shook his head. 'You really should have known better. Didn't your father tell you not to do that to people unless absolutely necessary?'

'Yes, but he never said why, and I assumed it was because I was so powerful I could kill them,' she said. 'That isn't a problem with you.'

'That's right, but he should have mentioned the side effects for Immortals. When Emma finds out that he never told you, she'll tear his shell off.' He pulled himself back to his feet, raising his hand to stop her from assisting him. He put his hands on his knees and breathed deeply, then stood and winced down at himself. 'Let's clear these demons so I can find some clean clothes.'

'I can conjure you new clothes ...' she began.

He shook his head. 'Once we clear the demons, Semias will change from an empty husk of a city to something similar to the Celestial Palace. He can provide us with food, shelter and clothing.' His expression filled with determination. 'Let's kill some demons.' He turned to Semias. 'Can you arm us? We can't conjure our weapons here.'

'Not until the demons are gone,' Semias said. 'My abilities are severely restricted by their corrupting presence.'

'Let's ambush a patrol and take their weapons to use on the main force,' Simone said, and turned to Semias. 'Can you find us two or three demons who are out on their own and exposed?'

'I have a pair that are patrolling near the wall,' Semias said. 'Simone, be aware that as you move closer to my centre, the gravity will reduce. It is about one-third Earth normal, to facilitate the height of my glorious spires.'

'I see,' Simone said, and grinned. 'Sounds like fun. Where are the demons? Point us at them and we'll take it from there.'

A map appeared in the air before them, showing the city's precincts. The city wasn't much larger than a modern suburb, with a wall around it. A mass of red dots clustered in the centre, with a few smaller groups patrolling around the edges.

'Where are we?' Michael asked, and three green dots appeared on the far-left side.

'I see, that's the gates,' Simone said. 'Closest demons?'

Two red dots grew larger as they worked their way around the edge of the city, beneath the wall.

'Coming to us,' Michael said, and smiled at Simone. 'We've never fought demons together, have we? I mean, we've sparred—'

'That's all very cute but they're fifty yards away and they'll see us soon,' Semias said.

'We can't make ourselves invisible,' Simone said, and a pearly aura appeared over her vision. 'Thank you.'

'My pleasure,' Semias said. 'There they are.'

Two black winged demons holding spears were strolling along the bottom of the wall and talking to each other.

'I get that it needs to be guarded, but no more of them have come since that big black one and the mud monster, and we scared him off,' one of them said.

'Eh, as long as the boss is happy, I'm content to wander around here and do nothing,' the other said.

'On the left,' Simone said softly.

'Got the right,' Michael said. 'Remember the gravity—'

Simone's training kicked in and she didn't think. She was unarmed, the demon was one of the spiky winged black things and much taller and heavier than her, so the immediate strategy was to rush it, hit it with her left shoulder into the wall and stun it, then crush its head with a brute force punch. None of this filtered through her brain, it was automatic from years of work to ensure that she wouldn't hesitate to have the advantage of speed when at the disadvantage of arms or strength.

She threw herself at the demon on the left, closing the distance of twenty metres in the blink of an eye. She didn't realise what had happened until she'd slammed the demon into the wall, turning it into something that resembled a crushed insect, and shattered her own shoulder blade, left arm and a couple of ribs as she hit the wall after it.

The demon was a mashed mess of flesh and shell beneath her, but all she knew was the pain of her destroyed left arm. Blood blossomed on the left sleeve of her sweater, and she ripped it off to see the bone poking through the skin. The pain dragged a scream out of her, and she collapsed.

A brilliant burning shot of light passed over her—Michael's Inner Eye—and the other demon was gone, destroyed by the brilliance of his Eye.

'Can you block the pain?' Michael asked, his voice strained, as he shifted her off the remains of the demon. 'Oh god, it's all over her.'

Simone was in too much agony to reply.

'No,' Semias said. 'Get rid of the demons and I have a full medical centre for you. Right now ... nothing.'

'Simone, concentrate on my voice and block the pain,' Michael said.

Simone was in a haze of torment, but his words made it through. She tried to concentrate on her energy to block the suffering. The overwhelming pain was interfering with her ability to reduce it.

Michael's consciousness stepped in and worked its way through her energy centres, filling the acupuncture points so that the pain eased enough to clear her head. She joined her energy with his and pushed it into her points, blocking the pain. She threw her head back, closed her eyes and sighed with relief.

'Hold her arm straight while I knit the bones back together,' Michael said. 'Simone, stay still and keep those points blocked. This will hurt a lot without pain relief.'

She kept her eyes closed and nodded, concentrating on the energy points. One of them took her left hand and pulled it, and she had to work even harder to keep the pain at bay. It turned to a dull ache that threatened to flare to full-on agony again, and she winced.

Michael's healing energy—still replete with the energy she'd gifted him minutes before—spun around her arm and shoulder, and the bones shifted back into their correct positions. He held them in place then began the process of knitting them back together with skill and patience.

'Remarkable,' Semias said softly.

As Michael's energy moved up her arm to her shoulder and onto her back, the pain reduced enough for her to add her own attention to the healing process. Their energies touched, and she felt his devotion for her—and he became aware of her yearning for him. Their souls wove around each other, resonating with a growing harmony that made the healing easier than any she'd ever experienced. It was a dance between their souls, uplifting and joyful, and the similarities of their experiences magnified the differences in their inherited Yang and Yin natures and thrummed with the love both of them had denied for so many years.

'Done,' Michael said softly with awe, and his energy withdrew, leaving her chilled.

She shifted the arm—the bones were back together but

hadn't knitted completely, and her arm would be out of action for at least a week—then pulled herself up to sitting with her back against the wall. She was covered in disgusting demon bits, so she conjured a flush of water over herself and then drained it until she was dry. She rested her head on her knees. Even with her extra strength and stamina, the travel, injury and lack of rest were starting to take a toll.

'I am so sorry,' she moaned. 'What a stupid thing to do—right after you warned me. Please don't tell anyone I did something so idiotic. I'd never be able to handle the shame.'

Michael fell to sit next to her, gasping, and put his head between his knees. Using his Eye and healing her had drained most of the energy she'd gifted to him, and he again was close to exhaustion.

'I'm glad I'm not the only one who does stupid things like that,' he said. 'At least nobody died this time.'

She turned to see him. 'People died?'

'I didn't tell you the whole story of my last visit here.' He looked up at the sky, cloudy with grey miasma from the presence of the demons. 'When I was still Dad's Number One, his Number Two, Rohan, called me in to help out on a big Nest. Up in Central Mongolia or something, in the desert. Miles from anywhere. We went in—me and Rohan were the only Immortals. This was just before the war, all the Horsemen were out on reconnaissance, so the West was short on warriors. We took six of the best Horsemen we had, but none of them were Immortal, just Rohan and me.' He looked down at his knees. 'Twelve massively big Mothers were waiting for us. It was a trap. I could have destroyed them all with my Inner Eye, but I was too stupid to think of it at the time. They killed all of my brothers, grabbed me, knocked me unconscious, and brought me ...' He looked up again, studying the walls around them. 'Here.'

'Dad taught me never to use the Eye unless it's a major emergency, because it can kill everything around you,' Simone said. 'It's the training, same as what just happened to me. You don't think.'

'So I found Clarissa and my mother here, being held captive,' Michael said, not appearing to hear her reassurance. 'I knew there was a good chance they were demon copies—they were a pair of the really good copies, almost undistinguishable. Even Semias wasn't sure. Semias helped me to get them out, and we escaped, but we were followed by a group of big demons, too big to fight, so I've learned my lesson and this time I'll be clever, right? I turned my Inner Eye on the demons and destroyed them. Go me, I did it. I smiled the biggest smile ever, turned around to share how clever I was with my wife and mother ...'

'Oh no,' Simone said.

'Gone in a blast of my Eye,' he moaned. 'I mean, I knew there was a good chance that they were copies, but they were self-aware—Clarissa had a meltdown at the possibility of being a demon copy when I first met her. They *knew*. And they were still my wife, and my mother, and ...' His voice hitched. 'I killed them because I'm a fucking idiot.'

She put her hand on his. 'We're a pair of fucking idiots together.'

He grunted a short laugh and repeated what she'd said. 'Don't tell anyone, I couldn't handle the shame. Nobody else knows how stupid I was, except for Semias, and he's stuck here.'

'You know I'll keep your confidence, lad,' Semias said gruffly.

She tapped his hand. 'Deal.' She sighed. 'Well, we have these spears now, and my right arm is still good, so I guess it's time to play Exterminators, because I'm *hungry*.'

'I saw your energies resonate. I've never seen two people who are a better match—why are you not together?' Semias asked.

'Do *not* take that concept any further,' Simone said. 'You remember the Clarissa copy?'

'Yes, she was brilliant and brave, but you—'

'The real Clarissa was his wife, and she was smart and courageous and kind and wonderful—and died in childbirth three days ago,' Simone said.

'And you don't even care, Michael?' Semias asked with disbelief. 'You seemed totally devoted to the copy ...'

'Our Supreme God took my grief away so I can ... *focus*,' Michael said bitterly.

'Oh.' Semias nodded. 'I understand. Don't mind me, the city is blunt sometimes. I'm not a person, so I can occasionally be a little too honest.'

'Autistic city,' Michael said, standing and helping Simone to her feet.

'I don't know what that means,' Semias said. 'How many demons can you take down now that you're armed? I can make some spectral images to draw them out in small groups for you.'

'Three at a time with only one arm,' Simone said. 'For both of us, I mean. Michael's exhausted.' She looked down at the smashed demon corpse. It hadn't dissipated into black goo, its corpse was like that of a living thing with a hard, black shell. 'What's going on with these? Why don't they vaporise?'

'Do Western demons not dissolve into goo?' Michael asked Semias.

'They used to, but they seem to have more human in them since they invaded, and now they die like living things,' Semias said. 'Most disturbing.'

Michael glanced at Simone. 'You're okay with that?'

'With what?' Simone asked.

Michael waved one hand at the smashed corpse. 'You were covered in it. You didn't seem bothered at all.'

Simone looked away. 'When these Western hybrids first turned up, Emma called a family meeting about it. They knew I'd be fighting them. She and Dad offered me desensitisation training.'

'Good lord, you didn't—'

'Pigs,' Simone said. She raised one hand at his horrified expression. 'Dead ones, don't worry. We must have gone through at least fifty of them before I stopped throwing up.' She glanced down at the corpse. 'I still have nightmares, but you see enough of it, and it's not the shock it used to be.' She looked up at Michael. 'It isn't bothering you, either.'

'If you want to be a Horseman you have to work for six months in the medical centre,' Michael said, and quirked a smile. 'I'm probably registrable as an OR nurse.'

'That's a good alternative, I should suggest it to them,' Simone said. She turned to Semias. 'Let's go hunting. Can you bring some more for us?'

'Yes,' Semias said, shifted to his stained-glass structure, and then fell vertically into the ground. He spoke from somewhere beneath their feet. 'Making spectral bait for a patrol now. On their way.' He shot back up out of the ground and changed to human again. 'About a hundred yards, on the right. If you listen, you can hear them.'

Simone cocked her head and heard the demons' footsteps—three of them. She hefted the spear in her right hand and tapped its tip on the ground to feel its weight, balance and flex. It was terrible. She held her left arm against her side and bound it to her with energy like a sling, then spoke to Michael telepathically as the pearly aura of Semias's invisibility appeared in her vision.

I'll have a go at binding them, and you take them down.

If you can hold them, I can experiment and see where their weak points are for a single-hit kill, he replied.

She nodded, he nodded back, and the demons walked into view around the edge of one of the stained-glass buildings. She used the most basic demon binding manoeuvre—pulling half their demon energy out—and all three of them froze with expressions of confusion.

'Got them,' she said out loud. 'Go play.'

He leapt forward and shot over the ground without touching it, landing in front of the demons in an impressive display of control. He shoved his spear through the head of the one on the left, and it didn't seem damaged.

'Still got them?' he asked.

'Yeah,' she said. 'Try slicing its head off, that didn't do anything, it's still active.'

He took the demon's head off with a swing of the spear—its bluntness making it require more effort than a good spear would—and the demon fell into two pieces, obviously dead.

He shoved the spear into the next demon approximately where a human heart would be located, and it made some awful gasping noises, scrabbled at the shaft of the spear, and fell as well.

'Weak point found,' he said with grim amusement. 'Let's try energy.'

He turned to the last one and hit it with a ball of chi. The explosion was three times larger than it would have been with an Asian demon and he was knocked back. He did a graceful cat-like somersault in the air and skidded backwards to a halt close to Simone and Semias.

'Harder to control, but the energy rush is sweet,' he said, and spun the spear in his hands. 'Damn, I feel good.' He turned to grin at Simone and Semias. 'Next!'

15

'How many more to go?' Simone asked twenty minutes later. She picked up one of the dead demons' swords and gave it an experimental swing. It was an interesting design, obviously based on a Japanese katana, curved with a simple handle wrapped in leather and a minimal guard, but it had been modified to be a Western-style wider, double-edged weapon. 'Terrible balance, their forge is worthless. Rubbish, but it'll do.'

'There are just over ten of them left, in my centre, and they've worked out that their patrols aren't coming back and called for reinforcements,' Semias said as he dragged the most recent bodies to the growing pile of dead demons. 'It should take them about half-an-hour to arrive at the least—there aren't any demons closer than that.'

'More than half of their number gone before they got smart,' Michael said. He shook out his shoulders. 'Let's finish this.' He turned to Semias. 'Once we have them out of your city, can you open a portal for Hades and Persephone to take over?'

Semias paused, watching them, and Michael opened his mouth to say something, but Semias interrupted him.

'Not until a new High Lord is on the Throne of Heaven. I suggest you have a quick sit on the throne, open the portal, bring them up and hand it over.'

'Not Simone?' Michael asked. 'She's much more powerful

than me.'

'Her demon nature precludes her from taking it,' Semias said. 'It must be you.'

'Okay.' Michael studied Semias with a penetrating look. 'I won't be tied to the throne or anything? I can pass it to someone else?'

'Absolutely, yes. You can pass it to someone else if you choose.'

'Can I stay after all the demons are gone? With my corrupted nature?' Simone asked.

'Not corrupted!' Michael said, protesting.

Semias gestured towards Michael. 'If he takes the throne, he can grant you permission to stay before he expels the demons.'

'The "Food of Heaven" that Persephone mentioned—can you make it for me?'

'Once all the demons are gone—all of them—yes, I can, but he'll already be on the throne so it will be irrelevant,' Semias said, and smiled. 'I never thought I would see these Heavens alive again. Thank you.'

'Good.' Michael nodded to Simone. 'Ready?'

'I suggest you start by running your Inner Eye over them to thin the ranks, then both of us take the leader—' Simone started, then spoke to Semias. 'Any idea how big the leader is?'

Semias shook his head. 'Afraid not, Highness. Free me from the corruption of the demon presence, and I'll be able to do everything you ask and a whole lot more.'

'Okay,' Michael said. 'Let's go.' He swung his sword. 'Using my Inner Eye is draining me, so let's get this done and out of the way and we can stop for a while.'

'Before you do,' Semias said. 'What is this "okay" thing you keep saying? It's obvious it means "yes" or "let's go" or general affirmative—and I can see that it's two letters from your alphabet, but why those two letters? O and K? What do they *stand for*?'

Michael's expression went blank. 'I have no idea.'

'I know why, but it's a long story and I'll explain when

we've cleared your city,' Simone said.

'Looking forward to hearing it once we have Semias settled,' Michael said.

They shared a nod and followed Semias as he walked towards the centre of the city.

'My human body can fly when I'm free of demons,' Semias grumbled quietly. 'I really miss that. I'll make you invisible when we approach them, so you can strategise.'

The demons had set up a makeshift camp in the middle of the city on the raised avenue in what appeared to be a dead park that sat at the level of the roofs of the two-storey houses around it. An expanse of dirt, which would originally have been lawn, spread over the area, dotted with planter boxes, and a flowing shell-like sculpture of opalescent white stone stood in the centre. The demons didn't require shelter or much in the way of food or water, so only weapons racks, surrounded by piles of dead plant matter stood at the edge of the clearing. Half the demons were, interestingly, lying on the ground in an impersonation of sleep, something Eastern demons didn't do—Eastern ones just stood upright, parked and unresponsive. The rest sat in a small circle and talked quietly while three guarded the perimeter.

There were ten of the big black things, five smaller human-shaped demons who looked like male British skinheads—shaved heads and cruel expressions—and a single leader that made Simone stop and stare until Michael pulled her behind a planter box. The leader was a copy of Simone.

I can't distinguish you from the demon, he said telepathically. *You have about the same amount of demon essence and as far as I can see, she's you.*

What's your daughter's name? Simone asked him.

His expression filled with wonder. *I'm a dad! I have a daughter!* He went grim. *Larissa, after her mother.*

That's the code word.

Gotcha. He poked his head up to see the demons—they were standing quietly in the middle of the park, armed and alert.

Reinforcements are on their way, Simone said. She had a brilliant idea. *They may not be able to tell us apart either. Be ready to back me up, I'll pretend to be the reinforcements and take the leader by surprise.*

He stared at her. *I can't let you—*

Too late, she said, hefted the rubbish sword, and shot into the air. She flew a hundred metres back from the gathered demons in the centre of the city, then spoke to Michael.

Ask Semias to take down the invisibility.

Done.

The pearly edge to her vision disappeared. She gathered herself and broke the sound barrier—throwing the dead vegetation into the air—as she rushed to the centre of the city and screamed to a halt, then dived to land next to the shocked demons, sending a spray of gravel around her from the impact. She bound her left arm to her side, hopefully looking natural, and strolled to the leader of the demons. 'You sent for help.'

The demon tossed her head, and the expression on her face was cruel. 'Help, yes. You, no.'

'Deal with it. I was ordered here, probably to replace you because ...' Simone glanced around. 'This is all you have left? Didn't you have like ... thirty or something?' She grinned at the copy. 'You are in *big* trouble.'

The other Simone's face went cunning. She grabbed a sword from a rack, hesitated, then spun and swung at Simone's neck in a vicious sweep. Simone easily fended her off with her own sword, pushed her arm in the direction it was already going, then struck the copy's hand with the hilt of the sword to disarm her, making the sword spin away. The other Simone stopped, stepped back, and studied her with loathing.

The demons gathered to watch, some of them grinning with anticipation.

'You forgot everything you were taught while you've been sitting here fucking around,' Simone said with vicious delight as she moved the copy closer to where Michael was hiding. 'I, on the other hand, have been learning from the best. I managed to snag one of the young ones that was taught by that Emma thing, and it gave me a bunch of nice techniques.' She raised her sword, facing the other Simone copy. 'Go on, get the sword. Bring it. This'll be fun.'

'You're supposed to be my reinforcements!' the other Simone said. 'Something's been taking out my thralls and you need to help me!' She sounded desperate. 'Weren't those Rhonda's orders?'

Simone nearly dropped the act when she heard Rhonda's name, then gathered herself. 'Yeah, until you attacked me,' she said. 'Now it's personal.'

The other Simone edged backwards without taking her eyes off Simone, picked up her sword, and rushed her.

The demon copy was trained, but Simone had been learning from the best since before she could walk. The demon made a swing for her head so fast that it would have been invisible to a human, but Simone had already cut her in half horizontally at waist level. The two pieces separated and collapsed into a heap, looking like a pile of cow entrails from the market.

Simone didn't give the demons time to think. She strode to the centre of the garden area and turned on the spot to eye them. They stood looking at her and she scowled. 'Why aren't you kneeling? I just took out your lord!'

The five skinheads fell to one knee and lowered their heads, but the big, winged things stood uncomfortably watching her.

'You want me to kill you too?' she asked them. 'I haven't eaten yet.' She glanced down at the pieces of Simone-demon at the other side of the clearing. 'Shall I eat her, or you?'

One of the winged demons fell to its backwards knees, and the other four followed suit. They still seemed hesitant, and she recognised the need to press the advantage before they realised she wasn't who they thought she was. They appeared much more intelligent than the ones they'd already encountered, and she had to move fast.

'Rhonda said I was to come here because something has killed about half of her ...' She waved dismissively at the other

Simone. 'Thralls. What was it?'

'We don't know, ma'am,' one of the black demons said. 'Something is sitting at the edge of the city—probably near the gates—and started picking off the patrols. We sent a larger group out and they all disappeared as well.'

'Brilliant,' she said with scorn. 'Shall we go and see what's going on, then? All of you, with me.'

The demons nodded and rose, collecting their weapons from the racks.

Simone sensed the reinforcements—five demons flying in at speed. She didn't glance at Michael, hoping that he sensed them as well. 'Form up around me, you two ...' She indicated a couple of black demons. 'In the van, in front, and the rest around and behind me.'

'Why don't we have to obey her?' one of the skinheads whispered to a black demon. 'It's like she's just talking, there's no will behind it.'

'Because I'm such a good copy that you're not sure if I'm the real thing or not!' Simone shouted. *Any time,* she said to Michael, then switched to out loud. 'Feel free to disobey me, you'll end up like my other copy. So, let's go find out what's been killing our thralls.'

'No, this is wrong,' one of the black demons said.

The reinforcements landed into the clearing. They were more of the big winged black things, and Simone hoped that Michael was paying attention because there were now more demons than she was comfortable taking down one-handed.

Duck, Michael said.

'About time!' Simone shouted, hit the ground and lay flat, wincing as the shock went through her injured left arm. Michael's Inner Eye seared above her, and the demons were gone. She pulled herself to her feet, brushed herself off and heard something hit the ground behind her. She turned to see that Michael, his face slack, had fallen to his knees. He toppled over, hitting his head hard as he fell.

'Oh no, his head!' she shouted, and flew to him, correcting her low-gravity rush at the last second, and slid to a halt next to him. She rolled him onto his back and concentrated on his head, unable to see inside.

Semias appeared next to her as she sat and placed Michael's head into her lap as she checked him. He was limp and unconscious.

'You were supposed to thin the ranks, not destroy them all, you idiot. I could have handled the big ones.' She looked up at Semias. 'Do you have medical facilities here?'

'Not yet, the demon corpses need to be gone before I can fully reassemble,' Semias said. 'He hit the ground hard, but I don't think he's done any major damage—'

'He's had a brain injury before, there's a great deal of scarring here,' Simone said. She ran her fingertips over his scalp, not finding any major lumps or blood. 'I can't see inside while I'm contaminated like this. You'll need to check inside his head.'

'I don't see any bleeding inside his skull, I think it's exhaustion,' Semias said. 'Can you carry him? We can take him into one of the residences and you can rest and wash and eat, and he can recover.'

'All right,' Simone said, and rose. She bent and lifted Michael to carry him over her good shoulder. 'Where to?'

'This way,' Semias said, and led her past the garden and onto one of the raised walkways. 'About a hundred yards.'

'I hope you can provide us with something to eat and drink,' Simone said, concerned by Michael's extended unconsciousness. He was completely limp in her arms. 'If he has a brain injury, can you fix him?'

'Not as long as that pile of demon corpses sits next to my gates, contaminating my essence,' Semias said. 'Basic food and drink, yes. Healing, no.'

He led Simone to a small, square, balcony-type extension off the soaring walkway with a waist-high barrier around three sides. The ground of the walkway and balcony was covered in what appeared to be glass tiles, deep blue and glossy, but they didn't feel slippery underfoot. They were smokily transparent, and the ground below was dimly visible through them. Semias gestured towards the balcony. 'Stand on this and I will take you down to the residence.'

'When I've settled him, I can remove the demon corpses,' Simone said. 'If we leave them for a couple of days, will they dissolve into black goo by themselves?'

'You've seen these ones before,' Semias said, and a third wall appeared at the edge of the balcony. It became an open-air lift, large enough to hold ten people, that slid downwards without any feeling of movement. 'That would not be a good option, as their essence would contaminate my soil. If you can remove their bodies, I'll be able to start mending myself, and see about …' He touched Michael's head. 'Mending him too.'

'He's not waking up,' Simone said, her voice full of urgency. 'Don't you die on me here, Michael MacLaren, I need you.'

'He said the Inner Eye was draining him,' Semias said.

'I hope that's all it is.'

Simone followed Semias along a lower-level avenue that appeared to be a pedestrian boulevard, shaded by the causeway above, and not broad enough to accommodate vehicles that were more than a couple of people wide. Empty planter boxes dotted the footpath, again with dead vegetation in them. Two-storey mansions, made entirely of stained glass, stood on either side of the boulevard, behind waist-high stained-glass fences that led into gardens the size of a modern front yard. The glass walls of the houses were splintered and broken between the metal pillars and stained with mud. Many of the roofs had fallen in, but some of them still had intact towers and spires that looked much too tall and slender to stay upright.

'This is all very suburban,' she said, and looked around. 'Which one?'

'Michael and the demon copies of his wife and mother were in the mayor's palace before, and I don't think it would be an idea to put you there again,' Semias said. He opened the metal-and-glass gate of the mansion in front of them and gestured her through. 'This way.'

The mansion had white stone Corinthian columns holding

the roof of the stained-glass portico on the front. The front door was a single sheet of shattered, opaque blue-green glass in a metal frame, which rebuilt itself as she approached. She entered the building, holding Michael, and stopped.

It was shaped like a stained-glass version of a traditional Roman building, similar to the ones she'd seen when she visited Pompeii during her gap year. It reconstructed itself as she walked past the shallow, rectangular marble fountain in the central courtyard to the stairs at the back leading up to the first floor. The walls and ceiling were all frosted glass, and its transparency filled the interior with a blue-green morning sunlight.

'To the left,' Semias said. 'In the dining room.'

She turned left and went through another glass door that was in the process of recreating itself. The walls reconstructed themselves to show elaborate scenes of revelry in stained glass, showing the ancient gods in a feast with wine, music and song. The exterior wall's transparency again filled the room with a glowing golden light.

'Can't do anything until those corpses are gone, this is so frustrating,' Semias grumbled behind her, then his voice changed to chagrined. 'Not blaming you, Princess, you've done so much for me already. I just wish I had full control of my city so I could show you all I'm capable of.'

Simone nodded and stopped in the dining room. There was a central silver-and-glass organically curving table surrounded by similarly constructed chairs. The table deconstructed itself to its glass and metal components and remade itself into a bed. A feather ticking mattress, covered in rough grey linen, appeared on the frame but there was no pillow. She laid Michael on the bed, shook her sore left arm, then fell to her knees next to him. He was still unconscious, and she was unable to see him internally to ascertain whether it was brain damage or just being drained.

'Can you see inside his head now that we're in a house?' she asked Semias without looking away from Michael.

Before Semias could reply, Michael stirred, and she gasped

with relief. He winced with pain, and she took his hand. He opened his eyes and blinked at the ceiling, obviously confused.

'It's okay, I'm here,' Simone said, squeezing his hand.

'Simone? Where? Oh.' He struggled to sit up and failed. 'What happened?'

'You knocked yourself out with your Inner Eye,' Simone said. 'Over-used instead of under-used, this time.'

He flashed a quick, wry smile and sighed. 'I take it they're all gone?'

'All gone, lad. Thank you,' Semias said.

Michael touched his temple with his free hand. 'Whoa, that's the headache from hell.'

'You fell flat on your silly face,' Simone said. She turned to Semias. 'Food? Water? Rest?'

'The kitchen is the room next door. What would you like to eat? What do people today eat? This region's specialties are roast boar, apples, cow's milk cheese, soft bread, and pickled cabbage. Some nice pig pancreas? Clarissa and Rhonda—'

Both Simone and Michael winced, and Semias stopped.

'I don't eat meat,' Simone said. 'Anything vegetable. Mushrooms. Pasta?'

'What's pasta? They never mentioned that.'

'Never mind,' Simone said. 'Just whatever you gave ... the copies.'

'My head hurts like hell, I think I hit it pretty hard,' Michael said. 'Can you heal me, Semias?'

'I can't help you until those demon corpses are gone,' Semias said.

'I can transform to heal the injury, but I'll be stuck in Tiger form for a while,' Michael said to Simone. 'But if I eat in tiger form ...'

'Good idea, it will help you rebuild your energy as well,' Simone said. 'And I've seen your father eat, it doesn't bother me. Get some protein into you, it'll do you a lot of good. I'm okay with you having half a haunch of wild boar as a tiger. Go for it.'

Michael nodded and grunted as he climbed off the bed,

shifted down to a crouch, and changed to a gold-and-white tiger, paler than a natural animal but not as white as his father.

Simone smiled. 'Pretty fur.'

'Thank you,' he said, and shook his head, making his bushy tiger mane swing. 'I feel much better.' He looked around with his golden tiger eyes. 'Semias?'

'Right here, lad,' Semias said, entering the room with a large metal platter of grilled vegetables floating next to him. The bed transformed back to a table, and the platter laid itself onto the surface. Another large platter of fruit, bread and cheese landed next to it, with apples, grapes and small apricots. 'That's the best I can do, I have trouble conjuring food when it's out of season. Did you say raw haunch of boar? How about deer?'

'Sounds good,' Michael said, his voice a throaty growl, and another platter entered the room and landed in front of his nose, holding a raw, bleeding lump of meat with a deer's leg and hoof sticking out of it.

'Wine to drink?' Semias asked. 'Ale? Mead? Posca?'

'Water, please,' Simone said, and a jug and two cups, all made of earthenware pottery, appeared on the table next to the food. 'Thank you.'

'Eat and rest while I rebuild the rest of the house so that you can wash and sleep,' Semias said. 'Then I need to rest as well.' He changed to his automaton self and fell straight into the ground to disappear. The rest of the house made grinding and clinking sounds as it put itself back together.

There weren't any individual plates, so Simone grabbed an apple and crunched into it. It was harder and sourer than modern apples, but she was too hungry to care. She tried a grape from the bunch of red ones in front of her and found it as sweet and juicy as any modern version, although it had multiple large seeds. She emptied the grapes out of their pottery bowl onto the platter, filled the bowl with water, and placed it next to Michael's gruesome meal so that he could drink.

He stopped crunching on the bone and looked away.

'Don't stop eating, I'm fine with it,' she said. 'My father's

Turtle form makes the most *disgusting* noises when he's eating a bowl full of the most *gross* stinky cat food. And I don't even want to talk about him and Emma's Serpents eating, that's even more gross. This—this is normal.'

'You sure?' he asked, blood staining the white fur of his jowls.

'Absolutely positive,' she said. She tore a hunk of bread from the circular loaf and used a knife to cut a slice of cheese to put on top of it. She took a bite and it tasted as good as any modern food. The cheese was tart, and the bread was soft and warm. She tried a grilled purple root vegetable and it turned out to be a purple carrot, and there was squash and broccoli but no potatoes. 'I guess people weren't vegetarian in the Iron Age.'

'They were, but they called it "fasting" on holy days and it was for religious reasons. Spiritual purity. That sort of thing,' Semias said from somewhere near the ceiling.

'That's why I'm vegetarian,' Simone said, bit into an apricot, and winced. It was harder and sourer than the apple.

When they'd finished eating, Michael lay on his side in tiger form on the stone floor and licked himself clean. He lifted one front paw and cleaned the pads, then nibbled between his toes, his eyes half-closed with bliss. He lifted his hind leg like a cat, sat with it in the air for a long minute, then put it back down again and busied himself licking the back of his front paws.

Simone went to the floor and sat next to him. She rested her chin on her knees and wrapped her arms around her legs. 'How much do you remember about what happened before you passed out?'

He looked up from his paws. 'I heard what she said.'

Simone lowered her head. 'I am so sorry.'

Michael dropped his head onto his paws with a throaty sigh. 'I knew it was a possibility. My father warned me about them.' He licked the back of his paw again, his tongue making a rasping sound over his fur. 'Mostly copies of Emma, Rhonda, and you—serpent women. Not so many of Clarissa, because she was …' He swallowed it. 'She wasn't a fighter, and she was an ordinary human.' He studied his paws. 'If we see my mother …' He looked up at her, his tawny eyes intense. 'Could you do it for me? I don't think I could.'

'Ditto if we meet an Emma copy?' Simone asked.

He raised one paw and she tapped it. 'Deal.'

'It's dark now, I guess we sleep here the night and then tomorrow we find this throne.' She glanced up. Semias wasn't visible. 'Where is the throne, anyway?'

'Close to the region's centre, next to the river Musell, in a city called Treurorum or Treverorum for the Romans,' Semias said. He shot out of the floor and sat on one of the chairs to speak to them with his elbows on his knees. 'It's floating crystals, and you'll have to fly to the topmost one. It's close to the top of the air layer, so I hope you're capable of dealing with a very thin atmosphere.'

'I've seen those crystals,' Simone said with wonder. 'I didn't go up and visit them, I was looking for a way back out of these Heavens.'

Michael stopped grooming his paw, stretched his claws out and yawned. 'I'll have to stay in Tiger form overnight, and I'll be in clean human form when I change back.' He glanced at Simone. 'You rinsed yourself off after you killed that demon, but you should know that…'

'Yeah, I stink. I'm sweaty and gritty and there are still gross demon bits on me.' Simone turned to Semias. 'Is there a bathroom where I can wash?'

'Yes, it's across the other side of the atrium,' Semias said. 'No hot water, but there is a bath for you, and I can put a fire underneath it …'

'No need, I can heat the water myself,' Simone said, and patted Michael's tiger rump. 'I'll be right back.'

She stopped halfway across the courtyard, next to the marble fountain in its rectangular glass pool, which was empty of water. 'Semias?'

'Yes, Princess?'

'I need to use the latrine. Can you show me the way?'

'It's at the back of the house, past the kitchen, in its own outbuilding,' Semias said. 'The demon copies of Michael's wife and mother told me some most interesting things about modern latrines, and I hope I can see how they work very soon.'

'Thank you.' Simone went through the echoing, empty rooms to a small yard attached to the back of the house, bare of greenery. A long, narrow outhouse—a single building with a sloping roof—stood against the back fence. Interestingly, it was made of glass bricks rather than the sheets of glass used for the rest of the building, with a sloping, glass-tiled roof. She opened the door and there were five stone toilet seats in a row over what appeared to be a cesspit, with wooden covers on the openings to keep the smell out. She saw the sponge attached to a long stick sitting in a bucket of water to one side and shook her head. It was straight out of a history lesson.

'Communal?' she wondered aloud as she looked for the cleanest-looking seat.

'No, everyone had their own,' Semias said from somewhere above her. 'If someone was using it, others would wait—unless it was really urgent.'

'Out. This is private,' she said.

'I can't see you,' he said.

The bathroom was in one of the rooms at the front of the house with a single bath, no basin, and the drain running out into the street. The bath was a rectangular, glass-tiled area with sides raised from the floor, and it was already full of lovely clear water. Simone disrobed, heated the water, and sank into it up to her waist. There was a glass bottle full of some sort of bath oil to one side and she pulled off the stopper and sniffed it. It smelled of sweet clover and she studied it. She hesitated about asking Semias, as the spirit had been very clear about his sexual enthusiasm, and she didn't want to be naked in front of him.

She poured some of the thick liquid onto her hand, put the bottle down and rubbed her hands together to discover with delight that it was a floral, sweet-smelling liquid soap. She exited the bath to wash Japanese-style, covering herself in the frothy soap and lathering her hair. She rinsed herself off with conjured water, and then returned to the bath, feeling clean for the first time in ages. She sighed and closed her eyes, then sank under the water completely to soak. She was tempted to spend the night in the water, but it would cool quickly without her conscious attention, and the night was promising to be cold.

She dried herself and conjured fresh clothing that was more suited to the fight she expected the next day—a good, supportive sports bra, yoga pants and a long-sleeved T-shirt with a simple leather vest over the top for armour. As she braided her long hair, she mourned not being able to pull her lovely custom-made armour to herself—Moaner at Wudang Mountain's forge had spent weeks tweaking it to fit her perfectly. She headed back towards the dining room, then stopped and went out to the yard. There had been gardens, but everything was dead. She looked up for a while, appreciating the Celestial stars, then went inside.

16

She returned to the dining room to find Semias sitting at the dining table and Michael, still in Tiger form, reclining on the floor. The food on the table was reduced to a single earthenware bowl of apples, pears and grapes next to the jug and cups, looking like a mediaeval still-life painting.

'So there were human farmers who provided the bulk of it,' Semias said, obviously in the middle of explaining something to Michael. 'If there was a delicacy that the Gods needed *right now*, I transformed the dirt into the food, and of course there's the Food of Heaven, which I made the same way.'

'The food we just ate was transformed *dirt*?' Simone asked.

'All food is transformed dirt, Princess,' Semias said. 'I just have the ability to skip some of the steps.'

Michael raised his tiger head and his nostrils flared. 'You smell really nice!' he exclaimed. 'Like flowers.'

'What was that soap?' Simone asked Semias. 'It made my hair lovely and clean, and it was so gentle I didn't need conditioner.'

'What's conditioner?' Semias said, then waved it away. 'It's a decoction of soapwort. The lye soap the Celts use is too strong for skin, but it's good on clothing.'

'What's soapwort?' Michael asked.

A bunch of tiny white five-petaled flowers appeared on the

ground in front of his nose.

'That is,' Semias said. 'Now for your sleeping arrangements.'

'He's running low on energy with those demon corpses sitting next to the gate,' Michael said to Simone. 'The best he can do is re-make the bed out of the dining table. I'll sleep on the floor, I'm comfortable like this.'

'I can move those demons now—' Simone began.

'In the morning,' Semias said. 'I can see how tired both of you are.' His smile turned knowing. 'I can make a bigger bed for you to share, if you like.'

Michael shot him a glare under his tiger brows. 'You are trying to throw us together.'

'You belong together.'

'Not yet,' Michael said. 'So make me a mat and I'll sleep like this on the floor, and make a bed for Simone.'

Semias shot a querying look at Simone, confirming Michael's choice.

'If you could, please,' Simone said.

'Very well,' Semias grumbled and stood. A mat made of finely woven reeds appeared on the floor, and Michael moved onto it.

He grinned a tiger grin. 'This is spongy, like rubber tubing. I love it.'

Simone sat on the reed mat next to Michael and put her hand on his side to stroke his fur as she watched the bed assemble itself next to the mat. She realised what she was doing and jerked her hand away. 'Oh God, I am so sorry. I'm so exhausted I forget where I am, and for a moment I thought you were your dad.'

'It's fine, I'm wrecked too,' Michael said. He lowered his head. 'But there's something we need to talk about. We'll be going to the throne tomorrow, and I have this ... premonition. Future view. I *know* what will happen, and it's not good.'

Simone watched him silently.

'Oh,' he said. 'You've seen it too, of course you have.' He looked away. 'I'll be imprisoned, and you'll return alone, and

...' He turned back to gaze at her. 'It'll be the right thing to do.'

Simone looked down at her hands and shook her head.

'Is that what you see as well?' he asked.

'I see ...' She looked up to gaze into his tawny eyes. 'I see me. Going home. By myself. Full of rage, because I left someone I ...' She didn't finish it. 'I left them behind.' She shrugged. 'That's all. But I've seen it at least a dozen times now.' She put her hand on his paw. 'I don't want to lose you! And you've suffered enough. You need to come home with me when this is done and put yourself back together.' Her voice broke. 'Please come home with me.'

'Semias?' Michael asked.

There was no reply. The spirit had finished the bed and disappeared again.

Michael turned back to Simone. 'Semias has never lied to us. Both of us can tell. Everything he's said to us has been absolutely truthful. When I sit on the throne, I can pass it off to Hades. But ...'

'Yeah,' Simone said. 'The stories of the Fae. They couldn't tell a lie, so they'd find clever ways to bend the truth, and have loopholes in all their agreements ...'

'And that's where we are now.'

'Let's skip this throne business, find a portal and go home.'

He shook his head. 'You know that isn't an option. Even if we did have one of those skinhead demons to smash so we can open the portal, we don't know where the portal is. The only way we can leave this place is if I go and sit on the stupid throne.'

'Just promise you won't get stuck on it.'

He put his other paw on top of her hand, and the pads were cool, like soft chamois. 'I promise. I want to go home, and sort myself out, and then maybe, one day, have my daughter back again.' He stretched out his front paws and rested his head on them. 'Sleep now, and tomorrow we'll try to fight fate.'

Simone peeled off the leather vest, climbed onto the bed and rolled onto her right side with her injured arm on top. She hesitantly stretched her hand out, and Michael shifted so that he was directly next to the bed, and she could touch his fur. She buried her fingers in it, then stroked it.

'Thank you,' she said. 'Your fur is lovely. You don't take tiger form nearly often enough.'

'It scared Clarissa,' he said, his voice rough. 'I wonder if Larissa will be able to transform? Sometimes the transformation ability carries down through the generations, if the ancestor is a very large Shen.'

'Did you warn Clarissa's mother—what was her name?'

'Christine, and I couldn't, because she doesn't know about us.'

'Oh, Michael. I think you made a terrible mistake when you allowed her to take your daughter.'

'When I have my grief back, I don't think I'll care. Sleep now, and we'll try to fight fate and our own ability to see the future—tomorrow.'

Michael was in human form and dressed in his white jeans and a yellow V-neck sweater over a polo shirt when Simone woke the next morning. He and Semias were sitting together on the floor mat with a platter of bread, cheese and fruit between them.

Michael smiled at her. 'We were talking for ages, and you didn't wake up.'

'Yeah, I think I was nearly as wrecked as you were,' she said. 'And that bath felt *amazing*.'

He gestured towards the platter. 'So is the bread.'

'In a minute,' she said, rolled out of the bed and raced into the back yard to the latrine.

She returned to sit with them and pulled a pie-shaped, pre-marked chunk out of the round loaf, then placed some of the tasty cheese on it. An earthenware plate appeared in front of her, and she took a bite of the bread, placed it onto the plate and added a small bunch of grapes next to it.

'After not eating for a couple of days, the fibre from all this fruit has hit my digestion hard,' she said ruefully. 'I hope I don't have to run for a loo break halfway through you sitting on the stupid throne.'

'I thought you could handle this with your manipulation of water?' Michael asked with a cheeky smile that showed his charming dimples.

'Not water,' she said, quirking a smile back at him.

He looked down. 'Emma used to call it that. "You kids need a loo break? Go now because you won't have a chance later! This shopping centre has no public toilets."'

'And you'd respond with—'

'I'm not a kid!' they said in unison.

He shook his head, rueful. 'I was such a little kid.'

'We both were.'

He glanced up into her eyes. 'In many ways you were more mature than I was. After losing your mother, then having to protect yourself while your father faded away ...' He looked away. 'Sorry. They say girls mature faster—but it's more that you see a heap of ugly shit from a very young age. I remember the girls in my high school class—sharing self-defence tips for moving through a world that could attack them at any time.'

'You've seen more than your fair share as well,' she said, putting her hand on his. He turned his hand over to hold hers, and they shared a moment of contented closeness. He understood what she'd been through, and was probably the only man in the world who truly did.

He gazed into her eyes, and the world disappeared. 'One day we will be together, and it will be wild, and perfect, and wonderful, and infuriating.' He kissed her hand and released it. 'Remember that through the lonely time ahead. It will happen for us.'

She wiped the tears from her eyes. 'Don't give up, we can still change the future and go home together. Emma did it. She went to Hell, even though all their advisors told her that she would *die* if she did. My little brother popped up in Hell, was his usual random, powerful self, and pushed her into a timeline that nobody predicted—one where she didn't die.'

'Why did she go if she knew she would die? Why would your father let her go?'

'They went together as a last-ditch effort to forge a new treaty with the demons and avoid the war,' she said. 'They knew that if she didn't go with him, we would lose my dad instead. He would be imprisoned there, and we'd have no chance of winning the war.'

'We lost the war anyway,' he said grimly. He shook his head. 'I didn't know she did that. What an incredibly courageous thing to do.' His voice filled with awe. 'And he went along with it? Knowing she was walking to her death? Just, "Let's traipse into Hell so you can die"? I would never sacrifice the one I love for the Heavens.'

'She made it very clear that it wasn't his sacrifice to make. He tried to talk her out of it, and apparently—I wasn't there— she told him, "If you respect me, then butt out, because it's my decision." Mention it now and she'll refer to it as "My most stupid and pointless Hell junket of them all".'

'I believe it.'

Semias appeared next to them. 'When she was here, she was fearless and powerful and never gave up. She would be a tremendous asset to these Heavens.'

'She's already ruling a quarter of the Heavens with my father back home, and doing a terrific job,' Simone said. 'She will never agree to that.'

'After the lad is enthroned, you can bring more than just Hades and Persephone up,' Semias said, brightening. 'Gods of European heritage from other Centres can help us to rebuild and repopulate these Heavens. More gods here will have a cleansing effect on the Earthly Plane below. I may be able to conjure food from dirt, but I'm certainly not capable of making people.'

'We sent an Immortal woman of European heritage to the European Earthly Plane with her husband, and she wandered around for three months with no success,' Simone said.

'Tell her to return once Hades has the throne,' Semias said.

Michael and Simone shared a nod and rose. Simone put her leather vest back on, then turned to Michael. 'Would you like some armour? Just in case?'

'Please,' he said, and she conjured it and passed it to him. He slipped it around himself and zipped up the front opening.

'Hold on, what is that closure method?' Semias asked and moved closer. 'May I touch?'

'Good job asking permission,' Michael said, and showed him how the zipper worked. 'This?'

'That is *so clever*!' Semias said with awe. 'A simple mechanical design that is much faster than laces. Leave this behind when you go, so that I can copy it.'

'Wait until you see mobile phones,' Michael said. 'After we work out how to get some signal up here. Do you still have yours?'

Simone pulled her phone out of her pocket and checked it. 'Yes. Still no signal, and battery's at twenty per cent.'

He held his hand out. 'May I?' She passed the phone to him, and he held it with an expression of concentration for a couple of minutes, then handed it back, fully charged. He shook out his shoulders. 'Ready to go? Let's shift these demons, then find the throne.'

'Once we're outside the city, one of you will have to carry me again, I'm afraid,' Semias said ruefully.

'Can you make your human body smaller? You're a little unwieldy,' Simone said.

'No, because it's a skin over my mechanical self,' Semias said.

'I'll hold him, you take point,' Michael said, went to Semias, and lifted him like a child. Semias put his hand on Michael's shoulder and smiled at him.

'Okay, let's go,' she said, and lifted off.

'You still haven't explained the source of that "okay" expression,' Semias called as Michael lifted off behind her.

'And so it became a catch-phrase,' Simone said as they followed the glittering Little Muse River to reach the floating crystals. 'Oll Korrect, because it was super-trendy at the time to use comedic misspellings, and they shortened it to "okay". Sometimes legacy business names do the same thing, usually with the "K"—misspellings in an effort to be cute.'

'Krispy Kreme,' Michael said with awe.

'Kwik Kopy,' Simone said. They arrived at the crystals, and she looked up. 'You said it was the top one, Semias? I can see bridges from the higher ones, but none that link the crystals to ground level. The bridges glitter! They look like spider webs.'

'That's because they are,' Semias said. 'Land on the ground next to the river and we'll find the entrance crystal.'

The river wasn't wide and curved through a valley that had steep hills—almost mountains—on one side and a small plain that held the ruins of a large town on the other. The town's buildings were made of amber-coloured sandstone that glowed in the morning sun.

The crystals floated in an area that spread far further than the town itself. They varied in size from that of a bus close to the ground and becoming larger as they gained altitude to become big enough to carry an entire town high above. Each had a curved, faceted underside and a flat top to carry either a single or a cluster of ruined buildings. The crystals varied in colour, with those closer to the ground being a deep green-blue that faded to sky blue as they reached higher. The crystals at the top weren't visible, they were too high.

Silver bridges that were patterned like thick cobwebs, woven with threads as wide as steel cables, were strung between the crystals. The webbing was damaged, with some pieces hanging down from the bridges, and others having collapsed into a bundle of hanging threads still attached to the crystals at either end.

They landed on the ground, below the lowest crystal, which was a deep grass green. The multitude of tiny facets on its underside made it glitter.

'You said they *are* cobwebs?' Simone asked and shivered. 'How big were the *spiders*?'

Semias glared at her. 'The construction spiders who lived with the Gods on these crystals were intelligent and dextrous and revered craftscreatures. Some of them even had rewarding and respectful romantic relationships with my fellow city guardians when we visited with our mayoral masters.' He quirked a small smile. 'Remarkable lovers. Exquisite.' His smile disappeared. 'They are gone, and no god has the power to return them to life. A great loss. Our new master …' Semias nodded to Michael. 'Will need to be ingenious to think of ways to rebuild the bridges on the crystals without them.'

'What's holding the crystals up?' Simone asked, running her hand over underside of the lowest one. It was the size of a shipping container, and something gold was moving inside it.

'Gravity engines embedded within them,' Semias said, gesturing upwards.

Michael took the hint and lifted Semias onto it, and the cobweb bridge up to the next one hadn't collapsed, so Simone followed them across it. The bridge was as sturdy and unmoving as a steel suspension bridge, with the cobweb a thick mat below her feet. She touched the spiderweb railing, expecting it to be sticky, but it was smooth and slightly fuzzy beneath her hand. She stroked it as she walked up the bridge, enjoying the velvety feeling.

'Michael mentioned these gravity engines in his report,' she said, stepping onto the next crystal up. It was the same size as the first one, with no barrier around the edge, and had a gazebo on it that was almost completely destroyed, with only the lower part of two walls remaining. 'Four-dimensional mechanisms.'

Michael looked down and pointed. 'You can see the engine within this crystal.'

Simone moved next to him and saw that the shell of the crystal was less than a metre thick, leaving the cube-shaped mechanism and its golden clockwork cogs visible working within it.

'This must be the smallest they could make the crystals,' Michael mused. 'Any smaller and it will shoot off into space.'

'Precisely,' Semias said.

'Smaller?' Simone asked, then, 'Oh yeah, I remember. The smaller the engine is, the more powerful it is. I would love to see one working directly, outside of the crystal.'

'Didn't you make one to demonstrate when you made it

home?' Semias asked Michael.

'I didn't take the blueprints with me,' Michael said ruefully. 'I didn't take *anything* useful back except for some basic knowledge.' He lowered his head and shook it. 'I failed miserably.'

'You were lucky the demons didn't have the skill to use the blueprints,' Semias said.

'No, I left important details out, because I didn't want to lose you,' Michael said. 'If they had succeeded in building it, your city would have shot into space, so I made the blueprints incorrect.'

'Clever,' Semias said.

'No,' Michael said. 'I failed completely. You had a library full of vital information, and I didn't take single bit—I didn't even remember anything I'd read. I murdered the copies of my wife and mother by mistake. I couldn't even salvage the blueprint for the gravity engine.'

'I probably would have done exactly the same thing,' Simone said.

'I should have done better,' he said.

'Today, you will have a chance to redeem yourself, by freeing these Heavens from the demon corruption, and returning them to the Gods,' Semias said. He clapped Michael on the shoulder. 'That will more than make up for any mistake you have made in the past.' He pointed. 'The next bridge has collapsed. Can you lift me?'

Michael nodded, lifted Semias, and carried him the fifty metres higher to the next crystal. This one had an ankle-height barrier around the edge, and empty dirt surrounding a ruin the size of a suburban house.

'Is this a little farm?' Simone asked, fascinated, as she approached the house. It was made of brown bricks with a thatched roof that had collapsed a long time ago.

'Small meditation garden and pavilion,' Semias said. He guided them to the next bridge. 'We have at least fifty crystals to traverse, children, and the ones further up are much larger. Shall we move?'

It was mid-morning by the time they were close to the summit. The crystals that high up were nearly transparent, and so large that the gravity engines within them weren't visible from the outside.

The topmost crystal glowed, but it was more than just a shine; brilliant, blinding rays of light emanated from above them, like a miniature cool-white star. An energy similar to shen energy—the energy of the soul—radiated from it, and it lifted Simone's spirits and filled her with vigour. She was concerned that when they were next to the throne the radiance would be overwhelming.

Simone shaded her eyes as she looked up—the light was too bright to observe directly and left blinking after-images if she did. 'Is that the throne glowing? I can feel the energy coming from it.'

'That's it without an occupant to moderate its output, and with demons reducing its power,' Semias said. 'When it's occupied, the radiance is controlled and diverted to maintenance of the Heavens.'

The crystals' flat upper surfaces were now large enough to hold a modern suburb, and the buildings consisted of golden sandstone houses and squares with dry fountains, untouched by the high winds of altitude and completely empty. The gardens were bare earth and the buildings echoed around them with hollowness.

'Nearly there,' Semias said, and shook his head. 'It hurts to see the throne so unconstrained. The residents here would never allow it to run so out of control.' He raised his head. 'At least its energy is adequate to rebuild. You should have little trouble clearing the demons from these Heavens once you have its power in your grasp.'

'Totally terrifying,' Michael said under his breath.

'I agree,' Simone said.

The spider-web bridges at that level were untouched as well, and the atmosphere was so thin that Simone needed to use energy to keep herself alive. There weren't any strong stratospheric winds, but they were in the high, sweeping clouds of altitude, and it was so cold that everything was covered in a rime of frost.

'You okay?' Simone asked Michael as they trekked along an avenue through deserted houses towards the bridge leading to the highest crystals with their glowing aura. 'There isn't much air here.'

'No, I'm good,' Michael said. 'After our stupid trip to the Kunlun Mountains where we nearly died, my dad kind of apologised to me—as much of an apology as that asshole will make, anyway—and taught me some better techniques for dealing with altitude. I'm capable of staying on the moon for more than an hour at a time.'

'I love moon walks,' Simone said. 'The absolute silence and the stars that don't sparkle, but the best part is the lower gravity. Bouncing around up there is like a private jumping castle.'

'How about a quick trip when we get back?'

'Maybe when you have your head back together,' Simone said sadly.

'Ugh. I forgot again.'

They were at the edge of the crystal and Simone looked up, then away. The brilliance coming from the higher crystal was dazzling. She conjured two pairs of sunglasses and handed a pair to Michael. He put them on and stared, open-mouthed, at the island.

'Is there anything we should be prepared for?' Michael asked Semias without looking away from the crystal. 'Demons? Traps? Defences?'

'No,' Semias said. 'The demons can't approach that purity without being destroyed. And the throne itself is its own defence.'

Michael glanced back at Simone. 'Your demon nature okay?'

'It kind of feels like an unpleasant buzz, like being low-level electrocuted,' Simone said. 'Like standing in a really good seal.'

'We'll have that stuff out of you in no time. First thing I'll do when I sit on this stupid throne,' Michael said, and walked onto the bridge up to the final crystal. The bridge was three times as wide as the others, spanning the width of the final, topmost crystal.

The highest crystal was smaller than the previous, with only a single hall on it. The hall was the size of a middle-ages cathedral, and a similar structure to Semias's city—taller than it was wide, and made of silver, with stained glass between the soaring pillars of the walls, which ended in arches at the top. Light shone from inside the building—blinding light—that hit the stained glass and filled the sky with a rainbow of brilliant colours. The roof was covered in spires and spikes, all of gleaming silver, with what appeared to be crystal balls of all hues sitting on the top of the spikes.

'It looks like a madman's design of an electrical transformer,' Michael said.

'I think that's what it is, except for celestial energy instead of electricity,' Simone said. She squared her shoulders. 'Time to save all of Europe.'

'I can do this,' Michael said under his breath.

He started towards the building—the rest of the surface of the crystal was bare, but it was obvious there had once been gardens on this one as well—and Simone stopped him with a hand on his shoulder. He turned to her, questioning, and she threw herself at him and held him tight.

'Please come back with me,' she said into his shoulder.

He was slightly taller than her and buried his face into her neck. 'I want to, more than anything in the world. One day our souls will sing together, and the harmony will be wonderful.' He pulled back to smile at her, and when their eyes met, something rose and joined between them. The union felt like a completion of her soul.

His expression went intense, and he bent to kiss her, but she put her hand on his cheek to stop him.

'Not now,' she said. 'It would be wrong.'

He pulled back, released her, and nodded. 'It would.' He

turned and walked with determination towards the throne room. 'Let's do this.'

17

The throne room's gothic-arched doorway had a rose window above it and stained glass down the sides depicting a number of the Western deities in graceful, flowing robes, engaged in blessing the smaller figures of worshipful humanity.

As they approached, the immensely tall double doors—nearly as tall as the gates of the Heavenly Palace back in the East—swung outwards to reveal an interior of silver shimmering, pearlescent light that radiated in waves. Simone followed Semias and Michael to find the interior was a Western-styled long, narrow space with rows of pews constructed of pale pine timber. There was no altar at the end of the aisle; instead, a massive throne, made of silver, stood on a dais under more stained glass. The throne appeared to be constructed of woven metal in thick strands that curled into intricate designs reminiscent of Celtic or Norse motifs.

The light came from the throne. Its rays of silvery illumination were almost blinding. Simone reached out with more than her senses and saw the throne as it really was; it was a receptacle, processor and emitter for the Heavens' pure energy. It was more like a machine than a piece of furniture, and its energy was severely limited by the presence of all the demons. It was dazzling already; when the demons were gone it would be overwhelming.

'Whoever sits on that will have *immense* power,' Michael said with awe. He stepped back. 'Uh ...'

'You're the only one, lad,' Semias said. 'Sit on it, open the portal, and let the old ones up to take your place. Then you can go home.'

'It won't kill him?' she asked. 'That thing's like a nuclear reactor!'

'I'm a son of the Tiger, that sort of Yang is my element,' Michael said. 'It can't hurt me.'

'It won't hurt him, it will protect him,' Semias said. 'Go, Michael. Take your place.'

Michael glanced at Simone. He smiled shyly. 'If this goes wrong ...'

She tried to suppress the feeling of dread at the knowledge that she would be returning alone. She wouldn't let that happen. She touched his hand and he grasped hers. 'You'll be in charge. Make sure it doesn't.'

He brought her hand to his face and kissed her fingertips. 'It would not be right for me to say the words so soon after I lost Clarissa. But one day, I will say the words, and I'll mean them. If this goes wrong ...' he glanced at the throne, still gripping her hand, then turned back to her. 'Don't wait for me. Find happiness for yourself with someone else, until our time comes? Promise.'

'I promise,' she said, not meaning it at all. She opened her mouth to tell him not to do it, then closed it again. He was the only one who could, and the demons needed to be removed from these Heavens so that the wars would stop. 'Make sure that it doesn't go wrong. Sit and bring Hades here so you can go home and mourn like you should.'

'I'm not looking forward to regaining my grief, but being like this is completely wrong,' he said, then shook out his shoulders and turned to face the throne. 'Is there a ceremony or anything? Words to say?'

Semias held one arm out towards the throne. 'No. Just go and sit.'

'All right.' Michael shot a loving glance at Simone that

broke her heart, then strode to the throne, took three steps up onto the dais, and sat. His hands flew to the throne's arms, and he went rigid, then screamed a high-pitched sound of agony that pierced her through. Everything exploded in a light so dazzling that she couldn't see anything.

The rays of light shooting from the throne were mirrored by a deep bass thrum through the floor that didn't cover the sounds of Michael's anguished screams. The waves increased in frequency, like an energy cycle overloading, and Simone took two steps towards it but was stopped when the energy burst from the throne in a single blaze of white-hot brilliance that shot through her and hit her demon essence with a sear of pain.

All her breath left her, and she fell to her knees as she dissolved. It burned through her, and she lost her vision again and gasped for air.

'You may stay, demon,' a massive voice boomed, making the ground shake, and everything stopped.

She lowered her head and panted, trying to get her breath back, then pulled herself to her feet. She shook out her left arm where she'd landed on it and pinned it back to her side.

She blinked, attempting to clear the blinding afterimages, and when the interior of the building came into focus it was completely different. It matched Emma's description of the aftermath when the Jade Emperor had regained control of the Eastern Celestial Plane. Although it hadn't physically changed, everything was brighter, clearer and cleaner. All the dust motes had disappeared from the air.

Michael looked twenty years older, and had gained height and muscle mass, but more importantly, he looked pure-European and no longer had his half-Asian features. It was still him, but the change was dramatic. He sat on the throne with his hands on its arms and scowled at Semias, who cringed in front of him.

'Duplicitous spirit!' Michael boomed with the same voice, so deep and resonating that it was almost unrecognisable. 'Liar! Thief of life! I should have you destroyed.'

'Mercy, my Lord, you know I had no choice.'

'You sacrificed this child's life to return your own selfish power—'

'You can change the entire region for the better, my Lord ...'

Simone filled with desperation. Her premonitions were right. Something had gone completely wrong, and Michael didn't sound like himself at all. 'Are you in there, Michael?' she asked. 'You're supposed to let Hades up here, and then you can step down and we can go home. Don't forget.'

'I am now Throne Michael,' Michael said. 'Apt that I should gain the name of the one who is named to be like the Creator. Michael the individual—no longer exists.'

Simone stomped up to the base of the dais. 'Michael MacLaren, you get your half-tiger ass down off that ridiculous throne right now!' she shouted. 'We are going *home*.'

'Too late, child,' Semias said softly.

'Bring Hades up!' Simone shouted.

Michael stared at her, still radiating pure energy. The flood of power was making her head ache.

Michael returned to his normal form, but his arms were still stuck to the throne. 'Some angels were called Thrones for a reason, Simone,' he said, and his voice had returned as well. 'The Throne itself is the source of power and controlling nexus for the entire Heavens. The one who sits on it is just a lens. I've been absorbed by it, and I'm part of the machinery that runs this place.'

'But Hades—'

His voice returned to the booming Throne. 'Hades is guilty of kidnapping, imprisonment and treason. His sentence is to stay in Hell, administering the dead, for all eternity.'

'But the gods who sentenced him are gone!' Simone said, protesting. 'You're on the Throne now, pardon him or something, so he can come up.'

'He is not worthy of pardon.' He changed back to his own voice. 'The Throne doesn't trust him. It thinks he'll try to take over again.'

'Let him!'

'He led a demon rebellion against Heaven before, and that's why he's been cast out. The Throne is adamant that it doesn't want him back here, and it's controlling me, not the other way around.'

'It's the right thing to do, you don't know the whole story,' Semias said to Simone. 'Can you keep the demons out by yourself, lad?'

'I can,' Michael said. 'They cannot enter. But it will take a great deal of time for me to expel the demons that are here already.'

Simone rounded on Semias. 'Let me take Michael's place …' She waved her arms with disgust. 'I know, I'm too demon!' She turned to Michael. 'Remove the demon essence from me and I'll take your place and you can go home and be with your family.'

'Oh God,' Michael said, and collapsed forwards, still with his arms on the throne. They seemed to be glued in place. 'We've succeeded, Simone, I have my grief back.'

'I am going to *murder* the Jade Emperor,' Simone said. 'He had to know this would be the result.'

'I'm not stuck here forever,' Michael said. 'Every generation, the best and brightest from among the gods is chosen to sit on the Throne, and when a new generation emerges, they pass the Throne down to the next. Nobody sits on it for more than a hundred years.'

'*What* next generation?' Simone shouted and gestured angrily towards him. 'You're here by yourself!'

'You can stay with me?' He looked around. 'But I can't leave the Throne for more than a couple of hours at a time, and I can't leave these Heavens at all. I'm kind of trapped here.' He studied her. 'If you help me to repopulate these Heavens, I'll be freed.'

'You want me to stay here and make babies with you to repopulate the Heavens?' Simone asked, incredulous.

'The Throne says: Yes. I say: Go home, Simone, and tell the Jade Emperor that we succeeded and I'm working on a way to rebuild these Heavens without doing the old-fashioned thing of kidnapping humans to use as toys. Ask him for some volunteers to move to these Heavens and help start a new community here.' His face went strange. 'European heritage only? That's ridiculous! I have to fight the mechanism's inherent racism as well? Wonderful.'

'What about Hades and Persephone? What will you do about them?'

Michael went rigid and his voice changed back to the Throne. 'They were thrown from Heaven and have no relevance. Take my message to your greatest leader, and tell him that I am ready to negotiate.'

'Remove the demon essence from me first.'

'Only if you allow me to change you as I have changed Michael and stay here as his Queen.' Flashes of conflict swept across his expression. 'No. Yes. No. I want to!' He raised his head and yelled with pain, and the light shot through her again, burning half her existence away. The darkness was swept from her in a blaze of cold brilliance, and she fell to her knees and panted.

'If you have enough free will to do that, you have enough free will to come home with me,' she said to the blue-green floor, then pulled herself unsteadily to her feet. It would take some time for her own shen energy to refill the void that the demon essence had been occupying, and she felt completely drained. 'Or let me take the Throne so you can go back to your family.'

'Semias is right,' Michael said, his voice rough with grief. 'One of us needs to stay, and it should be me. It wants to imprison both of us here to repopulate, but you deserve your freedom. I've texted you—how about that, the Throne has already dissected your phone and reverse-engineered the technology—details of the location of the Gateway directly below the throne room. If you go there and touch the ancient Roman monument, I will know and bring you up to visit.' His voice changed to the Throne again. 'You are not of sufficiently pure heritage and are not welcome here. Begone and do not return.' He smiled sadly at her and his voice changed back to his own. 'Goodbye, Simone, it will be a long time—but it will happen.'

'How long?' she asked, but she was already back in the lobby of the Tiger's hotel in Paris.

18

Simone took a few gasping breaths, then summoned her swords, ignoring the pain in her left arm, and took her biggest Celestial Form, robe and armour and stars and everything. A few people in the lobby of the hotel made loud sounds of wonder. She ignored them. She went into the restaurant and floated up to the underside of the glass roof. She summoned a circle of Yin—she wasn't so out of control that she would drop glass on the diners—to make a hole in the roof, then shot straight up, probably leaving a blowback that knocked tables over. She didn't care as she screamed towards the East, her heart breaking at the fulfilment of her premonition—that she'd return alone. She arrived at the edge of the Eastern region and headed to the Asian Heavens.

She landed on the island that held the Celestial Palace, and the massive doors opened for her to reveal the main square. The area was the size of a football field with an ornamental stream that passed through it, traversed by three marble bridges. The square was occupied by a number of Celestials gathered to talk or walk in the afternoon breeze, and some phoenixes and dragons tumbled in the crystalline blue sky above her. The golden tiles on the roofs of the Celestial Palace buildings shone in the sun, but she didn't really see them.

The Primal Yin, her father's essential element, spiralled

around her hands and her long golden hair, and she smiled with grim satisfaction at the level of control she had over it, after so many years of being unable to touch it. Her robes were the full Celestial version, not just deep blue with printed stars but appearing to be a portal into the night sky itself, glittering with brilliant constellations. Her hair floated around her, long enough to touch the ground but floating above it, and she knew that her eyes were huge and black and shimmering.

The Jade Emperor was holding court in the Hall of Supreme Harmony, the largest hall facing onto the square, so she teleported as far as she could before she was blocked by Palace security. She landed at the top of the marble ramp that led to its doors.

The Door Gods, each three metres tall and bearded, saw the swords in her hands and moved to stop her. One was black-skinned, one was red, and they held their halberds diagonally in front of them, then planted themselves side-by-side in front of the doors.

'Princess, we've been ordered—' General Wei began, but she didn't give either of them time to finish it. She swept her swords in a spinning attack that cut both of them into three pieces, at a speed that would have her father smiling tightly with satisfaction. From the looks on the Door Gods' faces as they disappeared, they hadn't seen the attack at all.

She returned her swords to her back, pulled one of the doors open, and walked onto the golden carpet that ran from the door to the raised dais containing the throne. The usual large crowd of Celestial residents, in all forms, were standing in neat rows on either side of the carpeted aisle to watch as the emperor handed down his proclamations. She drew her swords again as she stalked towards the dais, and the room went completely still.

She stopped halfway to the throne with her robes floating around her and ribbons of Yin winding through her golden hair. The Jade Emperor was sitting on the throne in full Imperial regalia, complete with ridiculous beaded hat, with Er Lang standing as second behind him. She wanted the emperor to burst into flames where he sat.

'You knew,' she said, her voice tight with fury. 'You knew where he would end up.'

'Stand down, Princess,' Er Lang said.

'Clear the hall,' the Jade Emperor said.

'No!' Simone shouted and turned on the spot to see the crowd standing on either side of the carpet. 'Stay right here, all of you, and hear this!' She swung back and pointed the tip of her sword at the Jade Emperor, quivering with fury. 'Michael MacLaren is stuck on a throne in the European Heavens, absorbed by it. He's completely alone, he's lost his wife, his child, his individuality and his free will and *you did it to him*.'

She continued up the carpet but Er Lang appeared in front her with his hands palm down as if he was calming an enraged animal. 'Simone, please,' he said. 'You don't want to do—'

She went for his head with sweeping strokes from both swords, but he summoned his halberd in time to block her. The swords hit the carbon-fibre clad aluminium shaft of the halberd with a blow that rang through the hall, making the clerestory windows above them rattle.

'Simone, please,' Er Lang said through gritted teeth as he tried to hold her off. His feet slid on the carpet from the force of her push.

'No,' she said, unlocked her blades, and made three quick cuts that bypassed his guard completely and split him into four astonished pieces before he knew what was happening.

The Er Lang pieces disappeared, leaving blood stains on the carpet.

Er Lang's dog, who looked like a big black Doberman, raced down the stairs and stood in front of Simone to glare at her, and she glared back. She waved the point of her sword, Bei, in the dog's face, and he lowered his head, tucked his tail between his legs, and backed away.

Simone spun to face the Jade Emperor, who was standing in front of his throne with one hand on the arm as if to hold himself up. His face was ashen, and he looked very old.

As she continued towards him, she placed the ends of the

hilts of her swords together to join them and transformed them into a halberd with the chakra indentations along its length and onto the broadsword blade at its end. She loaded her energy centres into the blade—the first time she'd been able to do this since being filled with demon essence—and revelled in the brilliance of the light.

She spun the halberd in one hand and pointed the tip of the blade at the Jade Emperor as she strode up the stairs. 'He is stuck there—for who knows how long—mourning his wife, without his child, and you—' She took a breath and shouted it. '—Knew!'

The was a long, ringing silence as he gazed at her, his expression unreadable, then he said, 'I only know what happens inside my region. I didn't know—'

'You knew he wouldn't return!'

She ran the blade of the halberd straight through the middle of his chest. He looked down at it with shock, then up at her, gurgled an attempt at words and disappeared.

The silence deepened, then there was a rustle and a thump as everyone in the hall fell to their knees and kowtowed to Simone. 'Ten thousand years.'

She turned to see the neat rows of them prostrate before her. 'Yeah, to Hell with that.' She raised her voice. 'I abdicate the throne. The Qilin Jade Emperor is restored.'

The Jade Emperor reappeared behind her, standing in front of the throne. 'I knew that if he took the Throne, he would—'

She spun to see him. 'How? How did you know that? How did you know about the Throne?' She moved closer to glare into his eyes. 'Did you arrange this with Semias?'

'Not as such, but—'

'Don't lie to me!' she shouted, spun and cut him in half at chest height.

The pieces made a few wheezing noises and disappeared.

'I abdicate the throne. The Qilin Jade Emperor is restored,' Simone said.

The Jade Emperor reappeared, looking even more exhausted. He stood silently, waiting for her.

'Stop taking everyone I love away from me!' she shouted into his face and shoved the blade straight into his throat. He disappeared again.

The heat of her anger finally eased. She placed the butt of the halberd on the floor and sagged against it. She struggled to say the words through the choking misery. 'I abdicate the throne. The Qilin Jade Emperor is restored.'

The Jade Emperor reappeared, leaned on the arm of the throne and fell to sit. He put his forehead in his hand but didn't speak.

She wanted to kill him again but didn't have the energy. Her throat closed up, and she fell to her knees to release huge, gasping, wet, horrible sobs of grief and pain. 'He's all. Alone. Suffering. Trapped. Enslaved. It's ...' She put her hand on her chest where it felt like the halberd was in it. 'Made him into something that's not who he is, and ...' She glared up at the Jade Emperor and pointed one shaking finger at him. '*You did this to him*!'

'I know,' the Jade Emperor said softly, with infinite sadness. He waved one hand. 'Clear the hall, and I will tell you the truth.'

There were mumbles and rustles as the crowd departed. Simone didn't move from her spot kneeling on the floor, gasping with heaving sobs she had no control over—she felt completely drained, and couldn't move at all. The Jade Emperor gazed down at her from the throne.

'Yes. I arranged it with Semias. I was in contact with their Shen two thousand years ago, before they stupidly destroyed themselves and returned their spirits to the Earth. I knew about the Throne. Michael was the best choice to take it, second only to you. You would have been a preferable ruler, but your demon nature precluded that.'

'The demon nature is gone. Let me go back and replace him!'

'No. Your place is here, and his is there. Take time to recover and retrieve your stepmother. Return here when you have rescued the Dark Empress, and I will share the whole plan with you.'

'Simone,' Xuan Wu said from behind her.

'Daddy!' She dropped the halberd with a clatter, turned and ran to him. He enfolded her in an embrace that made the rest of the world go away, and she completely lost control, wailing into his shoulder.

Simone was aware of movement and being pushed to sit, but it was all a long way away. When she came out of her blur of grief, she was in her father's small residence in the Celestial Palace, sitting on a ceramic stool at an outdoor ceramic table in the courtyard, with a cup of tea in front of her. She took a sip, then a larger gulp. She grabbed a few tissues from the box on the table to blow her nose, then wiped her eyes. She felt like she'd been punched in the face and her throat was raw from crying.

Her father sat on the other side of the table, glowering down at his own tea.

'How long will Michael be stuck like that?' Simone asked him. 'Does the JE know?'

'At least a hundred years,' Xuan Wu said.

Simone slammed her teacup onto the ceramic table, shattering the cup, then stood and stormed around the courtyard, over the lawn and past the small pond and waterfall that stood at one side. Her father sat quietly and waited for her.

She went back and stood next to the table. 'Michael said that the Throne wants people of European heritage to repopulate?'

Xuan Wu nodded. 'But Michael himself is stuck there until all of the demons are gone—and that will take some time and effort.'

'At least a hundred years.'

He nodded again.

She strode backwards and forwards across the courtyard again.

'We can send someone to take his place,' she said as she paced. 'I'll do it. The JE said I'd be better at it.'

'Michael has contacted the Asian Region,' Xuan Wu said. 'We made him that offer. He said no, that he's the most suited for the position and asks for your understanding.'

She stopped and waved her arms with frustration. 'My understanding!' she shouted. 'Oh, I understand, all right. That *idiot* is punishing himself for losing Clarissa. I will *kill* him.'

'Let's go home,' he said. 'Frankie's been worried sick about you. And now that you're back and the mission was a success, we can free Emma from her cell in Hell.'

'That was not a success, that was a sacrificial execution,' she growled. 'The Jade Emperor tied a willing martyr to a stake and burned him alive.'

'I know.' He rose. 'Come on.'

They landed on her father's heavenly martial arts academy, Wudang Mountain, in the front yard of the family manor, a double-storey, courtyard-styled house with its back flush against the stone spine of the tallest peak.

She followed him into the entry, then through the courtyard to the living room on the right. Frankie was sitting with both demon servants, Smally and Er Hao, on the floor between the rosewood couches and the coffee table, with a mountain of toys. When he heard them, he dropped his toy car, spun and ran to Simone, hitting her hard. He buried his face in her stomach.

'You were gone for *so long*,' he said into her. 'Don't go away again, please?'

'It was only a couple of days,' she said to the top of his head.

He scowled up at her. 'You were gone for a *lot* of days.'

'You were up there for two weeks,' Xuan Wu said.

Simone straightened, still holding Frankie. 'Wait? Two weeks? It was only a couple of days ...' Her voice trailed off. 'Time flows differently there.' Realisation flooded through her. 'He'll miss most of his daughter's growing years!'

'It's a symptom of not having enough Shen residing there to control the Heavens.'

Simone squeezed Frankie. 'Did you notice that I can come up here now?'

He pulled back and his mouth fell open. Then he grabbed her and clutched her again. 'Finally,' he said, his voice full of tears. 'You can come and help us at Nanna's! We can get Mum out and have *Christmas*!'

'We can,' Simone said, and Christmas suddenly seemed like something to look forward to—delayed or not.

'The Tiger is here and requests an update on what happened to his son,' Xuan Wu said. 'I can tell him to do it later …'

'No, let me talk to him,' Simone said. 'All my stuff is still at his hotel in Paris—'

'Kimberly packed it for you, here it is,' the Tiger said from the courtyard, and pushed her suitcase towards her. 'Don't worry, I didn't touch anything.'

'Good,' Simone said, and gestured towards the couches. 'I'll tell you what happened.' She turned to her father. 'Clear the paperwork with Court Ten to get Emma out. We're done, she's in no danger, and he probably made it a month because he knew it would be two weeks and he doubled the time to ensure her safety.'

Xuan Wu nodded. 'You okay?'

She sighed with feeling and wiped the tears that had started again. 'I'm Immortal,' she said through them. 'Of course I am.'

Frankie was still holding her hand and shook it. 'Talk to Doctor Au if you need to. She can help if you're sad about Michael.'

'No,' Simone said. 'The person I really need to talk to … is Emma. Go and do her paperwork, Daddy, and we can be a family here on the Mountain and have Christmas at Nan and Pop's.'

Xuan Wu smiled. 'That is the best idea ever.'

19

While they waited for their father to return, Frankie made a spaceship out of Lego with Smally and Simone found some fruit and a lemon tea in the kitchen, then sat on the couch and checked the news on her phone. She was relieved to see that the war in Europe had abated, with the invading armies retreating for no apparent reason. Her mission with Michael had been a success, even if it felt like she'd lost part of her soul. She logged into her email account and there were a massive number of emails from Tokyo U, but not a single one asking her why she'd been MIA for two weeks. Maybe there was something to be said for using Celestial connections like this.

No messages from Graham. It would take her a long time to meet someone as smart, sweet and ... just overall *kind* as him. The tears sprang in her eyes, and she swiped her hand over her face as she heard her father returning.

Their father entered the living room in the full Celestial regalia of his administrative kit—flowing black robes without armour embossed in silver with the characters for 'North' and 'Heaven'—'Bei' and 'Tian'—as well as a few 'Xuan' among them. His belt had a ba gua symbol for the buckle, and a turtle-shell pattern along its length, again in silver. The front of his long hair was tied in a topknot and held back by the deco-styled twining platinum diadem that Emma had given him for a wedding gift, which stretched from his temples and across his forehead to enhance his Inner Eye.

He raised a dun-coloured scroll bound with a red ribbon. 'I have Emma's release document. You two stay here. Simone, please mind your brother while I—'

'No way, Dad,' Simone said. 'We're coming with you.'

'I want to see my mum!' Frankie shouted.

'This is not the place for a child ...'

'Dad!' Simone said, exasperated. 'He grew up there! He knows all about it! And ...' She touched the top of Frankie's head. 'He's not much younger than I was when I went down there to get her.'

'You're not allowed in Hell, either of you, you promised—'

'The Celestial side of Hell is part of the Celestial. I'm Immortal, so I'll go there if I'm ...' She didn't finish it, not wanting to scare Frankie.

Their father sighed with defeat. 'I've already lost this argument, haven't I?'

'Yes!' Simone and Frankie said in unison. Simone took Frankie's hand. 'Ready?'

'You betcha!' Frankie said. His expression faltered. 'Is there anything I shouldn't say? Or not do? I want to make sure we get her out.'

'Let us do the talking, stand at the back and look like a mad little brat who wants to burn the place to the ground,' Simone said.

Frankie lowered his head and glowered from under his brows.

'Just like that.'

'You two are impossible,' their father said with a smile. 'Let's go.'

Xuan Wu stepped forward and held his hand out, but Simone waved her father away and teleported herself and her little brother to Hell.

They arrived on the wide green lawn with perpetually flowering pink peach trees at the edge of the opaque, black lake that separated the Celestial from the Demonic sides of Hell.

The sky was a universal warm light with no sun above the Celestial side of Hell, which was a circular island at the centre of the lake. Causeways like spokes of a wheel led out from the island to the Ten Levels of Hell where the demons tortured the souls who were sentenced by the Courts of Hell for crimes committed during their lives, then fed the Soup of Forgetfulness and reattached the Wheel of Life.

Court Ten was presided over by Judge Pao the Uncorruptible, the most senior judge in the courts and a stickler for procedure. It was where all Immortals landed after they died—skipping the other nine levels where Mortals were judged—and it was the largest and most important courtroom because Mortals who had attained Immortality were also judged there, and Pao had the power to confirm their status and send them on to reside on the Celestial Plane.

The building itself was in an ancient style of a two-storey courtyard building with red pillars holding up the traditional pitched roof and decorative red lattices over the windows. A pair of huge, red-scaled tame demons guarded the entrance, and they fell to one knee as Simone's family approached.

'Ten thousand years,' they said.

Simone's father said, 'Rise,' and the demons stood and waited expectantly to obey him.

'Cool,' Frankie whispered.

'It's a pain in the neck after a while,' Simone said. 'You can't talk to someone because they have to do this stupid years thing.'

'Precisely,' Xuan Wu said. He grew from normal human size to his biggest Celestial Form, and Simone smiled at Frankie and took her own.

She grew in height to match her father, and her hair spread around her to float in a breeze that kept it from touching the ground. The scales were gone, and the skin of her hands was pale and glowing. Her robes shifted to the firmament of the night sky, with twinkling stars within them.

Frankie's eyes widened and his mouth fell open. 'What? This is?' He leaned in to speak softly to her. 'You look like a *magic princess*. Where did the scales go?'

'This is the Celestial me,' Simone whispered back. 'I like it more.'

'I like the snake one too, can you still do it?'

She shifted quickly to her demon form, then back to Celestial. 'Sure.'

He nodded. 'Nice.' He turned to face Court Ten. 'I need one too.'

'Call your robes. They'll come.'

Frankie raised his head and concentrated, and his new robes wafted into being around him. He'd chosen the style himself at the Celestial tailors, and they had three layers—a fine black silk under-robe, a heavier black silk robe over the top with a silver-embossed belt and decorative ribbons along the collar and cuffs embroidered with the character for North, and a final, gauzy black over-robe that floated over the other two. He looked like a little Chinese Prince, and Simone smiled. His sword, the Murasame, appeared on his back, held in place by its telescoping strap, and he touched the strap where it crossed his chest.

'Anyone tries to keep our mum from us, Muri says it will help convince them.' He glanced up at Simone and Xuan Wu. 'I want to be bigger.'

Their father had been watching them with quiet delight. He hooked his thumbs in his belt. 'You need to get bigger before you can be bigger. Do some growing—and a lot of training—and you'll be as magical as Simone is.'

'As soon as we're home, I'm doing a *lot* of sword,' Frankie said.

The Murasame spoke in a voice that grated like metal. 'Good.'

Xuan Wu moved between Frankie and Simone, put a hand on his daughter's shoulder, took Frankie's hand, and nodded. 'Let's find our Emma.'

'Yeah,' Frankie said softly with resolve.

The three of them walked up to the entrance to Court Ten and the demons opened the doors for them. The courtroom occupied the ground floor, with stairs behind a screen leading to Pao's residence on the floor above. The floor was simple slate tiles, and there were three rows of benches on either side for spectators, all empty. Demon guards, similar to those at the door, stood wearing armour and carrying halberds at the end of the room on either side of Judge Pao. Pao himself was sitting behind his desk on a raised dais, and Emma was in her prison whites, kneeling on the floor.

Frankie ran to her, and she turned and smiled when she saw them. Her face crumpled and she wailed softly, bent with misery and hugging herself, then exploded into streams of demon essence.

Frankie stopped dead in the middle of the courtroom. He looked from where Emma had exploded to Pao, then shouted, '*Where's my mother?*'

'That was a demon copy!' Xuan Wu shouted, nearly as loudly. 'Where is my wife?'

Pao sat grimly on the dais without responding.

'Holy shit, you *don't know*?' Simone shouted.

Pao again didn't respond.

Xuan Wu stormed up to the dais and stood below it to glare at Pao. 'Who took her?'

Realisation hit Simone in a bolt of horror. 'She isn't in European Hell, is she? She didn't rush over there to find me?' She jumped onto the dais to stand over Pao's desk and leaned into his dark-skinned face, toppling his ink-brush stand and splashing ink all over the sentencing scroll. 'Confirm that she wasn't taken to Europe!' Frankie jumped up to join her, eyeing Pao over the edge of the desk

'She was taken from her cell in the Sixth Level of Hell by one of five senior Asian demons,' Pao said, not looking her in the eye. 'The Celestial confirms that she is not in the European —'

Xuan Wu stomped up the stairs to the dais and stood next to Simone and Frankie, quivering with fury. His voice resonated as the room went cold. 'The Jade Emperor *knew* she had been taken?'

'We have to get her out!' Frankie said. 'They'll hurt her!'

'No, don't worry,' Simone said, putting her hand on his shoulder. 'She's too powerful to be held like that, she would have gone along with them to see what they're up to.' She glared at Pao. 'Did she leave any clues behind in her cell as to which demon it was? Come on! She's a freaking genius and would have left *something* behind for us …'

'She was here in snake form, Simone, she had no hands,' Xuan Wu said softly.

'Let's go check her cell anyway,' Frankie said.

'Give me the list of five demons,' Xuan Wu said, and Pao handed him a scroll. 'Number One, eh? She'd be thrilled to bits if Edu—'

Frankie made a loud, wordless sound of terror and stepped back.

'You can go home, Frankie, this might be—' Simone began.

'Not without my mum!' Frankie shouted. 'Promise or not, we're finding her! Edu. Who else? I bet Four's on that list, and the new Twelve, and Eight and Nine probably working together because those two were *mean*.'

Xuan Wu glanced at the scroll. 'You are absolutely correct.'

Frankie disappeared.

'He is too young to be doing that,' Pao said.

'I want a full report on *everything* that happened in the level of Hell where she was incarcerated, and I will return to collect it when I have found my wife.'

Pao hesitated, then said, 'Good luck, my Lord.'

'Come with me, Simone,' Xuan Wu said, and stormed out of the courtroom. Simone followed him across the lawn towards the lake that separated the Celestial from the Demonic sides of Hell, where they encountered Frankie striding backwards and forwards with fury at the end of the causeway to Level Six, the Hell of Poisonous Snakes.

Frankie turned and waved his arms at them. 'It won't let me go across!'

'Stay here, I'll look for her,' Xuan Wu said, and touched his crown. 'This is connected to her, it has her snakeskin on it. It will give me a good idea of where she is.'

'What—that sword and crown with the bits of you and her in them aren't creepy and weird? They're to *find* each other?' Simone asked, aghast.

'You thought they were creepy and weird?' Xuan Wu asked, even more aghast.

'I thought it was some bizarre Julia Roberts–Billy Bob Thornton—'

Xuan Wu now looked thoroughly confused, and Simone plunged on.

'Blood necklace bull … dust, I'll explain it later,' she said. 'I didn't realise that you always wanted the ability to find each other—'

'Wherever we are,' he finished with her. 'My shell, her scales—as we are senior Celestials, these things are imbued with immense power.' He waved them away. 'Move back. I'm about to use a great deal of that power.'

Simone took Frankie by the shoulder and pulled him back from the lake. Xuan Wu lowered his head, spread his hands palm-down, and rose gently on a wave of dark energy.

'Wah,' Frankie said softly.

Xuan Wu floated out over the surface of the lake, and the water rippled in circles below him. His energy thrummed across the surface of the water, then he summoned Yin around his head in a halo of darkness that formed a vortex in front of his Inner Eye. The water bounced in circular waves beneath his feet, then lifted into orbs the size of basketballs, which spun around him. The dark energy twined in ribbons around the water spheres and his hair writhed with a life of its own as his face was set in concentration. Emma's Serpent skin inlaid on the crown began to glow and formed threads of light that twisted with Xuan Wu's dark energy.

'I want to do that one day,' Frankie whispered with awe.

'He used to scare me to death,' Simone said with grim humour.

'Why? That's the best part of him being who he is.'

The Yin stopped moving completely and the spheres of

water froze, then fell into the water, sending a wave of spray towards Simone and Frankie, who both raised their hands to stop it from reaching them. The crown re-absorbed the Emma light, and Xuan Wu released the Yin and pulled it back into himself. He glided back, landed softly on the grass in front of them, and smiled. 'Definitely not Europe. She's to the south-east. Since we're in the middle of China, at first I thought Hong Kong, but it's further than that, but not as far as the Philippines.'

'Taiwan,' Simone said in unison with him.

'I know you don't want a part of it anymore, but you should be aware that the top levels of the demonic administration appear to be under siege from the new hybrids created by the previous Demon King,' Xuan Wu said. 'Let's head over to Yanluo Wang's office, obtain permission from the King for you two to enter their side of Hell, and get our Emma back.'

'Will the King let us in?' Simone asked. 'He's scared to death of us.'

'He'd better,' Frankie growled.

'Yanluo Wang has a direct line to the other side,' Xuan Wu said. 'This way.'

Yanluo Wang was Lord of the Dead and chief administrator of the Celestial court system in Hell. He ran it from a three-storey brutalist concrete building in the middle of the main Celestial Island, on a wide spreading lawn under the sunless warm light. They flew to the building, and he was waiting for them at the entrance. Yanluo Wang wore red Tang-style robes with the character for 'death' embroidered in black over them, and a traditional square hat with long extensions on the sides.

'Xuan Tian Shang Di, ten thousand years,' he said to Xuan Wu, saluting him. 'Come and talk to this asshole, then get him out of my face. That last Demon King was duplicitous as hell, but at least he was polite. This one insists on being "modern" and doesn't even salute and address me. He wants to shake my damn hand! Oh.' He saw Simone and Frankie. 'Welcome home,

Princess. You sent the Jade Emperor down here three times in quick succession, and I've never seen Pao so damn happy in my entire life.' He opened the door for them. 'Come on in, they're in conference room one.'

They passed through modern beige cubicles with officials wearing Tang-styled robes working on computers, and through to the conference room which was also beige with carpet tiles and a pine, rectangular conference table big enough to seat twelve. A whiteboard at the end had a projector showing a view of somewhere in Europe that Simone didn't recognise but appeared to be a Roman ruin. The Demon King, in a maroon silk suit, was already sitting at the table, accompanied by a pair of Snake Mothers in human form who both appeared to be gorgeous young Chinese women in traditional blood-red cheongsams standing behind him.

Xuan Wu bowed and saluted the King. 'Mo Wang.'

The King stood and saluted Xuan Wu back. 'Xuan Tian. Good, you're here.' He waved across the table at them and sat himself. 'Sit, sit. Let's be modern about this, and it won't take long.' He steepled his fingers as Xuan Wu, Simone and Frankie sat across from him. Yanluo Wang nodded to them and closed the door as he went out.

'When my father was in charge, he played so many games, leading you all around the place, purely to plant that Black Jade stone thing into your household. I'm not playing games.' The Demon King placed a late model mobile phone onto the table. 'Twelve's an idiot, and kidnapped Emma to ask for her aid to take down the European hybrid-demon running the campaign against me so that he can make an attempt at my throne himself.' He stopped and studied them. 'You know who that one is?'

'I do,' Simone said. She glanced at her father, and he nodded.

'Good. I'm dealing with it. Twelve has taken Emma to his Nest, so pop down there, destroy Twelve, and bring her out.' He pushed the mobile phone across the table to them. 'This has his location in the maps app. Twelve knows better than to hold

Emma in my dominion in Hell—I'd give her back to you immediately—so he's holding her in one of his Nests on the Earthly. Go and destroy Twelve, release your Empress, done deal.'

'What should we expect there?' Xuan Wu asked, taking the phone and passing it to Simone. She opened the maps app and noted the location on the southeast coast of the island of Taiwan.

'He's amassed a high-end Nest of Mothers, but it's nothing that the three of you can't take down. Good practice for the kids.' He smiled tightly around at them. 'It's possible that Edu's there as well, Twelve was stupid enough to believe her when Edu said she would help him.'

'Do you want Edu alive?' Simone asked.

'I think the answer to that is completely obvious from what I've done here,' the King said. 'And if you could do me a favour, and rid me of that piece-of-shit Rhonda as well—'

'Mind your tongue in front of the children,' Xuan Wu said.

The King shook his hands over the table at them in a casual salute, and the Mothers scowled. 'Forgive me, that was inappropriate in front of the *dear* child.' He placed his hands on the table and smiled. 'Rhonda and Edu are in the thick of some high-level infighting, and if you could take them out for me, I'd be in your debt.' His smile turned vicious. 'And I mean that in its fullest sense. I would owe you one, Turtle.' He rose and the Mothers moved behind him. They all saluted around the table, and Xuan Wu saluted back. 'Have fun.' They disappeared.

'Rhonda?' Xuan Wu asked Simone quietly as they headed down the stairs to leave Yanluo Wang's office. 'Michael's mother?'

'A Rhonda copy was running everything in Europe,' Simone said. 'Looks like the old King made multiple copies of Michael's mother. He knew she was one of the Celtic Serpent people.'

'They are in the European Heavens as well?' he asked.

'Michael didn't have to face one, did he?'

She shook her head. 'He had to face a copy of *me*.'

'So there are multiple copies running around. We need to inform the rest of the Celestial.'

'I know,' she said. 'We seriously need a thorough debrief on this, and the JE needs to share what he knows. If there's a Rhonda copy here as well, working with Edu—'

Frankie made another small sound in his throat.

'We're here, she can't hurt you,' Simone said, putting her hand on Frankie's shoulder.

He nodded and wiped one eye.

'So it's possible there's more than one Rhonda copy,' Simone said. She checked the phone again. 'Let's go see what this Nest looks like.' She glanced down at Frankie. 'You can stay here if—'

'Not happening,' Frankie said, sounding much older than his five years. He lifted off the ground. 'Let's go.'

'Nice control,' Xuan Wu said, rising next to him. 'No teleporting, though, you're too little and you're lucky you didn't hurt yourself when you did it before. Hand?'

Frankie put his hand out, Xuan Wu took it, and they teleported out of Hell. Simone followed them.

Simone had no difficulty flying as fast as her father as he carried Frankie, and they broke the sound barrier over the ocean. Frankie squealed with delight as they screamed through the thin atmosphere, and then went quiet and serious when they followed the coast of Taiwan south. That part of the island wasn't densely populated, having only small villages clinging to the cliffs that overlooked the water, and most of the landscape was dense with scrub. A few market gardens and rickety farmhouses appeared along the winding road skirting the coast, and there was the occasional inn overlooking the grey-brown rock-strewn beach.

'Here,' Simone said. Xuan Wu lowered Frankie, still holding his hand, and they hovered over the location.

It was a small, white, four-storey hotel, with balconies

overlooking the ocean beneath the cliffs. There appeared to be twenty rooms, and a larger administrative and conference area to one side. A generous infinity pool sat between the building and the cliffs, and the general air was of restrained indulgence. The facility had a gravel-paved car park next to it, which had enough space for ten cars, but held only three high-end luxury sedans.

Xuan Wu concentrated, and a small spiral of Yin appeared in front of his crown.

'There's a vast chamber beneath the hotel,' he said. 'Nest cavern.'

'Mummy?' Frankie asked.

'I cannot sense her.' He turned and knelt on the air to speak to Frankie. 'Remember, your mother is Immortal. If she is killed, she is taken to Court Ten—' He stopped speaking and his head shot up. 'Her stone just spoke to me.'

'What did it say?' Simone asked.

'To collect it, because she left it behind.' Xuan Wu rose. 'Stay here, I do not want you to see this.'

'I'm coming—' Frankie shouted.

Xuan Wu shook his head. 'The stone says you should not see what happened to Emma.'

'But—' Frankie began.

Simone took Frankie's hand. 'They're right. Wait for Dad. It might be messy.'

'Find my mum,' Frankie said.

'I will.' Xuan Wu spoke silently to Simone. *I have had this talk with him, but he may ask you questions that have difficult answers.*

He drifted down and made himself invisible.

The birds and bees talk? Simone asked.

No, that one was easy after what he saw in Hell. I mean— the difference between Mortal and Immortal, and why for some, death is permanent. Clarissa's death affected him greatly and he railed for some time about the unfairness of it. Here she is.

'He found her,' Simone said. 'It sounds like she left ...' Her voice trailed off, and she didn't say, 'Her body behind.'

'What about the demons? What about Twelve?'

Twelve? Simone asked her father.

No sign. Probably eaten. Don't let Frankie down, Emma left her Serpent body behind, and it looks like they shot her in the head at close range with a large calibre weapon. I'm collecting her crown, and her stone is awake and helping.

Hello, Princess, the stone that lived in Emma's engagement ring said.

Simone smiled. It had been a while since she'd heard the stone's affected English accent. *Hey there, stone.*

She left me behind! She's really not big enough to take the body yet? I'm disappointed in her training and she needs to work harder.

As soon as she's out of the cells in Court Ten and back online she'll call for you, so she must be ... It felt strange using the term. *Newly dead.*

Yes, it just happened. If you'd been half-an-hour earlier, you would have caught them.

Tell me everything that happened while my father looks around.

'This is taking too long, I want my mum,' Frankie said, and disappeared.

Dad, Frankie just teleported again!

He really needs to stop doing that, he will hurt—Xuan Wu started, and Simone jumped when Frankie screamed above the building, a wailing sound of terror that sounded like he was falling. There was a splash and the scream cut off—he'd fallen into the pool.

She raced down towards the sound to find Frankie lying in the water at the edge of the pool with a spreading blossom of blood around him. Her father appeared next to her, and lifted Frankie's sodden body out of the water. Frankie screamed again with the movement, and Xuan Wu put his hand on Frankie's forehead. Frankie went limp, unconscious, and Xuan Wu gently laid him on the slate edge of the pool.

'Both legs broken, internal injuries, he hit the concrete

hard,' Xuan Wu said, holding one hand over Frankie's torso. He glanced up at Simone. 'Move back.'

Simone flew back as her father changed into his True Form. He was a massive Turtle with a black, spiked shell, surrounded by a Serpent that twined around its body and disappeared into it. The Serpent separated from the Turtle and held its nose over Frankie, and Simone felt the healing energy coming from it— ice-cold, like the nature of her father. The energy coiled around Frankie and his little body went rigid, then relaxed. The water in his clothes changed to ice, then melted and disappeared, leaving him dry.

'Healed,' the Serpent said in its warm female voice. 'Come here, Simone, let me look at that arm.'

Simone held her left arm out for it and hissed as the freezing energy hit the newly broken bone there. The energy retreated, and the Serpent nodded with satisfaction. 'It didn't need much, whoever set it for you did a good job.'

'Michael and Semias,' Simone said, swinging her arm and nodding when there was no twinge of pain. The break was completely healed. She went to Frankie, knelt next to him, and put her hand on his forehead.

The Serpent re-joined the Turtle and changed back to her father's human form. 'Take him home while I check through—'

'No,' Simone said. 'Emma's dead, so she's in Court Ten. Take him there to collect her, because he's feeling abandoned and it's important that he sees she's okay.' She looked up at him. 'It needs to be you, to reassure him that he can trust you.' She stood and summoned her swords. 'I'll have a look around, kill some demons, usual stuff.'

'You said you didn't want to do this anymore,' he said. 'I can send a senior lieutenant from the Mountain or the Thirty-Five, you don't have to do it.'

'I want to find the demons who were stupid enough to kidnap our Emma,' Simone said with menace. 'And make sure that it never happens again.'

He slipped his hand into the side of his robe and pulled Emma's crown out of a pocket in his pants. It was made of twining platinum and shaped to fit her Serpent head. Her snake form couldn't wear the engagement ring that normally held the stone, so it morphed into the crown when she was a snake. 'Maybe wear this so the stone can help you. If there's anything out of the ordinary, you call for backup, okay?'

She was pleased that he didn't argue—he trusted her to handle herself in a high-level Nest, and his confidence in her was flattering. 'Sure.' She slid the crown onto her forehead, and it adjusted itself to fit.

'I am only allowing you to do this because you need my assistance,' the stone said from Emma's crown. 'Otherwise, I would be horrified that anyone but my Mistress dared to don me.'

'Sure, stone,' Simone said patiently. 'Let's see what the Rhonda copy and Edu are up to.' She crouched and touched Frankie's head. 'Look after them.'

Xuan Wu picked Frankie's limp body up and cradled him. He gazed down at his son with adoration. 'He's a brave little fighter and he will cause no end of trouble when he comes into his power.'

'I know, he's wonderful, isn't he?' Simone said. She touched her father on the arm. 'Go and find our Emma.'

Xuan Wu nodded, bent in to kiss her on the forehead, then shot into the air and screamed away.

Simone turned back to the building and sent her senses out. Empty—they'd cleared out, which was normal when they became aware that the Xuan Wu, the demons' worst nightmare, was on his way. There was a huge Nest of Snake Mothers—the senior demons who were mated with the King to breed the Princes—in a cavern underneath it, and it was deserted as well.

She went into the building. There was a hotel-style lobby, with a reception desk, and she pulled the locked door open to go behind it. The administration computer wasn't plugged into the wall.

'Unused,' the stone said. 'There's another door behind you,

to Twelve's office.'

'What happened to Twelve?' she asked as she forced the next locked door and entered. The office overlooked the pool and had a heavy-set teak nineties-style desk on it. Emma's serpent corpse covered most of the floor, and her father was right—instead of her snake head, there was a ragged mess of skin and flesh, with her spinal column sticking up in the stump, and the room looked like a flesh bomb had exploded in it. 'Ew.'

'Eaten. Edu and …' its voice softened. 'The Rhonda copy actually calls itself Rhonda. They ate him.'

'I'm sorry you had to see that.'

Its voice filled with grim humour. 'Me too, believe me. Check if there's anything in the desk drawers? Twelve was old-school and did everything on paper.'

She checked the drawers. Fortunately, they were on the lee side of the Emma explosion, so they were relatively clean. She found a bound stack of envelopes, checked inside them, and was astonished to find …

'Love letters?' the stone asked with mirth. 'From a human woman. Twelve was so stupid. Wow.'

Simone looked around, found Twelve's handbag—rectangular, brown leather, multiple pockets including one for a phone that was still present, with a long carry strap. 'This is an 'old boss man'—a Lao Ban bag?'

'He did the whole Lao Ban schtick,' the stone said. 'Expensive sateen polo shirt tucked into pants high up around his waist, belt with the gold buckle, the loafer-sneaker hybrid shoes, the works.'

'Keys on a chain?'

'Yes, them too. He was a caricature of … what did Emma call him? "A senior government bully".'

She slipped the letters inside the old-man bag. 'That's all that's here, have you infiltrated the network? Downloaded the data on the devices?'

The stone's voice was chagrined. 'Uh, Princess. I apologise, but the damage to my lattice from the war precludes any downloads. I'm too broken to hold data. Can you collect the devices that the demons left behind, and take them up to Emma's intelligence department on the Mountain? There are at least twelve high-end phones and four laptops here.'

'Isn't their data on the cloud rather than on the devices?' Simone asked. 'They're all about appearances, so they use expensive Apple gear.' She understood. 'You can access their passwords if we take the hardware with us.'

'That's correct,' the stone said. 'Some of them are making a show of performative patriotism and moving to Huawei, as well.'

'Okay, locate the devices, and let's round them up.' She went back out to the lobby and checked behind the desk for a luggage storage room and found one. She broke the lock on a high-end, hard-sided carry-on and opened it, then tipped out the maroon and black designer clothing. She snapped it closed and pulled the handle up. 'Let's get some data.'

'I may fade during the process, so here's a map of the building, with all the devices in it,' the stone said. It slotted the map directly into her head—through the contact of the crown—and it felt like a flow of lava through her brain. She hissed with pain.

'Sorry, I don't do that often,' the stone said.

'I'm okay,' Simone said. 'Let's go.'

She went up the lift to the first floor. The corridor had windows on her right and a row of four doors on the left. The first computer was in the second room to the left, and she went in and promptly covered her nose at the pungent, strong smell of expensive musky perfume.

'Ugh, I *hate* this fragrance,' she said through her fingers. 'It sticks to everything and it's impossible to wash off. It'll be in my nose for *ages*.'

'I think they use it because they feel that they smell of demon,' the stone said. 'On the desk.'

'They do smell ...' Simone stopped as she stared at the room with horror. It looked like one of the rooms in the student residence in Japan—when it was occupied by a spoilt rich girl. There were clothes thrown everywhere, a couple of dirty plates on the bed, underwear bunched on the floor, and litter on every surface—from chip packets to coke cans. The smell of rot from the food on the plates added to the strong odour of the perfume and her eyes watered.

'She probably ate the cleaning demons, then complained about the mess,' the stone said.

Simone went to the desk and unhooked the latest-model, high-end iPhone from the Apple laptop, and placed them both in the carry-on bag. She checked the map in her head. 'Okay. Next.'

She sensed it as she was taking the phone and iPad from the third Mother's dorm, which was as filthy as the first two. A massive demon presence—at least Prince level—had teleported into the Nest below the building. She summoned her swords, changed to her working form, and slipped the swords into their sheaths on her back.

'What do you sense?' the stone asked.

'A Prince-level,' she said. 'In the basement.'

'Can you handle it?'

'With one arm behind my back.'

'You sure? If you're out of practice ...'

'Do not question me,' she said, her voice flinty. 'I spend at least an hour training every day. There are always demons stupid enough to make a try for me.'

'Wah,' the stone said. 'You sound just like your dad.'

'Good.'

Simone went out onto the balcony and flew directly down to ground level. The lift to the basement Nest was at the bottom of some white concrete steps that passed through a large indent in the swimming pool, down to a basement lift lobby. The floor below her was sealed against Celestials and for the first time in ages, she could feel it. She resisted the urge to do a little 'I'm back in the Celestial' dance and pressed the button. The lift arrived immediately.

She drew her swords and held them ready as the lift descended. It took a long time to travel, and she went far further down than a single floor, finishing deep underground.

The doors opened and the Nest smell hit her—a stronger mix of the decay and perfume from the rooms above. It was completely dark, but she had no difficulty seeing, and she slid quietly along the short tunnel from the lift into the Nest cavern.

Usually, Nests held multiple shallow rounded indentations for the eggs, spaced apart so that the Mothers didn't attempt to eat each other's eggs. This one had the smooth black stone floor that was the norm to facilitate cleaning after a particularly nasty Mother altercation—but there were partitions between the hollows, which Simone had never seen before. The partitions looked like stage sets for a show located in a 90s love hotel—salmon wallpaper with small cream flowers, and skirtings and wainscoting of cream-coloured timber. The partitions weren't joined in the corners to divide the hollows into rooms, and they were only two metres tall so they didn't reach the high ceiling, but they would ensure that the mothers in their hollows wouldn't be able to see each other. Some of the partitions even had European-style landscape oil paintings on them. The splashes of black essence—or blood—on the lower walls of many of the partitions were a gruesome touch.

She heard them talking to each other before she saw them. Edu's little-girl voice was easily recognisable, and she was talking to another woman. Simone walked quietly, swords ready, around the edge of the cavern and listened to what they were saying.

'It will work,' Edu said. 'She loves him and won't be able to hurt his mother.'

'Are you absolutely positive?' the other woman asked, in a familiar voice.

'Shh,' Edu said. 'She can probably hear us. Trust me.'

'Trust you,' the other woman said, her voice heavy with sarcasm.

Simone rounded the final partition and stopped. Edu was in her little-girl form, ten years old with twin braids and a black frilly dress with many petticoats. The other demon was a copy of Rhonda. It broke Simone's heart to see Michael's mother again—but this obviously wasn't the Rhonda she knew.

The real Rhonda had been a snappily dressed White American businesswoman in a tailored suit, refined make-up and blonde hair neatly pinned back. She had died ten years before, when the Tiger had married her, made her his Empress, and given the Elixir of Immortality that had reacted with her Celtic Serpent nature to destroy her.

This Rhonda had her head shaved nearly bald and was taller and more muscular than the real Rhonda ever was. She wore traditional Chinese-warrior black leather armour and had a scimitar sheathed at her waist.

'This had better be worth it,' the Rhonda copy said, then she drew her sword and rushed Simone.

Simone stepped aside without drawing her own swords and neatly avoided the blade coming at her head. The Rhonda copy was well-trained, but Simone was the daughter of the God of War.

'Leave now,' Simone said. She ducked beneath another swing from the Rhonda copy's sword as she glared at Edu. 'I don't do this anymore. I don't fight stupid Mothers and Dukes and Princes who want to test their skill against me. I have my own ...' She jumped back as the Rhonda copy tried to get into her personal space and used a double-handed unarmed block to push the demon away. 'Life, and I'm not part of this anymore, and *leave me alone!*'

'But you'd love it if I attacked you, wouldn't you, honey?' Edu asked. 'You'd take my head in a *second*. I had *so much fun* making Emma and Frankie's lives *so miserable* when Dad owned the Heavens and kept them in Hell. Emma was *my* nanny—'

'Fight ... me!' the Rhonda copy growled, making multiple slashes at Simone's abdomen and then aiming a kick at her midriff. 'Show me what you have! I want to see!'

Simone lost her patience with them and drew her swords, lighting the chakras along their lengths to seal the deal. She was properly annoyed with Edu and the Rhonda copy now.

Edu changed from her frilly dress, little-girl form to a slender, graceful young man with short hair in his mid-twenties, wearing a tailored suit. He was heavily cosmetically enhanced, with a narrow nose and widened eyes, and looked like a Korean or Canto-pop star. 'Now it gets interesting. Let's see if you're as good as you say you are.'

Simone nearly snapped back about how good she was, then realised that Edu had been speaking to the Rhonda copy.

The Rhonda copy stepped back, facing Simone, and moved so that they were between the salmon-coloured partitions and the wall of the cavern. 'I can do it. I'll kill her and take her place, and the Dark Lord will never know.'

'Holy shit, you're stupid,' Simone said, aghast. 'You think we don't know that you're a copy?'

The Rhonda copy swung her swords. 'Edu says he won't look too closely at his own beloved daughter. Let's see if she's right.'

She attacked Simone in a series of beautifully formed butterfly swings of her sword, and Simone, fed up, parried them all with her own swords, the lights in the blades sparking as they hit the demon's dark essence. Simone's heart filled with grim joy at being able to use her full Celestial powers against the demon threat. It had been a long time.

Simone attacked back in a dual-bladed hurricane that made the Rhonda copy give ground in turn. Simone tried to turn the demon so that she would back into either the wall or one of the partitions and be trapped, but the demon kept free space behind her. She was exceptionally well-trained and some of her moves were reminiscent of Emma's elegant style.

'An Emma copy taught you?' Simone asked, stepping back, crossing her swords in front of her, and waiting to see what the demon would do next.

'We have all sorts of cute copies,' Edu said from the side, his male voice sounding bored. 'Can one of you win already and wind this up? I have places to be.'

'Sure thing, boss,' the Rhonda copy said, and made another flurry of strikes. Simone grew tired of playing with the demon and took her feet out from under her in a kick that the demon obviously never saw. The Rhonda copy lay on her back, panting, and stared up at Simone. 'You'd better be right about this.'

Simone lunged to spear the demon through the throat, and hesitated. The sword quivered as she tried to make the killing blow and couldn't.

She couldn't kill Rhonda—even if it was a copy of Rhonda. She couldn't destroy a demon that looked like Michael's mother. She'd loved that woman for the short time she'd known her, and Rhonda had been smart, compassionate and cared for both Simone and Michael with all her heart. She was the only true parent Michael had known after Rhonda left Michael's father, and she'd done a wonderful job raising the half-Shen with intelligence and common sense.

Simone stepped back and lowered her sword. The Rhonda copy was still on her back staring at her.

'Holy fucking shit I was actually right,' Edu said quietly with wonder. 'I don't believe it.'

'Just go,' Simone said wearily. 'Tell the other Princes that I don't fight stupid demons who are out to prove their superiority or training or whatever. I'm done. I'm not a part of that world anymore—'

'Your presence here today disproves that,' Edu said, still very quiet.

The Rhonda copy stood, and Simone readied herself for another attack. Instead, the Rhonda copy sheathed her sword, raised her hands and smiled. 'Thanks for a good bout,' she said, and glanced at Edu. 'You were right. Let's go.'

Simone turned to see Edu, who was standing with a gentle smile on his face. He blew Simone a kiss. 'Thanks for demonstrating your weakness. Later, darling.'

They both disappeared.

20

Daddy, I have a big bunch of data from the demon hotel, Simone said. *Where are you guys?*

On the Mountain. Can you bring the data to Emma's new intelligence department on the West side of the Mountain campus?

Will do.

Simone teleported up to the Mountain and stopped to appreciate its winter beauty. Most of the trees were leafless saplings, but there were some snow-cloaked young cypress trees flanking the red-pillared breezeways with their black-tiled roofs. The pine scent filled the Celestial freshness of the air. The traditional buildings with their stone or wooden walls spread over the pinnacles of the Mountain's seven peaks, surrounded by the high walls crowned with their snapping black banners bearing her father's emblem of the seven stars of the Big Dipper.

She took the roller case to the administrative complex on the western side, passing some Celestial Masters teaching weapons to junior Masters on the slate-paved main square, surrounded by its three great halls and below the Golden Temple perched on the highest peak. Emma's new intelligence department—four stones and a couple of dragons—had their headquarters in the administrative complex, housed in one of the original monastic residences.

She stopped when she saw the Jade Emperor, in full Imperial regalia, standing at one of the waist-high stone guardrails with his back to her, obviously enjoying the view of the sweeping mountains of Celestial Hubei province, green and cloud-misted with rainbows that appeared and disappeared as the clouds moved. He turned and smiled as she glared at him, then he raised one hand.

'I said I would explain everything when your stepmother had returned, and I chose to come here to do it rather than drag you to the Celestial Palace. Ask me anything, and I will tell you the truth.'

'Did you set Michael up to do it?' Simone asked.

'Yes.'

'With Semias?'

'Yes. We'd been talking for a while and decided this was the only way to clear the demons from the European Heavens.'

'Did you kill Clarissa to make sure he would go?'

He looked shocked. 'Goodness no, I would never kill anyone! But I knew—'

Simone shook with fury. 'You *knew*?'

—That there was about a one in three chance the childbirth would be lethal.'

'Why didn't you tell her that?' Simone asked.

'I did.'

'She did it anyway?'

'I advised her against it. She did it anyway.'

Simone waved one hand with frustration. 'You didn't order her not to have a baby? You could have saved her life!'

He slipped his hands into his long sleeves. 'Contrary to popular belief, I do not force orders on my citizens unless the need is dire. I warned Clarissa, but I did not try to stop her. The choice was her own.'

Simone shook her head as her eyes stung with tears. 'What a complete idiot.' She glared at the Jade Emperor. 'Look me in the eye and tell me you're not lying.'

'I am not lying,' he said, and it had the ring of truth.

'Anything else you want to share now that you're *so*

generously being completely honest with me?'

'You now have access to Primal Yin, yes?'

She nodded a reply.

'Pop down onto one knee, swear allegiance—just to me personally, rather than the whole Celestial, is sufficient—and we can both ensure that the Yin will never escape your control, and the realm is safe. Then I'll leave you alone.'

'Promise?'

'Promise. You have done all the Heavens a great service and you deserve a break. I'll leave you alone for at least six months after the allegiance thing, so relax. You know it's the right thing to do.'

She went down on one knee, lowered her head, and said, 'I swear allegiance to you. I vow to serve you for the rest of my life.'

'Thank you,' he said. 'Merry Christmas. Forget about me, and there won't be any more red boxes, I promise.' He gestured towards Emma's new intelligence department. 'Go give them the data, they'll be delighted.' He disappeared.

The intelligence office was a traditional double-storey courtyard house with red walls and pillars, and decorative carved lattices over its windows. She went inside and around the carved black demon-barrier screen, to find the courtyard set up to be a small modern shooting range. She turned left to go through the ground floor living room, which was equipped as a technology manufacturing area, with wide benches covered in circuit boards and soldering equipment. There were some interesting cameras and weapons on the bench, and she decided to return later to see what they had developed. Someone had pinned up a large poster of a scene from an early James Bond film with Q talking to the Sean Connery Bond with the subtitle, 'Pay attention, 007', and she snorted quietly with laughter.

She wandered further towards the back of the house, where the kitchen and dining room normally stood, to find a modern office with four desks in a standard configuration with dividers between them, reminiscent of a police station. She wheeled the case in and one of the agent's heads shot up above the partition. He appeared to be the only one present.

'Princess!' he yelled and threw himself out of his chair to race to her.

He was a stone Shen, looking like a Filipino in his mid-thirties, bald and heavily built, wearing a pair of tracksuit pants and an oversized fluffy hoodie.

He opened and closed his hands above the wheelie case. 'Is that the demon data?'

'Yes. All yours.' She pushed the case towards him, and he snatched it, then scurried away.

He skidded to a halt at the end of the room. He left the case where it stood, marched rigidly back to her, and saluted her with a small bow. 'Please excuse my ...' He appeared to be listening. 'Excruciatingly poor manners. Profoundest apologies, your ...' He hesitated again. 'Highness. I will—'

'Stone, leave the poor man alone and let him go do the data,' Simone said. She shooed him away. 'Go. Analyse! I want to know what they're up to.'

He collapsed with relief. 'Thank you!'

'But I was having fun,' the stone whined.

'Let's go find Emma and Frankie,' Simone said. 'I want to hug them and make sure they're okay.'

I'm in my office with Frankie, Emma said.

Simone went back around the administrative area, where her father's office perched on top of the western side of the wall. These buildings pre-dated some of the main halls and were smaller constructions of grey slate with traditionally styled, black-tiled roofs. A young Japanese maple tree stood outside Emma's office, devoid of leaves. Simone filled with sadness at the sight of so many of the Mountain's lovely gardens that had been destroyed when the demons had control over it. She hadn't seen it since the demons won the war and she'd gone into hiding, then killed the Demon King, absorbed his essence and been barred from the Celestial Plane.

She went inside Emma's office to find Emma's tame demon, Yi Hao, sitting with Frankie in the reception area, reading him a story from a picture book. Yi Hao saw Simone, smiled, and nodded to her. Yi Hao was identical in appearance to Er Hao—they were demons from the same clutch—and acted as Emma's personal assistant on the Mountain.

Frankie jumped up and tackled Simone, then pushed her towards Emma's inner office. 'Tell her to hurry up.'

Simone went through to Emma's office, where Emma was engrossed in her computer, scrolling through emails.

She jumped up and hugged Simone, then sat in one of the visitor's chairs and guided Simone to sit in the other, holding both her hands.

'You okay?' Emma asked.

Simone nodded silently and wiped another tear that had leaked out. She handed the crown to Emma, and it folded up into an engagement ring holding the jade stone and returned to Emma's finger.

'You've suffered a great deal of loss in the last few days. I'll take you to see Audrey Au,' Emma said.

'Maybe after the break. I just want to enjoy the fact that I have freedom of the Celestial,' Simone said. 'Just being here makes some of the pain go away. Can we do Christmas now? Have the demons retreated?'

'Yes, the demons have gone quiet,' Emma said. 'After Edu and the Rhonda copy took out Twelve, they all seem to have gone into hiding.'

'What about the King? This is full-on threat to him.'

'It is, but it's none of our business under the terms of the treaty. We'll deal with it when Rhonda and Edu make their next move.'

'Are Nan and Pop still okay for a deferred Christmas?'

'They are, and we'd like to do it tomorrow, because it's close to New Year and your father and I have a huge Celestial duty calendar booked. We'll have lunch in the Mountain residence now—it's nearly lunch time—then head over to my parents' to hang out for a while, have dinner with them and set up the Christmas stuff for tomorrow. My little nephew, Matthew, is staying with them, and the rest of the family will join us for lunch and gifts tomorrow. Are you okay with that?'

'Absolutely, I'm already packed, and that bag I have in the Residence has everything I need.' Simone studied Emma. 'Are *you* okay? You were in Hell … then went with the demons.'

Emma squeezed Simone's hands where she held them. 'What you said. Christmas. Family. I'm looking forward to it.' She brightened. 'Can you take Frankie over to the Residence while I sort out the last of my emails?'

Simone smiled. 'Sounds good.'

She rose and went out to the reception area. 'Frankie, I'm starving,' she said. 'Let's go get some lunch while Mum and Dad tidy things up here.'

'Yeah!' Frankie said and jumped out of his chair. He turned to Yi Hao. 'Thanks for reading to me, Yi Hao. Help Mum sort herself out so she doesn't get stuck here for the rest of the day, okay?'

Yi Hao nodded, smiling. 'Yes, my Lord.'

Frankie took Simone's hand and guided her out of Emma's office. 'Yi Hao is arranging for some of the Celestial Masters to teach me up here, when Mum and Lo Dau are busy!'

'Lo Dau?' Simone asked him. 'Who taught you to call Dad "Old Bean"?'

'Uh … Uncle Bai?' he said, using the name that they both called the White Tiger. 'Mum and Uncle Bai think it's really funny, and Lo Dau gets this cute smile when I call him that.'

'Good.'

Frankie continued to ramble excitedly without taking a breath as they walked back over the bridges and through the gardens to the Residence. 'I need to pack to go to Nanna's, I hope someone told Smally to pack for me, do you know if Freddo will be there? Cousin Andrew said it snowed. Did you know he has a *girlfriend,* and he was happy that Christmas was delayed because he said he wanted to spend Christmas with her family, and Nanna said that's a really big thing, and—' He took a deep breath.

'We'll have a lot of fun,' Simone said.

They crossed the bridge to the final peak, where the

Residence's front yard was a small open area, divided into a traditional Chinese garden with bamboo lattice edgings around the empty flower beds, and into the Residence. It was a double-storey, traditional-styled house with pillars and lattices over the windows, but completely black instead of the normal good-luck red. A depiction of Xuan Wu in his True Form—the Serpent and Turtle in the combined creature—was in a stone bas-relief over the front door.

'Smally!' Frankie shouted as they kicked off their shoes in the entry, and he took off running through the central courtyard towards the kitchen. Smally came out of the dining room into the courtyard, and he tackled her. 'Is lunch ready? I'm *hungry*.'

'Lunch is on the table. The Dark Lord says to help yourself and he will be along shortly.' Emma's tame demon who ran the household on the Mountain bowed to Simone, smiling with cute dimples on her cheeks. 'Your room is set up for you, my Lady, and I've placed your bag in there. Welcome home.'

Simone hesitated—she desperately needed a shower and a change of clothes—but she hadn't eaten since she left the European Heavens, and she was starving. Frankie made the decision for her and dragged her into the dining room, where a huge pot of fragrant vegetarian ho fan in soup, with straw mushrooms, shiitake mushrooms, snow and wood ear fungus, as well as bright green bak choy, sat in the centre.

Simone picked up a couple of big noodle bowls, but Smally took them from her, ladled some of the soup noodles into them, and proudly placed them in front of Simone and Frankie. 'Do you need help, my Lord?'

Frankie looked from Smally to Simone and obviously made a decision. 'I want to eat them myself.'

Smally bowed. 'Let me know if you need anything else.'

Simone watched as Frankie picked up his chopsticks and ceramic spoon—chopsticks in his left hand, as he was left-handed—and used the spoon to slurp some of the soup from the bowl. He clumsily used the chopsticks to guide some noodles onto the spoon—he was obviously still working on fine motor control—and Simone made a point of enjoying her own noodles and not making an issue of his minor struggles.

Emma and their father entered, in their scruffy human forms, both wearing black cotton Mountain uniforms without adornment. They sat at the table and Smally re-emerged from the kitchen to serve them.

'Need a hand?' Emma asked Frankie.

'I have it,' Frankie said as the noodles fell off his spoon. He set his jaw and scooped them back on, then smiled with triumph when he got them into his mouth without losing most of them.

Their father looked down at his noodle bowl, then around at the family. 'All of us all here together, and the rest of the family safe and loved. I am a very happy old Turtle.'

'Christmas!' Frankie crowed and raised both hands, still holding spoon and chopsticks.

When she had eaten her fill, Simone climbed the stairs at the back of the ground floor to the balcony that wrapped around the interior of the upper floor, with the bedroom doors opening from it. She went past the master suite at the back, which had the stone of the Mountain's peak one of its walls. Emma and her father were inside, checking what the demons had packed for them and arguing about him wearing something that wasn't black.

Simone turned left. There were two doors here that opened onto the internal veranda, the first opening onto Frankie's room—it was tidy, but full of the books and toys of a small boy. Smally and Frankie were inside together, packing.

'You have clothes there, sir,' Smally said. 'And toys. You don't need to take everything.'

'But I need to show them my car!' Frankie said. 'Freddo wants to see it!'

Simone was delighted to see that her old doll's house sat in the back of Frankie's room, with figurines of a family in it. Emma would be using it, in play, to teach Frankie how normal families worked. Good for her.

The second door was the shared bathroom, and she poked

her head inside to check. Everything she needed was there; she just had to find a change of clothes and then she could finally have that long, hot shower.

'I'm going to have a shower,' she yelled at nobody in particular. 'I really need it.'

'Take your time, and you can meet up with us at Nan's later if you want,' Emma shouted back.

'Nanna's!' Frankie yelled with joy.

She went to the second and final door, took a breath and opened it. She went in to find that nothing had changed. The room was larger than a standard single bedroom, and the spacious area was furnished with antique rosewood. Her double-sized four-poster bed, made up with dark grey bed linen and enclosed with gauzy black curtains, stood next to the window that overlooked the front garden. The wheelie bag that Kimberley had packed for her stood next to it. Her bookshelf filled with children's books that she'd asked Emma to keep for her was still there. Her rosewood desk, where she'd studied when she was at Celestial High, stood against the wall, next to an old-fashioned, solid-timber, stand-alone wardrobe. The five years that had passed since she'd destroyed the King and been filled with demon essence felt like an eternity, but at the same time it was if she had been there just the day before.

She went to the window to look out at the garden, and fat flakes of snow began to fall over the Mountain, adding to its loveliness. She sighed with bliss—she had a decision to make. She could move back into this room on the Mountain where her family spent most of their time, or an apartment in the Palace of the Northern Heavens as a Celestial Princess and help them with the administration of their realm. Or she could live on the Peak—but the family didn't need to stay there now that she was cleared of the demon essence, and the pollution from the demon presence in the upper Earthly administration, combined with the police harassment of both her and Emma, had been increasing to an unbearable level. She also had the option of returning to the apartment in Japan and completing her research and then decide what to do after she finished it.

The decision was easy. She found a change of clothes and her toiletry bag, carried them into the bathroom and locked the door behind her.

Ten minutes later she came out, pink and shining with warmth. She sat on the bed, then fell to lie on her back. A knot of tension inside her unravelled, and for the first time in what felt like forever, she allowed herself to completely relax and enjoy the feeling of being home and safe and loved. The hate-filled angry demon essence that had filled her when she killed the Demon King no longer poisoned her life. She was free and pure, and her soul was liberated. She had multiple agreeable options for the near future and the only negative aspect to her life was the lack of a partner to share it with.

She wondered how Michael was faring now that his grief had been returned to him. She filled with sadness of the memory of him alone in their Heavens suffering so brutally. Maybe she could go and visit him—if she could do it without causing a Celestial scandal. And maybe she should just give up on a love life until Fate had tortured them to its satisfaction and allowed them to be together.

She woke disoriented some time later, lying on top of her bed and under an old-fashioned silk wadding quilt that had been thrown over her. She checked around and realised where she was, then sat up and stretched. She hadn't intended to fall asleep, and the rest of the house was quiet.

Her clock said that an hour had passed, and there was a note on the nightstand, under her Hello Kitty bedside lamp. It was in Emma's neat hand in English and said, 'We went on ahead, so catch up with us when you're awake. You needed the rest.'

21

Simone arrived at her grandparent's estate in the Northern Heavens to find it covered in a layer of fresh snow. The estate's previous owner, Miss Toi, had been a huge fan of European styling, so the three-storey house looked like a British country manor. The concrete walls had been painted to appear as brown brick, and there was a small front porch with leafless climbing roses twining over it. Christmas fairy lights hung from the snow-covered roof and were strung along the walls, and it looked like something from a Christmas card. One of the demon servants opened the door and she went into the double-storey entrance with its stairs up to the bedrooms.

The house was deserted and quiet, and her grandfather shouted, 'In here, Simone,' from the kitchen.

She went through the living room, past the absolutely massive, heavily decorated Christmas tree, standing with its lights on and a mountain of gifts under it. She wound around the comfortable living room furniture, past the rectangular Western-style, ten-seater dining table, and into the country kitchen with its timber cabinets and fake-brick internal walls. There was another smaller table here, in a bay window overlooking the snow-covered garden, and Pop was busy in the kitchen, wearing a black-and-white-striped apron. He looked about sixty, but he was nearly ninety years old now, his lifespan

278

lengthened by living on the Celestial as a mortal. He was preparing everything the family would need for a make-your-own-pizza night, and the demon servants were helping him lay it out on the kitchen bench.

'They all went tobogganing,' he said as he tipped a packet of grated cheese into a bowl. 'You can go and catch up, they left not long ago.'

'You won't come?' she asked.

He shrugged. 'I'm from Queensland, and I hate the cold. Your Nan is from Melbourne and was a ski bunny from way back.' The expression on his kind, lined face softened. 'She looked an absolute treat in those skiing outfits, and she still does.' He put down the cheese bag and pointed at the back door. 'Head out that way—I know you can sense them or something—and go have a slide with them. Matthew and Frankie have decided to call it "butt-sliding" and now the whole family calls it that.'

She went out the back door and shrugged her shoulders inside her jacket when she felt the briskness of the cold air over the snow. The path the rest of the family had taken was obvious as there was a worn trail through the half-metre-deep snow—so she followed it past the barn and foaling stables, and into the forest of young fir trees Emma's parents had planted. The winter day was quickly fading, and a light appeared in front of her, high above and shadowed by the trees. After a couple of hundred metres, she heard Frankie's and Matthew's shrieks of joy, and emerged from the trees to find the family standing at the top of a gently sloping hill. A glowing ball of her father's shen energy floated above them, lighting the hillside so that it was easier to see in the growing dusk.

Her father and Emma were there, holding plastic toboggans by the cords. Her little eight-year-old cousin, Matthew, and Frankie had just hit the bottom of the run. They jumped out of the sleds, grabbed the cords, and raced back up the hill. Emma's mother was halfway up, wearing skis and a bright green skiing suit, Freddo towing her from a long belt around his neck.

Simone's father and Emma turned and saw her, and both of them lit up with smiles that warmed her heart. Emma gestured to Xuan Wu, who held his toboggan cord out to Simone.

'Race you to the bottom,' Emma said.

'Butt-sliding!' Frankie yelled from the bottom of the hill.

'Simone,' Frankie whispered in her ear. He shoved her and spoke in a hushed shout. 'Wake up!'

She nestled under her silk quilt and groaned. 'I'm asleep. Go away.'

'Presents, Simone! Let's go and wake up Mum and John and Nana and open ...' His voice was full of quiet joy. 'I have a present for you!' He shoved her again. 'Come *on*, it's morning and it's *Christmas*!'

She raised her head, saw that it was 6:30 and groaned again.

'Simone?'

'I'm coming,' she said, before clumsily pushing the covers off. 'Ugh. I need something to drink. Morning breath. Just a sec.' She pulled her fluffy bunny robe around her and went out to the bathroom. She stopped in the doorway. 'Do you need to go?'

He looked proud. 'I already went. By myself. And I didn't make a mess.' He shooed her away. 'You go, I'll wake up Mum!'

'You do that,' she said, and headed to the bathroom.

She sensed them in the living room when she re-emerged. She went down the stairs, still in her robe, and found them all sitting around the tree in various states of Christmas-morning scruffy. Frankie was in the process of giving Matthew a present, watching him excitedly as he opened it to discover a dinosaur discovery science kit. They studied it together and cooed.

Nan pushed a mug of tea into Simone's hand. Simone thanked her, then sat on the couch and looked around at everyone. Emma and Xuan Wu, still in their pyjamas—Emma's were old and purple and nearly rags—with fluffy robes over the top, and both of them with tangled hair. Nan and Pop in old-fashioned tartan robes and fluffy slippers. Matthew and Frankie, in little matching robes from a children's cartoon, both trying to read the back of the dinosaur discovery box. Even Freddo was present, lying on the floor between the couch and the dining table with his feet curled up beneath him.

Xuan Wu gestured towards Emma, and she rose and picked up a box from under the tree, passing it to Simone. 'Merry Christmas.'

Simone put her mug down and sat next to Freddo to open it, wondering what they would have given her that was double the size of a shoe box. She made a loud sound of appreciation when she saw that it was a high-end Japanese rice cooker with multiple functions for making congee as well as rice.

'A kitchen appliance, Emma?' Nan asked.

'No daughter of mine is putting up with second-rate rice,' Emma said.

'That is the most Asian thing I've ever heard you say,' Simone said.

'Do you like it?' Freddo asked.

'Yes!' Simone said. She'd already opened the box and was checking the functions in the user manual.

Emma picked up her mug and smiled behind it. 'I bought it for your little apartment in Japan, before you had the freedom of the Celestial. And I think you'll still be able to make good use of it.'

'I will,' Simone said, and placed it next to her. She turned to Nan. 'It's a fabulous gift, Nan, I wouldn't have spent that much on a cooker myself.'

'I know,' Emma said.

'If you say so,' Nan said, unconvinced.

Emma gave Frankie his gift and he opened it, squealed and ran in circles, then stopped and jumped up and down. Matthew saw that it was a new Nintendo and joined Frankie's excitement.

'Careful, you'll break it,' Emma said.

Frankie placed the console carefully on the couch, then ran and tackled his mother. He kissed her on the cheek then pulled back to look into her eyes. He opened and closed his mouth a few times, then threw himself at her again and hugged her tight. She hugged him back, her own eyes closed and her expression fierce.

'I have something for you as well, Frankie,' Xuan Wu said, and reached under the tree to pass Frankie a poorly wrapped sword.

'Don't let the Murasame see it,' Emma said with a smile.

'Whoa,' Frankie said, and unwrapped the gift. It was a wooden training sword, similar to the one that Simone had used when she was a child, and Frankie immediately held it out in front of himself in a perfect katana-wielding pose. 'This is great!'

'No waving it around in here, you'll hit something!' Nan said. 'Wait till you get it home and start training with your father.'

'Okay,' Frankie said and gently laid the training sword on the floor.

'I have a small gift for you, Simone,' Xuan Wu said, and picked a gold box that looked like a shoe box from under the tree and passed it to her.

She studied the box. 'You didn't need to get me anything, Dad, Christmas is a Western thing.'

He gestured towards the box. 'You may not even like it … it has no real monetary value. So open it and see.'

'No real monetary value?' she asked and opened the box. It contained a dun-coloured scroll with a brown ribbon around it, and she eyed her father suspiciously. There was also a red envelope, similar to those used to hold Chinese greeting cards.

'Read the scroll first,' he said. 'I promise it's not from the Jade Emperor.'

'Well, this is intriguing,' Pop said.

Simone placed the box next to her and opened the scroll.

The Princess Simone of the House of the North is hereby granted leave to visit the main land mass of Australia, including Tasmania, for the rest of her life. She is no longer prohibited from laying foot on the soil of our sacred homeland.

Uluru, Mother of All the Rocks.

Simone jumped to her feet and squealed. 'I can go to Australia!' She looked up at her father, who was obviously delighted at her reaction. 'How did you do this?'

'Two and half years of diplomatic negotiation,' Xuan Wu said. 'She drives a hard bargain.' He gestured towards her. 'Check the card.'

She sat again and opened the envelope. It contained a standard red greeting card, but had an embossed gold map of Australia instead of the usual Chinese characters. She opened the card and read the message written in gold on the interior:

Your actions have been exemplary, and the demon threat grows. You are invited to visit me, in person, to discuss plans for the future safety of all the realms without that annoying busybody poking his goddamn nose in.

Uluru ☺

She looked up at her father. 'Smiley face and everything?'

'They're all spooked by the ... new demons,' Emma said, glancing at Frankie.

'I know exactly who she means by annoying busybody,' Simone said, placing the card next to her.

'You have no idea,' Emma growled under her breath, and Xuan Wu choked with a short cough of laughter.

Simone went to the tree and pulled out her gifts for the family. She'd intended to give them on the Peak and was delighted to be doing it with them in the Heavens.

She raised the gift that she'd bought for Frankie and gave it to him. He went goggle-eyed at it, then reached down and passed a gift to her as well. They sat together and opened them, and Frankie crowed with delight at the Lego battery-operated mechanical car.

Simone smiled at her father. 'You have to help him build it, Dad.'

'I look forward to it.'

'Open yours!' Frankie said, jiggling on the couch.

Simone opened her gift from Frankie to discover a custom-printed desk calendar of photos of the Mountain, the Northern

Heavens, and Nan and Pop's estate.

'He took and chose the photos himself,' Emma said.

'I wanted you to be able to look at these cool places, even though you couldn't come,' Frankie said. 'And now you can!'

'I know!' Simone said and hugged him. 'This is the best gift ever!'

'The printing house asked if it was a movie set,' Emma said. 'And we're thinking of doing a print run next year to give to the Mountain students.'

'Great idea,' Simone said, flipping through the photos, and smiling at the idea that she could visit these places again. She rose to check for the gifts that she'd bought for Emma and her father, but Emma stopped her.

Emma gestured toward Freddo. 'Give him his present, he's dying of curiosity.'

'What *is* that thing with my name on it?' Freddo asked. 'It's huge!'

'Right,' Simone said, and moved the coffee table back to clear some space in front of Freddo. 'Let's see if we can work this.'

She pulled the large, flat box from under the tree, shifted it upright, and opened it for Freddo. She pulled a computer monitor out of it and set it up in front of him.

'Uh ...' Freddo began, then stopped.

'Yes, you can use a computer, just watch this,' Simone said with satisfaction.

She reached into the bottom of the box, pulled out the headset, and studied him. 'This had better fit you.' She placed it over the top of his head, and a long stylus protruded past the end of his nose. She stepped back and studied it. 'There. Good.' She plugged the monitor in, and it booted up with a smartphone operating system.

'This is a touchscreen, and your stylus works like a finger on the screen,' Simone said. 'It operates as one of the Dragon's hyper-intelligent AI phones, and it will respond to voice commands as well.' She glanced at Freddo, who was watching the screen boot up with his horse mouth open and his tongue hanging out. 'You'll have to train it to understand your voice commands, but once you have it, you have full use of just about all the internet, and we'll be able to video chat any time.'

'My friend at school has one of those,' Matthew said. 'She uses it in her wheelchair.'

'Freddo's in a wheelchair,' Frankie crowed. 'Freddo can't walk!'

'Freddo's got no arms!' Matthew said, waving his hands around.

'Dis-a-bled,' Frankie said in a sing-song voice.

'Hey!' Emma said, at the same time that Nan said, 'You boys quit this!' and both Xuan Wu and Pop said, 'No!'

Freddo disappeared, leaving the headset behind to fall to the carpet.

'Uh oh,' Matthew said softly.

'I ruined Christmas!' Frankie shouted, leapt to his feet, charged out of the room and clumped up the stairs wailing loudly.

'We'll handle the boys. Go to Freddo,' Emma said, rising to follow Frankie.

'Come with me, young man, we are having a talk,' Nan said sternly to Matthew.

'I'm sorry!' Matthew shouted and burst into tears. 'We didn't mean it!'

'Go to Freddo,' Pop said. 'Bring him back, because I have a lovely warm pot of boiled barley for him, and he loves that.'

The interior of the barn was warm and spacious, and smelled of the fragrant bales of lucerne and rice straw stacked at one side, next to large hessian sacks of oaten chaff and pony pellets. There were four loose boxes for horses down the side, with external doors opening out onto the home paddock. The donkey Simone had rescued a baby from the food market in Guangzhou when she was four years old was dozing in his stall. He gently shook his long ears when he saw her but didn't wake otherwise. The other two boxes contained contented-looking ponies munching on hay nets.

Freddo was curled up on the floor of his box, nestled in the rice straw, his nose leaning on the floor.

Simone went into the box and wrinkled her nose at the smell. She went back out, unwrapped her robe to hang it on a hook, and returned with the rake and wheelbarrow. She raked up Freddo's poop and put it into the wheelbarrow, then collected the urine-soaked straw and added it to the pile.

'Princesses don't muck out demon horses,' Freddo said without looking up. 'The mafoo comes to do that at eight am.'

'That was the first thing Hongie taught us in Demon Horse Management 101 at Celestial High, remember?' Simone asked. She wheeled the barrow of muck out of his box and left it near the barn door for the mafoo to drop into the muck heap—the snow on the ground was too thick for her to plow through in her pyjamas. She returned with an armful of rice straw from the bales and spread it over the rubber matting that softened the floor of Freddo's box. 'There. Much better.'

She sat next to Freddo and put her hand on his shoulder. 'They're just little kids. They see other kids being bullies in the playground sometimes and forget that it's not okay. And Frankie ...'

Freddo didn't look at her as he spoke. 'Frankie spent a lot of his life with demons. Demons are cruel monsters who delight in torturing people.'

She put her arms around his neck. 'He's learning. We have to help him. And he'll definitely be along shortly to apologise profusely and self-flagellate for being so mean to someone he loves so much.'

He sighed deeply, making a puff of dust rise from the straw. 'I'm just so damn *tired* of moving through a world that's not designed to fit me.' He turned his head to see her. 'Your grandparents didn't stop me from joining Christmas in the living room, but they were *freaking out* that I would break something 'cause I'm so big. I appreciate the phone thing, but I'm not disabled. I'm just me, and most of the time the world rejects what I am.'

'You are unique, you know that?' she asked. 'The Demon

King's breeding program produced some monsters, but I don't think he ever intended to make something as magnificent as you. Your father is sentient as well, but he isn't nearly as intelligent as you are, and wouldn't know what to do with his own computer. You, on the other hand, could probably go to Celestial High and get straight A's.'

'The study halls wouldn't fit me. The equipment wouldn't fit me,' he said softly into the floor. 'I'm such a freak.'

'I love you so much, Freddo. We're a pair of freaks together.'

'I would give anything to be human-sized and have arms to hug you back,' he moaned. 'Is there any way that I can be changed to human? Lok was a dragon who was changed to a dog. Your dad's the most powerful person anywhere—can he do something for me?'

'I'm an idiot,' she said. 'I assumed you knew—when of course you don't. You don't have access to the teachings or anyone to teach you.'

'I knew what?' he asked. 'What teachings?'

'When demons Ascend, they become human. I know that's what you want, and in enough time, it will happen.'

'No!' he said and looked away again. 'Demons who Ascend are born as humans and forget their demon lives. I never want to forget you. Ugh. Move back, please. I'm getting stiff on the floor like this, and I need to move around.'

She gave him room, and he pulled himself to his feet, then shook himself out.

'That's better,' he said. 'Is there a way for me to be made human *without* Ascending? I never want to leave you.'

'I've never heard of it, but I'm not an expert on demons.' She grabbed a body brush from the side of the box and ran it over his gleaming sides. 'You can use the phone I gave you to contact people in the Celestial and ask them? Contact the Archivist and see if another demon has done this? Research the teachings?' She stopped brushing. 'I seem to vaguely recall the horse in Journey to the West occasionally changing into a human, maybe you should check that out?'

He lowered his head and snorted. 'It was a brilliant gift, and I went all petulant and rejected it.'

'The boys caused that, your reaction was perfectly understandable,' she said. 'I didn't realise it would make you feel lesser. You are exactly who you are, and I want you to be happy.'

'There's only one way that I could truly be happy.' He turned his neck to see her as she brushed him. 'You know how I feel, Simmony. Is there …' He choked on the words. 'Is there any hope for us?'

She stopped brushing him. She knew this question had been coming for ages, and she'd already prepared a speech about power imbalances, inappropriate age differences—he was only ten years old—and the fact that she didn't see him that way. She couldn't have a relationship of equals with a tame demon who had no choice but to obey her every command. Introducing him to gorgeous demon mares had been ineffective, as he'd despised every one. She decided not to break his heart while he was hurting so badly, and fortunately the rest of the family were approaching with the television, headset and warm barley to rescue her.

'They're coming to say they're sorry for being mean,' she said. 'We'll have that talk later.'

He lowered his head. 'Then I know the answer. They weren't being mean, it was the truth. I would be *less* disabled if I was a human in a wheelchair—at least I'd be welcome in the house.'

'Have you ever thought about designing a house that would suit you?' she asked. 'If you stopped trying to fit into the human world, and made a world for yourself? What would that look like?'

He glanced around at the barn. 'It would look like this. Your grandparents asked me what I wanted when they built it next to the foaling stables.' He lowered his head and his ears sagged. 'It's a place for an animal, which is what I am.'

She hugged his head. 'I love you so much, Freddo.'

'Not the way I want,' he said miserably to the floor.

She sniffled and wiped her nose on her pyjama sleeve.

He saw her face. 'You're crying?'

She choked through the tears, devastated at his misery. 'I can never be what you want.'

'Oh.' He stepped back from her and turned to face her. 'Wow. Look at me. This isn't me.' He tossed his head. 'Now I know what Emma was talking about! She said I was being selfish and hurting you by wanting you to love me like that when it wasn't what you wanted, and she was right.' He stepped forward and touched her head with his nose. 'I was too wrapped up in what *I* wanted. How can I demand this of you when it's not what you want? I'm so selfish, so obsessed by my love for you, that I never considered what *you* want. If it was true love, I would be happy if you were happy, even if it is with someone else.' He moaned softly. 'I am so sorry.'

'You can talk to Audrey?' Simone asked.

'I already am. I'll talk to her again after the break. Hey.' He stepped back and lowered his head to look her in the eye, full of remorse. 'I'm so sorry. Emma was right. Audrey was right. I'm a selfish dick—'

Simone snorted with laughter through the tears.

'Yeah. And that chestnut mare? The one with the flaxen mane and tail?'

'I'll arrange for you to meet her again.'

The doors opened and Frankie and Matthew crept in, still sniffling, followed by the rest of the family.

'They need to apologise to you as well,' Freddo said. 'Everybody's always expected you to do things for them, Simmony, and it's about time you started doing things for *you*.'

22

Even though it was early Spring, the weather on the Great Barrier Reef was mild, warm and still suitable for swimming—a pleasant change from Japan's late summer heat. Simone was halfway through her research, and after six weeks of taking samples on the reef, she would return to Japan and take samples from the turtles in Asia.

The waveless ocean was almost completely transparent, making the reef they floated over clearly visible two metres below the boat. The research station cut costs by combining the research activities with the tourist excursions, so there were twelve tourists on the big launch as well as the skipper and two deck hands to assist her.

While the tourists snorkelled on the reef, Simone and one of the experienced deckhands, Ron, cruised the reef in a small inflatable boat seeking turtles. He was an Australian local in his forties, had helped many of the researchers find their way around the station, and she'd appreciated his assistance. She grabbed the net when she saw a really big leatherback—at least a metre long—floating on the surface. She stood with the large hoop-shaped net, scooped it around the turtle, and released the net from the frame to catch the turtle, which flapped its flippers in protest when it felt the constraint.

Simone dropped the hoop onto the sloshing deck of the

boat, grabbed the rope holding the turtle net, and secured it to the boat. Ron had done this with her before, and knew what to do, so he slowly eased the inflatable back to the large tourism launch, which was big enough to hold twenty people. There was a ladder and an examination table at the rear of the boat, and they went alongside, secured the inflatable to the launch, and Simone climbed up the ladder holding the rope.

'I need a hand, please,' Simone shouted to the tourists resting on the boat as Ron climbed up beside her.

The skipper and some of the tourists joined her at the side of the launch to help her tow the net containing the thrashing turtle towards the boat. A few of the tourists who were in the water snorkelling over the reef rushed to climb aboard and assist, talking excitedly about the turtle and commenting on its size.

The leatherback hit the side of the boat with an audible smack and Simone winced.

'Now, carefully lift it up the ramp and make sure we don't snag any of its flippers,' Simone said, gasping with feigned effort, as a couple more of the tourists joined her to help. 'If it catches on the side, we could injure it.'

'Carefully,' Ron said, and they lifted the turtle up the makeshift ramp she'd attached to the boat, and onto the examination shelf.

Simone nearly shrieked with horror when the turtle glared at her from the inside of the net, and she realised that it was a Shen.

She glanced around at the humans, then spoke telepathically to it.

I am so sorry—

Xuan Si Min Simone, yes? the turtle asked, sounding like a teenaged girl with a New Zealand accent.

Simone struggled to free the turtle from the net. *I'll get you out of there immediately, I am so sorry—*

No, the turtle said. *They can't know. Do everything you would do as if I was a natural turtle.*

But that involves a tag! And a blood draw!

The turtle raised her rear flipper, showing that she had a bright yellow tag attached to it already. *That MacPherson woman from University of Queensland would not stop chasing me until she had me tagged. Apparently, I'm one of the largest leatherbacks in the region.* The turtle's voice filled with amusement. *Buy me dinner at Airlie Beach or Port Douglas later and you can have your blood.*

Simone had the net unravelled from the turtle, and the tourists and boat crew made loud sounds of appreciation.

'It's so big the boat's leaning in the water!' Ron said.

'How old would it be?' one of the tourists asked before grabbing her son's hand. 'No touching. See that beak? It could take your fingers off.'

Yum yum children fingers, the turtle said, and Simone hissed with laughter.

'A turtle this big would be well over eighty years old,' Simone said.

Humph, the turtle said. *Four hundred and seventy-seven.*

Your honoured name, ma'am? Simone asked as she prepared the syringe for the blood draw.

My name in these waters is Te Anahera Hurinuri.

Pleasure to meet you.

You as well. I am glad I found you, Venus said you would be here.

Simone hesitated, holding the syringe, and spoke out loud. 'What?'

'What what?' Ron asked.

You were sent to find me? Simone asked.

Imagine my surprise when this hottie comes floating down in this gorgeous purple gown, glowing and everything, to give me an Edict from the higher-ups. I've lived in New Zealand for a hundred years and stayed very quiet during the Demon War, but if I'd known you were here, I'd have said hello—and thank you—anyway. Apparently, you will receive a summons soon, and Venus has briefed me. Do everything as if I was a natural turtle, then we will swap places. I will handle the rest of the cruise disguised as you. Don't worry, I will keep the natural turtles away until you return, it's the least I can do after all you've done for us—Celestial and Earthly turtles alike.

Simone's shoulders sagged as she prepared the syringe. *I thought he would allow me to finish my research before he grabbed me to serve him.*

You could have delayed swearing allegiance until your research was finished? We all know how important it is …

Simone hesitated with the syringe over the big vein on the turtle's front flipper. *Now that the demon essence is cleared from me, I have access to Primal Yin, just as my father does. I pledged allegiance to the Jade Emperor to protect the world from this power. There was a risk that I could summon it in nightmares and destroy everything around me … by accident.*

Simone slipped the needle into the vein and drew the blood. The tourists made soft sounds of wonder, and one rushed away to sit at the other side of the boat.

Oh, Te Anahera said. I understand. Your father is the most divine and powerful of us all, and you his daughter. When you return from your mission, I will lead some natural turtles to you to assist with your efforts.

Thank you, I would appreciate your help. The summons hit Simone and she winced. *I just received it.*

The Heavens speed you on your way and help you to return safely, Princess, Te Anahera said. On three?

Just a sec, I need to measure you and record your tag number before we can release you.

She pushed the blood into the vial and placed it into the cooler, then turned to Ron. 'Can you help me measure it, Ron?'

'Sure thing, Simone,' Ron said, and passed her the tape measure. 'What a fucking monster, eh?'

'She's beautiful,' Simone said, and smiled again when the turtle winked at her.

Simone landed at the entrance to the Celestial Palace, and the gates opened to allow her to enter the Square of Running Water.

'Audience Hall Two,' she said, and stepped forward,

arriving outside the Jade Emperor's own residence at the end of the long, high-walled corridor that was supposed to provide it with extra security but had failed miserably when the demons won the war. She'd expected to arrive at the audience hall, but the Jade Emperor had given her access to his own house—a substantial message of trust.

The Door Gods stood on either side of the entrance to the residence, one black-skinned and one red-skinned and both with goatees, holding their halberds crossed in front of the door.

Simone hesitated. 'Uhh ...'

The Door Gods snapped the halberds back so that she could enter, and the door opened by itself.

'Good job killing us, Princess,' General Wei on the left said. 'Stunning display of skill.'

'Welcome back, Simone,' General Qin said, and nodded to her. 'The Heavens are much safer with you on our side. We appreciate your sacrifice.'

'We've all wanted to do that to him for *ages*,' General Wei said quietly as she approached them. 'And you did it three times? Living the dream, Simone.'

'Assholes,' she growled, making both of them smile broadly, and stalked past them into the JE's residence.

It was a standard square courtyard building with a small pond in the open central area.

'In here, Simone,' the Jade Emperor said from the back of the house.

She turned right into the living room, which was decorated in traditional style with carved rosewood couches, set with gold silk pillows, a Ming-style coffee table, and a set of shelves with priceless ceramic vases on it. A few paintings of birds and flowers—made of semi-precious stones—adorned the walls, and there was a small sculpture of a peach tree, also made of semi-precious gems, on the coffee table.

It looked like something out of the China Arts and Crafts store's high-end flagship in Pacific Place, then her perception shifted, and she understood—the store was duplicating the

Celestial style. Someone at the store was obviously a citizen of both Planes. She went past the dining room with its ten-seater round table, complete with lazy Susan, and into the kitchen.

The Jade Emperor was in the kitchen, wearing a simple black silk robe over pants and his long grey hair tied up with a wooden spike.

'Simone, good, you're here,' he said, and took the kettle off the stove. A Palace fairy watched him with an expression of restrained concern.

The Jade Emperor waved at Simone. 'Sit, sit. Oolong? I have a mandarin oolong.' He raised the dried mandarin stuffed with pu'er tea, which would infuse the tea with a citrus flavour when it brewed.

'Just green tea, if I could,' Simone said, sitting at the dining table. 'Dragon Well?'

The mandarin in his hand changed to a foil tea packet and he tipped it into the two gaiwan—individual tea bowls with lids. 'Good choice.' He brought the tea and sat, and the gaiwan and a pair of cups floated with him. He left the tea on the table to brew, and steepled his hands in front of him. 'The Throne Michael requests that you attend him to make a decision that only you are qualified to make.'

She studied him suspiciously. 'What decision?'

'Whether to pass the Throne to Hades. He is desperate to leave the Throne but is unsure whether this is the correct path.'

'What is the correct path?'

He tilted the lid of his gaiwan to hold back the tea leaves, placed his index finger in the indentation on the top, and used it to pour the tea into Simone's cup and then his own. 'I don't know, Princess, that is outside my dominion. Whatever decision you make over there has the same consequences for us here in the East.'

'What about the consequences for me or Michael?'

'Same.'

'I don't have enough information! Is Hades leading a demon rebellion, or is he a legit Celestial with a tame demon army, like my dad?'

'I don't know.'

'Was Hades working with the European Demon King? Are they allied? If we give him the Throne, will he allow the demons to take the Heavens over again?'

'I don't know.'

'Does Michael know?'

'As long as there are still demons in his Heavens, he is heavily restricted. No.'

'What about your *old friend*,' she emphasised the meaningful term. 'Semias? What does he say?'

'Semias has stopped responding to my messages. Michael may have ordered him to back off so you will travel there and assist him.'

'Why is Michael so desperate to leave the Throne?' she asked. 'He was happy to sacrifice himself, the selfless idiot.'

'He can tell you that when you arrive there. Go to the city of Trier in Germany—on the Moselle River, near the border with Luxembourg—and touch the font on the highest floor of the ancient Black Gate. That's the portal. You will be transported to the European Heavens, and thence hear their cases and make the decision.'

She sipped the tea, not tasting it. 'I'm not wise or informed enough to do it.'

'Which is precisely why you're the ideal person. You are also the only remaining citizen of those Heavens.'

'Emma—'

'Emma renounced her citizenship when she swore allegiance to the Asian Heavens and took her position in our Heavenly administration. You're the only one.'

'Meredith—'

'*You*, Simone. You swore allegiance to me, the individual, not me, the Celestial. You have dual citizenship.'

'You suggested simple words yourself!'

He waved his teacup with an ironic expression.

'And if I ...' She wanted to say 'refuse' and couldn't. 'Damn you!' She slammed the teacup on the table and rose to leave.

'One more thing,' he said.

'There always is,' she growled.

'For you, it has been nine months since you left there. For him it has been—'

'Forty days,' she said. 'He'll still be grieving his lovely wife.'

'No,' he said. 'Now that the Throne is occupied, it is able to reassert its control over time—but Michael's control is not precise. Right now, time is moving faster there than it is here. He has been there for four years.'

'He's been there by himself fighting demons for *four years*?'

He nodded. 'Go with my blessings, Princess. I'm sure the decision you make will be the right one.'

Simone stopped above the city of Trier and pulled out her phone. The ancient gate she was seeking was halfway between the river and the hills, the location of the lowest crystal in the Heavens. She flew down to land next to it, ignored by everybody. The gate had two semi-circular towers with a pair of archways beneath them, and she went inside and up the stairs to the top floor. She passed some tourists, and found the half-broken font, looking like a dry fountain, in one of the towers.

Hades was standing at the arched windows, viewing the city. He was in the same form as when he'd regained his identity in Hell: muscular, tall and bronzed with short black hair and wearing a stylish suit. He turned and smiled at her.

'I can't come up with you,' he said. 'So if you'll allow me, I will make my case here.'

'Where's Persephone?' Simone asked.

'She's there helping him.'

Simone crossed her arms in front of her chest. 'Okay, go for it. Convince me.'

Hades planted himself in front of Simone and put his hands on his hips. 'The boy is suffering where he is, and he doesn't belong in this part of the world. He's not completely in tune with the Throne, and that's causing him untold physical and mental anguish.'

That was the truth. She let Hades continue.

'He doesn't have the age or experience to take full control of it. He can't even control the flow of time there effectively.' He turned and paced from one side of the tower to the other. 'Release him from his torment. He's grieved enough, and ...' He stopped and turned to face her. 'You two deserve happiness together. I know what it's like to be parted from your own true love, and I don't want to see you two suffering as we have.' He paced again. 'I am older, wiser, stronger, and this is my throne by birthright now that all my siblings are dead.' He stopped again, faced her, and crossed his arms over his chest, mirroring her posture in an obvious body-language challenge. 'So free that poor young man and take him home with you, so you two can be happy together.'

Half of this was lies—particularly about the throne being his birthright, which was interesting, but Simone gave him rope to see where he was going with it. The bit about Michael suffering, and Hades being a better choice by his own estimation, was unfortunately the truth.

'What about the demons?' she asked

He uncrossed his arms and shrugged. 'What about them?'

'Will you remove them from the Heavens?'

'I won't need to,' he said, full of confidence and telling the truth. 'I will be able to control them when I take the throne—something Michael doesn't have the power to do. They will become my army and obey me. Once I have the throne, I can retake our Heavens immediately, and the Earthly will know greater peace and prosperity than it ever has.'

She nodded and waved for him to continue, and he spoke with more confidence, obviously thinking that he was convincing her. He was right; her own father had an army of tame demons in the Heavens, and they were the greatest weapon the Celestial possessed.

'I have always been the mightiest fighter of the three of us,' he continued. 'I look forward to hearing from your chief ... leader?'

'Emperor,' she said.

He nodded. 'Fitting. It will be refreshing to speak to

someone at my level, and I look forward to liaising with him to control the demon threat throughout the world. So, what do you say?' He approached her and smiled kindly. 'The boy's had his period of grieving and you two can finally be together. Go and rescue him.'

'I can tell when you're lying, you know,' she said casually. 'You're undermining your own case by doing it.'

'Only on minor details? I may have exaggerated slightly.' He scowled. 'That doesn't change anything. You need to free Michael so I can take his place.'

'You said you can control the demons. Did you allow them into the Heavens so that you could make them your army?'

'I never allowed them into the Heavens. I do not have that ability.'

This was the truth, but she had a flash of understanding. 'Did Persephone?'

'I can control them.' He strode backwards and forwards again. 'Michael is suffering horribly on the Throne. His mind is too small to contain the power, and there's a good chance—'

She interrupted him. 'Changing the subject. When did she let them in, and why aren't you in control up there? Tell me the whole story. The truth. Did you ask Persephone to open the portal, or did she let the demons in for reasons of her own?'

'All right. The truth.' He sagged and lost his impressive demeanour, and sat on one of the arched openings, looking defeated. 'We were approached by the demons in the early sixties, and they asked us to let them into the Heavens. We made a blood pact—that if we allowed them in, they had to permit me to enter as well. I thought they weren't aware that once I was on the throne, I would be able to control anything in the realm, including them.'

Finally, the truth. 'Sixty years ago?'

He nodded. 'About that. Give or take a couple of years. I don't know how they broke the blood pact. It should have been impossible. When I realised what we had done, I considered suicide and joining my brethren. Penny begged me not to, so I decided that I should atone instead. I drank the water of the

River Lethe and lived an ordinary, miserable, human life. Persephone felt just as guilty and did the same.'

This was just before Simone's father had done his reconnaissance in Europe, and been unable to enter their Heavens, so the timeline fitted. The demons had been in those Heavens for *ages* preparing for world domination, and this asshole and his girlfriend had helped them get there. Hades didn't plan to remove them; he thought he could go up there and use them as a tame army, just as her father did. He spoke the truth about his motives, as well.

'Are you planning to extend your influence once you have this army?' she asked.

'Absolutely not.'

Again, the truth. He might conceivably have the raw power to control the demons, so she had a difficult decision to make.

'You are so stupid it hurts,' she said, took a step forward and placed her hand on the font.

23

She arrived in the Heavens on the ground below the bottom crystal. Persephone, in her small, round human form wearing the green silk gown, stood nearby, smiling and clasping her hands with her long auburn braid thrown over her shoulder.

'Welcome, Simone, thank you for coming,' Persephone said. 'Please allow me to escort you—'

'Don't talk to me,' Simone said, and shot straight into the air.

She flew up to the highest crystal, the journey taking less than five minutes at full speed. She landed lightly on the edge of the crystal and stopped to study the building. The ground around the building was covered in soft earth, with what appeared to be vegetables growing in it, but they were in the dried-up stage of post-harvest.

She walked towards the throne building, which still shone, but not as wildly as before. The doors opened and Michael flew out, floating above the ground, rushed across the surface to her, grabbed her and pulled her into a fierce embrace.

'You're here, you're here,' he gasped, and then he was kissing her, and everything fell away.

His arms were around her and she grabbed him as well, relishing finally being able to share her true feelings for him. His kisses were desperate and passionate and they melted into each other. Their energy spiralled together, and their love made the sky blaze around them as she felt a completeness she'd never felt before. She ran her hands over his back and up into his hair and wanted to crawl inside him. There were too many clothes between them, and she needed to find somewhere private and explore and touch and share with him—

'Ahem,' Persephone said behind her, and Simone was jerked back to where she was.

Michael stopped floating and thumped onto the ground, leaned his head on hers, and started to shake uncontrollably. The shaking turned to racking tremors she realised that he was crying.

She held him as he gasped for air, lost in his misery.

'Bring him to the throne room,' Persephone said, and Simone helped Michael—nearly carrying him—inside.

There was a pallet of a straw-and-linen mattress on the floor, and a small wooden table and two chairs to one side next to the Throne. Simone guided Michael to sit on the mattress. A box held some limp cabbages next to the table, and there was a terracotta jug and cups on it as well.

'He lives like *this*?' Simone asked, aghast.

'I grow food for him,' Persephone said. 'But I'm limited in what I can bring up that will grow in this weak soil.'

'Why don't you bring up some groceries? If you have access to the Earthly Plane?'

She smiled wryly. 'I don't have any money, and it is not in my nature to steal.'

Simone fell to sit next to Michael, who had stopped crying and seemed to have collapsed in on himself, sitting on his mattress. She put her arm around him, and he was gaunt and thin, with papery skin and tangled hair. He had lost a great deal of weight and muscle mass, and looked unwell.

'I can go shopping for you,' she said to him. 'If I brought you up a fridge and a stove, could you power them yourself?'

He didn't seem to hear her.

'Michael,' she said, and leaned into him. 'I can help you live better here.'

'Let me out,' he said into his knees. He turned to see her, his haggard face swollen with tears, and grasped her hand. 'Please, Simone, I beg you. Let me out.' He gasped and gestured towards Persephone, who stood nearby watching them indulgently. 'Her six months are nearly finished, so she'll be leaving soon, and I'll be left here by myself, all alone, with nobody to talk to and no food. If Semias brings me food, it fades away and he's pulled back to his city. Please!' He clutched her hand. 'Bring Hades up to take the throne. He's more powerful than me and will fix everything. I can't ...' He lowered his head. 'I can't do this.'

'Hades and Persephone let the demons in here in the first place,' she said. 'They gave the demons the ability to attempt a world takeover—and they nearly succeeded. I'm not sure we can trust them.'

'I know that,' he said. 'I don't care. I just want ...' He moaned the words. 'I want to go home. I'm so alone.'

She squeezed his hand. 'You asked me to come here and decide?'

He shook his head. 'The Throne won't let me abdicate, it's refusing. We came to an agreement because both of us trust you. If you say yes, it will let Hades sit.'

'I'll sit,' she said, standing and facing the Throne. 'We can take turns.'

'It won't let you, child,' Persephone said.

Simone rounded on Persephone and jabbed her finger at her. 'You. Leave. Now. Out.'

Persephone opened her mouth to argue, obviously changed her mind, and smiled tightly. 'Whatever.' She spun and walked out of the building, and the doors closed behind her.

Simone walked up to the Throne and took a deep breath. The energy coming from it wasn't painful, but its intensity made it difficult to keep her thoughts together. She took the three steps up to the Throne and turned to sit—and couldn't. She hovered with her butt above it, fighting the restriction.

The Jade Emperor had stopped her from taking it? Easy

fixed.

'I renounce my allegiance to the Jade Emperor,' she said, and tried to sit again. She couldn't.

She straightened and shouted, 'Let me take his place!'

Michael spoke with a voice of hissing silvery metal. 'You are unsuitable.'

'I'm the same as he is! Half-European! Half Welsh-Serpent! If he can sit, then I can too.'

Michael spoke with the Throne's voice again. 'You are of lesser intellect—'

'What?'

'An animal of base instincts and unfettered desire—'

'*What?*'

Michael switched to his own voice. 'It hates women, Simone,' he said. 'Iron-Age men regarded women as sex-crazed animals, and it still has that attitude.' He smiled sadly up at her. 'We've argued about it for *years* and the belief seems intrinsic to its programming. It's part of the way it's made.'

'Fuck!' she shouted, stormed down the stairs, and stood next to him.

'Your obscene outburst proves my point,' the Throne said through Michael.

'Okay,' Simone said, and sat next to Michael on the pallet. 'Let's allow Hades up, and he can do this.'

'We have an agreement,' the Throne said, and Michael nodded as it continued to speak through him. 'If you agree to permit that piece of filth up to sit on me, I will allow it. You may decide—but only after I have made my case that Michael is a more suitable occupant.'

'Go for it,' Simone said, already making the decision to free Michael whatever the cost.

'I will not have deceitful traitors sitting on me,' the Throne said. 'They have not stopped lying to you since you arrived here.'

'I know that,' she said.

'Persephone has been deliberately starving this poor child—I cannot feed him myself—and has been verbally haranguing him to give the throne to her Lord.'

'I'm not surprised,' Simone said.

'Hades attempted to kill his own family and steal me,' the Throne said. 'He led an army of demons to attack this divine realm—*twice*. The first time his brothers put him down and exiled him, and the second time, sixty years ago, he failed to control the demons, and was locked out of his own realm. He is incompetent and incapable.'

'I know that too,' Simone said, beginning to wonder if it was the right choice to allow Hades up. The man was a deceitful idiot.

'Right now, Michael is the only one who can sit on me, but we will rebuild. He will be freed.'

'After a hundred years,' Michael said bitterly. 'I can't control the time difference, so my daughter will be long dead.'

'Can she come up here to visit?' Simone asked. 'I'm here right now, aren't I? Can I come up to visit more often? Can I bring her? What can I bring up for him? Persephone's been denying him basic comforts to help her asshole boyfriend, and I know that she lied about the theft thing. Can we set up a house for him here, and I furnish it?'

'You are not welcome here, only those of pure heritage may enter,' the Throne said.

'But you're happy to use Michael, and his heritage is the same as mine. If I was allowed to visit, would you be able to handle it, Michael?'

'That would be wonderful,' he said. 'Sharing this realm with you? Removing the demons with you? I think the dream of having you here one day is the only thing that's kept me sane. But,' Michael shook his head. 'You have your own life, Simone. I can't ask you to do this, it's wrong.'

She shrugged. 'My research will be done in a year or so. How long is that up here?'

'Five years,' the Throne said.

'Could you wait that long, if I came up to visit occasionally?'

Michael nodded. The tears—this time obviously of hope—

had started again.

Simone stood and brushed herself off. 'That's the offer. Take it or leave it. I choose Hades, or you let me help Michael be more comfortable and allow me to visit, and sometimes bring his daughter to see him.'

'No, Simone,' Michael moaned. 'I love you too much to do this to you.'

Simone filled with delighted misery to finally hear the words she'd wanted for so many years and softened her voice. 'I love you too, but this is my choice, so butt out. You asked me to come up and decide, so deal with it.'

He choked a short laugh and shook his head again. 'You're as stubborn as your father.'

She snorted with disdain. 'So are you.'

'If it will keep Hades from the realm, then you may enter,' the Throne said without a hint of Michael's emotion in his voice.

'And his daughter,' she said, wondering how she would talk Michael's mother-in-law into allowing her to take his daughter and run away with her for indeterminate lengths of time in a no-contact situation. She squared her shoulders. Details.

'I wish you didn't have to do this,' Michael said in his own voice, and pulled himself to his feet. 'But I'm too broken from being here by myself to fight you.'

'Hey,' she said, went to him, and put her arm around him to allow him to lean into her. 'That's what love's all about, right?'

'I'm so happy,' he wheezed into her shoulder. 'Thank you so much.'

'You,' she said sternly, and pointed at the Throne. 'I'll allow you to keep using this poor man on those conditions. Allow me to visit and make him more comfortable, and allow me to bring his daughter for visitation. In fact, allow me to bring anyone else I please—except for Hades—to ease his loneliness and suffering.'

'No, only you or his daughter,' the Throne said.

She shrugged. 'Worth a try. Do we have a deal?'

'I agree, the pact is sealed,' the Throne said, again through Michael, and Michael collapsed against her with relief, still shaking with emotion.

Simone became aware that someone was banging on the doors of the building and yelling outside.

'Is that Persephone, pissed beyond belief?' she asked.

'Yes,' Michael said, shaking with both tears and laughter.

'Can you expel her?'

'No. She has right of abode or something for Heaven during the summer months.'

'When will she be kicked out?'

'Nine days.'

'Can you move her somewhere where we don't have to listen to her tantrum?'

The banging stopped. 'Done.' He shook his head. 'She'll be back.'

'If she comes back, she will see a Wudang One-Inch Punch to the face,' Simone said, and guided Michael to sit on his pallet again. 'Throne. Can you build him a house on one of the crystals, or on the ground below?'

'No,' the Throne replied through Michael.

'Can you build him a house at all?'

'No,' Michael said. 'Not until the demons are gone, and we've been destroying them one by one together.'

'Okay then, one thing at a time.' She bent to speak to Michael. 'Can you run electrical appliances with your Metal alignment?'

'For short periods, yes. When Persephone's gone and there's no food and I'm starving, I can't gather the energy to do it.'

'Portable gas stove it is then.' She pulled out her phone. No signal. 'I thought you'd reverse-engineered this, Throne.'

'I need to rebuild the communications network,' the Throne said, continuing to speak through Michael. 'And find a way to connect to the Earthly one.'

'Would you like technical assistance with that? I know some experts.' She jerked with shock when Michael spoke with both voices at the same time.

'No,' the Throne said.

'Yes,' Michael said.

'Michael's in control,' Simone said. 'I'll see what I can do about getting you help. But first I am heading down to a supermarket—I saw an Aldi near the gate—and buying you a great deal of fresh food. Okay?'

'I love you,' Michael said.

She bent to kiss him on the forehead. 'I'll be right back. Don't listen to anything Persephone says, she lies more than Hades does. No money my half-Turtle ass. I've seen you make gold bars myself.'

He nodded, and she waved at the Throne. 'Let me out.'

'This is entirely not what I was expecting when I agreed that you could make this decision,' the Throne said, and she was back in Trier, right outside the Aldi.

She turned to enter the supermarket, and ran straight into Hades, still in his large human form. He put his hand on her chest and she stepped back out of his reach, full of disgust at his meaty hands touching her.

'You know what I think, Simone?' he asked, walking forward and making her back away to give him ground. 'I think, that if I killed you right now ...' A long black spear with a simple black obsidian head appeared in his hand. 'After you relinquished your Eastern allegiance? You're a citizen of this region now, and I think if I killed you, you would go to my Hell here. And if you were sent to my Hell, under my control, then I could bind you there while it ate your soul. Your boyfriend would give me my throne back to stop you from losing your soul to it.'

Simone looked around. 'Not here,' she said.

He spun the spear in his hands—his technique was flawless, identical to her father's—and held it in a low guard position. 'You're actually planning to fight me? Let me send you to my dominion and get it over with.'

'Not. Here,' Simone said, rose in the air and flew back to the Roman black gate. There was an open square in front of it, with plenty of room for them to do this.

She didn't know if she had the ability to take him down. He was infinitely older than her and had thousands of years to perfect his technique with a spear that was obviously more than just a pointed stick. She switched to her Celestial form—wearing armour over her robes—and summoned her swords. The humans wandered away, not seeing her but sensing that something was amiss and that they needed to leave.

Hades floated to follow her, and his own clothing changed to flowing black robes with a gold geometric pattern around the edge. He grew in size to match her father at his largest, and a black metal crown—like a diadem, with black stones set into it—appeared on his brow.

Simone swung her swords experimentally. Every battle she'd had in the recent past had been a simple win and now she was facing someone who could potentially be more than a challenge.

Her sickle-shaped deep blue swords, Bo and Bei, had seven indentations in each blade to take the energy from her chakras and she loaded them, filling them with glowing light. She took a step up and floated above the ground, then swung her arms wide into a broad defensive position.

'Magnificent,' Hades said, and took position two metres from her. 'Ready? This will be a joy. I have not given anyone so young and talented a lesson in warplay in centuries.'

'Bring—' Simone began, but he went for her eyes with the tip of the spear.

She dodged easily and let him push her around the arena, watching him as he slowly and clumsily poked at her with the stick. He was feinting and pretending to be less skilled to put her off-guard—but she was doing the same thing. His casual, low-energy attacks suddenly shifted, and he moved faster than a human eye could see, attempting to take her legs off at the knees. She jumped over the spear, helped it in the direction it was already going with one sword, and sliced at his belly with the other one. He spun the spear—again too fast to see—and blocked the blades, then jumped back, spun it again, and held it in a guard position as he studied her without emotion.

Simone smiled tightly. He was rusty—really rusty. He'd spent too much time as a normal human without training, and it was obvious that his muscle memory had faded—meaning that he had to consciously decide what moves to make instead having of the training kick in like second nature, as hers did. He was bigger and stronger than her, but she was fast, and her Eastern techniques were profoundly more refined than his brute force. She trained as a daily exercise routine, and she had a chance.

'What's with the fairy lights?' he asked, pointing his spear at her blades.

'I thought coloured LEDs would look pretty on my swords,' Simone said, edging closer to him. 'I wanted pink swords with Hello Kitty—'

She didn't finish her sentence, instead going for a low sliding attack under his guard in an attempt to take his feet off. He blocked her and pushed her back, spun the spear and tried to slice her in half crosswise. She jumped back in time, with the point of his spear barely missing her abdomen.

Close.

She felt Persephone's presence behind her and leapt into the air, somersaulted backwards, and stopped above the other woman. Persephone was carrying a gun, and she pointed it at Simone. Simone filled it with water to make it useless, then threw a ball of experimental chi at Persephone. Persephone shredded as if she'd been hit by a thermal blast, and from her expression before she incinerated, she never saw it coming. Since that worked, she tried another ball at Hades, but he brushed it away with a dismissive wave of his hand.

Hades launched himself into the air at her. Her training kicked in—the muscle memory moving her before she was aware of it—and she slapped her blades together, then pulled them apart with the chakra energy glowing as ribbons between them. She swirled the blades to extend the ribbon, snapped it around his neck, and pulled her blades apart to take his head off. His body and head fell onto the ground separately, and she dropped as well. There was no blood; the chakra energy had cauterised the wounds. She stepped back when she saw that he was still breathing.

The body picked itself up and moved jerkily towards the head.

She tried Yin on his head, not expecting it to work, and was surprised when it did. His head disappeared into a black vortex that made a gentle sucking sound before it shrank to a point. The body flopped forward, then disappeared as well.

The crown and the spear fell from a metre above the ground to land at her feet, and she dismissed her swords and picked them up.

'Looks like by defeating you I won your dominion, and you have to obey me,' Simone said, putting the crown on her head. 'Look at me. Queen of Hell. I wonder how this will affect my allegiance to the Jade Emperor? I guess I should talk to him about how to control my Yin without Celestial allegiance to restrain it.' She changed back to her sports pants and T-shirt, and the spear and crown disappeared. 'But before that, I need to hit Aldi and see what's in the middle aisle. I wonder if they have any tents?'

Simone floated outside Larissa's bedroom window and watched as Larissa's grandmother Christine told her a favourite bedtime story, then tucked her in, kissed her goodnight, and turned out the light. Simone waited until Christine had gone to bed herself, then teleported into Larissa's room. Larissa was lying wide-eyed and awake, waiting for Simone, and shot upright to sit when she saw her. She was nearly five years old and had inherited her mother's dark hair but had fair skin from Michael. Her large brown eyes were full of intelligence, and she jiggled with delight.

'Ready for your dream trip?' Simone whispered.

Larissa nodded. 'Daddy's there on the floating crystals? I can fly with him?'

'Daddy's there waiting for you,' Simone said. 'Remember, it's all a dream, and you'll wake up tomorrow morning like none of it happened.'

'I wish it was real,' Larissa said, and put her arms out for Simone. 'Let's go see my dad.'

Simone lifted Larissa and held her in her arms, then conjured the lookalike that would hold Larissa's place until they returned early the next morning. 'He can't wait to see you.'

'Can you stay with us, Aunty Simone? Come flying with us?'

'This time I can, I can stay the whole two days with you. I think I can arrange another visitor for us as well—I have a talking horse that was born there, and we may be able to bring him in so you can have pony rides.'

Larissa held her tighter. 'I want to stay with Daddy forever.'

Simone kissed her on the cheek. 'So do I.'

313